A.D.M.

By

Cliff Peterson

Printed in the United States of America

ISBN   978-0-578-00115-9

Cover art by Joel Barger

ACKNOWLEDGEMENTS

I must admit that I write in long hand. This book would never have come to print without the help of the following people. First, my wife, Anne, who read through all of my hand written notes and typed the manuscript. Second, Janet Fitch for proof reading and Roxanne Malick and Gary Curry who recommended changes that have vastly improved the script. And finally, John Malick who researched the publishing process, led me through the computer maze and who has put in many hours of work getting this manuscript ready for publication. I am truly grateful to each of you for your support and encouragement through this long process.

CHAPTER 1

Angus Donald McGregor, age thirty-nine was the youngest General Officer in the U.S. Air Force. He had a distinguished career as a fighter pilot with two tours in South East Asia and five rows of citations under his Command Pilot Wings, topped by the Air Force Cross, the Silver Star, and the Legion of Merit. Shortly after his promotion to Brigadier General, he was picked to be the Defense Attache' in Cairo with the additional duty as the Air Force Attache' accredited to the Sudan. He was selected for his demeanor, his imposing manner, and his reputation for getting along with everyone. The fact that he had a working knowledge of Arabic, from a previous Military Assistance Tour in Saudi Arabia didn't hurt.

Adam McGregor was a bachelor. He was also independently wealthy. He was the only child of Douglas and Agnes McGregor. His father had died in 1975 and left thirty million dollars, split between Adam and his mother. Adam would be the only heir to his mother's estate when she would expire.

Normally, the Defense Attache' lived in a large Villa in the Cairo suburb of Maadi. Because Adam was a bachelor, he shunned the responsibility for entertaining and turned the Villa over to the Naval Attache', Captain Donald Sanford and his wife, Lydia. General McGregor was always invited to functions at the Villa, however, he left the official niceties to the Sanford's. He seldom arrived with a companion unless some woman's husband could not attend. He would then be paired up with the extra wife. There was some talk that perhaps Adam was gay. Few believed it.

Adam had taken residence in the Swiss Air Building on the West side of the Nile. The multi-story building had several luxury apartments above the Swiss Air Restaurant, one of the best and most popular eating places in Cairo. On those rare occasions when Adam was not occupied in the evenings, he would dine downstairs. Or if he was entertaining someone in the apartment, someone who didn't want to be recognized in public, he would have dinner catered from the restaurant.

The apartment was on the third floor. It was quite spacious. There was also a stairway that went to the back of the apartment. The floors above had a fire escape to come down, but no entry other than the main elevator. Adam had picked the third floor for two reasons. It was high enough to miss most of the dust from the street along the Nile, and for the additional entry in the back. The fantastic view of the Nile from the front balcony was a plus.

In addition to the Swiss Air apartment, Adam had a special arrangement with the Meridian Hotel. The hotel was directly across the Nile from his apartment. The Meridian had a pool. Adam was an accomplished swimmer and he was also an accomplished stalker.

Adam had first seen Sonya Olsen the previous week at the Cairo Airport. He took one look at her and decided she was unhappy. She had a young boy in each hand and was following a man who was probably her husband. He walked past them and checked a bag tag. The last name was Olsen.

Adam joined Captain Dave Baldwin and they departed the terminal to find their driver, Mustafa. Mustafa was in the parking lot beside an old gray Plymouth Volare that served the Defense Attache's Office. When they arrived at the Embassy, Adam told Dave that he was stopping at the Consulate and would join him in the Defense Attache's Office in a few minutes.

Adam went into the Consulate and asked if they had anything on a family named Olsen arriving on TWA that day. He was told that the Reverend John Olsen was arriving that day with his wife, Sonya and sons, John, Jr. and Paul. He's the new Pastor at St. Mathews Lutheran Church. They would be staying for a few days at the

Meridian.

Adam thanked the official murmuring that he thought he might have a mutual friend who knew the Olsen's. He went up to his office and went through the message traffic. After everyone else had departed, Adam called his contact at the Meridian and asked him for the room next to the Olsen's. He said he would probably need it for a week. His contact stated that the room wouldn't be available until Friday. It was Thursday and Adam said that would be fine. Adam stopped by the Meridian to buy his contact a drink then went to his Swiss Air apartment to shower and change before going to the Chinese Embassy for dinner.

Dinner at the Chinese Embassy was always a mixed blessing. It was the largest Embassy in Cairo with nearly two thousand people. All of the personnel lived on the Embassy grounds. The good part was there were five chefs from various areas from Canton to Shantung Peninsula. The food mixture was fantastic. It was the only Chinese Restaurant in Egypt. The beer and liquor were excellent. The Chinese Defense Attache' was a Lieutenant General in the People's Army. General Hwang was a lush and he was always trying to get guests drunk in hopes of getting someone to compromise themselves. The General's wife, Mai Lee was rumored to be from Chinese Intelligence and thought to be senior to her husband. Mai Lee watched and listened as her husband bounced from table to table with a glass of liquor in his hand toasting everyone with "Kampai", the Chinese equivalent of "Cheers" or "drink up". Adam stuck to the beer.

Adam enjoyed his drinks, but he preferred Scotch. Almost every Embassy served Scotch except the Chinese. The Russians were not in town having been expelled by Anwar Sadat several years before. The North Koreans were in town. U.S. Policy was to have no direct contact with them.

The other part of the evening that was hard to take was the propaganda films on the "glorious" Red Army, Navy and Air Force. Films were sped up, reminding one of the days of silent pictures. Guests were happy to have the films over so they could start to excuse themselves and go home.

Adam waited until a number of guests had departed before taking his leave. His driver Mustafa, was waiting and they immediately departed for the Swiss Air Building. Mustafa dropped Adam at his rear entrance.

Adam changed from his uniform to slacks and a shirt and headed for the Meridian in his 1973 Corvette. The staff at the Meridian were very familiar with the General and his car. He always used valet parking. He tipped well and the staff were always at his beck and call.

Adam checked with the Concierge and learned that Reverend Olsen and family had checked in and were having dinner in the dining room. Adam proceeded to the bar and took a seat where he could see the Olsen's table. Mrs. Olsen had obviously freshened up. The haggard look she had at the Airport was gone. She was gorgeous. The transformation was sufficient to make Adam question whether she was unhappy as opposed to showing fatigue from a long trip. He would have to find out. He finished his Dewars on the rocks and took another look at Sonya Olsen. She had a magnificent sun tan. Adam decided that Friday and Saturday, he would go for a swim in the Meridian Pool. He left for his apartment.

Friday was a slow day at the U.S. Embassy. It was the Muslim Sabbath and the Egyptian Government was shut down. After going through the daily message traffic, Adam left for an early lunch at the Meridian. He lunched on the patio overlooking the swimming pool. Just as he finished he looked down and saw Sonya Olsen arrive and take a lounge chair by the pool. She was wearing a large towel over her shoulders. She dropped the towel on the chair and walked to the pool. She was wearing a yellow string bikini. The bra was strapless.

Adam paid his check and proceeded to his room stopping at the ladies wear store. He purchased a yellow string bikini with a strapless bra. When he arrived at the room, he hung the bikini in the closet and undressed. He put on his boxer swimming trunks and headed for the pool. He went directly to the area roped off for swimming laps and proceeded to swim for twenty minutes. He was careful to never make eye contact with Sonya Olsen, although he had observed nearly everything she did during his swim.

Sonya was beautiful. She was about five foot seven and weighed one-twenty to one-twenty five pounds. She had a perfect figure in spite of having had two sons. She had a beautiful smile, although Adam had noticed she rarely smiled.

After finishing his laps, Adam picked up his towel and headed for his room. On his way, he stopped at the flower shop and bought a basket of flowers and a card. When he got to the room, he quickly checked the window over the pool. Sonya was swimming laps. He stripped and jumped in the shower where he rinsed off and quickly shaved with a safety razor. When he had dried off and used deodorant and after shave, he put on a robe and checked the window again. Sonya was gathering her towel and a book and then she headed for the hotel. Adam wrote "The Olsen's" on the card for the flowers. He set the flowers outside his door and left the door ajar.

Sonya saw the flowers as she came down the hall. She noticed the card, picked up the flowers and reached to put her key in the door. When the door opened, she stepped in, thinking the family was there. Before she could call out the door closed behind her. She started to turn when she felt something sharp in the middle of her back. Before she could scream her bra fell off. As she grabbed for it, the strings were untied from both sides of the bikini. It fell to the floor and she stood stark naked. She tried to scream, but nothing came out. She took a deep breath and turned to face her attacker.

"Are you going to rape me?" she asked trying not to panic.

"No," he said, "I'm going to make love to you."

"You're the swimmer!" she said in a whisper as he pushed her gently onto the king sized bed. She had been taught in health class in high school, not to struggle if rape couldn't be avoided. She decided to be passive but not cooperate. She spread her legs, thinking that would hurt less. Then she lay passive as he patiently moved his penis in and out. He was much gentler than her husband. The copulation went on for several minutes. At that point, he slowly increased the speed and Sonya began to rotate her hips in cooperation. She began to sob and moan. She had never enjoyed sex before.

They both laid still while their pulses slowed. Finally he slowly backed out and raised up. He put on his robe as she pulled a sheet over her.

"I need something to wear," she said.

He went to the closet and got the new bikini and helped her put it on.

She was about to say, "You think of everything," but decided not to speak. Instead she picked up her flowers and quickly kissed Adam on the lips. As she ran out of the room she said, "I'll return your bikini tomorrow."

The next day Adam left his office at eleven am. He told his secretary that he was going to the Meridian for a swim and he would return around two pm. He had intentionally worn civilian clothes so that he wouldn't be seen in uniform.

As soon as he could, he donned his swimming trunks and headed for the pool. Several minutes after starting his laps he saw Sonya appear in the yellow bikini. They did not make eye contact. When he finished his routine, he departed the pool, picked up his towel and went to the room. He observed Sonya diving into the pool through the reflection in the glass door entrance. When he got to the room, he checked the pool area and observed that Sonya was just leaving. He took off his trunks and put on a bathrobe and then he unlocked the door. Two minutes later, Sonya tapped on the door.

Adam opened the door for Sonya to come into the room. He put out the "Do Not Disturb" sign and locked the door. When he turned around, he saw that Sonya had taken off the bikini and left it on the floor. She was turning down the bed. She turned around and held out her arms. Adam joined her on the bed. Without a word being spoken, they proceeded to make passionate love until both had climaxed. Sonya pulled the sheet over them and they lay quietly. Finally, Sonya spoke.

"I don't know how this got started, but it has to stop. How long are you remaining here?"

Adam was taken aback for a moment. He wondered where she was going with this. Finally, he responded. "I'll be here until three pm tomorrow."

"All right," she responded emphatically. "I'll see you tomorrow at the same time. Then we'll say good bye and never see each other again. I'll admit that I've enjoyed the sex. I'm a married woman with two children and I can't continue this liaison. I hope you understand."

She got up from the bed and looked around. Suddenly, she realized that all she had with her was a towel. Adam was putting on his robe and realized her predicament.

"You're welcome to use the bikini. I wish you would keep it. I did ruin yours."

"I'll bring it back tomorrow," she said, as she quickly put on the bikini. "I can't keep it. I would think of you every time I saw it and I couldn't wear it without wanting you." She hurried out of the room.

Adam took a shower, dressed and returned to the Embassy.

CHAPTER 2

It was common practice for The Embassy to take advantage of VIPs visiting Cairo. If they could coerce the visitor to come to an Embassy function, the Embassy would send invitations to the head of state and many of the highest ranking members of the regime. If the titular leader of the country accepted, the entire cabinet would show up and hopefully the Embassy staff would make some contacts that would provide better access to the regime.

At six pm on this date, the Vice President of Egypt had come to pay his respects to an Ex-President of the United States and his wife. Brigadier General McGregor had been selected to introduce each person to the VIP couple.

Adam had seen the guest list. He wasn't surprised when the Reverend John Olsen and his wife Sonya appeared. He quickly announced them to the VIPs. The President was acquainted with Pastor Olsen through a mutual acquaintance. They immediately began a conversation.

The President said, "The Reverend Doctor Cameron and Mrs. Cameron of the World Council of Churches told me you were here. He suggested that I make arrangements for you to accompany them on a fact finding trip to Darfur. They have made arrangements to visit refugee camps in Geniena on the Sudan-Chad border. Could you go with the Embassy group?"

Pastor Olsen was completely surprised by this invitation. "I would love to do that, Mr. President, except I have just arrived and I have committed myself to a busy schedule," Pastor Olsen replied. "However, I would like to suggest that Mrs. Olsen take my place. She is perfectly capable of reporting to the Council the findings from the visit?"

The President turned to his Embassy Liaison, "Can that be arranged?"

The Liaison Officer replied, "General McGregor is the pilot. Adam, do you have room for Mrs. Olsen?"

"We have blocked a seat for a representative from the WCC. We need Mrs. Olsen's passport to enter the Visa," Adam replied. He immediately turned toward the next person in the receiving line avoiding any eye contact with Sonya.

Sonya was in a state of shock. She didn't want to make a scene by complaining publicly. She was shocked with the prospects of a trip away from her family. Being thrown into a long term contact with her elicit lover was frightening. She immediately wondered if her recent lover had maneuvered her into a trap right after she had promised to break off the affair tomorrow.

The next day Sonya was waiting for Adam when he arrived at the room. She was fully dressed and had the yellow bikini in a plastic bag. She handed him the bag and started to leave.

"Where are you going?" he asked. "I thought we were going to have one more day."

"I think I should go. We've moved out of the hotel. My family needs me," she replied.

"I ordered lunch for two," he added, hoping she would change her mind.

She was hesitant. Then she said, "I have to be out of the hotel by two." She followed him into the room.

Moments later there was a knock at the door. Adam motioned her into the bathroom while he let the waiter in with the lunch. When the waiter had gone he knocked on the bathroom door. Sonya appeared dressed in a bathrobe. They quietly ate their lunch.

Adam went into the bathroom, disrobed, and reappeared in another robe. They met by the bed and kissed for a long time. They pulled the robes down on each other and collapsed on the bed. They began to make love. It lasted longer than the previous two times.

"Is your name really Adam?" Sonya asked as they lay catching their breath.

"No," Adam replied, "It's an acronym for my initials, ADM.

"What does the A and D stand for?"

"Angus Donald." he replied.

"You didn't like Angus," she guessed.

"I have always preferred Adam. I don't object to Angus."

"Do you mind if I use your shower?" she asked.

"Of course not," he replied. "Do you mind if I join you?"

"Would it matter if I did?" she asked with a hint of sarcasm, "Won't it be a bit crowded?"

"Not at all! This suite has double shower heads. The French think of everything."

They went into the shower and each adjusted the flow and the temperature. Sonya looked over at Adam and noticed that he was washing his genitals first. "Is it pride that makes you wash there first?"

"Au contraire. Most men wash there first and I would think that you femmes would find that comforting," he replied with a slight smile.

"When you say 'most', how big is your sample?" Sonya asked.

"It's gigantic!" he responded. "I've been showering with males, men and boys since I was ten. Male shower rooms are generally open bay. You girls have separate stalls."

"And how many girls shower rooms have you visited?" she asked dripping sarcasm.

"Not many," he replied. "I certainly couldn't make any judgments about what most women do first. I can say that given my limited sample, you fit the majority."

"What would that be?" Sonya demanded.

"Most women wash their bosoms first," he replied.

"Oh!" she said as she stepped out of the shower and grabbed a towel. The more she thought about it, the more his cavalier attitude irritated her. She quickly dressed and gathered up her purse. She went to the door.

"I suppose you'll be bragging about your conquest to the rest of the boys in the locker room. Well, it's over!" she concluded. "Don't expect anything on our trip to the Sudan!"

He looked at her for a moment and then said, "I don't kiss and tell, Sonya. I must say that you are one of the most beautiful women I've ever known."

She started to respond. Instead her eyes filled with tears. She came forward and kissed him on the lips. She ran out of the room. As she walked to the elevator, she dabbed her eyes with a Kleenex and donned her sun glasses. By the time she reached her car she had composed herself. She drove directly to Mohandisin.

Reverend Olsen noticed that Sonya was not herself. He asked her if she was worried about the trip. She responded that she felt strange about leaving the boys and her husband and going into a strange country without knowing anyone except the passing introduction to that General.

CHAPTER 3

Captain Dave Baldwin and his wife, Marianne arrived at the Mohandisin apartment of the Olsen's just after seven am. They knocked on the door. Reverend Olsen answered almost immediately.

"Come in." he said. "Sonya is ready. She's just saying goodbye to the boys."

Sonya appeared a moment later carrying two small bags. "I guess I'm as ready as I'll ever be," she said. "I'm Sonya. We met at the Embassy."

"Don't worry about being ready," Marianne replied. "The Sudan is the most casual place you'll ever visit."

Sonya kissed her husband on the cheek and waved goodbye as they slipped out of the door. At the entrance to the apartment building sat another gray Plymouth Volare sedan. The driver, a young Egyptian named Alaa Adin, held the back door open for the two women. Captain Baldwin went around the car and climbed into the front seat.

"Are we picking up the General?" Marianne asked.

"No ma'am." Alaa replied. "Mustafa picked up the General and two people from the Embassy in Khartoum. They are returning from vacation in Greece. We'll meet them at Cairo East."

"What is Cairo East?" she asked.

"It's the Egyptian Air Force Base across the runway from Cairo International. We park the Embassy C-12 there," Dave Baldwin replied.

"What's a C-12?" Sonya continued, "Or shouldn't I ask?"

Dave laughed, "It's the military designation for a Beechcraft Kingair. It's a twin engine Turbo prop."

"It's not a jet then?" Sonya asked.

"It's a prop-jet. It's perfect for what we do because we can go into small landing strips. We have two pilots and seven passenger seats," Dave continued. "Believe me, you'll like it."

"Do you fly everyday?" Sonya continued.

"No," Dave said. "Last week, we made two trips to Tel Aviv, one trip to Sharm El Sheik, and a trip to Ras Banas. That was a pretty standard week."

They had crossed the Nile and were turning into the Salah Salem, the main road to the airport. Cairo traffic is always heavy but the Salah Salem is a six lane highway and the three outbound lanes were moving at high speed well above the speed limit. Sonya noted that Alaa was a very attentive driver, constantly checking his mirrors and very aware of the traffic around the old Plymouth.

Marianne broke the silence.

"Do you know Adam well?" she asked.

"I only met him in the receiving line the other night," Sonya replied. Suddenly she remembered Adam's real name.

"How did you know he was called Adam?" Marianne pressed.

"The liaison officer called him Adam when he asked about my going on this trip. Isn't Adam his real name?" she asked innocently.

"No," Marianne replied. "His name is Angus Donald McGregor."

"I guess I'll just call him 'General' or 'Sir' until I hear differently. I've never met a General before. Is he terribly formal?"

"No," Marianne replied. "He's really quite relaxed when you get to know him. Wouldn't you say he was relaxed, David?"

"What's that?" David responded.

"Adam, David," his wife responded. "I was just telling Sonya that Adam is very relaxed and not stuffy at all. Wouldn't you agree?"

"Yes, of course," David responded. "He has a great sense of humor."

"I guess I'll get to see him in action on this trip," Sonya said. Out of the corner of her eye she saw Marianne's head snap in her direction. Sonya busied herself looking for a Kleenex in her purse. She didn't want Marianne to think that the conversation had made an impression on her. Suddenly, it occurred to her that Marianne might have had an affair with Adam. Marianne might be having an affair with Adam now! After all, Sonya could only account for his midday activities.

Sonya continued, "I guess you see a lot of Adam, with all the social activities connected with the Embassy."

Marianne was about to answer when David piped in, "Marianne goes riding with Adam a couple of times a week, don't you, Dear?"

Marianne nodded, "Yes, we do ride on occasion."

"How neat!" Sonya said. "Where do you ride?"

"Out by the Pyramids," Marianne answered. "You and your husband should join us."

"I would love to join you!" Sonya exclaimed. "However, you'll never see John on a horse. He grew up as a city boy and I've never been able to get him near a stable."

Sonya glanced at Marianne to see if she was reacting. They were pulling into the Air Base so the conversation lapsed. Sonya looked across the tarmac and saw Adam standing beside a small airplane. "United States of America" was painted above the windows. She felt a strange twinge at seeing Adam for the first time since their meeting at the Meridien. Sonya glanced at Marianne and noted she was watching her.

"This is so exciting," Sonya said.

"What's exciting?" Marianne asked.

"The whole thing. Going to the Sudan, traveling in an Air Force or Government airplane. Not having to pay! None of this has ever happened to me before."

"I guess that is different," Marianne replied, satisfied for the time being that the presence of Adam had nothing to do with Sonya's excitement.

CHAPTER 4

Adam was having a discussion with another man, Beechcraft's Tech Rep, who handled aircraft maintenance for the Kingair. They had completed a walk-around and checked the aircraft forms. The aircraft was ready to go.

"Okay folks, we are ready to go. Mrs. Olsen, I have your passport. Do the rest of you have yours?"

Everyone indicated they had their documents and Adam passed Sonya's to her. Nothing in his manner indicated that she was anything but a casual acquaintance. If he was having an affair with Marianne, he certainly wasn't showing it.

Captain Baldwin and the Tech Rep had finished loading the luggage. Adam turned to Dave, "I'll take the leg to Luxor and you can fly it into Khartoum. Get the paxs settled while I run the checklist." Adam entered the Kingair and disappeared into the cockpit.

The State Department couple from Khartoum entered and took the two front seats across the aisle from each other. Marianne took the second seat on the left and pointed at the seat across the aisle for Sonya. Sonya didn't argue although she was not anxious to spend the remainder of the day making conversation with Marianne.

Captain Baldwin closed the entry door and checked the

passenger seat belts for security as he went forward to take the right seat. The right engine was already running and Adam had just started rotation on the number one. Two minutes later they taxied. They took off at eight-thirty.

"How long of a flight is it?" Sonya asked.

Marianne responded, "It usually takes a little over an hour to get to Luxor. We will be on the ground less than an hour and we should make it to Khartoum in another four hours or less.

"They can't fly direct to Khartoum?" Sonya asked.

"The C-12 can fly that far but the fuel reserve would be questionable for them to divert to Jidda, Saudi Arabia should they need to."

"Is that the closest airport?"

"No, but if a sand storm comes up, it may be the only alternate." Marianne replied, quite pleased that she could be so conversant on the subject.

The trip to Luxor was without incident. Refueling was accomplished in twenty minutes. The passengers had time for a facilities stop and a few minutes to stretch their legs and then they were back on board Spar 80. They were on the ground for thirty minutes.

After take off, the pilots pointed out Aswan, Lake Nasser, and Abu Simbel as they proceeded southbound into the Sudan. Soon the drone of engines and the boredom of sand and more sand had the passengers napping.

Spar 80 touched down at Khartoum Airport at three minutes after four in the afternoon. Adam left his seat as Dave taxied into the military parking area. As soon as the engines were shutdown, Adam opened the exit and invited the passengers to disembark. Colonel Tom Carson, U.S. Army Defense Attache', was there to greet everyone.

"Hello, General. How was the trip?" he greeted Adam.

"It was fine, Tom. You know everyone except Mrs. Olsen. Mrs. Olsen, this is Colonel Tom Carson, our host in Khartoum."

Sonya shook hands with the Colonel and he introduced her to his wife, Marty.

"What are our sleeping arrangements, Tom?" Adam asked.

"Unfortunately, General, our daughter and son-in-law are

here for a month. We only have one bedroom available. I've made reservations for you and Mrs. Olsen at the Hilton. Dave and Marianne will stay with us. I brought an extra car and driver to drop you at the hotel. He'll wait for you and bring you out to our house for dinner. We've invited a few guests for a barbecue, cocktails at five. Come as you are. We're very casual here in the middle of Africa!"

Adam replied, "It's four-twenty. We probably won't be there by five. We'll try not to hold up dinner, though."

Marty had been chatting with Sonya. She said, "Sonya, take all the time you need. We probably wont eat until seven or eight anyway. Don't let Adam scare you. He's all bark and no bite where beautiful women are concerned."

"Thank you!" Sonya replied. "He's quite imposing when you first meet him." She hoped that remark would not cause speculation.

They parted company and Adam and Sonya left for the hotel. As they drove to the Hilton, Adam gave a running commentary on Khartoum and Omdurman, pointing out where the Blue Nile meets the White Nile where General Gordon was beheaded in the 1880's, and finally the Hilton, the only good hotel in Khartoum, say nothing of the Sudan.

They checked into adjoining rooms on the top floor. Sonya didn't make an issue about the adjoining rooms. She wondered if Adam was responsible for the arrangements.

"I'm going to take a shower," she announced as she opened her door. She half expected a smart remark about joining her in the shower.

"Give me a ring when you're ready," Adam replied without further comment.

Sonya had very short blond hair with a natural curl. She was able to shower and dress in twenty minutes. She called Adam's room. He was ready. She checked the lock on her adjoining door and stepped into the hall. She was dressed in a sleeveless dress with a pleated skirt. The dress was yellow and nearly matched her hair. The neckline was high and the skirt was not tight. Her shoes matched the dress with three inch heels.

Adam was dressed in a blue shirt and matching slacks with black roper boots. "You're fast," he said and added, "dressing that is!"

"Watch your remarks, Adam. We are history!" she answered with emphasis.

He followed her into the elevator without further comment. They rode to the Carson's quarters without conversation. Sonya was not comfortable. She looked out the window.

Sonya was introduced to the Carson's daughter, Jane, and her husband. They made small talk about family and children. Sonya showed pictures of her two sons. The women had separated from the men to opposite ends of the walled in yard.

Jane asked, "Sonya, how did you get your husband to let you come out to the Sudan with Adam McGregor?"

Sonya's eyes widened, "Actually, my husband was suppose to come on this trip. He had commitments so he volunteered me. I've only met General McGregor twice—today and last weekend at an Embassy party. Is there something that I need to know about General McGregor?"

"Oh, I'm sorry" Jane backed off. "I assumed you knew about his reputation as a ladies man."

"Heavens, no! Thanks for the warning, though. I'll be sure to lock my door."

"Let's get a drink," Jane suggested. They walked to the bar.

"We help ourselves if we can't get a gentleman to help us!" Jane stated loud enough for the men to hear. Her husband responded, "What can I get you, Jane?"

"I'll have a Manhattan," Jane replied.

"What would you like, Sonya?"

"I think a scotch and soda," Sonya replied.

"We have Dewars or Johnny Walker," Tom Carson chimed in.

"I'll have a Dewars," Sonya replied.

"Good choice," Adam interjected.

"Are you an expert on liquor, General?" Sonya asked with a hint of sarcasm.

"No," Adam replied, "just on Scotch.

"And how do you arrive at Dewars?" she continued.

"After considerable testing! I was a fighter pilot in my previous life," he added with a grin.

"I've never met a fighter pilot before," she responded. "How do you tell when you meet one?"

Tom Carson jumped in, "They have big watches."

"I think we'll leave it at that," Adam said closing the subject to much snickering.

"Is that an inside joke?" Sonya asked.

"Most definitely," Adam replied.

Marty called out, "Soups on!"

Everyone lined up at the outdoor barbecue for ribs with all the fixings. Tom Carson brought out Brandy and Port for after dinner. After everyone was offered a drink, Tom explained the itinerary for the trip to Geneina. They would fly to El Fasher the next day. He suggested they leave about nine o'clock, arriving in El Fasher around Noon. The Governor, Ahmed Ibrahim, would put the party up at the guest house and in his quarters. There would be the two pilots, Mrs. Olsen, The Reverend and Mrs. Cameron, the Ambassador and his wife and Colonel Carson. Governor Ibrahim would be the seventh passenger for the flight to Geneina on Wednesday. They would save Thursday as an alternate in case there were thunderstorms on Jebel Mara, the eleven thousand foot peak between El Fasher and Geneina. It was the rainy season for the Sudan.

Adam suggested that he and Sonya should probably go to the hotel. It was after ten pm. He would be getting up at seven am to be at the airport by eight o'clock. Sonya said she was ready as she had promised to call home before going to bed.

Marty suggested that she call from their house through the Embassy lines as Marty doubted she would get through from the hotel. It took about ten minutes to get through to Mohandisin. Reverend Olsen was there, but the children were asleep. Sonya gave him a quick brief on her itinerary and promised to call as soon as they returned to Khartoum.

The Embassy driver was waiting. Adam and Sonya departed for the hotel. Adam made arrangements for a pickup at seven-forty five. They went up to their rooms. As they approached their doors, Adam asked if she needed a call in the morning. She said no.

Once inside her room, Sonya checked the double doors between rooms to make sure hers was locked. She undressed and put on a negligee and proceeded to read the novel she had brought for the trip.

It was just after eleven pm when the power failed and the lights went off. Sonya gasped. She was afraid of the dark and no where is as dark as Equatorial Africa when there is an overcast. She began to panic. She wondered if she should scream. Finally, she crawled on the floor to the adjoining room door. She unlocked her door and tried Adams. It was locked. She wrapped on the door gently.

"Sonya, is that you?" he asked in a low voice.

"Yes. Please let me in!"

"Just a moment."

She heard him moving and suddenly he opened his door. She couldn't see him. She reached out and grasped his leg and pulled herself up.

"Please hold me, I'm afraid of the dark and I've never seen darkness like this. It's making me panic," she pleaded through hard sobs.

He pulled her up to her feet and kissed her for a long time. He said, "Close your eyes and keep them closed. Pretend you're sleeping and try to breath normally."

They sat on the edge of the bed for a moment while he lifted her nightgown over her head. Then he laid her out on the bed and began to make love to her. She opened her eyes, though she still couldn't see anything. Her eyes were brimming with tears. She began to cooperate, rolling her hips and then the climaxes came, one after another.

"Are your eyes still closed?" he asked.

"No! They're so full of tears, I still can't see."

"That's because it's still dark. I can't see either."

He held her tightly and kissed her until her body went limp and she fell asleep. He slept also. At six ten, the lights came on. Sonya woke up and saw Adam. She started to get up and she remembered when the lights had gone out. She jostled Adam gently. She saw his eyes open.

"Did you cause the light failure to get me in bed?"

"I didn't know you were afraid of the dark," he replied.

"You didn't have any pajamas on. If you weren't plotting to get me into bed why were you naked?" she pouted.

"I never wear anything in bed," he replied. Just then his alarm went off. He cut off the alarm.

"I guess we weren't finished after all," Adam stated.

"Please don't make fun of me. I really can't help my fear of the dark. I've had it since I was little. I always sleep with a light on. You could have just helped me. You didn't have to make love to me."

Adam sighed, " I thought making love to you would get your mind off the blackout."

"I guess you were somewhat successful as I slept all night. Do these blackouts happen often?" Sonya asked.

"More nights than not," he responded.

"You're kidding!" she said with the sheet pulled up over her. "Are you sure you didn't plan all of this?"

"How could I plan for something I didn't even know about. Do you want to shower here or do you want to go back to your room?"

"I'll go back to my room. Please hand me my nightgown." Adam watched.

When she got up, Adam said, "Sonya, I can see right through your negligee."

"Please be quiet! Just be still." She stomped out of the room.

They were both ready to go in plenty of time. Adam was dressed in jeans and an open collar shirt. Sonya had on tan culottes, a shirt to match and a vest. She was carrying a wide brimmed hat.

"You look nice," Adam volunteered.

"I feel terrible."

"Why? Are you ill?" Adam probed.

"I think I'm going out of my mind." "Why?" he continued.

"I was sure when we left the Meridien, that I could put you out of my life. All of a sudden, I'm on a trip to Africa with the lover I'm trying to forget. The lights go out and the only person I can turn to is the same lover I'm trying to forget and today, I'm going to Far Darfur with that lover. Will the power go off in El Fasher, too? Will I be a basket case again until I crawl back in your bed and let you ring my bell again, so I can sleep through the night. I'm petrified that the lights will go out. I want to be rid of you, but I'm afraid to turn to anyone else. I want you to arrange for us to be together at night until I get home. Am I crazy or what?"

Adam took her by the shoulders and turned her around. Tears were flowing down her cheeks. He kissed her tenderly on the lips. She put her arms around his neck and kissed him back.

"Let's take this one day at a time," Adam said. "We can decide to call it off once you're back with your family. Okay?"

She nodded her agreement still trying to get control. She went into the bathroom and redid her make-up. When she reappeared, she was better. They left for the airport.

CHAPTER 5

Colonel Carson met the car as it pulled up to Spar 80. Adam and Sonya got out of the back seat. Adam retrieved their luggage from the car's trunk and tossed them to Dave Baldwin. They were still waiting for the Ambassador's party.

"Are we all set at El Fasher?" Adam asked Tom Carson.

"The accommodations are all set. You and Mrs. Olsen will be staying with the Governor. The Ambassador and the Pastor and their wives will have suites in the guest house. The only problem is fuel. The Governor couldn't promise a full load of Jet A-1."

"We'll reroute to Rub Kona and fill up at Chevron. That will assure enough fuel to get to Geneina and back to El Fasher. If there isn't fuel at El Fasher, we can still make Rub Kona. Has Dave filed the flight plan?"

"He's in the cockpit," Tom replied.

Adam leaned in the entry door and shouted, "How did you file us, Dave?"

"I filed both routes, Sir. We can activate either flight plan when we contact the tower for taxi instructions."

"Good work!" the General responded. "Let's go through Rub Kona."

"Yes Sir!"

Adam looked around for Sonya. She had wandered around to the other side of the jet. He followed her.

"Sonya," he called out. "Are you doing my walk around?"

"I'm just trying to get myself straightened out before all the people show up. I was going over my options and no matter what I do, I come up with downsides."

"Over the next three or four days, we should have time to talk about the options," Adam said.

"I think you mean nights. We must remember to do some talking."

Adam smiled, "I promise. Here comes the Ambassador's party. I'll introduce you."

Ambassador and Mrs. Barton arrived in the Embassy limousine. Reverend Cameron and Mrs. Cameron were in their company. The Ambassador had met General McGregor and Captain Baldwin on numerous occasions over the past eighteen months. General McGregor was accredited to Khartoum as the Air Force Attache'. The General usually visited the Sudan every three months.

Adam led Sonya around the aircraft to the limousine. "Ambassador Barton, I would like you to meet Mrs. Olsen," Adam said. "She will be available to help Dr. Cameron with his report."

Ambassador Barton then introduced the Cameron's to everyone and Mrs. Barton introduced herself to Sonya. They all boarded the aircraft. The Ambassador and Dr. Cameron took the two front seats nearest the cockpit. Mrs. Barton and Mrs. Cameron took the next two seats. Colonel Carson and Sonya sat across from each other in seats five and six.

General McGregor closed and locked the door. He quickly checked seat belts as he proceeded to the cockpit where Dave Baldwin was finishing the checklist. The General took the left seat and started the right engine. By the time both engines were running, Dave had called the tower, filed to Rub Kona, and had taxi instructions. They were airborne in six minutes and turned southwest toward Rub Kona.

Sonya turned to Colonel Carson, "Excuse me, Sir. Did you lose power last night?"

"Oh, yes," Tom replied, "It was no problem because we have a backup generator."

"I wonder why the Hilton doesn't have emergency power?" Sonya asked.

"They do!" Tom stated. "It only covers emergency lighting in the corridors, the air conditioning, refrigeration, and the elevators. Your power failed, I take it."

"Yes, I was reading. I understand power failures are quite common."

"Yes," Tom responded, "Everything mechanical in the Sudan has a high failure rate."

"Why is that?"

"The Sudanese don't have an understanding of the need for periodic maintenance. Nothing gets changed until it fails. Didn't Adam explain?"

"Well, by the time I saw him this morning," she lied, "I forgot to ask." She picked up her book and began reading.

Tom Carson looked at Sonya for a moment. He noticed that her cheeks were flushed. "How long have you known Adam?" he asked.

"Oh, I only met him at the Embassy last Friday. My husband was suppose to come on this trip. He had scheduling conflicts, so he volunteered my services. The next time I saw General McGregor was yesterday. He has been very nice to me, even though I hardly know him."

"I'm sorry we couldn't accommodate you at our home. Will you be all right at the Hilton when you come back through?"

"Yes, of course, it will be no problem at all."

Sonya went back to reading her book, however, she read the same page three times. She wondered if Tom Carson knew about her affair. Maybe Adam did kiss and tell.

The trip to Rub Kona was short and they were only on the ground for twenty minutes. Adam and David swapped seats and they were on their way to El Fasher.

The field at El Fasher was built in the early 1940's. The runway was only five thousand feet long. The first thousand feet of each end of the runway were covered with asphalt although the asphalt was badly in need of repair. The middle three thousand feet were covered with crushed rock. This was no problem when the field was dry eleven months of the year. However, during the short wet season occasionally the crushed rock was covered with water. Fortunately, the field was dry on the day of their arrival.

Governor Ibrahim met the aircraft with two vehicles. The Governor's vehicle was a new white Range Rover and the second vehicle was a military Land Rover driven by a Sudanese Army Sergeant. The Governor took Ambassador and Mrs. Barton and the Cameron's in his vehicle while Adam, Sonya, Tom Carson and David Baldwin climbed into the Land Rover. Adam took the front seat while the other three were in the back seat with Sonya in the middle.

Both Rovers were driven to the Guest House where Governor Ibrahim had arranged a luncheon. They dined on a buffet of Sudanese and Middle Eastern cuisine, drinking tea and/or Pepsi Cola.

As soon as the meal was completed, Governor Ibrahim invited everyone to board the Rover and they set out to visit a water project. The Governor led the way in his Range Rover, taking off in a northwesterly direction. There was no road. They crossed the semi-desert at maximum speed, slowing down slightly to cross an occasional wadi and to circumnavigate the sparse vegetation.

The passengers wondered if the Governor really knew where he was going. In a little over an hour, they arrived at an installation where three diesel engines were hooked to three separate pumps. One rig was pumping water into a large thank that overflowed into a larger pond. Numerous animals, primarily camels and donkeys, were drinking at the pond. Natives were busy filling goatskins with water, loading the full skins on a beast of burden and then striking out for their villages. The Governor explained that this was the only source of clean water within thirty kilometers for many villages.

The Governor pointed to the General and Colonel Carson saying, "You two were here last year when we visited. Remember the natives were getting their water from the pond where the animals drink? It took me until two months ago to get the wells and pumps working. President Numerie is still upset with me. He says Darfur is nothing but problems and I remind them that Darfur doesn't have a Nile. All the rest of the Sudan gets their water from the Nile system. In Darfur, we must have wells."

Sonya had been following Adam. She tugged at his shirt to

get his attention. "What is it?" he asked.

"He's good, isn't he?" she whispered.

"He's the best man in the Sudan and maybe the best man in all Africa," Adam concluded.

"Why does he have all those scars?" Sonya quietly asked.

"Those are tribal scars from his youth. They represent rites of passage. He may have killed a lion or survived a long trek," Adam replied.

"How exciting!" she said.

When they returned to the Rovers for the return trip to El Fasher, Sonya tried to think of a way to get Adam to sit in the back with her. However, she noted a certain protocol and decided that trying to make a change might draw further attention. The return trip was fast and uncomfortable.

Back at El Fasher, the guests were dropped off at the guest house and Adam and Sonya entered the Range Rover for the short drive to the Governor's quarters. The Governor showed Adam and Sonya to the guest rooms. The rooms were very nice by African standards. The rooms did not adjoin, however, they did share a bathroom.

Governor Ibrahim stated, "I'm sorry that you will have to share a bathroom. There are very few bathrooms in El Fasher and most of them don't work."

"I'm sure we can work out a schedule," Sonya said. She didn't trust Adam to not make an off hand comment.

"I'll be sure to knock," Adam promised.

Sonya glanced at Adam to see if his facial expression gave her away. He was his usual collected self. He must have been a remarkable liar as a child, she thought to herself.

"I've arranged for some drinks and supper at the Guest House around seven pm," the Governor added, "if the power is on you can walk there. If the power is off, we'll drive the Rover." He backed out of the room with a nod.

Adam followed and whispered as he closed the door, "I'll race you to the shower." By the time he unlocked his door and got his luggage set down he heard the shower running. He tried the bathroom door. It was unlocked. He opened it and peeked in.

"Is there room for two?" he asked.

"No, there isn't. You'll have to wait until we go back to the Meridien."

"I was hoping for a quickie," he said.

"I don't know what a 'quickie' is," she replied. "I want what I've become accustomed to experiencing and I wouldn't describe it as a 'quickie',"

"My place or yours?" Adam asked.

"Let's go to your bed. I can run back to my room if anyone should knock on the door. I'll be with you in a minute."

Adam looked at his watch. It was four-thirty pm. He knew that everyone would show up at exactly seven pm. There was just time for some love making, a short nap and a shower before they would have to leave. He stripped off his clothes and turned back the sheet and bedspread and laid out on the bed, closing his eyes.

A short time later, Sonya came in from the bathroom. She saw Adam laid out on the bed, totally naked. She dropped the towel she was wrapped in and laid down beside him. He opened his eyes.

"Would you bring me a towel from the bathroom?" Adam asked.

Sonya retrieved the towel quickly. She was back in bed in ten seconds.

"What do you want with a towel?" she asked.

"I don't want the towel," he explained.

"Why did you ask me to get it?"

"I wanted to see you walk in the nude."

"What for?" Sonya asked with emotion.

"I wanted to see if you were still as beautiful as the last time I saw you in the nude," he answered sincerely.

"And what's the verdict?" she asked.

"Do you want the truth or a compliment?" he asked teasing her.

"I've changed my mind. I don't want to know," she pouted.

He pulled her close to himself and kissed her on the mouth. She reached down to grab his erection and invited him to roll on top of her. They made love. They laid together and dozed for sometime. Then Adam got up and took a shower. They both dressed and were about to go down to meet the Governor. Adam grabbed her arm and pulled her to him. He kissed her tenderly and said, "You are the most beautiful woman I have ever known."

"Oh, Adam," she replied, "I think I'm going to cry."

"Don't you dare. You'll blow our cover." He patted her on the butt and added, "Go into your room and lock the bathroom door. I'll knock on your door in a moment."

She did as she was told. They were both smiling as they walked down the corridor to meet Governor Ibrahim. They all walked to the guest house. As Adam had predicted, everyone arrived at the lounge area of the guest house at seven pm.

Ambassador Barton and Pastor Cameron joined the Governor and the three military officers. Sonya joined the other two wives. There were no Sudanese women in attendance, a fact quickly noted by Sonya and Mrs. Cameron.

"Are we the only women invited?" Mrs. Cameron asked.

Mrs. Barton replied, "It's rare that women are invited to social functions in the Middle East and it's particularly rare in Africa."

"What about the Governor?" Sonya asked, "Surely he's married."

"He's married to an Austrian woman who lives in Khartoum with their two children. The President keeps Governor Ibrahim's family in Khartoum in hopes of having better control over the Governor."

"How terrible!" Mrs. Cameron exclaimed.

Just then the Governor approached to invite them to partake of some of the food. Governor Ibrahim spoke perfect English with a combination British-Arabic accent. He explained some of the dishes and offered the ladies a choice of Scotch, beer, or Pepsi Cola.

There had been considerable cloud cover that day so the temperature was relatively mild. That was fortunate as the Guest House was not air conditioned, except for window air conditioners in the two VIP bedrooms.

Sonya accepted a scotch and ice from the steward and sidled over next to Adam. "What's edible here, Adam?" she asked.

"Everything!" he replied.

"Really?" she questioned.

"If you can survive Cairo, you can survive here. It may not look that appetizing, but I have never gotten sick from eating here.

Have some camel's liver."

She took a piece of liver with a toothpick. It was covered with a red pepper sauce. It took her breath away for a moment.

"Whew, that's hot. How do they cook it?" she asked innocently.

"They don't." Adam replied in a whisper. "If you cook Camel's liver, it turns to stone."

"Isn't there a danger of picking up a disease?" she asked.

"Probably," Adam replied. "Drink your scotch. It should kill the germs."

"It's certainly strong enough," Sonya replied. Her ice had melted and she sipped on very strong scotch.

"Can we drink the water?" Sonya asked.

"You'll have to drink it," Adam replied. "If you don't, you'll dehydrate and that's worse than catching a bug."

"I hope I survive this trip," Sonya replied.

There were about ten different dishes around the table. Adam and Sonya tried them all. They were able to whet their appetites quite nicely. Sonya returned to join the other two women.

"Did the General steer you to some good food?" Mrs. Cameron asked.

"I just followed him around and ate whatever he did," Sonya replied. "I guess he's been here enough times to know what to eat."

"The food is different," Mrs. Barton stated. "It's quite good. We seem to have less illness in the Sudan than you will experience in Cairo."

The party began to break up. General McGregor thanked the Governor for the accommodations and the meal. He then suggested they meet at eight am for the trip to Geneina. That was also agreeable to the Ambassador.

Governor Ibrahim said there would be coffee and some snacks at the Guest House in the morning. They would be served a lunch at Geneina during their tour of the refugee camp. The Governor walked back to his quarters with Adam and Sonya. He observed his two guests as they each entered their rooms.

Sonya undressed and put on her negligee. When she entered the bathroom, Adam was brushing his teeth. She turned the light out in her room. Adam looked at her.

"I know," she said, "you can see right through it."

"I'll leave the door open," Adam responded.

"I'll be there in a minute. Leave the light on for me," she said.

When she came in the room, she slipped out of her negligee and crawled into bed next to Adam.

"Can I ask you a question?"

"Sure," Adam replied.

"Are you having an affair with Marianne?"

"Why are you asking about Marianne?"

"Her husband said you and Marianne go riding together," Sonya responded. "She's very nice looking."

"She's also married to my subordinate. I'm not ready to lose my career over an inter-office affair."

She rolled over and kissed him. The rest of the night went well.

CHAPTER 6

The group gathered at the Guest House for coffee and pastry sweetened with honey. As soon as everyone appeared to be satisfied they boarded the two Rovers and drove to the airplane. Adam seated the Ambassador and the Governor in the two front seats, followed by Colonel Carson and Revered Cameron. The three women took the last three seats with Sonya in the rear. She was happy to sit apart as she had much to think about.

Adam and David had looked over the available maps. There were no terrain markings except to note where the summit of Jebel Mara was located. There were a lot of clouds shrouding Jebel Mara. They decided to remain in visual flight conditions by skirting Jebel Mara on the south side. When they got around to the southwest of the mountain, they picked up a paved road and followed it south-southwest. They never were able to tune in the low frequency radio beacon. They picked up a view of some buildings and an increase in the number of huts and decided to continue on to the east. Fortunately, the visibility remained good and they were able to make out the control tower at the airfield. They passed over the field at fifteen hundred feet to pick up the wind direction from a wind sock on the field. Then Adam circled to land into the wind. There was no other traffic so the landing was uneventful and they had no problem finding their way to the parking area.

The terminal was constructed of red brick. It appeared to be the only building in Geneina that was over two stories high. As they entered the terminal, they were approached by a man who introduced himself as Mr. Abdullah. He would be their host for the day. He asked if anyone spoke Arabic or French. Ambassador Barton suggested that Arabic would be fine and the Ambassador or Governor Ibrahim would translate where necessary.

Mr. Abdullah led the group to the parking area where two Peugeot station wagons awaited them. Mr. Abdullah would drive the lead vehicle. A native driver was at the wheel of the second station wagon. The Ambassador suggested that the Cameron's and Governor Ibrahim join him in the lead car. Adam took the remaining five to the second Peugeot. Colonel Carson and Captain Baldwin volunteered to crawl into the back seat leaving the middle seat for Mrs. Barton and Sonya. Adam joined the driver in the front seat. The two vehicles sped off toward the center of Geneina. They proceeded to what appeared to be an administration building where they would be treated to a buffet lunch.

Sonya followed Adam around the buffet table. Mrs. Barton noticed that Sonya took whatever Adam had on his plate. It occurred to Mrs. Barton that Sonya was becoming dependent on the General. For a moment she contemplated the possibility of an affair. She immediately rejected the thought. However, out of curiosity, she decided to remain close to Sonya for the day. She noticed that Sonya never let Adam out of her sight. When they had finished their lunch, Mrs. Barton struck up a conversation with Sonya.

"What do you think of Africa, Sonya?"

Sonya's head snapped around. She was taken back by the question and immediately wondered if she had compromised herself.

"To tell you the truth, Mrs. Barton, if it wasn't for General McGregor, I would be scared out of my wits. Before we came to Cairo, I had only been out of Minnesota twice. My family went to Milwaukee to a wedding and we drove to the Black Hills for a visit once. I grew up in Northfield and attended St. Olaf. My husband is the only man I ever dated. We met in grade school, went to high school and college together. We attended the same church where my father was pastor. I nearly fainted when my husband volunteered me for this trip. I'm not sorry I came. I'm just very relieved to have the General nearby. Am I being silly?"

"Certainly not, my dear!" Mrs. Barton replied. "Adam does give one a secure feeling when he's around. I felt the same way about my husband when we first came to a third world Embassy."

Sonya was relieved when Adam came by and said they were ready to go to the refugee center. Everyone filed out and got into their vehicles.

The refugee center was about a mile away. It consisted of a number of buildings arranged around a quadrangle. None of the buildings had roofs. The buildings had rooms inside where individual families could set up beds if they had them, or sleep on the ground. Food was prepared and served at a central meeting place. Everything was very spartan.

Mr. Abdullah explained that the Saudi Arabian Government funded the center, including paying for all the food. He explained that the buildings didn't have roofs because the climate was so mild that roofs were not necessary. The refugees were all from Northern Chad where Libyan forces had invaded. The Chad government's main concern was that the refugees would probably never return to Northern Chad where they lived in tents and were mainly nomadic.

Ambassador Barton tried to talk with one of the women, but she couldn't understand him. Mr. Abdullah explained that her language was a local dialect although she was familiar with some Arabic words, her language was primarily native to the desert tribes of the Central Sahara.

Mrs. Cameron and Sonya had cameras. They asked if they could take pictures. Mr. Abdullah said that pictures of the facilities would be all right as long as they didn't take pictures of the refugees. He explained that the tribal people were afraid of cameras. If the camera wasn't pointed at them, they wouldn't be afraid. The two women took pictures being careful that the refugees were not the center of the subject.

Ambassador Barton asked the Cameron's and Sonya if they needed any more information. They replied that they were ready to go. The Ambassador thanked Mr. Abdullah for his help and patience. They all went back to their vehicles and departed for the airport. The experience had been quite depressing and all were happy to get back on the airplane.

The trip back to El Fasher was uneventful. Adam and David saw thunderstorms forming on the south slope of Jebel Mara. They decided to follow the route around the north slope. They were able to maintain visual contact with the ground and arrived back at El Fasher by four pm.

Governor Ibrahim invited everyone to gather at the Guest House at seven pm. Refreshments and a light dinner would be served. All the guests went to their rooms to shower and rest up. Sonya stopped at the Cameron's quarters and spent an hour with the Reverend and Mrs. Cameron while they drafted a report to be sent to the World Council of Churches. By the time Sonya returned to the Governor's quarters, the sun was setting. She had just arrived at her door when the sky turned black. She hurried in and turned on the light. She went to the bathroom and knocked on the door. Adam was just about finished shaving. He opened the door.

"You're certainly casual," Sonya commented as she noticed Adam was wrapped in his towel. "How did you know it was me?"

"Who else would it be?" Adam replied with a smirk on his face.

"As soon as you're finished, I'd like to take a shower," Sonya said ignoring his comments.

"Go ahead," he replied. "I'll be finished in two minutes."

She didn't reply. She retreated to her room, undressed and donned her bathrobe. When she returned to the bathroom, she knocked again and entered, thinking Adam had departed. Adam grabbed her, pulled her to himself and kissed her.

"I missed you this afternoon. What took so long?"

"The Reverend and Mrs. Cameron are sticklers for detail. We went over the draft three times before I could slip away. I just made it here before the sun crashed," she replied.

"If I had known you would be this late, I would have come back for you. The Governor will be here for us at six forty-five. Better hurry," he said as he closed the door.

Sonya quickly showered and put her traveling clothes on again. She was saving her last dress for the last night in Khartoum. At six forty-five, she heard a tap and immediately went to the door. Governor Ibrahim and Adam were waiting. It was very dark as lights along the walkway to the Guest House were out.

"We lost power," the Governor said. "We are on my emergency generator and we only have lights at my residence and the Guest House." The Governor was dressed in a white galabaya and had a white turban wrapped around his head. He led the way while Adam took Sonya by the arm. Because of the white robes, they had no problem following their host as long as they remained close.

The lighting in the reception room of the Guest House was adequate to take away the shadows. They all helped themselves to the bar. Adam mixed Scotch and ice for himself and for Sonya. The remainder of the party arrived a few minutes later.

The party was closed suddenly by the arrival of a thunderstorm. There was a flash of lightning followed immediately by a clap of thunder. The lights cycled off and back on. Sonya grabbed Adam's hand tightly.

"I think we'll make a run for it," Adam said to the Governor.

"You might as well. It'll probably rain all night," the Governor replied. "We'll meet here for coffee at eight am, if it's not pouring. I'll be along in a few minutes."

Adam took Sonya's hand and started out the door and across to the covered veranda. The lighting flashed long enough for him to see the board walk to the Governor's House. He picked Sonya up in his arms and started down the walk. She buried her face in his chest and closed her eyes. By the time they reached the veranda, they were both soaked.

"Your room or mine?" Adam asked.

"Yours, I forgot my key."

At the door, Adam set her down on her feet and got his key out. He opened the door and they went in. They both quickly stripped off the wet clothes. Sonya said, "I'll get some towels," as she went to the bathroom door. It was locked.

"Oh, Adam, I locked your door and I don't have my key. What will we do now? If we ask for the key, the Governor will suspect we are co-habituating."

"He probably suspects anyway. He's a pretty cosmopolitan guy," Adam responded as he took out his Swiss Army knife. He used it to open a slight gap in the molding around the door latch. Sonya watched intently. "Is that the knife you used to cut off my bikini?

She asked.

"Yes," he replied as he took out his wallet and extracted his identification card.

"You didn't have to cut it off," she said as he slid the card into the gap and popped the door open.

"What are you saying?"

"I knew it was your room and I had been looking for an excuse to see you. I had watched you all week. I would have taken my bikini off. I wanted you to make love to me from the first moment I saw you."

"You little vixen, you," Adam responded as he pulled her to him and kissed her passionately. "Just how many liaisons have you had?"

"You're the first and you'll be the last. I'll return to my husband and sons when we get back to Cairo. I'll be the sweet chaste preacher's wife once again. I'll never forget you, Adam. You've shown me a part of life I'll never forget," she said as he kissed her again.

"Sonya," Adam began, "Why don't you get a divorce and marry me?"

"I never considered it," she responded. "I was told you were a confirmed bachelor."

"Who told you that?" he asked.

"Marianne dropped the hint at the Carson's party."

"Actually, I've been married. I married my high school sweetheart when I graduated from the Academy. I went to pilot training, expecting my wife to join me. She was working in a legal office. She got an annulment and married her lawyer. I've never seen her since the annulment."

"How awful!" Sonya whispered.

"It was more embarrassing for the families than anything. I realized early on, that I was lucky to be out of the marriage. It really freed me up to concentrate on my career. I did two tours in Viet Nam and two tours at the Pentagon. I made three early promotions, including making Brigadier General in eighteen years."

"Oh, Adam! I wish I could get a divorce and marry you. I know I love you and I guess you love me if you really want to marry me. I can't get a divorce. My family and my husband's family wouldn't allow it. They have been close friends since before John and I were born. I'm afraid I'm stuck. That's why I must stop seeing you after we return to Cairo."

Adam watch her from behind as she talked. He noticed that she was trembling. He turned her around and saw the tears running down her cheeks. He held her by the arms and kissed her on each cheek tasting the salt from her tears. Then he kissed her tenderly on the mouth, holding her tight.

"Let's go to bed," Adam suggested.

Sonya turned and pulled the covers down. She sat on the edge of the bed noting that they had both been naked since taking off their wet clothes. Adam reached over and turned out the light. Sonya reached out and took Adam's hand and pulled him toward her. He slowly crawled over her, kissing the insides of her thighs, then her navel, and finally her nipples. They made love with slow easy motion for some minutes until Sonya had a climax, then they increased their speed until they both climaxed together. They lay motionless for several minutes, neither wanting to separate their bodies. Finally, Adam rolled off of Sonya and they both fell asleep.

They awoke when lightning struck nearby. They each made a trip to the bathroom to relieve themselves and brush their teeth. When they were both back in bed they made love again.

The thunderstorms stopped, but it rained all through the night. There was an overcast and it was quite cool. Sonya showered first and went to her room. By seven-thirty am Adam had completed his shower. As soon as he was dressed, he went out on the veranda and knocked on Sonya's door. She was ready and they walked to the Guest House. They were the first to arrive. Coffee and pastries arrived just before eight am. The remainder of the group made their appearance. Captain Baldwin had been out to the aircraft. He reported that the field was saturated from the rain.

"Is the macadam covered also?" Adam asked.

"No, the paving is wet, but there isn't any standing water," David reported.

"Let's check the C-12 manual for the short field take-off procedure," Adam said.

Dave Baldwin pulled the manual out of his briefcase and opened it to the area on short field take-off and landing procedures.

They went over it carefully.

Adam said, "It looks like we can make it if we back up to the edge of the macadam, go to full power before we release brakes and pull back on the column when we reach the water. If we can ride the air cushion we won't settle back down."

"Have you ever tried this, Sir?" Dave asked the General.

"No," the General replied, "but it's an authorized procedure. The worst thing that can happen is that we'll settle back into the crushed rock. With all that water, aborting will be no problem."

After everyone had coffee and a snack, General McGregor explained the problems with the weather and that if they couldn't get airborne in the first thousand feet, they would have to abort and wait for the rain to stop and for the water to drain away.

Ambassador Barton thanked Governor Ibrahim for his hospitality and suggested that everyone get aboard Spar 80. They all boarded the two Rovers and drove to the parking area.

By the time the aircraft was loaded and taxied to the runway the rain had eased to a drizzle. Adam taxied the C-12 on to the runway centerline and then reversed the propelors to back up to the leading edge of the runway. He brought the props back to idle and turned to Dave. "I'm going to run-up to full power before releasing the brakes," he advised. "When I get to the end of the macadam, I'll rotate if I have 60 knots of airspeed. If we don't have 90 knots by midfield, I'll abort the take-off. Notify the passengers."

Captain Baldwin activated the PA system. "Ladies and Gentlemen," he said, "we are about to implement a short field take-off. We'll go to full power before we release brakes. If we don't have flying speed by midfield, we'll abort the take-off and taxi back to the ramp. Check your seat belts, please."

Adam ran the throttles to one-hundred percent and released the brakes. Spar 80 responded immediately. As the aircraft approached the end of the paving, Adam checked the airspeed. At 60 knots, he popped the column back. The nose came up and he immediately released pressure to level the aircraft. Spar 80 was riding on ground effect, inches above the water covering the crushed rock. At midfield, the aircraft was approaching one hundred knots. Adam eased back on the column and began to climb.

"Gear up!" he ordered. Dave pulled the handle up and

responded, "Gear is up."

"Flaps up!" followed by "Flaps are up."

There was a resounding cheer from the cabin. The pilots turned Spar 80 to 090 degrees and headed for Khartoum. They had plenty of fuel and wouldn't need to stop at Rub Kona.

Sonya thought to herself, "My hero, the pilot!" She felt her face flush and she looked across the aisle to see if Mrs. Cameron had noticed her. Her secret was safe and she wondered if she and Adam would have adjoining rooms again. She would enjoy one last night together.

Over El Obied, the pilots contacted the Embassy to request transportation. The vehicles were waiting when they pulled into the parking area at the Khartoum Airport.

CHAPTER 7

It was just a little after noon when the vehicles departed the airport. Adam, Sonya, David and Colonel Carson all got into an embassy Land Rover. Colonel Carson suggested that they tour the area where the Battle of Omdurman had taken place. Everyone liked the idea, except Sonya. She would have rather gone to the hotel.

The tour of the battlefield took a little over an hour. When they returned to Khartoum, they stopped at the Hilton. Adam and Sonya took their bags and checked in. Colonel Carson would send the vehicle back for them at five-thirty. The Carson's were hosting a cocktail party and dinner. He had told Adam that he wanted him to meet John Baranga, a Colonel in the Sundanese Army. Adam and Sonya had the same rooms as during their previous stay. They each unlocked the adjoining room doors.

"Your place or mine," Adam called out. Sonya was in the bathroom. "I turned down my bed, I'll be with you in a moment." She appeared from the bathroom in panties and a bra. She saw Adam stretched out on the bed. She unhooked her bra as she crossed to the bed, dropping her panties as she reached the bed.

"Sonya!" he said getting her attention.

"Yes," she replied as she laid down beside him.

"You are unbelievably sexy and I love you," he replied.

"Adam, please don't say that," she said. "How can I leave you if I believe you love me. You just love the sex. Our lives are so different. How could we possibly make it? You'd tire of me in a month."

"I wouldn't tire of you in a century," he replied as he kissed her passionately. They made love again and they both slept for a long time.

Sonya woke with a start. Adam's arm was still around her, just below her breasts. She poked him lightly on the arm.

"What?" he said, as he awoke from a deep sleep.

"It's four-thirty," she said. "We are expected at the Carson's in an hour.

"Oh," he responded . "I guess we'd better shower."

They immediately headed for their bathrooms. Adam was dressed and sitting at the desk when Sonya came in the room. She was wearing a light blue sheath that matched her eyes. She was unbelievably beautiful. He rose to meet her.

"Are you ready to go?" he asked.

"No, I have to put on my makeup."

"And?" he asked.

"I came to kiss you before I put on my lipstick," she said as she entered his outstretched arms.

"You know what happens right after we kiss?" he asked with a smirk on his face.

"Yes, but not now! We can't be late or they'll really suspect we are lovers."

He kissed her long and tenderly. Then she returned to her room. She was back in ten minutes more beautiful than ever. They went down to the lobby. The vehicle was just pulling up. Twenty minutes later they arrived at the Carson's quarters.

Colonel Carson met them at the door. He escorted them through to the patio where a bar was set up. Adam had his usual Dewars over ice and Sonya had a scotch and soda. Then Colonel Carson introduced them to each of the six couples the Carson's had invited to meet General McGregor.

Colonel John Baranga and his wife had arrived a few minutes earlier. Colonel Carson introduced them to Adam and Sonya. John Baranga was a tall man, maybe six foot two and very muscular. His spouse was at least six foot five. John Baranga was of mixed blood. His wife was a Dinka. She was very slender as well as tall. They both spoke perfect English. John Baranga had just returned from the States. He had been at Iowa State University in Ames Iowa, where he had received a Doctorate in Economics. His wife had completed her high school education while they were in Iowa. She was planning to return to Iowa State for her Bachelors in Education. Adam and Sonya were both enthralled with the couple. They talked about many things involving the differences between the Sudan and Iowa. The Baranga's were very upbeat on the Sudan if the political situation could be resolved and the economic situation could be improved.

"Tell me," Adam asked, "What would improve the economic situation in the Sudan in the short run?"

"That's easy," John fired back. "We need to complete the Jungali Canal. This would open the Nile for navigation all the way to Juba. It would provide a way to get agricultural products to market all over the world. The oil discoveries in the Sud will provide the finances necessary for development, if the politicians in Khartoum will quit stealing the money."

"I hadn't thought of the area as an agricultural bonanza," Adam countered as they walked to the buffet table.

"Neither had I before I saw Iowa and until I visited the French community who are digging the Jungali Canal. They grow all their own vegetables. They grow tomatoes as big as your head. The soil is unbelievably rich, just like Iowa. The Jungali Canal will drain large portions of the Sud. All we need to do is teach the tribes to farm."

"That's interesting," Adam acknowledged. "Do you mind if I quote you in my report to Washington?"

"Please do. The more information we can get out to the world, the better chance that international pressure will be felt in Khartoum."

They all filled their plates and retired to chairs to eat their dinners. Shortly after dinner was over, the Baranga's excused themselves and departed. They explained that they were traveling south in the morning to visit family in the Juba area. Mrs. Baranga and the children would be leaving for Iowa within the week.

"What did you think of John?" Tom Carson asked Adam.

"He's the first Sudanese I've ever met, who could express himself in that depth of thought. What chance does he have in the Sudanese Army?"

"I have no idea. Usually, the Sudanese military eats it's young. I'll tell you this. If John goes to the bush, the civil war will be on again. All they need in the South is leadership. Their distrust of the Government in Khartoum is total."

"That's a shame," Adam replied. "He's the most impressive African I've met, with the possible exception of Ahmed Ibrahim."

"As long as Khartoum has a loyal Army, I don't give any of these movements much chance of succeeding. Let's face it, Africa is way down on the list of concerns of the Western World. The Middle East would be on the side of Khartoum."

They chatted on for an hour while enjoying the Carson's Brandy. When the time approached ten pm, Adam suggested it was time to return to the hotel. Marty suggested that they stay the night as the Hilton would probably have another power failure. She pointed out that they would be cooler there on the floor.

Adam responded immediately, "Thanks, Marty, Our rooms are already paid for and we would have to go back for our clothes in the morning."

"How about you, Sonya? I have a roll-away you could sleep on. At least you wouldn't have to worry about a power failure," Marty continued.

"It's tempting," Sonya replied, "I've gotten used to the Hilton. One more short night won't kill me."

Marty noticed that Sonya was blushing so she dropped the subject. Before anyone could make any more suggestions, Adam got up and suggested they depart. After goodbyes were said all around, Adam and Sonya went out to the Embassy car, aroused the driver, and departed for the Hilton. After the car had departed, Tom Carson looked at Marty. He shook his head.

"What's the matter?" Marty asked. "I was just being hospitable."

"You were putting Adam on the spot. Why?"

Marty looked around to see if their guests had gone to bed. She whispered, "I just wanted to see if Adam was screwing her."

"That's hardly any of our business. Adam has always been an enjoyable guest and a great host when we are in Cairo."

"I know, Darling. He's such a rascal. She's madly in love with him and he's going to make a mess of her life. Mark my words."

"Let's go to bed. We can't do anything about it," Tom concluded.

Meanwhile in the car, Sonya and Adam didn't speak. When they arrived at the hotel, Adam gave the driver instructions to pick them up at eight am. When they got to the room, Sonya admitted that she had left her key and they would have to go in through Adam's room. As soon as they were inside she checked the adjoining doors. They were open. Sonya breathed a sigh of relief.

"I was afraid I would have to go to the desk for a key," she stated.

"Why would that be such a problem?"

"I was hoping to get back to Cairo before the whole world knows I've been sleeping with you!"

"The whole world?" he asked. "Why do you think that anyone knows about us."

"Didn't you see Marty looking at me? I was blushing. I tell you, she knows!"

"I keep telling you! Get a divorce and marry me. Then you can quit worrying about it."

"If it were just that simple. I want to, but I can't."

"Do you want to shower before or after we make love?" he asked.

"I think after," she said quietly as she slipped out of her dress.

The return trip to Cairo was without incident, with one minor exception. While they were on the ground in Luxor, Sonya suddenly felt ill. She went into the Ladies room at the airport. Her first concern was that she was suffering from the food in El Fasher. Then, it occurred to her that she had suffered similar discomfort with both of her pregnancies. She looked in the mirror and started to count backward to her first encounter with Adam. Could it be that she was pregnant? If she was, it must have happened while she was making love to Adam at the Meridien. What would Adam say? What would her husband say? When she got back on the aircraft, she curled up in her seat, pretending to be asleep while she quietly wept. She finally went to sleep. She was able to doze toward the end of the flight. She and Adam parted without exchanging words.

CHAPTER 8

Sonya hadn't seen Adam for two weeks. He had gone to Venice with Spar 80. The airplane was getting a new paint job. Unfortunately, Aero Navalde had blotched the job and one side of the fuselage had to be repainted. They would be in Venice another five days. Marianne had gone to Venice with David and Adam. Sonya had no one with whom to go riding on the desert. She tried to read, but she couldn't concentrate. John was gone most of the day except on Friday's. On this particular day, Miriam, their maid, had taken the boys to the Cairo Museum. Sonya was alone. She was depressed. She was pregnant and she was definitely suffering from morning sickness.

The phone rang. At first, she wasn't going to answer. On the third ring, she picked up the receiver.

"Hello," she said.

"Sonya, is that you?" Adam asked.

"Oh, Darling!" Sonya replied. "I thought you would never call. I miss you so much."

"I miss you, too," Adam replied. "Can you talk?" There was a slight pause as she caught her breath.

"Yes, I'm alone. John is at a meeting and Miriam has the boys. When are you coming home?"

"Tomorrow," he responded. "I wanted to check with you. Can you get away for a few days?"

"I think so," she answered. "John has plans to take the boys to Sidi Barani for some swimming and playing on the beach. I begged off of going and I'm supposed to go to Germany with a group of ladies from the Embassy. We are leaving tomorrow."

"What time?" he asked.

"We're scheduled to depart at three pm."

"Can you back out at the last minute?"

"For you? Of course!"

"Good! Pack your bikini and some casual clothes. I'll meet you at the TWA counter."

"Where are we going?" she asked, "Or is it a surprise?"

"I wasn't going to tell you, but I guess I should. We're going to Cypress. David is taking Spar 80 to Athens to pick up a couple of Congressmen. I've made arrangements to take a weeks leave. David will drop us at Nicosia. We'll be staying at a beach hotel near Larnaca. We'll share a room and see how you feel about being Mrs. Adam McGregor. We'll fly back whenever you need to return. I have two open tickets from Nicosia to Cairo." He paused for an answer.

"Are you there?" he asked after an awkward pause.

"Yes, my Love, I'm here. I heard everything you said. I'll be at the TWA desk waiting impatiently."

"I love you, Sonya. I really missed you this week. We would have had such a fun time in Venice. I promise, I will bring you there someday. It's unbelievably romantic."

"Adam, anywhere you are is unbelievably romantic. I'll see you tomorrow. Good by Darling."

"Until tomorrow," he responded as they hung up.

Sonya busied herself with packing. She had packed for cooler Germany. Now she repacked for the beach. She packed her yellow bikini along with a blue one that matched her eyes. She packed three dresses, all mini skirts. She took out the pantie hose she had planned for Germany. She changed her mind. She would keep one pair for the return trip to look more like she was coming from Germany.

She stripped naked and looked at herself in the mirror. At the most she was just over four weeks pregnant. She tried to think back to her last pregnancy. When did she start to show? When did she start morning sickness? Surely it wasn't at four weeks. Maybe her morning sickness was caused by her apprehension. She was happy that there was no question who the father was. Would Adam feel the same? Does he really believe it when she insists that she and John never have sex?

After observing herself in the mirror from every possible angle, she decided that she was still able to wear a bikini. She finished repacking and then took a long bath, daydreaming about Cypress and making love with Adam.

The next day went smoothly. Sonya had called her contact for the trip to Germany and explained that she was going to the beach with her husband and sons. She told Reverend Olsen that she would be returning from Germany on the following Monday. With her alibis in place, she took a taxi to Cairo Airport. She was confident that she was late enough to miss the women going to Germany and in plenty of time to meet Adam. She showed up at the TWA desk at two-thirty pm. Adam had just arrived. She rushed to his arms.

They kissed and hugged for several minutes and then headed for Spar 80 parked about two hundred yards across the Tarmac.

Dave Baldwin greeted them with raised eyebrows. To say he was shocked was to put it mildly. There was no doubt now that their affair would be common knowledge by the time they returned from Cypress.

They were airborne by three pm, and arrived in Cypress at four-thirty pm. Adam rented a car and they arrived at their beach hotel by six-thirty. They checked in and went to their room. They had a balcony that over looked the beach. The beach area was still covered with sunbathers. The sun was sinking fast. Most of the patrons appeared to be from Northern Europe. All the women were topless.

Sonya turned to Adam and said, "Adam, all the women are bare from the waist up!"

Adam came to the balcony and looked out. "Most of them should be covered up. I've never seen so many overweight women in one place," Adam said. "Are you going to join them?"

"Certainly not!" Sonya exclaimed. "I'm not going to join the spectacle."

"You may draw more attention if you're the only woman with a bra on."

"What do you want me to do?" she asked.

"I want you to do what you want to do. After all, no one here will recognize us," Adam explained. "Let's go down to the restaurant, have a cocktail, eat dinner and turn in early. I want to take you on a drive to Larnaca and on up the shore to the British Military Base. I have an old friend and his wife who are stationed there. I want you to meet them."

The restaurant had a combo playing dance music. Sonya and Adam danced between cocktails and while waiting for their meal.

"You're a good dancer," Sonya commented.

"Thank you." he replied. "So are you."

"It's easy when all you have to do is follow." They returned to their table to eat Mousaka.

"How would you like to follow me back to the room?" he asked after they had finished dinner.

"And do what?" she teased.

"Take a guess?"

"I'm afraid to guess. I would disappoint you if I made the wrong guess. Why don't you surprise me?"

Adam motioned to the waitress to bring the bill. As soon as it was paid they went up to the room. They walked out on the balcony to look at the moonlight on the Mediterranean. It was beautiful. Adam thought about suggesting a late night swim. However, the breeze off the Med was quite cool.

"Would you like to make love before or after we take a shower?" Adam asked.

She giggled like a little girl and then she walked over and kissed him passionately. "Surprise me," she cooed.

He reached around her back and unzipped her dress letting it fall to the floor. She reached down, unbuckled his belt, unzipped his pants and began unbuttoning his shirt. He unsnapped her bra letting it fall. He pulled her panties down as he sat on the edge of the bed and took off his shirt, trousers and shorts. She crawled around him and proceeded to turn down the bed. When the covers were out of the way, they embraced again, kissing while their tongues entwined going from mouth to mouth.   They began to make love slowly at first, then increasing their speed. Their two bodies worked in perfect harmony until they both climaxed at the same time. The moon was shinning in the window. Adam looked at Sonya and saw tears rolling down her cheeks.

"Are you all right?" he asked.

"Don't you know? We women cry as much when we're happy as we do when we're sad. And I am very happy! I love you, Adam. I never knew what real love was until I met you. I was so frustrated this last week without seeing you. I was going to Germany with a bunch of women and I thought I wouldn't see you for another week. I was near desperation when you called."

"Well," Adam replied, "I'm certainly glad this all worked out. I guess the only way this affair can possibly have a happy ending is for us to either live in sin, sneaking around for the rest of our lives, or for you to get a divorce and marry me."

She turned her face away and began to cry. Adam decided to drop the subject. He got up from the bed and took her hand, gently pulling her up to her feet and leading her into the bathroom. The shower did not have two heads, but there was plenty of room for them to wash each other's bodies as they enjoyed feeling one another while occasionally stopping to kiss. After the long shower, they continued the intimacy by drying each other with large fluffy towels. They returned to the bedroom and proceeded to make love again. The moon shown in the window enough to remove the need for a light. A church bell sounded midnight as they completed their encounter. They slept for several hours.

Sonya was awakened shortly after dawn. She had her second bout with morning sickness in nearly four years. Now there was no doubt, she was carrying Adam's child.

Adam was awakened by the sun shinning in the window and the drapes flopping in a light breeze. The beach was still empty of bathers.

"Let's go for a swim," Sonya suggested.

"Okay!" Adam replied as he picked up his boxer style suit and pulled it up.

Sonya put on her yellow bikini including the bra. They left the room and headed for the beach. They dropped their towels on two of the lounging chairs and walked to the water's edge. Just as they were about to enter the surf, Sonya unsnapped her bra and dropped it on the sand. They swam out to where the gentle breakers were forming. They were both excellent swimmers.

"Why do you wear boxers?" Sonya asked.

"With all the sexy breasts showing, I have to keep covered up."

"I'm the only one on the beach," Sonya said.

"Yes, I know. It was difficult enough when you still had your bra on. Maybe next time we can find a nude beach."

"Oh, no!" she exclaimed. "This is as far as I go in public. Besides, I don't want all the girls ogling you."

"Let's grab some sun before a crowd gathers," Adam suggested.

They went ashore and grabbed their towels. After drying off they stretched out on the lounge chairs. The chairs were oriented toward the southeast and the morning sun. The beach was beginning to fill up and Adam noticed that a steady stream of sunbathers, mostly men, were passing them noting Sonya with furtive glances. Sonya had on sunglasses and Adam noticed that she was napping. He watched her for some time, noting that she was the most beautiful woman on the beach. She stirred and ran her hand over her breasts. They were quite warm.

"I think I need to cover up or I may have a real burn," she said as she put on her bra.

"It's time for us to leave," Adam said. "I'd like to stop in Larnaca for some Calamari."

"Isn't that squid?" Sonya asked.

"Yes, and there is no where on earth where it is any better than in Larnaca."

"Do I have to eat it?" she asked. "I'm just a little old country girl from Minnesota."

"Do you eat Lutefisk?"

"Of course!" she replied.

"If you can eat Lutefisk, you'll love Calamari!"

They walked to the room. Just before they entered the building, two men slipped out of their room. One had been watching

Adam and Sonya while the other was installing a camera and microphone, hidden, except for the camera lens, by the top of the drapes.

Sonya and Adam took a quick shower, dressed and went to the car. Adam headed for Larnaca and the little hotel he had visited months ago. They ordered Ouzo and two orders of saute'ed Calamari. When they had finished the Ouzo, Adam ordered two glasses of Retsina. At Adam's urging Sonya sipped the retsina. She made a terrible face. "That tastes like kerosene smells," she said.

"It's different all right," Adam replied. "It's aged in resin containers. It grows on you."

"What does it grow, spark plugs?" she responded.

Adam chuckled and poured them each some water. The calamari arrived. It was accompanied by three choices of dip, one dark, one yellow, and one reddish. Sonya watched Adam try each in turn and then sip his retsina. She tried the same order and found the bite sized pieces of Calamari were very tasty. Her second sip of retsina was much more pleasant than the first. In ten minutes, they had devoured the large platter of Calamari and their retsina.

"Is there any place in the world that I could take you where you wouldn't surprise me with some new and pleasant experience?"

"How about Minnesota after we're married. We could go for a family reunion and you could serve me Lutefisk."

"Surely you've tried Lutefisk?" she questioned.

"Yes. In Norway, not in Minnesota."

Adam paid the check and they went to the car. They were both silent until they had passed their hotel on the way east along the southern shore of Cypress, headed for the British Base near the demarcation line between Turkish and Greek Cypress.

"A penny for your thoughts?" Adam offered.

"Oh my!" Sonya sighed. "Where to start? I was picturing in my mind the family reunion." She paused.

"And?" he questioned.

"It would be very awkward at first. You see, I would be the first divorcee' in the Carlson family. Of course, all the cousins would be there for the first time in years. They would have to come and see this charlatan who had brought shame on the family name by breaking up the most perfect marriage in the Carlson clan. They would all be standoffish. Then my cousin, Veloris, would come over and she would say, 'Excuse me, General McGregor, have you been married before?' Of course, you would say, 'No, I haven't'. Veloris would say, 'You've done well on your first try.' and she would turn to me and say for everyone to hear, 'My God! He's handsome! Congratulations, Sonya'. And then everyone would file by and say hello and welcome us to Minnesota. The Olsen family would not be that kind."

Neither of them spoke for several seconds.

"Could you say that again in future tense?" Adam asked.

"What do you mean?"

"Say, will instead of would."

She didn't answer. When he looked over he saw that she was crying. He decided not to press her further. They drove for about thirty minutes without speaking. Finally, Sonya spoke.

"Tell me about the people we are going to see." she said.

"He's Wing Commander Brian Scott. His wife's name is Sandra. I met Brian in Thailand. He was on exchange duty with an Australian F-86 outfit in Ubon, Thailand. The Aussies kept the unit there under the auspices of SEATO."

"What's SEATO?" she interrupted.

"The Southeast Asia Treaty Organization. It's long since defunct. I was flying Phantoms out of Ubon into Laos and North Viet Nam. We exchanged visits to each others' Officer's Club. We played some poker and did some drinking together. An Aussie USO show came to Ubon to entertain the squadron. Sandra and her twin sister were lead singers for the troop. She met Brian and decided to stay. They got married and had four boys before Sandra gave up on having a daughter."

"We're you at the wedding?"

"I was the best man. The Aussies had a chaplain but no Church. They were married in our chapel."

"How did you keep in touch?"

"Their home is in Lincolnshire near RAF Cranwell. I was stationed at RAF Bentwaters and we spent numerous weekends together. Brian did a tour as an Attache' in Washington when I was at the Pentagon. We have had numerous opportunities to visit. I'm also Godfather to Brian, Jr., their third son."

"This visit has no ulterior motives other than to renew an old friendship and see your Godson?"

"I wouldn't say that. I wouldn't dare get engaged without Sandra's approval. I've avoided too many of her attempts to match me up with her friends."

"She'll hate me!" Sonya remarked.

"Betcha she won't!" he responded.

They didn't speak for several minutes. Adam looked over and noticed that Sonya was pale and her eyes were closed. "Are you all right?" he asked.

"I'm just nervous and the retsina isn't agreeing with me," she lied. "How soon will we be there?"

"Another fifteen minutes."

They arrived at the main gate to the British base in ten minutes. Brian Scott was there to welcome them. Brian took care of the paper work necessary to get them on the base and they followed Brian's Rover to the Scott's quarters. Sandra was at the door with her youngest, Timmy, who was four years old. The three older boys were at the bluffs overlooking the Mediterranean Sea. They were watching the troops para sailing on the up drafts from the sea.

Brian pulled in the driveway and jumped out of the car. "You were right, Sandra. She's really a beauty," he yelled.

Sandra ran to Adam and hugged him. Then she turned to Sonya and said, "You must be the one. He promised that if Miss Wonderful ever appeared, he would bring her to me for an okay!"

Sonya looked at Adam with wide eyes.

Adam replied, "Don't worry. You've already passed."

Sonya was blushing and she didn't know what to say.

"Brian, take Timmy and drive Adam over to the cliffs. See what the boys are doing. Come back at One and I'll have lunch ready. Come in the house, Sonya. We have much to talk about."

Brian and Adam took Timmy and drove off. Sonya was in a state of shock. Suddenly, she felt a hint of morning sickness. She followed Sandra into the kitchen.

"Could I use your bathroom," Sonya asked.

"Of course, love, the loo is the third door on the left," Sandra replied.

Sonya went in the loo and closed the door. She splashed

some cold water in her face and took several deep breaths. She decided that anxiety had brought on the attack. She took several minutes to check her make-up and to make sure she was okay. Then she went back to the kitchen.

"I'm sorry," Sandra said. "I jumped to conclusions. We've been complaining to Adam for several years that he should come see us. He would always promise that he would not marry without bringing the perspective bride for my approval. I knew he was joking but when Brian talked to him the other day, he told me, 'Adam is dropping by with a bird he wants you to meet'. I assumed he was in love. Is he?"

Sonya stammered, "Well, I don't know what to say. I've only known Adam for a little over a month. Excuse me!" She jumped up and ran to the bathroom.

It was several minutes before Sonya returned. Sandra had busied herself with kitchen duties preparing for lunch. When Sonya returned she handed her a cup of coffee.

"When is the baby due?" Sandra asked.

"What baby?" Sonya replied.

"Honey, I've had four babies and five pregnancies. I can spot morning sickness across the room."

"I've only missed one period. I've given birth to two boys and this certainly looks like morning sickness. I suspect I'm pregnant."

"Has he asked you to marry him?"

"Yes, but I'm married."

"Who's the father?"

"If I'm pregnant, Adam is the father," Sonya said quietly.

"How can you be sure?"

"He's the only man I've had sex with since my last pregnancy."

"What about your husband?"

"He says two children are enough,"

"Have you told Adam?"

"No."

"Why not?" Sandra pressed.

"Adam was away to Italy for about ten days. I hadn't seen him for over two weeks. I was planning to tell him last night. There was never a convenient time to break in and say, 'Oh, by the way, I'm going to have your baby'."

"Are you in love with him?"

"Oh! God! Am I in love with him? I think about him all day long. I thought I would go nuts while he was in Venice. We had such a wonderful time in the Sudan."

"Wait a minute!" Sandra said. "You were in the Sudan with Adam? What does your husband say about this?"

"He doesn't know about my affair. He was responsible for sending me to the Sudan. Of course, he doesn't know that we had adjoining rooms everywhere we went. At first, I accused Adam of arranging the rooms. I locked the doors between our rooms in Khartoum. Then the power failed and I panicked. I crawled on the floor to the door and begged Adam to let me in. He did. We made love all that night, two nights in El Fasher and another night in Khartoum. By that time, I was completely hooked."

Sandra shook her head. "Did you meet Adam in the Sudan?"

"No, I met him at the Meridien Hotel in Cairo," Sonya responded.

"How did you end up in bed?"

"I had watched him swim laps for several days. I assumed he was a businessman. I learned that he was in the room next to ours. I went up to our room and as I passed Adam's room, I noticed a basket of flowers. The card said 'The Olsen's'. I assumed they had been left at the wrong door. The door was ajar. I tapped on it lightly and walked in. Adam was standing there in a bathrobe. I was about to excuse myself when he pulled the bows on my bikini. I dropped the flowers and grabbed for my bikini string. He had already pulled the other string and reached around my back and cut my bra with a little scissors on a small pocket knife. I was naked and so shocked, or scared, that I couldn't scream. I asked him if he was going to rape me. He whispered that he was going to make love to me. I didn't protest. We made love for some time. I climaxed twice. I was hopelessly in love."

"My God!" Sandra said, "He knocked you up on the first encounter?"

"Either that day or in the next two days. I had asked him when he was leaving the Meridien. He said he was leaving in two days. I agreed to meet him after swimming for the next two days. He tried to introduce himself . I wouldn't let him. I explained that my husband was the pastor at St. Mathews Lutheran Church and that it was good that he, Adam, was leaving because we could never meet again. I was determined to blot the whole incident out of my mind."

"How did you end up in the Sudan?"

"We were invited to an Embassy reception on Saturday Evening. When we entered the receiving line, there was Brigadier General McGregor in all his glory. He was introducing the guests to the visiting dignitaries. As it turned out, the VIP was a friend of my husband's father. He, the VIP, suggested that John, my husband, should go to Geneina to visit a Chadian Refugee Camp. John declined because of commitments in Cairo and instead volunteered me. The following Monday, I flew to Khartoum. Adam was the pilot on the Embassy's Kingair. It was the most wonderful experience of my life for numerous reasons."

"Have you talked of marriage?"

"He asked me to get a divorce and marry him while we were in El Fasher. I explained to him about John, his family and my family, and, of course, my two boys. I said I couldn't think of divorce. Of course, that was before I realized that I was pregnant. Now I'm afraid he'll think I've trapped him."

The two women sat quietly, looking at each other. Sandra was slowly shaking her head in disbelief.

Sonya spoke first, "You must think I'm the dumbest blond you've ever met,"

Sandra laughed. "I might think that if I didn't know Adam. I can't count the number of women who have wanted to marry Angus Donald McGregor. Those are the ones that I know. You're the first one to get an invitation."

"You do believe me?" Sonya asked.

Before she could answer, Brian, Adam and the four boys came in the door. Sandra busied herself, putting lunch on the table with the help of her oldest son. When all was ready, she sent Brian, Jr. to invite everyone to the table. Sandra waited until after grace was said then decided to put Adam on the spot.

"I want a vote from the Scott family. Should Adam McGregor marry Sonya Olsen? All in favor say 'aye'."

There was a resounding "AYE" from all.

Adam frowned, "I've asked her twice and hinted on several other occasions. Sonya, will you marry me?"

Sonya's eyes teared up and she reached for her napkin to dab her cheeks. "Yes, I will marry you!"

Great applause followed. The conversation died for a few minutes while everyone dug into their sandwiches and fruit salad.

"How much longer will you be in Cypress, Brian?" Adam asked.

"We're due to rotate to Cranwell in the Spring. I'm on the Group Captains List and I'll be a department head at the school. We're thinking of taking leave and visiting Australia and the States on the long way home. We haven't seen Sandra's family since Will was a baby. When are you due to rotate, Adam?"

"My three years are up next August. I haven't a clue where I'll be sent. I'll be eligible for a second star next year. Flag rank assignments seldom go to volunteers, unless the three or four star in question have suggested that you volunteer. If you reject a job and you haven't been invited elsewhere, you're usually invited to retire."

Sandra chimed, "That's downright mean!"

"Mean or not, one can't expect much sympathy. Besides, retirement in my pay grade isn't a hardship. I have the further advantage of being wealthy. My mother and I split my father's estate of thirty million. As far as I know, I'm Mother's only heir. Maybe Sonya and I will spend our lives visiting old friends in exotic places!"

"Is Lincolnshire an exotic place, Dad?" Willy asked.

"It may not be as exotic as Hong Kong or Bangkok, but it's still a good place to visit," Brian answered.

"I hope you'll visit us Mrs. McGregor," Willy said to Sonya as he moved close to his mother. Sandra didn't try to explain to Willy that Sonya was not yet Mrs. McGregor.

"Why do you want Mrs. McGregor to visit, Willy?" Sandra asked.

Willy hid his face in his mother's dress and then he whispered something to her. Sandra grinned, "He wants you to visit because he thinks you're pretty."

Adam entered the conversation, "Willy, can I visit you with

Mrs. McGregor?"

"Sure, but last time you were here you didn't bring her."

"Did he ever bring a girl friend when he visited before?" Sonya asked.

"No Ma'am! You're the first Mrs. McGregor I ever saw."

"You've made me very happy, Willy," Sonya said, smiling.

The adults sat and chatted about old times. Brian asked Adam if he had ever heard what happened to his old girl friend from Thailand. She was one of the tall beauties from Chang Mai. Adam insisted he had lost contact within a year of leaving Ubon. They reminisced until four in the afternoon. Brian offered them cocktails. Adam said he wanted to get on the road before having anything to drink. The next day they would hit the beach and then return to Cairo Sunday afternoon. They had a lot to talk about. After much hugging and kissing they managed to break away. Adam had promised to keep them apprised of their progression toward matrimony.

As soon as they were on the highway, Sonya blurted out, "Adam, I'm pregnant! I've been meaning to tell you. Sandra spotted my morning sickness as soon as we arrived. She made me promise to tell you as soon as we got on the road." She waited several moments for Adam's reply. Finally he responded.

"If you are happy, I'm happy. I wonder if this may make it easier for John to give you up. What do you think?"

"I don't know," she replied. "Of course, he'll know he isn't the father. He is always opposed to divorce under any circumstances. He'll say he forgives me, but that we can't divorce because of the boys."

"Sonya, the only thing you can do is walk out and come live with me. I'll check with the legal office to see if we can proceed with a divorce while we are in Cairo. I suspect you'll have to file in Minnesota. If need be, I'll take leave and we'll fly back to Minnesota and file the papers. When I rotate to the States next year, we can finalize things and get married. I suspect our baby will be born before we can marry. I'm sorry for that."

CHAPTER 9

They drove along in silence for most of the way to the hotel, neither one wanting to start a conversation. When the hotel came within sight, Adam looked at his watch. It was four-thirty. "It's early," he said, "Let's take a swim before dinner."

"I'm up for that," Sonya answered. "I need some exercise or I'll start gaining weight too soon."

When they reached the hotel, they hurried up to the room. They each used the bathroom while the other changed. Sonya wore the blue bikini bottom and covered her top with a sleeveless blouse.

"You're going native after all," Adam said with a lascivious grin.

"I'm throwing caution to the winds. I want all the male attention I can get. I want to make you insanely jealous for the remainder of our time on Cypress!"

"And just why this new woman? What happened to little Miss Pris from Minnesota?" he asked.

"She is coming to grips with the reality of pregnancy. Too soon my belly will begin to swell followed by my breasts lined with ugly blue veins. Your eyes will start to wander as beautiful women flirt with you trying to pry you loose from that fat cow to whom you're now married"

Adam took her by the shoulders and turned her around. Tears were streaming down her cheeks. He pulled her into his arms and kissed her tenderly. "Let's go swim," he said.

They walked to the beach in silence. Sonya dropped her towel and blouse on top of Adam's towel and they both waded into the surf. They swam side by side to the float and climbed out of the water.

"You're a pretty good swimmer for an old pregnant lady," Adam said in jest.

"You better not start patronizing me already. You'll need to save that for the two months at the end. I warn you, I will be a total bitch. You'll wish you had never met me."

"Sonya, you're too far ahead of schedule," he said quietly. "We're going to take this one day at a time. All that matters today is that I love you and you love me. We can't change the schedule. Our baby is in charge. We'll take over again when he or she arrives."

"Oh, Sweetheart, I'm such a fool!" She leaned her head on his shoulder and tilted her face up to kiss him. As he kissed her, he cupped her breast in his right hand.

"What are you doing?" she asked.

"I'm enjoying your naked body. Why don't we go back to the room and make love. The exercise will do us both good."

"I'll race you to the shore," she answered.

They raced toward the shore. Adam made sure that he won. He had her blouse in hand when she came up out of the water.

"Why are you in such a hurry to cover me up. I thought you wanted me to go topless," she pouted.

"That was before I found out you were going to be the mother of my first born. I'll be a jealous husband."

"You keep this up and I may believe you really love me," she replied as he pulled her up the beach.

They hurried to the room, pealed off their suits and rolled into bed oblivious of the camera that quietly filmed their passion. They slept for an hour. Then they got up, took a shower together, dressed and went down to the restaurant. There wasn't much conversation while they enjoyed Rack of Lamb, vegetables, a Greek Salad and a local Red Wine. After they finished eating, they danced to the combo.

"You dance divinely, Mrs. McGregor."

"You inspire me General McGregor."

The music was slow and mellow. They glided around the floor like they had been dancing together for years.

"I haven't danced this much since college," Sonya said.

"Didn't your husband dance?"

"We danced quite a bit while we were dating. After we were married we rarely danced. After my first pregnancy, we quit altogether. Will you quit dancing with me when I'm so big I waddle?"

"I promise to dance with you the rest of my life," Adam replied. "I just hope you'll always want to make love."

"Of course, I'll always want to make love to you," she responded. "Why wouldn't I?"

"You'll notice that I'm always the first to suggest that we make love and I'm always the first in bed."

"You always use the bathroom first," she replied. "I can't very well beat you to the bed. Let's go make love right now. There, I suggested it first."

"I have to pay the check," he replied.

"I'll be waiting in bed for you," she said as she started for the door.

"You better wait," he said holding up the room key. "We are going to have a fair race."

She waited while he paid the check. They walked together back to the room. He put the key in the lock and Sonya positioned herself to be first in the door.

"What are you doing?" he asked.

"Ladies first! Remember?"

"All right," he responded, "I'll let you go in first but you'll have to take the other side of the bed!"

"Okay," she promised as she reached behind her for her zipper.

"No fair starting until you're in the room!" he ordered.

"I won't," she replied.

He pushed the door open. Before he could get it slammed she had jumped across the bed, kicked off her shoes, unzipped her dress and unhooked her bra. Adam had sneaked his zipper down so he was keeping up with her. They both pulled off their underwear and fell into bed together laughing uproariously.

"Okay," Adam laughed, "It's a tie."

"What do you mean, a tie?" she complained. "You still have your socks on and I'm here with my legs spread waiting for you!"

"Under those rules, I can't win," he complained.

"That's right, Darling. Take off your socks and come make love to me."

"You're a Jezebel!"

"I am what you've made me, a sex maniac," she giggled with glee.

They made passionate love for a long time and then slept until first light.

They got up and put on swimsuits and went down to the beach. They were all alone. They swam out to the float. The water was warm and the sun was rising rapidly. Sonya took off her bra and they both stretched out on the float to sunbath. They laid there on their backs until they heard two young boys thrashing in the water, swimming toward the float. Sonya quickly put on her bra before the boys arrived.

"What are two young boys doing on a topless beach?" she questioned indignantly.

"Looking for thrills, I imagine," Adam replied. "Maybe they're guests at the hotel."

"We certainly aren't going to take our son to a topless beach!"

"It's a boy?" Adam asked with a smirk on his face.

"I hope so," Sonya replied leaning her head on his shoulder. "We can have a girl in a couple of years."

"But you already have two sons. I'm sure we'll be able to have custody for at least half the time. I vote for a girl," he concluded.

"What will we name her," Sonya asked.

"How about Sonya? She's sure to be as pretty as her mother."

Suddenly a motor boat appeared and approached the float just as the two boys neared the ladder. One of the men in the boat grabbed both boys by the hair and pulled them to the boat ladder. Harsh words, in Greek were exchanged and the boys were hauled off to the shore.

"I don't think they're guests at the hotel," Adam said.

"I hope they won't hurt them," Sonya replied.

"Only their pride," Adam replied. "Let's go have some breakfast."

They stood up on the edge of the float and dove into the water together. They swam to shore went to the room and dressed. They went down to the dining room. After breakfast, they took a drive along the beach west of Larnaca. Around noon they stopped in a bar and had an Ouzo. Adam suggested that their next trip should be to Istanbul.

"Why Istanbul?" Sonya asked.

"Istanbul is one of my favorite cities," he replied.

"Were you there with a lover?" she asked.

"No, I wasn't there with a lover. I want to return with someone I love. I love you. You're elected!"

"Adam, I do love you and I swear I will never love anyone else as long as I live."

"So you see!" he exclaimed, "It has to be you."

"Where else will you take me?"

"My other two favorite cities are Sidney and Hong Kong."

"Are they both romantic?"

"Yes," he replied. "Istanbul is still the best. There is nothing as romantic as a night cruise on the Bosporus."

"When can we go?" she asked.

"We could sneak off for a couple of days. I would rather go there after we are married. The first thing we have to do is get you a divorce."

"I know that's going to be a problem," Sonya replied. "John is not going to cooperate."

"When he finds out you're pregnant, I would think he would see things differently," Adam replied.

"John has a pension for martyrdom. He will promise to forgive me and he will say that he wants the baby. The truth is neither would occur. I would be more miserable than before I met you."

"Would he want you to get an abortion?"

"Oh, no!" she stressed. "Abortion would be out of the question. And it would be for me, also. That's one subject John and

I have always agreed upon."

"The more you tell me, the more convinced I am that we are doing the right thing. Maybe the fact that you are pregnant will be a plus."

I'm sure that will arise," she agreed. "Both my parents and John's parents will take that into consideration. They may decide that I'm a whore for allowing you to make love to me. They will consider the primacy of parentage."

"That tough?" Adam asked.

"I will be the first divorce' in either the Olsen or the Carlson family. It's going to create quite a stir."

"Surely your happiness would be important to your parents?" he asked.

"I believe they will accept us in time. We will just have to bear with the innuendos and whispers for a period. Once they get to know you and love you as I do, the family will come around. I can guarantee you, it won't happen over night!"

"I guess we'll just have to work this out in the quiet of our bedroom," Adam said as he paid the check. They departed. They were very quiet as they drove back to the hotel. Each wondering if the other one was having second thoughts. When they arrived back at the room, they embraced and kissed. Then they quickly stripped and began making love. After they had exhausted their ardor, they laid quietly side by side.

"I always feel better after we make love," Adam began. "All of the problems are worth solving as long as we love each other."

Sonya rolled up on her elbow and looked at Adam. She reached over and kissed him. "Everything is fine," she added. "I'm so happy that I'm carrying your baby." He kissed her lovingly.

"Tomorrow," he began, "We have to go back to Cairo. When does John expect you?"

"Not until Monday, sometime. I'm still supposed to be in Germany."

"You can stay with me at Swiss Air, until it's time to drop the bomb," Adam replied.

"Do you want me to go with you when you confront him?"

"I don't know yet. We can discuss it on our flight to Cairo. For now, let's get ready and go to dinner. I want to have a couple of drinks, a good meal, and some wine. Then I want to dance with you until it's time for us to go to bed and make love one more time."

"You're insatiable!" he declared.

"I'm in love, my Darling! What can I tell you?" she replied with a broad smile.

They took a shower together. Sonya stayed in the bathroom putting on lotion and combing her hair as it dried. Adam went to the sink in the room and shaved. When Sonya came out to get dressed, Adam went back into the bathroom. While he was gone, she quickly checked Adam's drawer in the dresser. She noted that he still had two pairs of socks and two sets of underwear. She put on her dress, a sheath with a short hemline about four inches above her knees. The neckline was scooped just enough for a little cleavage to show. Adam came out and slipped on his loafers. They departed for the bar.

"Adam, I was just reminiscing about our time together. Do you realize that the short time we've been together, we've spent more time naked than we have with clothes on?" Sonya waited for a reply. They walked on and Adam didn't say anything.

"Did you hear me?"

"Yes." he replied.

"Well, say something!"

"Are you bragging or complaining?" he responded with a smirk on his face.

She was taken aback. After some thought, she replied, "I'm certainly not complaining, but!"

Adam stopped her. She had a tear in her eye. He kissed her tenderly. "I'm sorry!" he said. "I didn't mean to treat our love making lightly. We better enjoy as much as we can while we can. It won't be long and we'll have to wear pajamas in case the baby walks in."

"Are you dreading that?"

"No!" he replied emphatically. "I'm looking forward to having two beautiful women in my life."

"I'm looking forward to having two handsome gentlemen in my life!"

They arrived at the bar and took a table in a corner. The waiter came and took their order for scotch. One with soda and the other on the rocks.

The regular combo was just arriving and the bar began to fill up. As they watched couples come in, they made guesses as to which were in love and which were married. Most were having fun but a couple were definitely having a strained relationship.

"I'm happy that we came early, Adam," Sonya began.

"Why is that?" he asked.

"Because we are back in the corner where we can't be seen by everyone. I would hate to have everyone talking about us the way we are talking about them."

"Don't you think that's a little unfair?" Adam asked.

"How did you ever become such a great lover and know so little about women?"

"I've never claimed to be a great lover," Adam replied.

"You must have had affairs," Sonya pried. "You are unbelievably handsome. Any woman would be proud to walk arm in arm with you just to make other women jealous, if nothing else."

"I take that as a compliment," he said.

"I mean it as a compliment, but why me?" she pressed.

"When I saw you in the airport on the day you arrived, I watched you follow your husband with a boy in each hand. Your figure was perfect. You were quite tall. With your heels on, you were taller than your husband. You looked like the perfect family. I walked by to see your baggage tags. I saw the name Olsen. Your husband spoke to you and I saw your face. Your face was very unhappy. I thought probably you were tired from the trip. I was determined to see you again. When I got to the Embassy, I checked with the Consulate to see if you were State Department or Military. That's when I found out you were Clergy. The Consulate confirmed that you were staying at the Meridien and I had my friend there get me the room next to yours. I began stalking you from the moment I laid eyes on you."

"I suppose I should be appalled," she replied. "I must admit, I was attracted to you the first time I saw you by the pool. I watched you swim. I wondered how old you were, if you were married, why you were in Cairo. I even fantasized about making love to you. I saw those flowers in front of your door and I was like a fly in the web. I knew I shouldn't go in but I had to find out who you were. It turns out we were stalking each other."

"You really were unhappy then?"

"Yes, Darling!" she exclaimed reaching out to take his hand. "If I had stayed in Minnesota with all my family and friends around me, I could never have broken away. After those first three encounters at the Meridien, I thought I could break off the affair and be satisfied to live with a cherished memory while I went back to being a loving wife and mother. Then we were thrown together on the trip to Khartoum. After that first night in the Hilton, I knew the only way I could break it off was if you left me."

"That will never happen," he added.

"Adam," she said passionately, "I'm so afraid. I can't imagine how things can turn out the way we want them to turn out. I just wish it was over and we were married. I worry about our baby."

"Have you had more morning sickness?" he asked.

"I had to get up once last night. It wasn't bad. I think all of our loving has kept my mind off of my pregnancy. I was afraid I might miscarry because of all the turmoil. Now, I think I'll have a good pregnancy."

"How about a dance? They're playing 'In the Mood' and I'm in the mood!"

They were alone on the small dance floor so they were able to improvise. When they finished and came together, Adam noticed that Sonya's breasts were soft.

"Darling," he said, "I could swear that you aren't wearing a bra."

"I hope it doesn't show," she replied. "My boobies are sunburned and my bra was chaffing."

He nodded his understanding. As they continued to dance closely, his hand slipped down over her buttocks. He couldn't feel her panty line. He eased her away and looked her in the eyes.

"Sonya, you don't have any panties on either." he said in a whisper. "Would you like to explain that."

She blushed as she nodded in the affirmative. "You see, Darling, while you were in the bathroom, I happened to check your drawer and I noticed that you had two pair of underwear and socks remaining. We only have tomorrow left. I said to myself, 'Why isn't my lover wearing shorts and socks? Is he planning another race for the bed?' I decided then I wouldn't wear a bra and panties. I did a quick time check. I can strip naked in five seconds."

"Let's go eat!" he said feigning displeasure.

She followed him to the dining room. They were seated in a dark corner. "Are you angry with me?" she asked.

"No. I thought I was stealing a stodgy old housewife who happened to be beautiful and unhappy. Now I find I have a sex kitten on my hands. I think I can adjust to it quite well. If you ever go out without panties again, please tell me. I want to be sure you don't slip and fall. I also want to be sure we are not far from our bedroom. I would hate it if we got arrested for a public display of affection."

She slid her chair around by Adam's. She kissed him and said, "Thank you for teaching me to love you."

They ate hurriedly and went back to their room. The moon was bright and they left the curtains open. They didn't turn on the lights. The microphone picked up the sounds associated with their love making. Sonya whispered, "I told you I could strip in five seconds." For once, there wouldn't be any pictures. They awoke in plenty of time to make their ten-thirty flight to Cairo from Nicosia.

CHAPTER 10

They arrived in Nicosia in plenty of time to turn in the rental car and have a quick breakfast. When their boarding was called, they joined the queue and followed the airline hostess out on the tarmac. The queue was headed for an old airplane with Cypress Air markings.

"Are we flying on that?" Sonya asked with emphasis on 'that'.

"It would appear so," Adam replied. "It's an old Hawker-Siddely. One of British Air's first jets with the engines on the sides instead of in the wing roots. I'm sure it will get us to Cairo. It's only an hour and a half and the weather is perfect."

"What are those tubes on the back of the engines?"

"I suspect they were a feeble attempt at sound suppression," Adam replied.

They boarded the aircraft and took two seats in first class. They were immediately offered a glass of champagne.

"You're not nervous are you?" Sonya remarked.

"No," he replied. "they do too many safety checks on airliners for me to worry."

"There are crashes," she came back.

"Yes. The vast majority of crashes are pilot error," he replied with authority.

"How much flying experience do you have?"

"Six thousand hours," he replied.

"My God! How long have you been flying?" she asked, taking a swallow of her champagne.

"Twenty years."

"How old are you?"

"Forty-one," he replied.

"You're thirteen years older than I am," she said. "When I'm seventy, you'll be eighty-three."

"I hope you're not going to leave me for a younger man already."

"Of course not!" she said. "John is my age and he acts like he's older than you are already."

"I don't know whether that's a compliment or not!"

"It's a compliment, believe me. When was the last time you were sick?" she pried.

"January thirty-first, 1967," he replied.

"What did you have?"

"A world class hangover. I had just finished my two hundredth mission in Viet Nam. I was celebrating with a cohort. We drank champagne, martinis, and something else I can't remember. I really don't care much for champagne to this day and I haven't had a martini since then."

She stared at him and started to laugh until he looked at her. "Doesn't anything ever phase you?" she asked.

"Yes!" he looked at her longingly. "Every time I look at you, I have the urge to rip off your clothes and make love to you."

She looked up into his eyes and replied, "That's so nice!"

The doors closed and engines began to turn. Within five minutes they were at the end of the runway. Two aircraft landed while they waited.

"Do pilots get frustrated when they have to wait like this?" Sonya asked.

"No," Adam replied. "They have check lists to complete. Besides, they know that landing aircraft have priority. What really irritates pilots is when they have to abort an approach and go around because some VIP gets to take off regardless of landing traffic."

"What kind of VIP can interfere with traffic?" she asked.

"Probably a head of State or an Ambassador. They won't change priorities for a Rock Star!"

"Why do you say 'abort'? I thought that abortions were reserved for babies."

"In the case of flying, abort means to stop. If I was on take off roll and something went wrong, I would immediately inform the tower that I was aborting the take off. Everyone on frequency would know what that meant. How it originated, I have no idea. It may have been started by the Wright Brothers."

"Is there anything you aren't an expert about?" she said coyly.

The pilot was taking the runway and as the power was added, the noise level increased. Adam didn't answer immediately. As in most older jets the noise level and vibrations increased as the aircraft rumbled down the runway. When the aircraft broke ground, the rumbling stopped and was replaced by the noise of the gear coming up. With each new noise, Sonya's grip on his arm tightened. Finally, take off power was reduced to climb power and the noise level was reduced so that voices could be heard again.

"You didn't answer my question," she prodded.

"I know absolutely nothing about women," he answered.

"How can that be," she began, "with all those women you've made love to?"

"What makes you think I've made love to so many women?"

"Well, you admitted you had an affair with Marianne and Sandra mentioned the Thai girl from Chang Mai. There must have been others. What about other wives?"

"You are entirely too nosy!" he whispered.

"If I'm going to be your wife, I think I should know a little bit about your past. If I don't know about the mistakes others made how can I keep you?"

"First of all, you are the only married woman I've ever had an affair with. I've avoided married women before, because I didn't want to be a home wrecker."

"Why did you pick on me?"

"Because you looked unhappy. Because you are unbelievably beautiful and because I fell in love with you."

"And because I'm going to have your baby," she interjected.

"If you'll recall, Sonya," he replied. "I suggested divorce and marriage to me in the Sudan before I ever knew about your pregnancy."

She noticed that he was getting irritated with this line of conversation and she decided it was time to let it be.

"I'm sorry, Darling," she whispered. "I believe you love me and I'm beginning to believe you don't know very much about women." She kissed him on the cheek.

"You've been baiting me, haven't you?"

"It's the woman in me. We're all like this. Can you stand it?" He leaned over and kiss her on the lips.

"The fringe benefits make it all worthwhile," he responded.

"Thank you, Adam. I love you!" she answered smiling.

They sat quietly for the remainder of the short flight. They were served some more champagne along with a plate of cheese and crackers. Adam had taken time to fill out their entry paper work. They were ready to go as soon as the exit door was opened. They walked across the tarmac to the terminal entry for out-of-country passengers. As soon as they were inside, Adam looked for a familiar officer. The officer recognized Adam. He took one look at Adam's Diplomatic Passport and waved them through.

"I've never traveled with a VIP before," Sonya remarked. "Is it always this easy?"

"It helps to come through often. I probably see that guy twice a month," he answered.

"We spent forty-five minutes in the queue when we arrived. They went through all of our bags even the kids toy bag. I was ready to go back to America by the time we got through customs."

"Aren't you glad you didn't?"

"Yes, I am!" she answered emphatically. "I wouldn't have missed the last six weeks for anything. How's that for a testimonial, General McGregor?"

"Would you put that in writing?" He quipped.

"I want it engraved on our marriage license when I show it to my parents," she replied quickly. "Otherwise, they'll call the police and have you arrested for molesting their goody two shoes daughter!"

Adam noticed that she was not laughing. He didn't reply, just put the conversation in his memory bank. He would want to talk about this encounter before he met the Carlson family.

Mustafa was parked right outside the terminal. He saw them emerge and immediately got out and opened the trunk. They tossed their bags in the trunk and got in the back seat.

"Where to, General?" he asked.

"Let's go by the Embassy. I need to check the message traffic."

Sonya leaned over and whispered in Adam's ear. "Darling, could you drop me at the Swiss Air Building first? I really don't want to be seen with you at the Embassy until I've confronted John."

Adam nodded, "Mustafa, on second thought, drop us at my apartment. I'll pick up my car and go to the Embassy. There's no need for you to wait as I don't know how long I'll be at the office."

"Shukran!" Mustafa replied in thanks.

Cairo would be a beautiful city, except for three things. First, there is always construction in progress. The city is over a thousand years old. There is constant deterioration. Sometimes it's hard to tell if buildings are going up or if they are falling down. The second problem is dust. There are many beautiful buildings and the Nile is lined with lovely Acacia trees. Everything is covered with a layer of dust that never quite goes away. The third problem is traffic. There are autos everywhere. There are many, many trucks and there are a large number of wagons pulled by a donkey or two donkeys depending on the size of the load.

The Corniche is a major thoroughfare that runs along the bank of the Nile through Cairo. They were traveling north on the Corniche toward the Giza Bridge when a black Mercedes cut in front of them. Mustafa braked the old Plymouth, avoiding a collision. When they reached the intersection, the Mercedes was in the next lane. The driver rolled down his window and yelled at Mustafa.

"Maallish, Maallish," meaning "God didn't will it."

Mustafa acknowledged the driver with a nod of his head. As the driver raced away on the green light, Mustafa addressed the General. "You see that, General? He say Maallish. If he kill me he say Maallish."

"I know what you mean, Mustafa," Adam replied.

They crossed the bridge to the west side of the Nile. As they did, they passed a flat bed wagon load of four camels pulled by two donkeys. The camels were marked for slaughter. The driver was beating the donkeys to make them go faster. The camels were hobbled and couldn't get up. One camel was on each corner of the wagon, facing outward. They nonchalantly chewed their cuds, oblivious to their destination and fate.

When they arrived at the Swiss Air building, Mustafa drove to the rear of the building and dropped them off. Adam released Mustafa and the car. Adam checked his Corvette. It was covered with a shroud. The shroud was covered with dust, however, the car was as good as new. They went up the stairs to Adam's apartment. As soon as the bags were in the room, Adam reiterated his need to go to the office.

"I'll miss you," Sonya said as she came forward to kiss him. They kissed passionately.

"How can you leave me?" she asked. "We haven't made love in over twelve hours."

"I promise to remedy that as soon as I get back," he said.

"Remember, tomorrow we must face the music."

"There's no turning back," he added.

"I know," she replied. "I just can't imagine how much turmoil we will have to endure."

"I have a number of friends who have gone through divorces. One thing that seems to help is separation. The farther apart the protagonists live, the better they get along."

"That will make custody a big problem," she replied.

"We'll just have to cross that bridge when we come to it. In most cases, that I'm familiar with, the mother gets primary custody. Since I'm wealthy, I think we can make a strong case for primary custody."

"John will fight it!" she concluded.

"We'll fight back," he added as he kissed her again. "I'll be back in about an hour and a half."

She followed him to the back door and watched as he uncovered the Corvette. She noted that he looked underneath the car and then raised the hood and thought he would check the oil, but he didn't. After closing the hood, he got in the car and drove off waving as he left the parking lot. Sonya locked the door and went in to take a long bath.

Sonya stripped out of her clothes and observed herself in the mirror. There was no swelling in her middle. She wished Adam was there to hold her. When he was around she felt assured that she could face John. When Adam was away she lost her nerve.

She put on her negligee and went to the living room. She turned on the TV to the one Egyptian station. The sound was in Arabic. She couldn't understand what was being said. The camera panned on the entrance of a building where smoke was coming out. It was St. Mathews Church. There was so much background noise that she couldn't understand what was being said. She recognized one of the parishioners from her first Sunday at St. Mathews. She backed further away through the open doors onto the balcony. She was still shaking her head in disbelief when she went over the railing. Her eyes were full of tears as she fell onto the roof of a Mercedes Sedan parked on the sidewalk below.

CHAPTER 11

Captain Baldwin was in the office when Adam arrived. "General," he said, "I need to talk to you for a minute when it's convenient."

"Come on in," Adam replied. "I just dropped by to read the traffic. Shoot."

"Well, Sir. I don't know how to say this. I'm afraid my wife is meddling in your business."

"How's that?" Adam asked.

"Last week after we dropped you off in Nicosia, she asked me if you were alone. I said, no. She said, was Sonya Olsen with you? I said, yes. She said she knew you were having an affair with Sonya. I said, what business is that of ours? She didn't answer. This morning, she told me she had called Reverend Olsen and told him that his wife wasn't in Germany. She was in Cypress with you. I chewed her out for meddling, but I'm afraid the damage is done."

"Dave, I'm sorry that Marianne decided to get involved. It really doesn't matter now. Sonya has agreed to get a divorce and marry me. She was prepared to confront Reverend Olsen tomorrow. I suspect it may be a little more contentious now. He had to know some time. Sonya is at my apartment. I'll prepare her before she talks to her husband tomorrow."

There was a knock on the door. "Come in," Adam ordered. It was his Secretary.

"General, the Consulate would like to speak to you on line one. They said it's very important."

Adam nodded and picked up line one. "This is General McGregor." The General was listening. As soon as he had the message he said, "Thank you, I'm going right over." He hung up the phone and slumped in his chair.

"Two terrorists just rolled hand grenades down the aisle at Saint Mathews Lutheran. They killed Reverend Olsen and the Olsen's two sons. Is your driver here, Dave?"

"Yes Sir, Alaa is waiting to take me home."

"I need to go over to Saint Mathews and check everything out. You can drop me back here on your way home." He got up and they headed for the door. He stopped at the desk to speak to his secretary.

"Emma, we're going to Saint Mathews to check this out. Let the Ambassador's Office know that I'll be at my apartment all evening."

Alice made a notation and nodded her understanding.

They were at Saint Mathews in twenty minutes. Two people from the Consulate were there to claim the bodies.

Adam took one look at the three bodies and saw that they had all died instantly. One of the parishioners was talking to the Counselors.

Adam spoke to them. "Excuse me, I'm Adam McGregor, the Defense Attache'. Could you tell me what happened?"

"What does the military have to do with this?" the parishioner asked.

"I know Mrs. Olsen quite well. She traveled to the Sudan with us last month. I'm going to have the unpleasant task of telling her what happened."

"I see," the parishioner backed off. "My name is Paul Stevens. I'm with USAID. I understand that Mrs. Olsen is returning from Germany sometime tomorrow. I would be available to help in anyway I can."

He continued, "We had just completed Communion and were about to sing our closing hymn when two men in military fatigues burst in the main entrance. They yelled, Allah Akbar at the top of their lungs and rolled two grenades down the aisle. Reverend Olsen came out from behind the pulpit and yelled, 'stop'! The grenades went off almost simultaneously. Reverend Olsen was killed instantly as were the two boys. The boys were in the front pew and had no protection from the blast. All the rest of us were seated further back and the wooden pews absorbed the shrapnel. You can get a feeling for the power of the blast by looking at the damage to the pews."

They hurried back to the car. "Alaa, take me to the Swiss Air building as fast as you can. I must get to my apartment before Mrs. Olsen learns of this disaster."

"Yes, General," Alaa replied. As soon as the doors were closed, Alaa sped off. When the car reached the high point on the Giza Bridge, they could see the Swiss Air building to the left. A large crowd had gathered in front of the building. When they reached the west side of the Nile, Alaa turned south to follow the river. They were about two blocks from the building when they ran into blocked traffic. Adam and Dave got out and ran toward the building.

Adam could see a body, lying on top of a Mercedes sedan parked in front of the restaurant. They pushed through the crowd and finally reached the car. Adam's worst suspicions were confirmed. The body was Sonya. He pushed through the crowd to the car. A well dressed Egyptian was feeling Sonya's pulse.

"Is she alive?" Adam asked.

"She has a very weak pulse," he said.

"Are you a doctor?" Adam asked.

"Yes," the man replied. "I'm a pediatrician. There is nothing I can do for her. We must get her to a hospital. The restaurant has called for an ambulance."

"Dave," Adam directed, "Have Alaa take you back to the Embassy. Get a hold of Doctor Ambrose and ask him to meet the ambulance at the hospital. Also check to see if there is a Medivac available to take Sonya to Germany. I'll stay here until the ambulance comes."

Dave rushed off to find the car while Adam talked to the police in Arabic to get the traffic cleared. It seemed like an interminable amount of time before the ambulance arrived. Adam stayed by Sonya while he waited for the ambulance. She was covered by her bathrobe. It appeared that she had fallen from the balcony of his apartment. "Did anyone see her fall?" he asked.

A young Egyptian came forward and volunteered information. He spoke highly accented English.

"I was walking by the river with my finance'. We heard a noise on the third floor. We looked up as that woman backed on to the balcony. She backed straight up to the railing and tumbled over backward. She didn't scream or anything. She hit the car in a horizontal position. We covered her body with her robe."

"Thank you very much" Adam replied as he pressed a ten pound Egyptian note into the young man's hand.

"Shukran!" the young man replied. "Is she your wife?"

"Yes," Adam replied.

Finally an ambulance arrived. The attendants moved Sonya's body to a stretcher. Adam watched for any reaction to pain. There was none. Sonya was in a coma. It was amazing that she was alive. He joined the body in the ambulance. He assured the ambulance crew that he would pay for all costs.

Dr. Ambrose met the ambulance at the nearest Cairo Hospital. Captain Baldwin was with him.

"General," Dave said, "There is a Medivac plane at the airport. I have them waiting in case she is able to travel."

Dr. Ambrose checked her pulse. It was weak. He suggested that she stay in the ambulance and go directly to the airport. Adam stayed with Sonya until they arrived at the D.C.-9 Medivac. While they loaded her on board, Adam called the Ambassador and suggested that he accompany Sonya to the hospital in Germany. He explained that her husband and two sons were both dead. The Ambassador agreed.

"Keep us informed of her progress and get back as soon as you can, Adam," the Ambassador concluded.

Adam got back to the D.C.-9 in time to talk to the aircrew. Since there was no immediate family to accompany the patient, the Aircraft Commander agreed to take the General without orders. Adam addressed Captain Baldwin.

"Dave, I'm going with Sonya," he said. "Have the office cut orders for me and send a message to Ramstein. I may have to accompany her to the States. She's not military so she won't be eligible to fly beyond Ramstein on the Air Force. Have my secretary cut leave orders so I can go on to the States. I will keep you posted."

"That's really nice of you, Sir!"

"Not really! I feel responsible for her situation. She may have jumped off the balcony after hearing what happened to her husband and her two sons. She was planning to confront her husband tomorrow."

"I understand, Sir," Dave replied. "I'll try to keep any rumors from spreading if I can."

"Don't lose any sleep over it," Adam replied. "I made my bed and I'll have to sleep in it. I just hope the doctors can keep her alive. For the first time in my life, I'm actually in love. I'll keep in touch."

Adam ran to the aircraft as the crew was closing doors and preparing to taxi. Sonya had been placed on a bunk. She was strapped down to preclude movement. She was hooked up to a monitor. The head nurse explained that Sonya's pulse was weak but steady. They had hooked up an IV to provide her some nourishment and to prevent dehydration. Oxygen was immediately available. Adam took his seat for take-off. As soon as they were airborne and the seat belt sign was off, Adam went to the head nurse.

"Excuse me, Major," he interrupted. "Can you tell me how Sonya is doing?"

"According to the monitor, she's doing as well as could be expected," the nurse replied. "I understand she fell a story and a half. She's in a coma and that may be a blessing. At least, she's not in pain. Are you her husband?"

"No," Adam replied. "Her husband was killed along with her two sons this morning. I believe she fell as a result of learning about her family."

"And you are?" the nurse asked.

"I'm Brigadier General Adam McGregor, the Defense Attache' at our Embassy in Cairo. I'm a close friend of Mrs. Olsen. She was in my apartment when she fell."

"Where were you at the time?"

"I was en route from her husband's church. Two terrorists rolled grenades down the aisle. Pastor Olsen and their two boys were killed. I was hoping to get back to the apartment before Sonya found out about the terrorist attack. It appears I was too late."

"You're the closest person to a relative to escort the patient?" the nurse continued. "Is there anything else you can tell me about her medical history?"

"She's twenty-nine," Adam began. "I believe she was in very good health. I think she's pregnant."

"How long has she been pregnant?" the nurse asked.

"Our best guess is at most five weeks."

"That's awfully early to be certain of a pregnancy," the nurse continued. "Why are you certain?"

"She had morning sickness a couple of times over the last week. She compared it to the experience she had with her two children. She seemed certain."

The nurse was a woman in her late thirties. She had been married and divorced. She was a career Air Force nurse on the Lieutenant Colonels list. She realized that she was grilling a General Officer about a private affair. The General didn't seem to mind.

"General McGregor, I don't want to pry," she began, "but you seem to be the only person available who could be responsible for approving medical decisions. Is that correct?"

"Yes, Major," he replied.

"That's an awesome responsibility for a friend to assume. How well did you know her husband?"

"I met him once at the Embassy in Cairo."

"How well did you know Mrs. Olsen?"

"I met her at the Meridien Hotel a couple of days after they arrived in Cairo. We've been intimate ever since. If she is pregnant, I'm the father."

"If she's pregnant, we should be able to determine if you are the father through blood tests," the nurse continued. "That should qualify you as an interested party who could be trusted to make decisions for Mrs. Olsen. You realize, of course, that we can provide emergency care, however, the Air Force may require reimbursement. Is that a problem?"

"No." he answered without hesitation.

"Why would you assume such a responsibility?" she asked.

"I'm very much in love with Sonya. We planned to marry as soon as she could get a divorce. As for the financial responsibility,

I'm independently wealthy. That's not a problem." he concluded.

"Thank you for being so candid. I will tell the doctor on board that you have sufficient interest in Mrs. Olsen's welfare to approve medical treatment and procedures. We'll have you fill out an affidavit."

The nurse left Adam to his own thoughts. He sat quietly by Sonya's bunk. For the first time in many years, Adam prayed.

CHAPTER 12

It was still daylight when they arrived at Ramstein. An ambulance was waiting. As Sonya was the only passenger on the critical list, she was taken off first and placed in the ambulance for the short trip to the Army Hospital in Landstuhl. Adam went with her. At the hospital, Adam explained her situation. He filled out forms explaining his relationship with the patient. In the absence of anyone else who could provide information, the staff was happy to have the General assume responsibility. After a short conference with several doctors, there was agreement that Sonya would be better off in the States. Adam dropped in on the Hospital Commander. He explained his situation and asked if he had a nurse he could spare for a few days. The Commander stated that he had a young lieutenant who was scheduled for two weeks leave. She was going to the States if she could get space available out of Rhein Main Air Base. Adam asked if he could talk to her. The nurse was called to the office.

"General," the doctor began, "This is Lieutenant Maggie McNamara."

"Hi! Lieutenant," Adam stated, "Can I call you Maggie?"

"Yes Sir!" she replied.

"I understand you need to go to the States. Where are you going?"

"I'm trying to get to Worthington, Minnesota,"she said.

"I'm flying to Minneapolis on Lufthansa this evening. I'm taking my friend, Sonya Olsen, to the Mayo Clinic. If you would be available, I would appreciate your accompanying Sonya as far as Rochester. As soon as she's in the Mayo Clinic, you'll be free to go on leave. I will take care of the tickets and your rent-a-car. Would you prefer another route or should I get a round trip on Lufthansa?"

"A round trip would be just fine," Maggie said enthusiastically.

"Great," Adam responded. "I'll see you at eighteen hundred. We'll be going to Frankfurt in the ambulance with Sonya." Adam thanked the Colonel in Charge and left for Ramstein. It was only fifteen minutes away by staff car.

His first stop was the base exchange where he purchased a uniform and insignia to identify him as a Brigadier General. He then checked in with the base commander. He explained his situation. The base commander had his secretary reserve space on a Lufthansa flight from Frankfurt to Chicago O'Hare for that evening. Lufthansa had space for an emergency bunk. The cost would be over two thousand dollars, including a ticket for Maggie. Adam put the charge on his credit card. He then checked into the BOQ to get some sleep.

Before going to bed, he called his office in Cairo. He had his secretary extend his leave for a week. He took a shower and tried to sleep. It was ten am in Germany. At two pm, he awoke and checked in with the Base Commander's Office. They had confirmed his flight reservations. The ambulance would pick Sonya up at four. Their flight departure would be seven pm, arriving in Chicago around eight pm Chicago time. They would then transfer to a Northwest flight to Minneapolis, arriving around eleven pm. An ambulance would be standing by to transport Sonya to the Mayo Clinic in Rochester.

At three pm, Adam placed a call to Sonya's parents home in St. Paul.

"Hello," a man answered.

"Am I speaking to Reverend Carlson?" Adam asked.

"I'm his son, Earl. My father is sleeping. We've had a family tragedy."

"I understand," Adam responded. "My name is Adam McGregor. I'm a friend of your sister, Sonya, from Cairo. I'm in

Germany with Sonya. We will leave Frankfurt in a couple of hours. We will change planes in Chicago and be in Minneapolis around eleven pm. I have arranged for an ambulance to take Sonya to the Mayo Clinic. The Emergency Room at the Clinic is expecting Sonya."

"Then she's alive?" Earl questioned.

"She's in a coma, but she is alive. The doctors here and in Cairo feel that she will be best off in the States. Where better than the Mayo Clinic?"

"My parents will be pleased to know that she is going to Rochester. I don't know how long we can afford to keep her there. We are working with Lutheran Missions to see what kind of insurance benefits are available."

"You don't need to worry about the finances. I know where I can get the money to cover medical expenses. It's not a problem," Adam concluded.

"I don't know how my parents will feel about taking money from an unknown source," Earl stated.

"Let's tackle that problem as the need comes up. I'll see you tomorrow," Adam hung up.

Adam awoke at three pm. He showered and donned his new uniform. Fortunately, he was able to get a complete set of his decorations. He was properly dressed. The ambulance picked him up at three-thirty. When they arrived at the Emergency Entrance of the Landsthul Hospital, the staff was there with Sonya's stretcher. Maggie was ready to travel. They loaded Sonya in the ambulance. Maggie got in beside her. The General followed Maggie in the back. The attendant joined the driver. They departed for Frankfurt.

Maggie watched Adam as he reached over and touched Sonya's forehead. She wondered what the connection was between them. When she met Adam that afternoon, she had thought he was quite good looking for an old guy. Now, when he was decked out in uniform, she saw him as unbelievably handsome. She thought he looked like a movie star. Adam looked up and saw that she was starring at him.

"Is there something wrong, Maggie?"

"No Sir!" she replied. "I was just admiring your decorations. You must have seen a lot of action."

"Most of the ribbons attest to the fact that I was in the wrong place at the right time or vice-versa, depending on how you look at it. How long have you been in service, Maggie?"

"Almost three years," she replied.

"How long will you stay in the Air Force?"

"I don't know. I have a little over a year to go on my commitment. My parents want me to come home and marry my high school sweetheart. He just inherited his family's farm. I promised I would try to get home on leave. Your kind offer of a free trip has insured that I will get home to discus the subject with my parents and my boyfriend. How long have you been in the Air Force, Sir?"

"Twenty-two years," Adam replied.

"How long have you known the patient?"

"Just a little over a month," he replied.

"Oh!" Maggie exclaimed. "I assumed you were old friends. Of course, it's none of my business."

"Maggie, do you know how they determine parentage in the case of," he paused, "in the case of, shall we say, surprise pregnancies?"

"They use blood tests. They aren't always definite. In most cases they are well over ninety percent reliable. I noted by the patient's file that there is a possibility that she is pregnant. Why do you ask, Sir?" she concluded politely.

The General stared off into the scene along the autobahn for several moments. Then he answered.

"Sonya is convinced that she is pregnant and she is certain that I'm the father," Adam concluded.

Maggie waited to be sure he was finished, then she proceeded.

"How do you feel about the pregnancy?"

"I'm very much in love with her. I hope that the blood tests will be conclusive. I have asked her to get a divorce and marry me. Initially, she said she couldn't. While we were in Cypress, she experienced morning sickness. She told me I was the father and that she wanted to marry me. I was ecstatic. She was going to confront her husband the day after we returned from Cypress. Sunday, the day we returned, her husband and two sons were killed by a terrorist attack at St. Mathew's Church. She fell from the balcony of my apartment on the third floor of the Swiss Air Building."

"Not to pry," Maggie began, "Did she say why she was sure you were the father?"

"She said that she hadn't had sex with anyone else since her last pregnancy."

"You believed her?" Maggie asked skeptically.

"I believe her. Maybe it's because I want to believe her. She has been totally honest with me about everything. I have no reason to doubt her."

They reached the Rhine and were turning north toward Frankfurt. The ambulance was proceeding down the right lane. Cars with flashing lights were streaming past in the left lane. It was not long before they were turning off to the airport.

Their accommodations were in the upper deck of a 747. Sonya was brought up on a stretcher by four men. No one else boarded until Sonya was secured on her bunk. Maggie checked Sonya's vital signs and hooked up oxygen and a monitor. Then she and Adam took the two facing first class seats on the opposite side of the section. They engaged in small talk until they were airborne.

They were served drinks and dinner shortly after take-off. Adam had two Dewars on the rocks. Maggie stayed with soft drinks. They both caught short catnaps. Each time Adam awoke he would check on Sonya to see that her oxygen hook-up still indicated breathing. Maggie checked on her patient every hour. Adam was very aware of her attention to Sonya and he was most pleased with her efforts.

Maggie was dying to know more about their relationship but decided she shouldn't pry. She wondered if she should offer to pay some of the cost of the trip. She looked at her ticket to see if there was any information on the cost. It noted that she was a medical attendant and the ticket included a first class return in two weeks. There wasn't any cost information other than it was marked prepaid.

When they arrived in Chicago, the transfer from one airplane to the other was done quickly and efficiently. The Northwest Boeing 727 had removed two first class seats to make room for a bed for Sonya. Adam and Maggie had facing seats next to the bed. They were airborne to Minneapolis/St Paul in thirty minutes. In a little more than an hour they arrived.

The ambulance was waiting on the tarmac and Sonya's stretcher was loaded on board. They pulled around to the front of the terminal and Adam went in to the Northwest counter and ask them to request that the Carlson family come to the Northwest Counter. He waited five minutes. Then he instructed the Northwest agent to tell the family that they were leaving for Rochester in the ambulance. Just as he was about to leave, Earl, Sonya's brother, arrived. He pleaded for the family to see Sonya before the ambulance departed. Adam relented. He urged them to get there as soon as they could. Earl came back in a few minutes with the Reverend and Mrs. Carlson. They appeared to be in their late fifties.

Adam introduced himself and they went immediately to the ambulance. Adam introduced the Carlson's to Lt. McNamara. He explained that she was on leave and had offered to accompany Sonya on the trip from Germany. They looked in on Sonya and saw that she was hooked up to an IV and seemed to be asleep. They asked if she had spoken.

Maggie responded, "She is in a coma. Her vital signs appear to be stable. I'm sure that if you could come to Rochester tomorrow, the doctors there will be able to give you a more complete prognosis."

Adam interrupted, "If you could come down tomorrow by eleven, I can arrange to have the staff member bring us up to date. We can then go to lunch and I can fill you in on the details involving Sonya's fall and the unfortunate demise of Reverend Olsen and your two grandsons."

They nodded their assent and took another look at Sonya. Adam and Maggie got in the Ambulance and left for Rochester. They arrived at the Mayo Clinic Emergency Entrance about twelve-fifteen am. The trip had been blessed with light traffic. Sonya was taken off the stretcher and placed on a gurney. The Emergency Room Doctor checked her vital signs and sent her off with a nurse and orderly. They went to the office to check in. The administrator noted that they had all the information they needed between discussions with the family and information forwarded from the Embassy in Cairo and the hospital in Germany. All they needed was a signature from General McGregor. Adam signed. The hospital had made reservations at a nearby hotel for Adam and Maggie.

When they arrived at the hotel, Adam asked Maggie how she was planning to get to Worthington.

"I guess I'll rent a car," she said.

"Let's meet at nine in the morning and I'll find you a car. We can get you on the road by ten and you'll be home by early afternoon. Do they know you're coming?"

"I sent a telegram from Germany that I was coming if I could get a flight. They will be really surprised when I show up so soon," Maggie responded.

"Good," Adam replied.

They checked in and went to their rooms. The next morning Adam and Maggie met in the lobby at nine am. Adam announced that he had rented two cars from Hertz. They took a taxi to the Hertz Agency. Adam had rented a Lincoln for himself and a Mustang for Maggie. He instructed her not to let anyone else drive the car as the insurance was only good for her. She was to turn in the car when she caught her return flight to Germany.

"What do I owe you?" Maggie asked.

"Nothing," he replied. "I appreciate your help with Sonya. I hope that someday you will get to meet her under better circumstances."

They were both in uniform. She saluted with tears in her eyes. They went their separate ways, knowing they would probably never meet again.

Adam went back to the hotel and checked out. He drove to the Mayo Clinic. He was in the waiting room when the Carlson family arrived. Reverend Carlson and Mrs. Carlson were accompanied by their son, Earl, and his wife, Rachel. After introductions, they took seats in a corner of the waiting room. Sonya's mother was the first to speak.

"How long have you known our daughter?" she asked.

"I met her in the Meridien Hotel in Cairo the day after they arrived. They were staying in the Meridien while their apartment was being cleaned," Adam responded.

"Were you on the trip to the Sudan with Sonya?" Reverend Carlson asked.

"Yes, I was one of the two pilots on the Kingair," Adam replied. "It was a very interesting trip. Sonya and I spent a lot of time together."

"Yes," Sonya's mother continued. "I guess you are the General she referred to in her letters."

"I was the one General present. I'm sure she was referring to me."

"She was very complimentary concerning your flying skills," Reverend Carlson added.

Adam laughed. "I fear that the experience of a dash into far Darfur may have overwhelmed Sonya's judgment of David and my abilities as pilots. The trip was actually quite normal for the time of the year. The Sudan can be very exciting to the first time travelers."

"Have you spent a lot of time in the Sudan?" the Reverend asked.

"That was my eighth trip to the Sudan," Adam responded. "I visited there from Saudi Arabia several years ago. In my present assignment, as the Defense Attache' to Cairo, I have an additional duty as Air Force Attache' to Khartoum. We try to spend a week to ten days in the Sudan every three to four months."

"Sonya didn't mention meeting you at the Meridien. She indicated that she met you at an Embassy Reception," Mrs. Carlson explained referring to the General's earlier statement concerning the Meridien.

"Our meeting at the Meridien was quite informal," Adam replied. "Our paths crossed at the pool. There was no formal introduction until we met in the receiving line at the Embassy." Further conversation was interrupted when a staff surgeon arrived.

"Mr. and Mrs. Carlson?" the Doctor asked.

"Yes," Reverend Carlson spoke as he rose to greet the doctor. "This is my wife, my son, Earl, and his wife, Rachel. I presume you know General McGregor?"

The doctor shook hands with the family and acknowledged Adam. "I'm Dr. Steven Snyder." he continued.

"General McGregor did a fine job of delivering your daughter to our care. She remains in critical condition. Shes in a coma. That may be a blessing as she has a broken back. Thanks to the coma she is not in pain. That is she doesn't feel pain. There is plenty of pain. My main concern is for the baby. Her pregnancy is just beginning. We would guess that she is less that two months along. We may have to consider abortion if the baby is sapping too much of her strength."

"That would have to be a last resort!" Mrs. Carlson interrupted. "Both Sonya and her late husband were opposed to abortion under any circumstances."

"I understand," the doctor replied. "We will certainly talk with you before any decision is made."

"How did you know she was pregnant?" Earl asked.

"General McGregor informed us that she was experiencing morning sickness last week," the doctor replied.

"Oh!" Mrs. Carlson said, "Were you in Germany with Sonya, General?"

"Please call me Adam, Mrs. Carlson," Adam responded. "I was not with her group in Germany. I did talk to her." He didn't elaborate on how they had communicated. He allowed them to assume it was in Germany.

"I hate to bring up finances," Reverend Carlson interjected, "but I doubt that their insurance will cover the costs."

"Don't worry about that. We will notify you if the present payment plan is interrupted," the doctor concluded.

The meeting broke up when a nurse appeared and invited the Carlson family to visit Sonya at bedside. When the Carlson's had departed, the doctor turned to Adam.

"I take it that they are not aware that you are the father of Sonya's baby?"

"No, Doctor," Adam replied. "I decided they have had enough shock for our first encounter."

"I can't blame you for that," the doctor countered. "I must advise you that you will have to show some kind of proof if you intend to make decisions concerning Sonya's health. As it stands now, the Carlson's are the next of kin with the Olsen family having a claim with regard to the baby."

"Can you take a blood test?" Adam asked..

"Not at this early stage. However, as the baby develops, we can. Blood tests are always subject to challenges as they are not one-hundred percent proof. They are accurate well over ninety percent of the time. I suggest you leave us a blood sample."

"I'll do that," Adam replied. "I'm leaving tonight for Cairo.

Please direct me to the administration office. I want to set up a payment plan."

The doctor pointed the way. "They will tell you where to go for blood work. I'll see you before you leave. I want you to leave me a contact number."

"I appreciate that, Dr. Snyder. I'll call you from Cairo."

"What's the time difference," Dr. Snyder asked.

"Nine or ten hours, depending on the season. Cairo keeps the same time year around."

"Call me about eight am my time. I usually have a few minutes before surgery."

"I will. Thank you, Doctor!"

Adam concluded his business with the hospital administration office. He then stopped by the laboratory and gave them a blood sample. He left his Cairo phone number at Dr. Snyder's office and departed for Minneapolis. He arrived at the airport in time to turn in his rental car and board his flight to O'Hare. At O'Hare, he had to hurry to get transportation to Lufthansa where he caught his flight to Frankfurt.

Adam called the U.S. Air Forces Europe Command Post at Ramstein. There was a C-141 leaving for Cairo West in two hours. There was a seat available if he could get to Ramstein. He called the Rhein Main Command Post and they dispatched a car and driver. "It's nice to be a General," Adam murmured under his breath.

He made the flight without any problems. He asked the air crew to call the U.S. Embassy and have the Defense Attache's Office send a car to Cairo West. They were able to make the contact on High Frequency Radio. Mustafa would meet the plane at Cairo West. Adam was the only passenger. He stretched out on the bucket seats along the cargo section wall and slept all the way to Cairo.

CHAPTER 13

Mustafa was at Cairo West, waiting for the C-141 to land. As soon as Adam had cleared customs, no problem for a person with a diplomatic passport, they left for Cairo. It was about a forty minute drive to the Nile.

"General," Mustafa began, "I have a message from our office." He handed Adam a note from Adam's Secretary.

The note read: "A man named Smith has called your office several times since you departed. He says he has some photographs from Cypress that he is sure you would like to see. He hasn't left any telephone numbers. He said he would keep checking your apartment. The man has an accent. Maybe a Cockney or possibly an Aussie. Thought you would want to know." Emma.

Adam thought for some time. He wondered if someone had taken pictures of Sonya when she was braless. There were so many topless women on the beach. Why would anyone have singled out Sonya? Although, she was the most attractive woman on the beach, he thought.

"Mustafa, take me to my apartment. I want to shower and pick up my car. Tell Emma that I'll be in the office by one this afternoon."

"Yes, Sir!" Mustafa replied.

Adam was deep in thought trying to retrace their steps in Cypress. The only time they were on the beach alone was when they swam early and went out to the float. Why would a photographer find that interesting? After all, it was a topless beach.

When they arrived at the parking area behind the Swiss Air Building, they noticed an old Mercedes parked along the perimeter fence. There was a man in the car. As soon as the man saw them, he started the car and drove away. He was far enough away so that they couldn't identify him.

"I wonder if that's our mysterious Mr. Smith?" Adam said to Mustafa.

"Maybe," Mustafa answered. "Should I try to tail him?"

"No, he'll probably call the office this afternoon," Adam responded. "I'll find out what he wants and then we'll decide how to proceed."

Adam went in the apartment. He checked around to see if anything was missing. There didn't appear to be any discrepancies. He took a shower and put on a clean uniform. As he was about to depart he looked back and realized how empty the apartment seemed. He realized how much he missed Sonya.

He went down to the parking lot and began to remove the shroud from his Corvette. The guard who seemed to be present at all times came over and helped him. The man appeared to be somewhere between twenty-five and forty years old. It was impossible to tell. Adam wondered when he ate and slept. Adam gave him a generous tip.

"Shukran!" the man said.

"Masalama!" Adam replied as he departed.

At the office, Adam was busy going through the message traffic when Captain Baldwin came in.

"Hi, Dave!" Adam said, "What's up?"

"Everything is fine except that my wife has pulled a boner," Dave replied.

"How's that?" Adam asked.

"She sent a letter to the preacher who was killed at St. Mathews. She told him that his wife was in Cypress with you instead of being in Germany with the Embassy wives group."

"Had Revered Olsen opened the letter?" Adam asked.

"Apparently not. At least it appeared to be unopened. It was on Embassy stationary."

"I guess it's been overtaken by events, if that's the case," Adam replied.

"I thought sure you'd fire me!"

"It was inevitable that our trip to Cypress would get out. There were others on the C-12 that were aware of our trip. It was going to come out. You might as well know that Sonya and I were planning to marry as soon as she could get a divorce."

"How is she, Sir?"

"She's still in a coma. I took her to the Mayo Clinic in Minnesota. If they can't save her, no one can. I will call the Neuro-Surgeon, a Doctor Snyder, at eight am Minnesota time. That's nineteen-hundred our time. I have to keep in touch with him if I'm to have any say in her medical treatment. She's pregnant and I'm the father. Her family and her in-laws are not aware that her husband was not the father."

Captain Baldwin didn't respond to this information. He suddenly realized that he didn't have a need to know.

"I appreciate your confiding in me, Sir. I assure you, I will not discuss this with anyone."

"Thanks, Dave. There is nothing anyone can do. The less said about the situation, the better I will feel about it. I'm going over to my apartment for awhile. I would like to see if I can contact Mr. Smith."

"Mr. Smith, Sir?"

"Emma left me a note about a Mr. Smith who has been trying to contact me. I think I may have seen him in the parking lot. My guess is that he has in mind to try to blackmail me. He claims he has pictures of Sonya and myself from Cypress. We were staying at a resort and most of the women, all Caucasians, were topless. If he thinks I care about that at this point, he has another surprise coming. Call me if anything exciting comes up. Otherwise, I'll see you tonight at Her Majesty's Birthday Ball."

"Yes Sir." Dave saluted and departed the office.

Adam informed his Secretary that he would be at home. He would be attending the function at the British Embassy that evening, and he would be coming to the office to check message traffic on

Sunday.

When Adam pulled into the parking lot, he saw the old Mercedes parked at the far end of the lot. He parked his car and walked over to the Mercedes. The window was open and the driver appeared to be sleeping. Adam yanked the door open and the man nearly fell out. Adam caught him by the hair before he could hit the ground.

"What the hell do you think you're doing?" the man shouted.

"Are you Mr. Smith?" Adam asked in a quiet voice.

"That's right, Governor. I'm Ian Smith from Melbourne, Australia. I came to offer you some pictures from your trip to Cypress with Mrs. Olsen."

The man was wearing a loose Hawaiian shirt. Underneath the shirt Adam had felt something as he kept the man from falling to the ground. The man was wearing a wire.

"Now why would I want pictures of myself and Mrs. Olsen? Mrs. Olsen is near death in a stateside hospital."

"I'm sorry about the woman, but you still have your career to think about. It wouldn't look good for a General Officer to be seen naked with another man's wife, particularly when she's the wife of a clergyman."

"You have a point there, Ian," Adam replied. "Let's get out of the hot sun. It's much cooler in my apartment."

"That's fine with me, Governor. I could use a cold beer if you happen to have one."

Adam motioned Smith toward the steps going up to his apartment. Ian insisted that Adam lead the way. "I'd rather follow you, Governor. I get nervous when people follow me."

"I wonder why!" Adam replied as he led the Aussie up the steps. "You must have a lot of enemies, considering your line of work!"

"Actually, this is our first caper. We met a bird who works at the Australian Embassy. She rides with a friend of yours. Your friend told her you were in Cypress with Mrs. Olsen."

"You decided to come to Cypress to make an album for us," Adam interjected calmly.

"Precisely, Governor," he replied with sarcasm. "Originally, we thought we would sell the pictures to the Reverend Olsen. By the time we got back, he was dead. We decided we would sell the pictures to you."

Adam opened the door and motioned for Ian to enter. Ian pulled a snub-nosed 38 from his belt. "After you, Governor," Ian replied. Adam entered the apartment followed by the Aussie.

"What kind of beer would you like?" Adam asked.

"I'll have a Heineken," Ian replied.

"It appears you've been here before. I thought my houseboy had taken up drinking. I won't ask how you got inside." Adam went to the kitchen and retrieved a Heineken. Smith followed him.

"Be careful how you handle the beer. I wouldn't want it to get all over me in an effort to get my gun," the Aussie remarked.

"I'm not sure what I'm going to do. I would like to take your gun away from you, take you out on the desert, shoot your ass and leave you for the scavengers."

"That's a dangerous line of thought, General. You might get killed in the interim."

"I realize that's a possibility. Why don't you go get your buddy, the guy on the other end of your wire and we'll all have a chat on the advantages and disadvantages of our respective positions."

"What makes you think I have a wire?" Smith asked.

"Just a guess. I didn't figure you would come up here alone, without a backup. He's in the parking lot, right?" Adam asked. "I need to take a shower and get dressed. I'm due at the British Embassy at nineteen hundred hours. If I'm not there by nineteen-thirty, there will be people here looking for me."

Adam went into the bedroom and locked the door. He took a long, leisurely shower and then put on his dress uniform. It was six-forty five in the evening when he emerged from the bedroom.

"Well, Ian, who's your friend?" Adam asked.

"This is Ian Jones. Ian, meet General McGregor."

Adam acknowledged the stranger with a nod. "Smith and Jones! How original," he added.

"Look, Governor," Smith began, "We've fallen on hard times. We need some money to get back to Australia. When we heard about your soirée with the preacher's wife, we decided we might be able to put the bite on you."

"Okay. Hold that thought," Adam began. "I have to make a

call to the States. Have another beer." Adam started for the bedroom.

"Wait a minute," Smith said. "Make your call here. We want to listen."

"Okay," Adam said with a shrug. He picked up the phone and dialed the International operator. He spoke in Arabic and got his number in minimum time. He noticed that his two companions were very nervous.

"Hello, Dr. Snyder, please," Adam spoke. "Tell him Adam McGregor is calling from Cairo." There was a pause. The two Ian's glanced at each other furtively. Then they turned their attention back to Adam.

"Hello, Dr. Snyder. This is Adam McGregor. How is Sonya?" Adam listened for sometime as the Doctor provided information.

"How critical is it?" Adam asked. He listened.

"I see," Adam spoke. "I may be able to rectify the situation. Can you recommend a good Lawyer?" Again, Adam listened. The two Ian's began to fidget.

"Can you make an appointment with the Lawyer and give me a number where I can call him tomorrow?" Adam asked. He took a note pad and wrote down a phone number and a time. "I'll call tomorrow at his office." He hung up.

"Okay, Smith and Jones, what have you got for me?"

"What do you mean?" Smith asked.

"You alluded to some pictures. I need to see them."

The two wannabe crooks looked at each other and then brought out several blowups. The pictures were copied from a black and white movie film. The quality wasn't good. They were snapshots of Adam and Sonya in the buff and they were certainly recognizable.

"Does the film have sound?" Adam asked.

"Yes, Sir," Smith replied.

"Okay. What are you asking for the film?"

They looked at each other. Jones nodded to Smith. Smith said, "We need two tickets to Melbourne and money to live on until we get there."

Adam pealed five, ten pound Egyptian notes from his money

clip. "Get something to eat. Meet me here tomorrow night with the film. I want to see the whole thing. If it has the information I'm looking for, I'll give you your tickets and enough money to get you to Melbourne. I've got to run to my function. I'll see you tomorrow."

Mustafa was waiting in the parking lot. The British Embassy was very close to the American Embassy. They arrived in ten minutes in spite of heavy traffic. Adam instructed Mustafa to return at ten pm.

Adam's counterpart, Brigadier Alistair Ames of Her Majesty's Marines, was introducing the guests to Sir William Hull and Lady Agatha Hull, the Ambassador and his wife.

"Good to see you, Adam," Alistair said softly. "I have a message for you from Brian Scott. I'll catch you at the bar." He passed Adam on to the Ambassador knowing that an introduction wasn't necessary.

"Good evening, Sir William!" Adam began.

"Ah, Adam," Sir William replied. "I understand you escorted Mrs. Olsen to the States. Do you have any news about her condition?"

"I talked to her doctor about an hour ago. She remains in a coma. She has several broken bones from her fall. That's all I can tell you for now."

"Where is she now?" Lady Agatha asked.

"She's in the Mayo Clinic in Rochester, Minnesota. I'm in daily contact with Doctor Snyder. He informs me that her condition is complicated by the fact that she's pregnant."

"Did you know the Olsen's well?"

"Reverend Olsen volunteered Sonya for a fact-finding trip to a refugee camp in the Sudan. She was representing the World Council of Churches, along with another couple. We were gone six days. We became well acquainted."

"Please let us know how she is progressing," Lady Hull concluded.

Adam wandered toward the bar talking to several acquaintances on the way. As soon as the receiving line was closed, Alistair Ames came to the bar in search of Adam.

"Have you checked the seating chart, Adam?" he asked.

"No, should I?" Adam replied.

"You're sitting beside Lady Agatha. Be prepared for a grilling. It's all over town that you and Sonya Olsen were in Cypress together."

"News travels fast!" Adam replied. "Bad news travels faster!"

"It seems that Mrs. Olsen missed a trip to Germany on your account?" Alistair questioned. "I suspect Lady Agatha will try to satisfy her curiosity."

"Thanks for the warning, Alistair. We really didn't try very hard to cover our tracks. What did you hear from Brian Scott?"

"Brian's been called to Cranwell. It seems his predecessor at the War College had an accident and was killed. Brian's been promoted to Group Captain and they are packing for the U.K. as we speak. He had heard about Sonya Olsen. He and Sandra send their best."

"Did Brian say anything about our visit to their home?"

"Sandra said you were quite smitten with Sonya Olsen and that the feeling was mutual. How do you feel about it?"

"We were planning to marry as soon as Sonya could get a divorce," Adam replied. "If Sonya survives, I intend to marry her assuming that she will still have me."

"I wish you luck," Alistair concluded. "Ah, there's the dinner chime. Good luck with Lady Agatha!"

Adam acknowledged with a nod and proceeded to the head table. Lady Agatha was apologizing to the US Ambassador for changing the seating.

"Your Excellency," she began, "I've placed you in the delightful company of the wife of our Charge'. I simply must complete my conversation with General McGregor."

"Of course," the Ambassador said, "I understand completely."

Adam helped her Ladyship with her chair after the completion of "God Save the Queen". When everyone was seated, Lady Agatha turned her full attention to Adam.

"May I call you Adam?"

"Yes, Your Ladyship," Adam replied.

"I'm hearing the most exciting things about you, Adam. Is Adam your real name?"

"Actually, it's taken from my initials. A.D.M. stands for

Angus Donald McGregor. I never cared for Angus, although it was my grandfather's name."

"You may call me, Agatha," she said.

"As you wish, Agatha," he replied.

"I'm hearing a great deal about a clandestine trip to Cypress with Mrs. Olsen. Is any of it true?"

"Yes, Agatha. I'm afraid it is all true. I took Sonya, Mrs. Olsen, to meet Wing Commander Brian Scott and family at the British Base on Cypress. They were the first to know that Sonya would seek a divorce and we would marry as soon as her divorce was final."

"You're being very open about this considering that her husband and two children were killed," Agatha replied.

"I can't very well sweep it under the table at this late date. If she hadn't been with me she would have been killed by the same grenades that killed her family."

"I guess that's true enough. How did she fall from your balcony?"

"I can only surmise that she was watching the television and saw the carnage at St. Mathews. It appears that she backed over the guard rail while distancing herself from the television."

They were interrupted by the arrival of the soup course. Agatha didn't get to respond. Once everyone was served, Lady Agatha tried her soup. She announced that it was quite good. She turned her attention back to Adam.

"Adam, my husband tells me that Mrs. Olsen's condition is aggravated by a pregnancy. You seem to be intent on marrying Mrs. Olsen. Does that mean you are prepared to accept responsibility for her condition?"

"Yes," Adam replied as he tried another taste of the soup.

"You've only known her for a month or so. How can you be sure?"

"Sonya told me that I was the only one she had slept with since her last pregnancy."

"You believed her?" Lady Agatha pressed on.

"Yes, I do," Adam replied without looking at Lady Agatha.

"This may be shattering to your career. Are you sure you want to be so, how shall I say, up front, with your position?"

"I've had a great career. If it ended tomorrow, I would have no regrets. You see, Lady Agatha, I've never been in love before. I must do everything I can to see that she survives. That means I must have a major say in her treatment. The sooner I can prove that I'm the father of Sonya's child, the more leverage I'll have in dictating her treatment."

"Excuse me!" Lady Agatha said, rising from her chair.

Adam looked at her. Tears were streaming down her cheeks. Mrs. Ames jumped up and took Lady Agatha by the arm. She led her toward the Ladies Room.

"Sit down, Adam!" she said. "I'll be right back. Don't you dare leave." The two ladies departed. They were gone for fifteen minutes. Lady Agatha had repaired her make-up.

"What happened? Did Adam say something to upset you?" Mrs. Ames demanded.

"Heavens no!" Agatha replied. "I pried into his life, thinking I was going to get a lot of lies and a cover up. Instead, I uncovered a real hero. He would give his life for that woman, Mrs. Olsen. All of a sudden I was crying. I'm all right now. Let's return."

When they returned to the table, the gentlemen all stood while the two ladies took their seats. Idle conversation began immediately. Sir William would have none of it.

"Agatha, the last time you had an outburst at dinner you were pregnant. That was twenty years ago!" Sir William began. "Please tell me you're not pregnant."

"Of course not, Dear. I'll explain. Adam, were you ever in the Strategic Air Command?"

"Yes, I was, in the early sixties," he replied.

Agatha began, "When William and I were in Washington, we were invited on a tour of SAC Headquarters near Omaha, Nebraska. After a briefing on the mission of SAC, we were taken on a tour of the Command Post. As we entered, I noticed a poster hanging on the wall. The poster showed this beautiful kitten crawling over a barrier. Below the kitten, written on the barrier, were these words. 'Curiosity is not a need to know.' I was prying into General McGregor's private life when suddenly I realized I didn't have a need to know. I can only say, Godspeed, General."

Adam recovered from the surprise. He kissed Lady Agatha's

hand and whispered, "Thank you!"

Everyone applauded.

Sir William turned to Mrs. Ames and said, "I love to put Agatha on the spot. She has such ingenious ways of recovering."

"That was quite good. I would have melted into the floor," Mrs. Ames concluded.

Adam left the reception shortly after the dinner was complete. He explained to Lady Agatha that he must call the States and talk to Sonya's Doctor. Lady Agatha understood. Adam went back to his apartment and placed the call. Dr. Snyder was in his office.

"Dr. Snyder, can I help you," he answered.

"Yes, Doctor Snyder, this is Adam McGregor. How is Sonya?"

"There is no change. There is no reason to believe she is any worse either. I have a lawyer for you, Adam. He wants to know if you can get back here in the next month."

"I'm meeting with a couple of scumbags who have some film of Sonya and me, during our trip to Cypress. They wanted to blackmail me. However, the film may have some conversation between Sonya and myself that will add credence to my claim to being the father of her baby. I'm seeing them tomorrow night. Once I've reviewed their film, I'll make plans to come to Minnesota." They concluded their conversation.

Adam poured himself a Scotch Whiskey and ice. He turned on the TV and watched a film. It was dubbed in Arabic. He had seen the film before. A lot of the Arabic translation didn't follow the plot as originally laid out. He decided to call it a day.

The following day, Adam went to his office. He used the time to catch up on his correspondence and plan his itinerary for the next three weeks. He called the Ambassador's Office to arrange a two week's leave to the States. He then sent a message to the Defense Intelligence Agency, DIA, to clear his travel plans. By the end of the day, both offices had cleared his leave request. He called TWA and made a reservation from Cairo direct to JFK with a connection to Minneapolis-St. Paul on Northwest. He left the office. When he arrived at his apartment, Smith and Jones were waiting for him.

"Have you got the film?" Adam asked.

"Yes, and we brought our projector," Smith replied.

"Okay!" Adam responded as they entered the apartment. "Set it up to project on that wall. I'll close the curtains."

The room was as dark as it could get for that time of day. The film quality was poor, but the sound track was fairly good. Adam could feel his ears and cheeks burn with embarrassment as the film continued from one sex encounter to the next. The quality was good enough to show both himself and Sonya in the nude, but the film was scratchy. Identifying them would be difficult unless the viewer knew them. On the other hand, the sound track was nearly perfect. It had picked up all of the sounds of passion. Adam could close his eyes and feel the excitement of each sexual impulse. His passion for Sonya raised with each filmed incident. At the same time his hatred for Smith and Jones increased with each tither of suppressed giggling that he could hear. He was about to give up when he heard the words he was hoping to hear. It was Sonya's voice.

"Everything is fine as long as I'm assured of your love. I'm so happy that I'm carrying your baby."

It was Sonya's voice and the film had caught her looking at the camera.

"Stop the film!" Adam ordered.

They shut off the projector.

"Do you have a copy of this film?" Adam asked.

"Of course," Jones replied.

"Okay. Leave this copy with me. I'll need your real names for your tickets and your passport numbers. What airline do you want to fly?"

"Qantas," Jones replied. "And Smith and Jones are our real names."

"When do you want to travel?" Adam asked.

"As soon as you can get us tickets," Ian Smith replied.

"Have you got your passports with you?"

"Yes," they both responded.

"Let me have them. I'll get your tickets for the day after tomorrow. Meet me here at four pm. Bring the other copy of the film.

Adam reached into his pocket and pulled out an envelope. It

contained Five Hundred Egyptian Pounds.

"This should help you clear up any expenses you have in Cairo," Adam concluded. "Until tomorrow then. Don't forget the other copy or copies if you have them."

Smith and Jones gathered up their projector and prepared to leave. As they were about to leave Smith turned to Adam.

"We appreciate the money," Smith said, "How do you know we don't have a third copy of the film?"

"We'll discuss that tomorrow," Adam replied as he ushered them out the door.

After Smith and Jones left, Adam put in a call to Dr. Snyder. They discussed Sonya's condition, which had not changed. The conversation went on to Adam's legal position. Dr. Snyder recommended that he call the lawyer that the Doctor had recommended. The lawyer's office would be open at nine am, Central Daylight time. The lawyer's name was Donald Johnson.

Adam waited until ten after the hour before he put in his call. The phone was answered immediately. Adam informed the receptionist that he was calling from Cairo for Donald Johnson.

"Is that Cairo, Illinois, Sir?" she asked.

"No Ma'am, it's Cairo, Egypt. I'm Brigadier General Adam McGregor. Dr. Snyder recommended Mr. Johnson."

"Please hold," she replied.

Ten seconds later the lawyer answered. "Hello, General McGregor. This is Don Johnson. Dr. Snyder briefed me on your requirement. When can you come to Minnesota?"

"I've requested two weeks leave. I'm planning to leave Sunday and I should be in Rochester during the day on Monday."

"We're you able to get any proof to back your contention that you are the father of Sonya Olsen's baby?" the lawyer asked.

"Yes, I'm in possession of a film in which she states that I'm the father."

"You'll bring the film with you?"

"Yes, I will," Adam concluded.

"What kind of film is it?" the lawyer asked.

"It's eight millimeter."

"Not exactly high tech. I'll work on finding a projector. Call me as soon as you're in town.

"I will," Adam responded. "See you Monday."

"Have a good trip. Goodbye."

Adam showered, dressed and went downstairs for dinner at the Swiss Air Restaurant. He ordered a Scotch on the Rocks and a steak dinner. He went over the last seven weeks in his mind. It was Sonya, Sonya, Sonya. God, how he missed her.

The following day he was in the office at seven am. He checked his calendar. He was obligated to functions every night but Friday. Tonight, he was going to the German Embassy. On Thursday, he was invited to the Sudanese Military Attache's home for dinner. That would involve a lot of Scotch drinking. For once, he was happy that he wasn't married. At a Muslim home, the women were always separated. This left the English speaking spouse to depend on her knowledge of Arabic or possibly French in order to participate in a conversation. It was always a tough night for the women. All the men were conversant in English, plus Adam's Arabic was quite good. Also, the men had plenty of Scotch while the women were drinking tea.

At eight am, all the Defense Attache' Office staff arrived. Adam went into Captain Don Sanford's office. Don was the Naval Attache' and the number two, seniority wise, in the office.

"Hi, Don," Adam began. "I'll be away on two weeks leave starting Sunday. I was wondering if you could cover an invitation to the Indian Embassy on Saturday night?"

"I'm invited also," Don said. "I'll be there. Was there anyone in particular that I need to talk with?"

"Yes. I think you know Group Captain Vanic. I swap a lot of information with him. The last time I talked to him, he mentioned that the Chinese may be selling F-7's to the Sudan. If he has anymore on it, I would like to know. You don't have to press him. If he needs a Quid Pro Quo, tell him about the Pakistani's F-16's that will refuel at Luxor on their way to Karachi. That way he can beat the political section. They won't hear about it until it's in the Cairo papers."

"Can do! Have a good trip," the Captain replied.

Adam went back to his own office and picked up the phone. He called the Australian Embassy and ask for the Consulate. He inquired about Ian Smith and Ian Jones. The Consulate was aware that Smith and Jones were in country. They verified that the names were authentic. They also verified that their visas would expire and they did need to leave the country before the first of July. They also verified that Qantas had two flights a week from Cairo to Sidney. Adam's next call was to the Qantas Office. He made reservations for Smith and Jones for Thursday. At lunch time he went by the Qantas Office and picked up the tickets.

Adam left his office. Smith and Jones were in the parking lot at his apartment. He invited them up for a beer and when they were all comfortable, Adam spoke.

"Did you bring me your copy of the film?" he asked.

"Yes, Sir," Smith replied as he handed over the canister.

"Here are your tickets," Adam volunteered as he gave them each an envelope.

"We were afraid you might back out of the deal. We decided not to make another copy," Ian Jones insisted.

"Good. I put an extra five-hundred Australian dollars in each envelope. I expect you to use that money wisely as there won't be anymore. If I ever hear of any publicity concerning myself and Mrs. Olsen, I will feel obligated to send someone out to Australia to look you up."

"Not to worry, General. We appreciate your generosity and we will keep your secrets," Ian Smith concluded. Ian Jones nodded in agreement.

Adam stood up and motioned to the two men that it was time for them to leave. They both got up and departed without further comment.

CHAPTER 14

Adam was due at the West German Embassy at seven-thirty pm. He decided to take some time to make some notes about the film and how he would present his position to Donald Johnson. The first question that came to mind was how much of the film would have to be shown to the Carlson family. Could he get by with a copy of the sound track? It's Sonya's words that provide the information, not the film. If they don't see her face, will they believe the words are truly hers? He kept hoping that she would recover and be able to tell her family and the Olsen family that she had decided to leave her husband under any circumstances. He made notes for over an hour, trying to prepare himself for a number of outcomes. In the end, he wanted Sonya as his wife no matter what the two families thought or said about the situation.

He started to write a letter to his mother. She still lived in the Georgetown Townhouse the family had owned for two generations. After his father died, his mother had installed an elevator so that she wouldn't have to negotiate stairways. He started a letter to tell her about Sonya. He tore up the letter. He decided to write a short note.

Dear Mother,

I will be in the States for a couple of
weeks. I have some business that needs
my attention. After it is complete, I'll
stop in D.C. for a couple of days. I hope
you will be at home over the Fourth of
July weekend.   I'll call you when I
get to the States.

Love,
Adam

It was time to get ready for his evening at the West German
Embassy. His invitation read informal for cocktails and dinner. That
meant suit and tie. He got out his white linen suit and an olive shade
tie. He took a shower and dressed. Just before leaving, he put in a
call to Minnesota. Fortunately, Dr. Snyder was in his office.

"How is Sonya doing?"

"She remains in a coma. Her condition remains the same.
When you get here, we must talk about an abortion. The baby is
growing normally. It may be sapping her strength."

"I'll be in your office on Monday morning if my flights are on
time. As soon as Don Johnson has a talk with the Carlson's maybe I
can make the decision," Adam replied.

"I'll be here Monday morning. Where are you staying?"

"I'll be at the Marriott," Adam said. "I should arrive late
afternoon on Sunday."

The doctor gave Adam his home phone number and
suggested they have dinner on Sunday. Adam agreed. It was six-
forty five pm. Adam could still make it to the German Embassy by
seven.

******

Oberst Gerhard Ehrlich of the Luftwaffe was the West
German Embassy's Defense Attache'. Adam had met Gerhard a

number of years previously when they were both involved in NATO Exercises. Gerhard was unaccompanied because he had two children in high school and his wife had remained in Germany with the children. Adam and Gerhard spent a lot of time together. So it was always a pleasant evening when they got to chat.

While they were enjoying a Scotch Whiskey before dinner, Adam brought Gerhard up to date on Sonya and told him that he was going to the States to see Sonya and to work out some problems with her family.

Adam and Gerhard sat together at the dinner table. Their conversation got around to the annual visit to El Alemain, the famed battlefield and high water mark of the German advance in Africa during World War II. The Germans and the Italians have burial grounds on the Axis side. On the Allied side there were troops from all over the Old British Empire. Attending officials usually included the Ambassador or Charge' d'affaires of the Embassies involved as heads of the delegations. There was always representations from the Defense Attache's offices. Attending from the Allied side were representatives of New Zealand, Australia, India, Pakistan, South Africa, Greece, the United Kingdom, France, Norway, Canada, and, of course, the United States. It made for quite a weekend. Gerhard asked Adam if anyone from the U.S. Embassy would be available to attend ceremonies at the West German and Austrian burial grounds.

Adam replied, "Our delegation usually attends the British Empire ceremonies. However, I will make a note of your thoughts. I'll discuss it with the Ambassador before November and I'll give you an answer."

Adam didn't commit the American Delegation as there was still a lot of hostility in the American Press toward the Nazis. Of course, any World War II German Forces burial ground was bound to contain some Nazi Party members. It was a bit ridiculous as the West Germans were a valuable NATO Ally.

Adam was not as fluent in German as he was in Arabic, but he knew enough German to get the gist of most conversations. This was more valuable when he was around the East German Delegation. Egyptian President Anwar Sadat had expelled the Russians from Egypt because they were proselytizing Communism, particularly among military officers. The East German Delegation had increased significantly since the Russian departure as they were Russia's surrogates in Cairo. Adam's ability to eaves drop when he was around the East German's had become a genuine asset to all of the US Delegations, including the CIA. Gerhard Ehrlich was the only German who was aware of Adam's talent. Adam was careful not to speak German casually.

When the function was over, Adam went directly to the apartment. He was up and at his office by eight am. Adam told Mustafa to pick him up at the apartment at seven pm. He wanted Mustafa to take him to the function at the home of the Sudanese Defense Attache', Major General Bashir El Ahmad, Sudanese Army. He had met General Bashir in the States when Bashir was attending the Army War College in Carlisle, Pennsylvania. Bashir was promoted to Major General when he was assigned to Cairo. He had always been well connected as he was related to Gaafar Numerie the Sudanese President.

Adam spent the morning catching up on all the correspondence. He wanted to be sure he cleared his desk before turning the office over to Don Sanford. He knew Captain Sanford would leave a clean desk for him when he came back. At four pm, Adam headed for the Meridien to swim some laps. He swam for thirty minutes and then hurried home to get ready to go to General Bashir's party. At six-forty five, he called Minnesota. Dr. Snyder had just arrived in his office.

They talked for ten minutes. Dr. Snyder suggested again that they abort the baby for the mother's sake. Adam wondered if Sonya would ever forgive him for that option. He asked if there wasn't another choice. Dr. Snyder admitted that he could do a Cesarean Section in another month or so. The baby would have to spend a long time in an incubator. That might be the best option to save both baby and mother. Dr. Snyder didn't mention the cost as he knew that Adam wouldn't care about that. They agreed they would talk some more on Monday morning.

Mustafa was waiting with the old Plymouth Volare in the parking lot. Adam jumped in the car and they raced off to Maadi, the upscale community south of Cairo where many foreigners and diplomats lived. The US Defense Attache's Villa was just a block away from General Bashir's Villa. Adam and Mustafa arrived at five after seven in the evening. Adam suggested that Mustafa return by ten thirty pm.

There were seven officers gathered in the living room. General Bashirs deputy, Colonel Ahmed, was Sudanese Air Force. Adam had met him and knew that he was a pilot. Other guests included Attache's from Nigeria, Tanzania, two from the Emirates and an Omani. Adam noted that they were all Sunni Muslims. He had hoped that Attache's from Syria and Iran might be present. He guessed that the Shiites were somewhat estranged. The final guest was an Egyptian Air Force Colonel, Khalid Ibrahim who arrived just as introductions were being completed.

A servant arrived with a tray containing eight glasses. The glasses were filled with thin shards of ice, chipped off a block. A second tray arrived with a large pitcher of Pepsi Cola and a bottle of Johnny Walker Red. It was not Adam's favorite Scotch. It certainly beat Pepsi Cola, however. Adam knew the cola was Pepsi as the Arabs had banned Coke because it was sold in Israel.

Adam took a glass and presented it to the servant who promptly poured it nearly full with Scotch. Adam noticed a couple of bits of sawdust on the top of the glass. There was no doubt it was 'street' ice. He sipped the scotch slowly and hoped he wouldn't be too sick in the morning.

The conversation turned to an aircraft accident involving an F-4D Phantom out of Cairo West. The Phantom was one of eighteen aircraft in an Egyptian Air Force Squadron at Cairo West. According to Colonel Khalid, the pilot and Systems Operator were the best in the Squadron. They had taken off, air refueled from a US KC-135 tanker, and proceeded on a low level mission across the desert Southwest of Cairo. Shortly after they finished the first leg of the low level the two engines failed. The aircrew zoomed up and ejected. Both aviators survived. The Egyptian Air Force was investigating the possible causes of the flame out of both engines.

Adam suppressed a smirk as he had been told of the accident by a US officer who had been at the accident scene. The refueling receptacle on the crashed Phantom was in the open position. If the pilot had not closed the receptacle, the external tanks and the wing tanks would not pressurize, trapping all fuel not in the fuselage tank. The engine failures were almost certainly due to fuel starvation.

The discussion of airplanes gave Adam an excuse to ask Colonel Khalid how the Egyptian Air Force liked their F-7s that they were buying from China. The F-7 was a Chinese version of the Soviet Union's Mig-21. After Anwar Sadat had expelled the Soviets from Egypt, Egypt's Mig-21 fleet rapidly fell into disuse due to the lack of spare parts. The Mig-21 fleet would now be a source of spare parts to keep the F-7s flying. This conversation gave Adam the opportunity to ask the Sudanese about their acquisition of Chinese F-7s. He caught General Bashir off guard.

"How did you find out we were buying the F-7s?" the General asked.

"I first heard about it at an Attache' luncheon last week. One of the Attache's from South Asia was the first to mention it. Several others appeared to have heard similar reports," Adam replied. Fortunately, dinner was served and Adam didn't have to do any more explaining.

The dinner was served at a long table by a house boy. Only the Attache's were at the table. The women were served in another part of the home. Once again, Adam was glad that he didn't have a spouse attending.

After dinner the men returned to the living room. They were offered more Scotch. Adam explained that he was leaving for the States on Saturday and he had to catch up on some reports before he left. He said his goodbyes, thanked his host and departed. Mustafa was waiting for him in the car. They drove to Adam's apartment. Adam told Mustafa to pick him up at nine am the next day. Adam went directly to bed.

The next morning Adam awakened at a little after dawn. He did not feel well. His sufragie, or houseboy, a Sudanese male named Mohamed arrived at seven am. Mohamed cleaned the apartment every other day. Mohamed was somewhere between forty and fifty years old. He spoke Arabic except for a few English expressions. Adam explained that he wasn't feeling well.

Mohamed replied, "I fix, I fix," and went off to the kitchen with a mischievous grin on his face. When he returned he had a concoction of Castor oil and herbs that he offered to Adam. Adam was nearly delirious. He was able to drink the concoction. He laid down and tried to sleep. In a very short time he woke up and rushed to the bathroom suffering from vomiting followed by diarrhea. He returned to the bedroom and slept for three hours. He got up a little after ten. His temperature was back to normal. He could still taste the concoction. It reminded him of how motor oil smells. As uncomfortable as he had been, he now appeared to be normal.

Mohamed just grinned and said, "I fix, I fix." Adam nodded his agreement.

Adam was feeling good enough to drive himself to the Embassy. Mustafa had come for him earlier, but he had departed when Mohamed had explained Adam's illness. At the Embassy, Adam went to the Canteen and had a bowl of soup and a sandwich plus coffee. He was pleasantly surprised that Mohamed's concoction had not left him with a queasy stomach. After lunch, he went to his office and wrote up his report on his meeting with the Sudanese and Egyptian Attache's. Adam had just completed a note to his Secretary leaving her his expected itinerary when his phone rang.

"General McGregor," he responded. The call was from the Consulate. An Iraqi citizen was requesting to speak to the American Defense Attache'.

"I'll be right down," Adam replied.

He stopped by the desk of his Secretary and turned on the coffee pot. She always left coffee set up in case someone needed a cup at odd hours. At the Consular Services desk, Adam met Brigadier General Ahmad Mohammad Abdul Jabbar, Iraqi Army. Adam led the General up to his office. He poured two cups of coffee and they went into Adam's office. Adam motioned the visitor to an easy chair and Adam took his chair at the desk.

"What can I do for you, General?" Adam asked.

"It's what I can do for you," General Ahmad replied. "I want to spy for America."

"We are always interested in good information concerning the Middle East, but why would you want to provide information to us?"

The General explained that he had two sons. They were in school in England. They would graduate shortly. If they returned to Iraq, they would be drafted into the Army and sent to the front in the war with Iran. He feared for their lives. If he could get his two sons in College in America, he would do whatever the US asked of him.

Adam nodded his understanding. He picked up the phone

and dialed the number of the CIA.

"Richardson, here," answered Tom Richardson, Deputy Chief of CIA, Cairo.

"Tom, Adam. I have a gentleman with me who needs to talk to you."

"I'll be right there!"

Tom Richardson arrived in less than five minutes. After a quick introduction, he suggested General Ahmad come with him. That was the last time Adam saw General Ahmad.

Adam called the Embassy and left a message for Mustafa to pick him up at nine am to be at the airport by ten. Adam returned to his apartment, then went to the Swiss Air Restaurant and had a couple of drinks and a steak dinner. By seven he was back in his apartment to call Minnesota. Dr. Snyder confirmed that Sonya's condition had not changed. He thought about calling his mother, but decided he would save that until he got to New York. He had a two hour layover in New York.

CHAPTER 15

Adam's TWA flight to New York was forty-five minutes late leaving Cairo. Head winds over the North Atlantic delayed the flight another half hour. He thought he wouldn't have time to call his mother. When the flight finally landed the 747 had to wait thirty minutes for a parking spot. By the time Adam got out of the airplane, he had already missed his connecting flight to Minneapolis. He asked about flights from La Guardia. The last flight to Minneapolis was departing as they spoke. The best connection he could make was to take a shuttle to Washington National and get a six am flight to Minneapolis Sunday morning. He called his mother. She was playing bridge. Her housekeeper said she would be home about ten pm. Adam told the housekeeper that he was flying into National and would be there between eight and nine.

"Would you like me to pick you up, Sir?" she asked.

"I assumed Mother had the car," he replied.

"She does. I have my own. I'll be happy to meet your flight."

"Okay. I'll be on the Eastern Shuttle from La Guardia. I should be there in about an hour and a half. I've got to take a cab to La Guardia. By the way, what's your name?"

"My name is Cecilia. I'll be driving an eighty-one Olds Omega. It's blue."

"Thanks, Cecilia. See you soon."

Cecilia hung up the phone and went to the living room. There was a portrait of Adam McGregor hanging on the wall. She had looked at it many times. She had heard Mrs. McGregor talk about Adam. Usually, she was angry with him for not writing. They had had a conversation that very morning. She was dusting Adam's portrait and had stopped to admire it when Mrs. McGregor saw her.

"Cecilia, don't even think about my son!" Agnes McGregor said.

"I know I'm not good enough for him. He's so handsome," Cecilia replied quietly.

"Ha! Not good enough? He's a no good womanizer. You're far too good for the likes of him. Besides, he's too old for you. Marry someone near your own age so you don't have to live out your old age alone."

Cecilia was a student at Georgetown. She had been working for Agnes McGregor for over two years. Their arrangement had turned out to benefit both women. Cecilia went to her room to study until it was time to go to the airport.

Cecilia left for the airport a little after nine. She took Rock Creek Parkway to Memorial Bridge, crossed the river to the George Washington Parkway to National Airport. When she got to the eastern Shuttle exit she stopped. A traffic cop ordered her on so she made a loop and came back for a second look. Adam was standing on the curb. She pulled up.

Adam opened the back door and tossed in his B-4 bag. He opened the front door and eased in as his large frame was cramped in the small car. "Cecilia, I presume," he said.

"You presume correctly, General McGregor," she answered as she slipped the car in gear and drove off.

"It's great of you to pick me up at this late hour," Adam remarked.

"I'm glad to finally meet you. Your mother speaks of you very often."

"Not very kindly, I'll bet."

"You could write a little more often. She worries about you."

"Does she know I'm here?"

"No. She'll be surprised."

They chatted about family and how Cecilia had come to work for Agnes. Adam asked how her school work was progressing. She volunteered that she would be starting her senior year and expected to get a degree in International Relations the following Spring. They arrived at the townhouse. Adam grabbed his bag and followed Cecilia into the house.

"Do I still have the bedroom on the third floor?" he asked.

"Yes Sir, the one facing the street. Your mother never lets anyone else sleep there."

Adam smiled and raced up the two flights of stairs. He was back down within two minutes. He had left his uniform blouse and overseas cap behind.

"Is there any Scotch in the house?" he asked.

"I'm sure there is. Your mother keeps some Dewars just in case you should drop in," Cecilia replied as she went to the liquor cabinet. "How do you like it?"

"On the rocks, please."

She reappeared with an old fashion glass filled with ice and Scotch. Adam took the drink and sat down in his favorite easy chair.

"Aren't you going to join me?" he asked.

"I'll wait until your mother arrives. We usually have a glass of wine before we turn in."

They heard a car at the back of the house. The garage door went up. "That has to be Mother," Adam stated as he took a drink.

Cecilia went to the back door to usher Mrs. McGregor inside. "We have a visitor, Agnes," she whispered.

Agnes frowned. "Is that you, Adam?"

"Yes, Mother," Adam arose and met his mother at the middle of the room. He tried to kiss her. She turned her cheek.

"You've been drinking Scotch. You smell just like your father. Why didn't you tell me you were coming? Marianne Baldwin's mother was at bridge tonight. She told me you were in the States. Now you drop in without warning. Explain yourself," she concluded.

"You should be in intelligence, Mother. You have such great sources!"

"Never mind my sources. Why didn't you tell me you were coming? Cecilia, be a dear and get us a glass of wine."

"I'm on my way to Minnesota. My flight from Cairo was late and I missed my connection. The quickest option was to come to Washington and catch a six am flight in the morning. I called to tell you I was coming. Cecilia was nice enough to meet the Eastern Shuttle."

Cecilia returned with the wine. She looked at Adam expecting him to be perplexed. He was suppressing a grin.

"What about this woman?" Agnes continued. "Are you trying to ruin your career. I understand she was hiding out in your apartment when her husband and children were murdered. Marianne told her mother you were in Cypress with this woman when she was supposed to be in Germany. Is that all true?"

"I must remember to thank Marianne for all the help. Is Marianne in Washington?" Adam asked.

"Let's not talk about Marianne," Agnes shot back. "Is it true?"

"There is some truth in what she has said. I was in Cypress with Sonya. She had opted to go to Cypress with me, rather than to Germany with a bunch of gossiping women."

"Never mind the snide remarks about women. Just explain yourself," Agnes continued.

"Do you want Cecilia to hear all the ugly details?" he asked.

"Yes, if she can stand it. I want her to know what a rake you are."

"Okay, Mother, here's the long and the short of it," Adam began. "I met Sonya at the pool at the Meridien Hotel. We had a short affair for three days. She thought I was leaving Cairo. The next Saturday, she and her husband were invited to the Embassy to meet our ex-President. Her husband was invited to go to the Sudan with a couple from the World Council of Churches. We were to visit a refugee camp at Geneina on the Chad border. Reverend Olsen could not go. He volunteered Sonya in his place. Sonya and I spent the next five days in adjoining rooms. Before we left the Sudan, I told her I loved her and asked her to get a divorce and marry me. She said she couldn't because of family concerns. When she suspected she was pregnant, she agreed to go to Cypress with me. I took her to meet Brian and Sandra Scott. Sandra spotted Sonya's morning sickness right away. On the way back to our hotel, Sonya told me she was pregnant. We agreed that she would sue for divorce and we would marry as soon as we could. That's about it."

"What makes you so sure you're the father?" Agnes asked. "She had a husband."

"I asked the question. She said they had not been intimate since her second pregnancy. I believe her," Adam concluded.

"Why did she attempt suicide?" Agnes asked.

"We can only guess. I don't think her fall was intentional. I think she was watching television. The incident coincided with a broadcast concerning the attack on St. Mathews and the deaths of Pastor Olsen and their two sons. I think she backed over the railing accidentally. She fell less than fifteen feet and landed on the roof of a Mercedes sedan. She was in a coma. I had her flown out to Ramstein that afternoon. In Germany, we transferred to a Lufthansa flight to Chicago and on to Minnesota. She's in the Mayo Clinic in Rochester. The baby is still alive and Sonya is still in a coma. The doctor wants to abort the baby. Sonya's family and in-laws are opposed to the abortion. I have proof that I'm the father of the baby. I hope I can get the courts to leave the decisions up to me. That's the purpose of this trip. I was planning to stop here on my way back to Egypt. You should get a letter this week saying I would be here over the fourth."

"Who's paying for her stay at the Mayo Clinic?" Agnes asked.

"I am," Adam replied.

"Can you afford it?" Agnes pressed.

"Without blinking, Mother."

"How much of your inheritance have you spent?"

"I haven't touched my inheritance, Mother. At last check, it had nearly doubled. The Air Force pays me very well. In Cairo, I'm invited out nearly every night. I have to make myself an appointment to stay home. If I entertain guests, I get reimbursed. Believe me, I can afford anything I want to do."

"You said you have proof that you're the father of this baby. What kind of proof?"

"I have a recording of Sonya saying that I'm the father," Adam replied.

"Can I hear it?" Agnes pressed.

"No, Mother, you can't!" Adam responded.

"Why not?"

"Because it's on film."

"I have a projector," she responded.

"It's eight millimeter film," he countered.

"I think I still have an eight millimeter projector in the attic. It may still work."

"Mother,"Adam responded emphatically. "You cannot see the film."

"I want to know why not!"

"Because the film was taken in an effort to blackmail me."

"You mean it's X-rated?"

"Yes, Mother, it's X-rated!"

"What kind of woman is this Sonya?"

"She is a wonderful person and you will love her."

"How can she be so wonderful if she got you in a porno movie?"

"The film was taken clandestinely by two Aussies who had in mind to blackmail me. I reviewed the film. When I found the proof I needed, I bought the film for two one way tickets to Melbourne and a little cash. Sonya is not aware of the film's existence."

"They'll be back for more!" Agnes persisted.

"If they do reappear, they will regret it," Adam concluded.

"I guess you know what you are doing. It does seem that you live on the edge. If this Sonya survives and you marry, will you be able to settle down and behave yourself?"

"As far as I'm concerned," Adam replied, "Sonya and I are already married and I have settled down."

"I must meet this woman," Agnes said. "However, now I must go to bed. What time are you leaving?"

"My flight is at six am. I'll call a cab to get to the airport."

"I'll be glad to drive you," Cecilia volunteered.

"At four-thirty!" Adam exclaimed.

"Sure," Cecilia replied. "I'll set my alarm for four."

"I'll say goodbye now, Adam," Agnes interjected. "I'll look for you next weekend." She kissed Adam and went to the elevator.

They all retired.

CHAPTER 16

Adam's flight to Minneapolis was on time. He arrived before seven am local. It was too early to call anyone. He rented a car and left for Rochester. He checked into the Marriott and called Dr. Snyder. There was no answer. He tried the attorney, Don Johnson. Mrs. Johnson answered and informed Adam that her husband was on the golf course. She expected him home around one-thirty in the afternoon. She would have him call the Marriott as soon as he came home. Adam went to the dining room and had breakfast. When he returned to his room, there was a message from Lawyer Johnson. Adam returned his call. They agreed to meet at the lawyer's office at three-thirty pm.

Adam was waiting in the parking lot when Donald Johnson arrived. Dr. Snyder was with him. "Adam, this is Don Johnson, your attorney," Dr. Snyder offered. "Don thought that I might make a credible witness to what you have on film."

"I've always understood that you shouldn't keep secrets from your mother, your doctor or your attorney," Adam responded as he shook Don Johnson's hand.

"Glad to meet you, General. I've got a projector set up in my office. Let's go see what we can glean from your film."

Adam had marked the film for the frames where Sonya had

identified him as the father of her baby. He fast forwarded the film to the marked area and then played the frames with Sonya's words. He stopped the film.

"Does that make my case?" he asked as he looked to Don Johnson for an answer.

"It's certainly an admission by Sonya that she's sure you're the father. Do you mind if Dr. Snyder and I view the full film to see if we find any other testimony that would help your case?" Don Johnson asked.

"No," Adam responded. "I'll excuse myself. I'll go down to the bar and watch the golf tournament. I've never seen the remainder of the film after Sonya's statement. There may be something more that would help." Adam left the room wondering if he could depend on client privilege with the doctor and the lawyer.

There was a Sports Bar on the ground floor of the building where the lawyer's office was located. Adam took a seat at the bar in front of a TV set featuring golf. He ordered a draft beer. It took the two professionals about forty minutes to run through the reel. This included some rewinding to be sure that they understood the dialog that went with the pictures. When they were finished, Lawyer Johnson called the bar and asked for General McGregor.

"Is there a General McGregor here," the bartender asked.

Adam got up and took the phone. "Adam, here," he said.

"Adam, we are finished with the film. Can you come up?" Don Johnson asked.

"I'll be right there," Adam replied. He left his beer and went to the elevator immediately. He was in the lawyer's office in five minutes. The three men looked at each other for several moments. Finally Adam broke the ice.

"Did you find anything that helps my case?"

"Not that we would want to show your prospective in-laws," the lawyer responded. "Do you happen to know if Reverend Carlson owns a gun?"

"No, I don't," Adam replied. "I guess I should avoid contact with the Carlson's until you have tried to convince them that I'm the father of Sonya's baby. How much of the film will you show to him?"

"None, if I can help it," Don Johnson replied. "I'll ask

Reverend Carlson to come to my office tomorrow. I'll tell him that I have proof that you are the father. If he insists on seeing the film, I'll show him the clip where Sonya acknowledges that you are the father. If he insists on seeing more, I'll show the film until he can't stand it. There are two scenes that are particularly revealing. I take it that there was some kind of race to see who could get in bed first?" he looked at Adam for an explanation.

Adam didn't answer immediately. He looked down at his feet and took a deep breath. "I assume that since you are both married that there are incidents in your sex life that you wouldn't want to make public. Everything that is on that film falls in that category. We were at dinner. I made a comment to the effect that I was always in bed first waiting for her. She responded that I always used the bathroom first and she had to wait. This banter went on all the way to the room. As soon as we closed the door, the race began. You saw the rest."

"Yes," the lawyer responded. "There was a second time that took place with the lights off. There was moonlight in the room but we couldn't see what was taking place. We heard Sonya say, 'I can be buck naked in five seconds'. What was that all about?"

Adam rubbed his forehead and looked out of the window. He shook his head in the negative. Finally he answered. "I want you two to know that I have a gun," he said, letting the obvious implication go unexplained. "I guess I should have edited the film."

He continued, "That was our last night in Cypress. As a prank, I was going to beat Sonya to bed. I left my socks and underwear off. I had a shirt and trousers on and my loafers. We went to have dinner. We danced a little after dinner. I noticed that she wasn't wearing her bra. I commented on that. She responded that she had checked my drawer and noted that I hadn't used my extra socks and shorts. She asked if I was prepared for a re-run of our previous race. I ran my hand over her bottom and realized that she didn't have any panties on. Needless to say, she won the race."

There was an awkward pause. The lawyer spoke. "I don't think we'll show that to anyone," he responded. "What do you think, Dr. Snyder?"

"I was thinking about how I could start that fight with my wife." Amazingly, no one laughed.

Don Johnson called the Carlson residence and made an appointment for Reverend Carlson to come to the lawyer's office the next morning.

"Do you want me to attend?" Adam asked.

"I don't think so. Why don't you hang out in your room and I will call you if a meeting would seem appropriate," the lawyer concluded. "Reverend Carlson will be here around nine. I will call you as soon as our meeting is concluded."

Adam returned to his room. He turned on the TV and searched for the golf tournament. It was the last day of the PGA Colonial in Forth Worth, Texas. He went down the hall and got some ice. He had settled in with a Dewars on the rocks when there was a knock on the door. It was Sonya's brother, Earl.

"Hello, Earl," Adam greeted. "Come in. Do you like golf? I'm watching the Colonial."

"I like golf," Earl replied. "That's not why I came."

"How about a Scotch?" Adam offered.

"No thanks," Earl replied. "I want to know what is going on between you and my sister. Why are you paying for her care? What do you expect to get for it?"

Adam put some ice in a glass and poured in some Scotch. He added some water and handed it to Earl. "Here," Adam said. "It's a long story. I'll try to shorten it for you. I first saw Sonya the day they arrived in Cairo. Later, I saw her at the pool of their hotel. I went there regularly to swim laps. Your brother-in-law, John Olsen, volunteered Sonya for a trip to the Sudan. I was one of the pilots. We fell in love. I asked Sonya to get a divorce and marry me."

"Why do you think you're the father of Sonya's baby?" Earl asked.

"Because Sonya told me I was the father."

"You believe her?" Earl pressed on.

"I believe her because I want to believe her," Adam responded. "You've known her for a longer time. Was she ever inclined to lie?"

Earl looked down at the floor for several seconds. He leaned back and looked up at the ceiling slowly shaking his head in the negative.

"The only time she ever lied was to protect me," he

answered. "She did that many times. Then she would chew me out for being stupid. I really owe her."

"I love her," Adam responded. "For the first time in my life, I've met someone who needs me and I need her."

"Are you divorced?" Earl asked.

"I was married the day of my graduation from the Academy. I went off to pilot training. My wife stayed behind to keep her job at a Washington Law firm. She had our marriage annulled and married her lawyer. I never saw her again. I never met another woman I wanted to marry until I met Sonya."

"What if she dies?" Earl asked.

"I refuse to contemplate that possibility until I have to face it," he replied. "She must live."

"What about the baby?" Earl asked. "Dr. Snyder has recommended an abortion to improve Sonya's chances. My parents are totally opposed to abortion."

"Sonya also expressed objections to abortion," Adam answered. "I've told Dr. Snyder that I'm opposed to abortion because Sonya is opposed to it. I won't change my mind unless something dramatically changes in Sonya's condition. I hope you'll convey that to your parents."

Earl was speechless for a moment. Then he spoke. "You sound like you should be making the decisions concerning Sonya," Earl stated. "My parents aren't going to like that."

"Don Johnson, my lawyer, will meet with your father tomorrow. He will explain my position. I hope that your father will concur," Adam concluded.

"If my father disagrees, will you terminate your financial support?"

"No. I won't even threaten to do that," Adam responded, "However, if we take it to a Judge, there will be a lot of unfavorable publicity. I will not be able to keep our love affair out of the proceedings. That will be difficult for your family and devastating for the Olsen's."

"That's comforting to know," Earl replied. "My parents would be hard pressed to pay for her care. I agree that nothing would be gained by publicity." Earl looked at his watch. It was time to leave.

"Did you drive down from the Twin Cities today?" Adam asked.

"Yes," Earl replied. "I'll be driving my dad down tomorrow for his meeting with your Attorney. I appreciate your hospitality. For what it is worth, I'm convinced that you have Sonya's best interests in mind. You can depend on me to be in your corner. Sonya had indicated that she was unhappy in her marriage when they were getting ready to go to Egypt. She put on a good front for our parents and the Olsen's. Privately, I knew she was unhappy."

"I appreciate that information, Earl," Adam replied. "I'll see you tomorrow." When Earl departed, Adam decided to go out for a couple of drinks and an early dinner. He was back in his room by nine and turned in at ten.

The next morning, Adam went to the Clinic early to see Dr. Snyder. They went together to see Sonya. There was no change in her condition except that she was losing weight. The doctor pointed out that the baby was beginning to show more because she was so thin. He also had Adam listen to the baby's heartbeat. The doctor pointed out that the baby was getting nourishment at the expense of the mother. He stressed that at some point, they would have to make a decision on whether to save the mother or the baby. Adam nodded his understanding.

"What's the earliest that a baby has been born and still survived?" Adam asked.

Dr. Snyder looked at Adam. "Are you thinking of a 'C' section?"

"What's the earliest that a baby can be born and still survive?" Adam pressed.

"I don't know what the record is. With incubation, we can save a very tiny baby. I'll check around today. You realize that it will be expensive."

"How expensive?" Adam asked.

"It could double your costs until the baby can survive without special care," Dr. Snyder replied.

"No problem, Doctor. Please check and see when we could consider taking the baby and expect both mother and baby to survive. I will let you know before I leave if I can make the decision legally. I may know the answer to that before the day is over. I need to get back to my room. Don Johnson is meeting with Reverend Carlson at nine. He wanted me to hang out at my hotel room in case he has some need of me."

Dr. Snyder nodded his understanding and they parted company. Adam hurried back to his room. There were no calls. He watched television for thirty minutes and picked up some International News. There was even some news from the Middle East. It looked like the Israelis and the Egyptians had reached agreement on a comprehensive peace treaty. The treaty called for a return of the Sinai to Egypt. Israel would gradually withdraw over the next two years.

It was nearly ten when Adam's phone rang. It was Don Johnson. He suggested that Adam come over to his office. Adam left immediately. On the short drive over to the lawyer's office, Adam tried to think about what he would say to Reverend Carlson. As he approached the office building he saw Earl's car leaving the parking lot. Reverend Carlson was with Earl. He parked in the first available space and hurried up to the lawyer's office. Don Johnson greeted him with a smile and a hand shake.

"You won," the lawyer stated.

"I can make the decisions?" Adam asked.

"That's correct," Johnson replied.

"Did he see the film?"

"Earl talked him out of viewing the film after I provided him with the results of the blood test on the baby."

"It proved that I'm the father?"

"You or your twin brother which you don't have," the lawyer replied. "I had Reverend Carlson sign an affidavit authorizing you to make decisions with regard to Sonya and the baby. Once he was satisfied with the parentage, he seemed to change his attitude completely."

"Have you told Dr. Snyder?"

"No, I thought you would like to do that in person. My secretary has prepared a copy of the authorization for you and one for Dr. Snyder. You can drop the copy off personally. What are your plans?"

"I'm planing to spend a couple of days with my mother in Washington. I leave for Cairo Saturday and I'm due back at work on

Sunday. I'll go see Dr. Snyder immediately. I can make my plans after I talk to him. What about your bill?"

"I'll send you a bill after you've taken action concerning the baby. If everything turns out all right, we should be able to close the case without further litigation."

"I hope so." Adam responded. He shook the lawyer's hand and gathered up the copies of the affidavit. "Thanks, Don," Adam concluded.

"It was my pleasure," Don Johnson replied as Adam went out the door.

Adam departed for Dr. Snyder's office. The doctor's administrator informed him that the doctor was in surgery. Adam left the copy of the affidavit and asked that Dr. Snyder call him at his hotel room. As soon as he arrived at his room, Adam called the airline and confirmed a reservation to Washington for the next morning. He had just hung up the phone when it rang.

"Hello," he answered.

"I'm calling from Dr. Snyder's office," a woman spoke. "The doctor wanted you to know that he has scheduled the 'C' section for this afternoon at two pm. He should be out of surgery no later than three. Would you like to be present?"

"Yes, I would."

"Come over about one forty-five."

"I'll be there," Adam said as he hung up.

Adam was not allowed in the operating room as Dr. Snyder was very concerned about the possibility of infection. Since Adam had been overseas recently, it was prudent to keep him away from both mother and baby. Adam waited outside of the operating room until Dr. Snyder was finished in surgery.

"Good news," the Doctor began, "both mother and daughter are doing well. The baby is in an incubator. All signs are good. Sonya remains in a coma. I believe that the best chance for Sonya is for her to gain strength. If she can regain her weight, she has a better chance of snapping out of the coma."

"That sounds pretty good," Adam replied. "I don't imagine we could expect much more under the circumstances. Is there anything else that I can do?"

"Yes, you need to fill out the birth certificate. Do you have a name?" the doctor asked.

"I hadn't even thought about that."

"Most first time fathers haven't," Dr. Snyder replied, smiling. "By the way, you are the father."

"Can I use your phone?" Adam asked. "I need to call the Carlson's."

"Take the one in my office."

Adam dialed the Carlson's number and Mrs. Carlson answered.

"This is Adam McGregor. I called to tell you that Sonya had a C-Section in the last hour. The baby is in an incubator and Sonya is still in a coma. The doctor thinks this is the best chance for both mother and daughter to survive."

"It's a girl?" Mrs. Carlson asked.

"Yes, I need to provide a name for the birth certificate. Could I ask your name?" There was a pause before Mrs. Carlson answered.

"My name is Carol Anita," she replied.

"Then I'll name our baby Carol Agnes McGregor. Agnes is my mother's name," Adam stated.

"You are satisfied that you are the father?" she asked.

"The doctor assures me that the blood test left no doubt," he said.

"You realize, General, that you led our daughter astray. I'll have a hard time forgiving you for that."

"I completely understand. Please remember if I hadn't taken her to Cypress, she would probably have died in the attack on St. Mathews with her two sons," Adam responded. He waited for a reply. It was not forthcoming as Mrs. Carlson had hung up.

Adam thought back to the conversation he had with Sonya about her family's difficulty accepting a divorce. She had described a probable first family reunion. There would be a very awkward introduction. They would eventually be welcomed by her cousin, Veloris. Adam decided that he would call Veloris on his next trip.

Adam packed his clothes and prepared to leave. He made one last call to his lawyer and left his mother's phone number for his stay there until Saturday. He had left a message at Dr. Snyder's office that he would call there daily until he left for Egypt. He departed for the airport to catch his flight to Washington National.

CHAPTER 17

It was after three pm when Adam reached the Northwest Airlines desk at Wold-Chamberlain field. There was a vacancy in first class on a flight leaving in forty-five minutes. Adam went to a pay phone and called his mother's number. Cecilia answered.

"Cecilia, this is Adam. I'm about to depart Minneapolis for National. I'm on Northwest Flight Number 92. Can you meet me about six thirty this evening?"

"Yes, of course," Cecilia answered.

"Bring my mother and we'll go to dinner at Army-Navy Country Club," Adam said.

"Your mother is playing bridge. She should be home by five," Cecilia replied. "I'm sure she will be pleased."

"They're calling my flight. I've got to run. Bye," Adam didn't wait for a reply.

The flight to National Airport was routine. Adam was the first one out of the plane. His luggage had been in the overhead rack. He hurried to the exit. Cecilia's car was at the curb. Adam's mother was in the front seat. Adam jumped into the back seat.

"Hi, Mom!" he addressed his mother. "Guess what?" he continued. He waited for a reaction.

"What?" Agnes replied.

"You're a grandmother," Adam replied.

"How can that be? The baby wasn't due for months," Agnes countered.

"Sonya had a C-Section this morning. It's a girl. I named her Carol Agnes McGregor after her two grandmothers. The baby is doing well in an incubator. I won't have any word on Sonya for a while. It appears that she survived the delivery without a set back. She had begun to lose weight while she was carrying the baby. It will be a week or so before the doctor will know if she has stabilized. I'll call on Friday to check. I'll be leaving for Cairo Saturday morning."

"I thought you were going to be here for the weekend?" Agnes complained.

"Sorry, Mom. My leave is up on Sunday."

"Which way do I turn?" Cecilia interjected.

"Get on I-395 South, get off on US one and take the first right into Army-Navy Drive. Continue straight past Pentagon City. Army-Navy Drive curves left. The entrance to the Club is marked," Adam concluded. Their conversation subsided as Cecilia maneuvered across lanes of heavy traffic. Once she got passed Macy's turnoff, the traffic eased.

"Do you have a reservation, Adam? Agnes asked.

"I didn't think I would need one on a Tuesday night," Adam concluded.

"Probably not," Agnes stated. "We can always go to the Grill Room. However, I do prefer the Sun Room."

Cecilia turned off Army Navy Drive passing under I-395 and up the long driveway to the Clubhouse. The parking spots were directly in front. Agnes always had her handicap sign in the car. They went into the cocktail lounge where they were met by Kim, a diminutive Vietnamese refugee. Kim had been at Army-Navy since the early seventies.

"Ah! General McGregor! Where you been?" she cried out. Kim was known for remembering everyone's name.

"Hi, Kim! I'm visiting from Cairo."

"You want window table like always?"

"That would be splendid."

"You want Dewars first?" Kim asked.

"Yes, please," he answered. "Mother, do you want a glass of wine?"

"Yes, Kim, Cecilia and I would each like a glass of Chardonnay."

"Yes, Ma'am!" Kim replied as she hurried to get their drinks.

"Do you still come here often, Mother?"

"We usually come every Friday night," she answered. "I've made a reservation for the three of us for this Friday."

The drinks appeared. Kim also delivered three menus for them to peruse while they finished their drinks. Agnes started the conversation.

"Adam, are you going to stop at the Defense Intelligence Agency while you are in town?" she asked.

"I wasn't planning on doing that. Why do you ask?" Adam questioned.

"Your affair with this Sonya woman has spread all over the Pentagon," his mother answered. "The rumor is that you are distracted from your duties."

"Is that right," Adam responded. "Does your bridge club know the source of this rumor?"

"Marianne Baldwin told her mother all about your soirée in Cypress. Marianne has left two calls for you since she found out you were stopping in Washington."

"Did you tell her that I would be here this week?" Adam asked.

"Yes. Why shouldn't I? She says you two dated when you were at the Pentagon."

"I had one date with her. I found out she was eighteen as opposed to the claim that she was twenty-four. I told her that our difference in age, eighteen years, was too much. It's still too much!"

"Why did you go riding with her?"

"I went riding with her twice. The first time she invited herself. When she showed up at the stable a second time, I decided it was time to break it off and I quit riding. I don't encourage liaisons with wives whose husbands work for me."

Kim returned with a second Dewars on the rocks. "Thank you, Kim," Adam said. "I believe we are ready to go to the dining room." He was hoping this would change the conversation.

However, as soon as they had ordered their dinners, Agnes continued in the same vein.

"What are you going to do about these rumors?" Agnes asked.

"I'll drop by DIA tomorrow. I'm sure the Middle East Office will tell me if there has been any concern about my taking leave. After all, I had sixty days leave on the books. Last year, I lost fifteen days because I didn't take any leave."

The dinner hour was passed without further rancor from Agnes. There was small talk. Adam encouraged Cecilia to enter into the conversation. He was able to find out about her academic progress at Georgetown. As soon as dinner was over, they left for home. Agnes was ready for bed by ten pm. Adam asked to use Agnes's car the next day. She insisted that she needed it. He decided he would rent a car for a couple of days. This turned out to be a good idea. The next morning Cecilia dropped Adam at National Airport. He rented a Mustang for the rest of the week. His first stop was at DIA Headquarters on Bolling Air Force Base.

The nice thing about being a general officer, even a Brigadier, was one got immediate attention. A female Staff Sergeant escorted Adam to the Middle East office. A Lt. Colonel was at the Egyptian Desk. Adam explained that he was on leave and that he would be returning to Cairo on Saturday. He had dropped in to see if any problems had arisen while he was away.

"We're glad you stopped in," Lt. Colonel Thomas began, "General Murphy would like to see you." He picked up the phone and dialed an intercom number.

"This is Lt. Colonel Thomas. I have General McGregor with me. General Murphy said he would like to speak to General McGregor." There was a slight pause, "We'll be right over."

Adam decided that maybe his affair with Sonya had caused a stir. He had only met Lt. General Murphy one time. He wasn't sure what to expect.

"Hi, Adam!" General Murphy said as he came around the desk ignoring Adam's salute. "It's good to see you. When are your returning to Cairo?"

"I have a reservation on Egypt Air for Saturday. I'll get into Cairo early Sunday morning," Adam replied.

"Great!" General Murphy responded. "We received your report along with Tom Carson's on your meeting with John Baranga. The CIA wants to arrange a meeting with John Baranga probably in Juba. Could you take the C-12 to the Sudan next week?"

"No problem," Adam replied. "I'll have the Egypt desk send a cable setting up the trip. We'll info the Ambassador's Office to preclude any conflict with VIP travel."

"Good," General Murphy replied. "Now what are your plans for the day?"

"I was thinking of playing golf," Adam said.

General Murphy picked up the phone and dialed the Army-Navy Country Club. "Hello, Pro Shop?" he asked. "Can you get a twosome off around noon?" There was a pause. "Eleven forty-five will do just fine. It'll be Jack Murphy and Adam McGregor."

"Adam," General Murphy continued. "I need to talk to you in private. I swear that around here the walls have ears. I hope the time suits you."

"I'll have time to pick up a set of clubs at my mother's. I'll be back to Army-Navy by eleven-fifteen at the latest," Adam replied.

"I'll see you on the range," General Murphy replied. "By the way, Adam, on the golf course, I'm Jack."

Adam nodded as he saluted and departed. He wondered how much of a grilling he would get in the golf cart.

Jack Murphy tossed a tee in the air. It pointed at himself. "How about ten dollar Nassau, Adam?"

"Sounds good, Jack," Adam replied.

"Medal or Match Play?" Jack asked.

"Medal play sounds good," Adam replied. "I'm a six handicap."

"I'm an eight," Jack replied as he teed up his ball. They both drove in the middle of the fairway.

As they headed down the cart path, Jack broke the silence. "Tell me about this Sonya woman, Adam."

"There isn't much to tell," Adam replied. "I'm very committed to her. As soon as she comes out of her coma, I expect to marry her."

"Is that wise?" Jack Murphy asked as he pulled up to his ball. When they had both hit their second shots onto the first green, the conversation continued.

"Considering that our first born is already here," Adam picked up on the conversation, "I would be something of a cad to abandon her now."

"First born?" Jack questioned. "I thought this started in April."

"It did. I decided upon the doctor's advice to have the baby taken by C-Section. This appeared to be the best chance to save both mother and daughter. Abortion was not an option for Sonya or her family.

"Her family let you make the decision?"

"My lawyer pointed out to her father that since I was the father of the baby, and her husband was deceased, I was legally her common law spouse. Faced with that fact and the fact that they could not afford the care that Sonya needs, the Carlson family backed off. Her husband's family has refused to get involved."

They putted out and went to the second tee. As soon as they were back in the cart the conversation continued.

Jack began, "The reason I'm bugging you about this, Adam, is the Chief of Staff's daughter, Marianne told her father that you had talked Mrs. Olsen into spending several days with you in Cypress. The Chief is concerned that there might be a nasty divorce with a lot of publicity. Publicity that might effect the Air Force."

Adam cleared his throat. "The divorce problem has gone away. I don't expect a fuss from the Olsen family although the situation certainly has strained relations between Sonya's parents and Reverend Olsen's family. That's unfortunate as the families had been close friends for many years. I guess if Sonya and I had known what a tangled web was being woven, we would have thought twice about our affair. Hind sight is always clear!"

They stopped at their drives. Jack was two hundred twenty-five yards out and he laid up short of the creek in front of the number two green. Adam was about two hundred yards out. He hit his three wood to the front edge of the green.

Jack spoke as Adam returned to the cart, "The Chief asked me to pry into your personal life, Adam. Don't take it out on me!" He was smiling and Adam laughed. He birdied the hole to take a one stroke lead.

"Do you think the Chief wants me to retire?" Adam asked when they returned to the cart.

"Not as long as this doesn't make the front page of the Post," Jack concluded.

"I don't expect that to happen unless the Olsen family decides to get involved," Adam stated. "Rest assured, I will not be interviewed by the press. I will keep you informed of Sonya's progress. I'll do it by mail so that only the two of us will have access. You can keep the Chief informed as necessary."

That proposal seemed to satisfy General Murphy and they got serious about their golf game. Adam won the front nine by three strokes. General Murphy won the back by one stroke and paid Adam ten dollars for the eighteen.

"Keep in touch, Adam," Jack said as they parted.

"I will General," Adam stated.

The remainder of Adam's stay in Washington passed without incident. He played golf a second afternoon and met his mother and Cecilia for dinner at Army-Navy on Friday. The next morning he caught an early flight from National. His flight to Cairo departed on time and arrived at Cairo International at nine am local. Mustafa met him at the airport and Adam was in his office by eleven am after a short stop at his apartment to change into his uniform.

CHAPTER 18

Captain Baldwin was waiting in Adam's office when Adam arrived. "How was your trip, General?" Dave Baldwin asked.

"It was a little hectic, Dave. I did get a lot done," Adam replied. "I understand there has been some traffic from DIA concerning a trip to the Sudan."

"Yes Sir," Dave replied. "We are all set to depart tomorrow morning. Khartoum has four paxs for the trip to Juba. Colonel Carson has made tentative arrangements for us to meet with John Baranga in Juba. He says its too dangerous for Baranga to commit to travel more than a day ahead. We'll be contacted at the Juba Hilton as to when and where we will meet. Khartoum has put a price on Baranga's head so his people are reluctant to guarantee a meeting until the last minute. We've made arrangements to go on to Nairobi if necessary."

"It sounds like that's about as good as we can get for the time being," Adam replied. "Does Marianne want to go to Khartoum with us?"

"Marianne is in Washington," Dave replied. "I'm surprised you didn't see her."

"I heard that she had been in Washington. My mother heard from her, so I assumed she had returned," Adam replied. Adam wanted to be sure Dave knew that he hadn't contacted Marianne.

"I've called for a staff meeting," Adam continued. "I want to bring everyone up to date on my situation. We'll all get together at fifteen-hundred hours."

Adam busied himself with reviewing the message traffic he had missed while he was traveling. As it approached fifteen-hundred, he opened his door to let the staff come in without having to wait. The staff consisted of four military personnel; Warrant Officer Bob Charles, US Army was in charge. Staff Sergeant James McKinnon, US Army; Staff Sergeant Dave Wilson, U.S. Marine Corp, handled Navy and Marine Corps traffic and Staff Sergeant John Brown handled Air Force traffic. There were three secretaries. Emma Charles, Bob's spouse, was Adam's secretary. Alice Smith worked for Captain Don Sanford and Paula Priest was secretary to Colonel Pete Marshall, the Army Attache'.

Adam greeted everyone and then began, "I want you to know about my trip to the States and Sonya Olsen. Sonya remains in a coma, however, we believe she may be making progress. Her doctor felt that her pregnancy was favoring the baby. We decided, the doctor and myself, to take the baby by C-Section. She was opposed to abortion. That was accomplished and the baby, Carol Agnes McGregor, is doing well in an incubator. Sonya is beginning to regain her strength. I anticipate going back to Minnesota in a few months and returning with my wife and daughter." There was a very awkward pause. No one wanted to speak first. It was his secretary, Emma Charles who broke the silence.

"General, we really don't want to pry into your private life and we are shocked to say the least, with the speed that all of this has taken place."

"I understand," Adam replied. "Certainly, if the murders of Sonya's family hadn't occurred, I would not have moved with this speed. The reason that Sonya's parents have allowed me to make the decision for her are twofold. First, blood tests have confirmed that I am the father of Carol Agnes and I'm the one person who can afford to take care of hospital expenses. The Mayo Clinic is very good, but it is also very expensive."

He continued, "I don't expect any of you to approve of my behavior in this situation. There is no reason that you shouldn't know the facts of the matter. There will probably be a lot of speculation around the Embassy and I would appreciate it if you would, at a minimum, let people know the truth as you know it. If you feel that I'm being cavalier about the situation, nothing can be further from the truth. I'm just eternally happy that I could be in a position to help Sonya when she really needed the help."

"Now," Adam went on, "let's get into the DIA business. Is there anything I need to do or anything that I should know about before Dave and I leave for Khartoum tomorrow?"

Emma replied, "Captain Sanford is covering your most important invitations next week. You had a call from Lady Agatha. She asked if you could stop for a cocktail this evening around six. We made arrangements with Nairobi. You will be able to go there from Juba if necessary. I've prepared the paper work to go with you tonight. Colonel Carson called to assure you that you and Captain Baldwin will be welcome at their quarters."

"Congratulations on the daughter," Don Sanford volunteered. "Did you have any trouble getting agreement on paternity?"

"Not after the blood tests," Adam replied. "Sonya's family were not pleased. They aren't able to pay for Sonya's care or for the baby's care. Reluctantly, they agreed to accept the situation as best for all concerned."

The meeting broke up. After making arrangements for the pick up in the morning, Adam returned to his apartment. He took a shower and changed into civvies, wearing a blue sport coat, a gray shirt and tie, and gray slacks. He went down to the parking lot and found the corvette, tipped the old man and jumped in the car and sped off to the British Embassy.

Sir William and Lady Agatha were waiting in their drawing room when Adam arrived. The butler led Adam to the drawing room and poured Adam a Dewars on the rocks. Lady Agatha was interested in Sonya's condition so Adam recounted the Minnesota portion of his trip.

Lady Agatha asked, "Adam, what will you do if Sonya doesn't recover?"

"I refuse to consider that possibility for the present," Adam replied. "I've been looking for Sonya all my life. Now, with the birth of Carol Agnes, I need Sonya more than ever."

"Of course you do," Sir William interjected. "We will be thinking about you. Please keep us up to date on the progress of both mother and daughter."

"I'll do that," Adam replied. "I'm going to call the Mayo Clinic before I turn in tonight. If there is any news I will leave a message for you before I leave for Khartoum in the morning."

Adam departed, returning to the Swiss Air Restaurant for dinner. After dining he went up to his apartment and put in a call to Doctor Snyder. The Doctor was not available, however, he had left a message and his head nurse was pleased to inform Adam that Sonya was cognizant of her situation. She had spoken several words. She was able to express her desire to see the baby. She was taken to the incubator room in a wheel chair to see Carol Agnes. She was very pleased and left no doubt that she knows the baby is yours." The nurse concluded, "It is obvious that Sonya's pain threshold has subsided. We expect her to progress steadily. Will you call tomorrow, General McGregor?"

"I will if I can get through," Adam replied. "I'm going to Khartoum in the morning. I'll attempt to call from there. After tomorrow, I expect to be out in the bush. You probably won't hear from me for five or six days."

The nurse acknowledged and said she would pass on the information to Dr. Snyder.

Adam called the British embassy to leave a message for the Hulls. Lady Agatha was still up and she was very pleased to know that Sonya was on the mend. He promised to keep her informed. He turned in early.

The next morning, Mustafa was waiting in the parking lot when Adam appeared. Dave Baldwin was already with him in the car.

"General, we have two passengers for Khartoum. They work for Colonel Carson. They should be at the TWA desk. I can pick them up and meet you at the airplane.

"Did they just arrive?" Adam asked.

"They came in on TWA early this morning. They called the Consulate to inquire about a ride to Khartoum. I had left word at the Consulate that we were leaving this morning with an empty aircraft. The Consulate called me early this morning."

"Good," Adam said. "I always hate to fly down empty when there are people who need the ride."

Mustafa dropped Captain Baldwin at the civilian side of the airport. He took Adam to the military side. The Beechcraft tech rep was busy preparing Spar 80 for the flight. Adam did a quick walk around and then went to the cockpit to run the checklist. By the time he was ready to start engines, Dave Baldwin had arrived with the two Staff Sergeants. Fifteen minutes later they were rolling down the runway.

They made their standard refueling stop in Luxor. By three pm, they were in the traffic pattern at Khartoum International. Tom Carson was waiting in the military parking area when they taxied in. He was there to meet them with two embassy vehicles. The two Sergeants got into one vehicle and sped off. Adam and Dave joined Colonel Carson for the ride to his quarters.

"So, Tom," Adam began. "Do we know where we can meet John Baranga?"

"No," Tom Carson replied. "We were told to go to Juba and await further instructions. No word on how long we will have to wait."

"Who's going with us?" Adam asked.

"There is a guy from USAID named Derek Douglas who asked about a seat on the plane to Juba," Tom began. "I called USAID to see if he was legitimate. The boss at AID said he was listed as an Agricultural Attache'. However, he gets his directions from Washington."

"Sounds like he's our CIA contact," Adam said.

"That would be my guess," Tom replied. "He's supposed to stop by for a drink tonight. You'll get to meet him."

They arrived at the Carson's quarters at four pm. Marty Carson was at the door to greet them.

"How is Sonya?" Marty asked Adam before anyone could say anything.

"She is much improved," Adam replied. "What have you heard?"

"Only that she fell from your apartment after hearing of the deaths of her husband and sons. Where is she?"

"She's at the Mayo Clinic in Minnesota. Let me get a shower

and I'll fill in the details during cocktails," Adam replied.

Adam finished showering and got dressed in casual slacks and a shirt. He made his way to the kitchen where he found Marty Carson. He quickly filled her in on Sonya's condition, the birth of their daughter, and his intention to marry Sonya as soon as she is able to repeat the vows.

"Are you sure Sonya will want to marry you? After all you hardly knew each other," Marty replied. "You only met her because she came to Khartoum for the trip to Geneina. I got the impression from her body language that she was not comfortable being with you in the Hilton."

Adam filled Marty in on the time that he and Sonya had spent together first at the Meridien, then at the Khartoum Hilton and finally on their trip to Cypress. He expounded on their visit with Brian and Sandra Scott and the fact that he was the father of Sonya's daughter.

"Wow!" she said. "Tom and I had no idea you two were that involved. Are you absolutely certain you are the father of her baby?"

"My doctor said the blood tests were conclusive unless I had a twin brother, which I don't. I even got to name her, Carol Agnes McGregor."

"You aren't married!" she replied.

"Legally, my lawyer says, I'm her common law spouse because I'm the father of her child and her husband is no longer alive. Her family agreed, not because they are pleased with me, but because I'm the only person who can afford the cost of caring for both mother and daughter."

"Oh, what a tangled web!" Marty responded.

"Yes, it is." Adam said. "We won't know how it will turn out until Sonya has recovered and can speak her mind."

"What is it costing you, Adam?" Marty probed. "With both mother and daughter in the Mayo Clinic, the cost has to be astronomical."

"It's high," Adam replied. "I'm a very wealthy man and I can afford whatever is necessary."

"Generals get paid well, but not that well," Marty stated.

"When my father died, my mother and I split his estate. My half has been invested well and I haven't had any reason to tap it. I easily live on my Air Force salary particularly as an Attache'."

"Thank you so much, Adam," Marty continued. "I just hope Sonya progresses fast enough to join you and come visit us. I really did like her when she was here. I asked Tom if there was something between you and Sonya. He said, no way. I wasn't sure. Now that I know how you feel, all I can say is you are welcome at our home anytime."

They were interrupted by the arrival of Derek Douglas, USAID Attache'. He was a sight to behold. He was about five feet, eleven inches tall with a very large girth. It was difficult to guess his weight as he was wearing a Hawaiian shirt over Bermuda shorts. The shirt fit like a tent. Colonel Carson made the introductions.

Tom Carson offered Derek a drink. Derek asked for a Beefeater Martini, on the rocks with olives. Tom and Adam took their drinks and ushered Derek into Tom's den for some private conversation.

Adam spoke to Derek in Arabic. Derek's response showed a good understanding of the language. Adam asked him how long he had been in the Sudan. He responded a year and a half. He volunteered that he had been all over the country except Juba. They switched to English for which Tom was grateful as his Arabic was not particularly good.

Douglas had a second martini and began to expound on his travels in the Sudan. He had been to Atbara, Kassala, Dongala, El Obeid, Nyala, El Fasher, Wau, and Malakal and now, Juba.

"How did you know we were going to Juba?" Tom asked.

"I saw some traffic about clearances and I put two and two together."

"Do you know John Baranga?" Adam asked.

"John Bananga?" Derek miss pronounced the name. "I never heard of him."

"I guess you won't be much help to us. We are trying to arrange a meeting with John Baranga. I was told by DIA that the Agency wanted our help in making contact with John Baranga," Adam responded. "We assumed you had a connection with the Agency."

"My only contact is the Agency for International Development. I hope that doesn't preclude me from flying with you," Derek replied. His expression gave no hint that he was anything other than an agricultural expert.

There was no reason not to take him along on the trip. However, Adam and Tom were wondering how CIA intended to make contact with John Baranga if they didn't send someone with the flight to Juba.

Derek Douglas was at the airport when Adam, Tom and Dave Baldwin arrived at the airplane. Adam explained the important safety precautions to Derek while Dave did the walk around. They were ready to go in twenty minutes. There was no immediate traffic problem and they were cleared for immediate take off. It was a typical hot summer day. The haze layer would go to over twenty thousand feet. There was very little wind. They took off to the south and turned southwest. Once again they were headed for Rub Kona. They would fill up with fuel in case there was no fuel in Juba. It was about three hundred nautical miles to Rub Kona and about the same to Juba. The Kingair trued out at about two hundred twenty five knots. With the stop they would be in Juba by noon. As soon as they arrived in Juba, Captain Baldwin went in search of jet fuel. Fortunately, since they only needed a top-off, they were able to fill up. They locked the aircraft and left for the hotel.

The Juba Hotel was laughingly called the Juba Hilton. It was not a Hilton Hotel. The accommodations were spartan, at best. There was a kind of festival going on and most of the hotel rooms were filled. USAID had a couple of projects in Equatorial Province. Derek Douglas knew the people involved. Through his contacts, he was able to get two rooms at the hotel. The rooms had two single beds each. The beds were rigged with mosquito netting. Derek suggested that he and Adam take one room and Colonel Carson and Dave Baldwin would take the other.

The bathroom was at the end of the hall. There was a bathtub with a shower head rigged over the middle of the tub. There was no shower curtain. There was a sink on one wall and a toilet on the opposite wall. There were no barriers between any of the facilities. Everything was filthy. By the time they had all showered the floor was covered with mud. Derek commented that the toilet seat was so dirty he had to wash it three times before he could stand on it. Picturing this nearly obese man standing naked on a toilet seat left

Adam, Tom and Dave in raucous laughter.

Derek Douglas seemed to know a large number of people in Juba. He had made arrangements with the local military commander for a visit to their office. He also got the four of them invited to dinner at the home of the leader of the AID project.

"Derek," Adam stated, "I take it that you've been here before."

"Yes," Derek replied. "I try to get to all of the projects at least once a year."

Derek had arranged for a vehicle, a Range Rover, to drive them around the city. The city was not large even though it was the Capital of Equatorial Sudan. They drove down to the Nile which ran through the city. There were a number of hippopotamuses lolling in the river. Most of the city consisted of native huts. Only the main area of Juba had permanent buildings. Equatorial is well south of the Savannah of the Sud. There were many tropical trees, mostly palms. There was ample rainfall for vegetation, but not so much as to support jungle.

The population was mixed. Dinkas seemed to be the most prominent, always noticeable because of their height. Most of the shops and street vendors seemed to be operated by men from the north. Most seemed to be Muslims judging by decorations in their shops.

The four of them arrived for dinner at the residence of the AID Chief and his wife a little before four to beat the afternoon thunder shower. These occurred daily for about a month and a half as the sun passed nearly overhead. The rains would stop when the path of the sun slipped below the equator about three hundred miles to the south.

The hosts, Tyler and Ann Gordon were there to greet them along with several other AID families. Adam had a feeling he had met Ann Gordon previously. He couldn't remember where.

Ann Gordon opened the conversation. "Hello, Adam. Long time no see."

Adam was put off, "Yes, I remember the face, but I can't place the place."

"How about Uban Rachitani? You were dating that beautiful Thai girl from Chang Mai and Brian Scott was with that saucy sheila from Melbourne. What was her name?"

"Sandra," Adam replied. "Sandra Scott."

"Oh!" she replied. "Then they married?"

"Yes, I spent a few hours with them in Cypress in May. Brian was promoted to Group Captain and they've been assigned to Cranwell in Lincolnshire. They should be in Britain by now."

"Any children?"

"Yes, they have four boys," Adam replied.

"What about you? I know that you are a General. You don't have to tell me about your success. I just want to know about your love life. What happened to the Thai girl?"

"I don't know for sure. I heard once that she married an Aussie and moved to Singapore. However, that was never confirmed. Let's talk about you. Where did you meet Tyler?"

"I met him in Laos. He was a colleague of my friend, Woody. You remember Woody?"

"Yes, I was sorry to hear about Woody," Adam responded. He remembered that Ann and Woody were dating when Woody was killed in an aircraft accident.

They dropped the subject and went to the bar. Adam had a scotch on the rocks. Ann helped herself to a glass of Muscadet.

"Where do you get the Muscadet?" he asked.

"You know the French contingent that's working on the Jungali Canal?"

Adam nodded.

"We have access to an old Cessna 206 that stops at their strip. The pilot gets a few bottles of wine for us every time he stops there. It brings a little civilization to our spartan existence," Ann concluded as her husband came up.

"Tyler, do you remember Adam from Ubon?" she asked.

"Certainly, hello Adam. I understand you are the one in control of Spar 80," Tyler continued.

"I am when we're on a trip. In Cairo, I have to check with the Ambassador's office before I make a commitment."

"We understand you are going on to Nairobi. Would you mind dropping Ann and me at Yei on your way?"

"Where is Yei?" Adam asked.

"It's about fifty to sixty miles up the road toward the Zaire border. We are invited to spend the weekend with the Karras'. They are an old Greek family that own a coffee plantation in the tri-border area of Sudan, Zaire and Uganda. They asked us to find our way to Yei and they will meet us with a couple of Land Rovers."

"What kind of an airstrip do they have?" Adam asked.

Dave Baldwin interrupted, "I was there once, General. It's a fifteen hundred foot dirt strip. They have a homing beacon. As long as we're in and out before any afternoon thunder storms, we should be fine."

"You're on Tyler. We're always glad to help out the folks from USAID." Adam concluded.

"Soup's on!" Ann Gordon shouted from the kitchen. Everyone queued up for the buffet line. The conversation dwindled as everyone enjoyed their meals.

After dinner there was more tale swapping about Southeast Asia and the fate of mutual acquaintances. The party broke up at ten pm. The Gordon's would meet the Khartoum foursome at Spar 80 at eight am the next day. Adam went next door to confer with Tom Carson and Dave.

"Did either of you pick up any hint as to the whereabouts of John Baranga?" Adam asked.

"Not a word," Tom replied.

Dave Baldwin shook his head in agreement.

"Okay!" Adam replied. "We'll see what happens tomorrow. Tyler and Ann Gordon are Air America folks from the Viet Nam era. I suspect we've made our CIA contact. My guess is we'll find out about Baranga at Yei."

They split up and went to their respective rooms. All four were up at six thirty for breakfast. They arrived at Spar 80 at seven thirty. They were airborne at eight am and landed at Yei thirty minutes later after making two low passes over the runway to check the area for security.

The runway was packed earth cleared of all grass and weeds. It was a mere twenty feet wide with a circular area at each end for turning around and taxing downwind to prepare for take off. An olive drab colored Land Rover followed the aircraft back to the take off end. As soon as Adam had shut down the engines the doors of the Land Rover opened and six passengers appeared. Adam recognized John Baranga and his Dinka wife. There were two young native children with them. The other two, a man and a woman, must be members of the Karras family. Adam went forward and greeted John Baranga.

"Good to see you again, General," Baranga said. "I understand you are taking my wife and children to Nairobi. They have a late afternoon flight leaving for the States. I would appreciate it if you could see to them getting passage without trouble."

"We understand your concern," Adam replied. "We will be in Nairobi in four hours or less. We'll see to it that your family makes the necessary connections."

It was obvious that Colonel Baranga was on the move to avoid confrontation and/or capture by the government forces controlled from Khartoum. The Karras' vehicle was ready to depart as soon as Spar 80 was airborne.

Captain Baldwin was in the cockpit watching the activities on the ground. Adam raised his finger in the air and gave Dave the signal to start number two. The passengers were helped into their seats by Derek and Tom Carson. Adam closed the door as Dave started number one. As soon as number one was in full idle, Dave slowly advanced both engines to full power. They were airborne in a minute . Adam watched the Land Rover disappear to the Southeast.

It was two fifteen local when they landed in Nairobi. They had contacted the Embassy in Nairobi by HF radio. The aircraft was met by an official from USAID. Derek knew the person well. They took Mrs. Baranga and the two children to the VIP lounge where they entered the necessary VISA information in the three passports. Derek returned to Spar 80 in a little over an hour. He announced that everything was set and that the Baranga family was boarding a BOAC flight to Heathrow. They would continue on to Chicago and were due to arrive at Iowa State in Ames, Iowa the following afternoon.

Spar 80 departed Nairobi for Khartoum. Adam and Dave spent the night at the Carson's Villa and returned to Cairo the following day. Adam submitted a trip report to DIA. He left out any mention of the Karras family involvement at the request of CIA's Chief of Station.

CHAPTER 19

Things were not going well for Sonya. She had come out of her coma and her physical condition was slowly improving. Her mental condition was another problem. She was depressed. She was slowly coming to grips with the deaths of her husband and her two sons. She wished she had died with them. She expressed that feeling to Dr. Snyder when he visited her on his regular morning rounds.

"Why hasn't Adam come to visit me?" Sonya asked Dr. Snyder.

"Adam is in the Sudan," Dr. Snyder responded. "I expect to hear from him as soon as he returns to Cairo. I'm sure he will come to get you as soon as he can."

Sonya turned her face to the wall and began to cry.

Dr. Snyder went to his office and called Sonya's mother. He described Sonya's depression and suggested that the Carlson's pay her a visit.

Carol Carlson asked Dr. Snyder if he had a number for Agnes McGregor. The Doctor had his nurse look up Agnes' number. They had gotten it from Adam when Adam was at his mother's house.

"Hello," Cecilia answered.

"Hello, am I speaking to Agnes McGregor?"

"Just a moment, I'll put her on the line."

"Hello," Agnes responded.

"This is Carol Carlson, Sonya's mother. I had a call from Dr. Snyder this morning. Sonya came out of her coma a few days ago. Physically, she seems to be improving, but he is concerned about her mental state. He suggested that I pay her a visit. I thought maybe we could visit her together.

There was a long pause. Finally Agnes responded. "I was under the impression that you were not sympathetic with my son's attentions to your daughter."

"That's putting it diplomatically and I thank you. My husband referred me to Second Samuel and the story of David and Bathsheba. I decided that if the Lord could forgive David and let Bathsheba birth Solomon, I could cut Adam and Sonya a little slack."

"I think I can catch an afternoon flight to Minneapolis," Agnes replied.

"I'll tell Dr. Snyder that we'll be there tomorrow, midday," Carol answered.

Reverend Olson and Carol met Agnes at the airport. They insisted that Agnes stay at their home in St. Paul. Carol and Agnes stayed up until eleven, swapping tales about Adam and Sonya in their youth. They were up early the next morning and departed for Rochester after breakfast. Reverend Olson opted to stay in St. Paul. He suggested that the situation called for motherly care.

Both Carol and Agnes were shocked when they saw Sonya. She was nearly bald. Her head had been shaved when they tapped her skull to remove pressure. She was very thin and pale. Her hospital smock hung on her like a tent. Her face was gaunt and her eyes were red. She had been crying.

"Hello, Sonya," her mother greeted. "We came to see how you are getting along. This is Adam's mother, Agnes McGregor."

"Momma," Sonya whispered, "I'm a terrible person. I killed my sons. I was suppose to be with them."

"We know all about what happened," Agnes interjected. "You couldn't have protected your sons, even if you had been there. Do you remember Adam?"

"Did you know that I'm Adam's whore?" Sonya asked. Tears

were cascading over her cheeks.

"I know of no such thing. What I do know is that you are the mother of your's and Adam's daughter. Your mother and I came to see you and Carol Agnes. Did you know that Adam named your daughter after both of her grandmothers."

"Yes," Sonya responded in a whisper. "I want to see Adam, but I don't want him to see me like I am. I'm so ugly.

"You have been very sick," Carol said. "Adam knows you have been sick. Dr. Snyder says that you are getting well and Adam will be coming soon. Won't he, Agnes?"

Agnes was quick to assure Sonya that Adam would be coming to Minneapolis as soon as he returned from the Sudan.

Sonya continued to mope and blame herself for everything that had happened. She was convinced that God would never forgive her for her sins.

Carol sat Sonya down and took her by the shoulders. "Listen to me, Sonya!" she began. "King David saw Bathsheba and wanted her. He sent Bathsheba's husband, Uriah, into battle where he would be killed. Then King David married Bathsheba. The Lord punished King David severely but he didn't punish Bathsheba. She was to be the mother of Israel's wisest King, King Solomon. You must remember that you were going to Germany until Adam invited you to go to Cypress. If you had been in Germany, your husband and sons would still have been killed. You should ask God's forgiveness for being unfaithful to your vows. Now you have a new child and a new husband. You must start thinking ahead."

"I don't have a new husband," Sonya responded.

"In the eyes of the law, you do," Carol continued. "Your common law husband has spent a fortune saving your life and the life of your daughter. Adam loves you. He wants to marry you. You must put your fears behind you."

Sonya looked at Agnes. "Do you think Adam loves me?"

Agnes answered, "Adam told me that he loved you and wanted to marry you when he first brought you to Rochester. I scolded him for being involved with a married woman at the time. Since then, he has convinced me that you are the best thing that ever happened to him. He convinced me that he really loves you and that he wants to marry you."

They began to plan for the wedding.

******

Adam had an early dinner at Swiss Air and went up to his apartment. He waited anxiously for the time to pass to place his call to Dr. Snyder.

"Hello," Adam replied. "This is Adam McGregor calling from Cairo. Could I speak to Dr. Snyder, please?"

"Dr. Snyder is at the hospital. I'm to give you a number to call at the hospital." She repeated the number twice. Adam repeated the number back and then redialed. A female voice answered.

"My name is Adam McGregor. I'm calling from Cairo for Dr. Snyder."

"Is that Cairo, Illinois or Cairo, Egypt?" the voice inquired.

"Cairo, Egypt," Adam replied impatiently.

"You must be General McGregor then. Are you inquiring about Carol Agnes or Mrs. McGregor?"

"There is no Mrs. McGregor!" Adam responded through gritted teeth.

"I'm sorry, Darling. Our lawyer told me that because you are the father of our child and because you are my common law spouse, you get to make all the decisions. I want to know when you are going to come and get me."

There was a long pause.

"Sonya?" Adam asked with emphasis. "Is that really you?"

"I don't know if it's really me. My voice is gravely. I look a mess. I have some gray hairs. I have scars all over from where they pinned broken bones and I have this foot long scar from my vagina to my belly-button. Of course, that's your fault, Mr. Common Law Husband."

"When can you leave?" Adam asked enthusiastically.

"As soon as you get here and sign me out. Of course, Carol Agnes will have to remain here for several months. They want her to gain quite a bit more weight before they take her off the incubator. I'll have to come back and get her. Don Johnson says that once we are legally married, I can sign for her."

"Would your father marry us?"

"He's already agreed to join in the ceremony," Sonya replied. "We're going to be married at the National Cathedral, so naturally one of the Rectors will also participate."

"Why the National Cathedral?"

"That was your mother's idea. The reception will be at the Army-Navy Club. All we have to do is set the date. The Cathedral and Army-Navy need ten days notice."

"You met my mother?"

"Yes, Darling, she came out here yesterday with my parents to see Carol Agnes. We had a nice chat. We talked about the wedding. I thought her plan was just fine. She stayed in Minneapolis overnight with my parents and apologized for your behavior. They agreed to our wedding plans. Isn't it wonderful?"

"Apologized for my behavior!" Adam exclaimed. "What about your behavior?"

"I got off scott free. It helps to be sick, of course. Your mother is wonderful. She already likes me better than she likes you. She says you're a terrible rake. I agreed, but admitted that I was hopelessly in love with you. She said, 'Yes, I know, so am I!' Aren't you pleased?"

Adam didn't answer immediately.

"Are you still there?" Sonya asked.

"Yes! Are you available at this number all hours?"

"Yes, my love."

"I'll call you tomorrow with my travel arrangements. You and mother can set the dates. I'll come to Rochester to get you. I want to see Carol Agnes before I return to Egypt. I think it's wonderful that you and mother had such a good beginning. I knew she would love you as soon as she met you. I told her she would. I'll call you tomorrow. I love you, Sonya!"

"I love you, too!" she responded as they hung up.

Adam called his mother. "This is the McGregor Residence, Cecilia speaking."

"Cecilia, this is Adam. Is my mother available?"

"She's gone to play bridge. She told me to get your travel plans if you called."

"I just returned from a four day trip to the Sudan. I need to spend a few days in the office. I'll try to get away this Friday. That will put me in Minnesota Saturday. We can fly to D.C. on Sunday. The wedding could be any day that week. I want to return to Cairo as soon as possible after the wedding," Adam concluded.

"What! No honeymoon?" Cecilia asked.

"Can you keep a secret?" he asked.

"Certainly," Cecilia replied.

"We're going to honeymoon in Istanbul as soon as we are settled in Cairo and before the baby comes. I promised Sonya we would go to Istanbul sometime before we left Egypt. That was before her accident. It will still be a surprise."

"That sounds wonderful! How can we notify you about the dates?" Cecilia asked.

"I'll call you a couple of times this week. I should have my itinerary completed by Wednesday. Thanks for the help."

They said goodbye and hung up. Adam called TWA for reservations to New York with a connecting flight to Minneapolis on Northwest. He decided to wait on return reservations until the dates were more certain. He turned in early and was up at six am.

As soon as he got to the Embassy he checked in at the Ambassador's office. The Ambassador would not be in until ten am. He left a message explaining his need to spend a week in the States. When he got to his office, he scratched out a quick message to DIA explaining that he needed another weeks leave in the States. He added that he was going to visit his daughter and bring his new spouse back to Cairo. That should shake them up.

Suddenly Adam had a thought. What was the waiting period for a marriage license in the District? He called Captain Baldwin into his office.

"Dave, were you married in the District?" he asked.

"Yes Sir. We were married in the chapel at Bolling Air Force Base," Dave replied.

"How long did it take you to get a a license?"

"I don't remember exactly. We had the blood tests taken at Bolling Dispensary. I think we had to wait three days for the final approval," Dave concluded.

"Thanks for the info," Adam replied as he picked up the phone. He called DIA and asked for his mother's residence. It was nearly eleven pm D.C. time. Cecilia answered. Adam explained his dilemma and Cecilia said she would let him know what resident and non-resident requirements applied to the District.

There was nothing further to do concerning the wedding. Adam went out of his office to talk to his secretary.

"Emma, could you check on reservations again? I need to be in Minnesota as early as possible on Friday."

"This coming Friday, Sir?" she asked.

"Yes, I need to pick up Sonya and go to Washington for the wedding. I want to get to D.C. in time to get a marriage license so that Sonya and I can be married early next week. If all goes well, we should be back in Cairo late next week. Don't confirm reservations yet. I'm expecting to hear from my mother or her companion, Cecilia, later today. Then we can confirm reservations."

"Yes Sir," Emma replied. "You have a dinner invitation at the British Embassy for Thursday. Should I cancel it?"

"No, I would like to honor that invitation. I promised Lady Agatha I would keep her informed. I should know all the dates by Thursday."

Adam spent the next two hours going through the message traffic that had piled up while he was in the Sudan. By noon, he had caught up with his basket. After lunch in the canteen, Adam stopped by the Ambassador's Office to discuss his travel plans. The Ambassador approved his travel and leave. He wished Adam well and said he looked forward to meeting Sonya again.

When Adam returned to his office, he had a call from Group Captain Vanic, Indian Air Force friend. They agreed to meet at the Pyramid's Golf course at three pm. Adam's clubs were in his Corvette. He had driven himself that morning. He stopped by his apartment to change out of his uniform. By two-thirty, he was on the Giza Highway. The traffic was not heavy. He arrived at the Pyramids in twenty minutes. Jason Vanic arrived a short time later. While they were on the golf course, they swapped some information. They finished nine holes before five. After having a beer at the clubhouse, they parted company.

Brian Scott was on temporary assignment at the National War College. He picked that morning to call Agnes McGregor to check on Adam and Sonya.

Cecilia answered the phone, "I will check and see if Mrs.

McGregor is available." She put Brian on hold.

Agnes picked up the phone. "Is this Brian Scott from England?" she asked.

"Yes, it is, Mrs. McGregor. I'm not in England, I'm seconded to the National War College for a month. I'm calling to inquire about Sonya and Adam. It's been quite a while since I've had an update," he concluded.

"How long will you be staying and is Sandra with you?" Agnes asked.

Brian replied, "Sandra is joining me this weekend. She will stay for the two weeks that I have remaining."

"That's wonderful," Agnes exclaimed. "How would the two of you like to be in a wedding?"

"A wedding?" Brian asked after a short pause.

"Yes, Adam and Sonya will be married late next week. They would be so pleased and surprised if you would be the Best Man and Sandra would be the Matron of Honor."

"I'm sure Sandra will love it. She really adored Sonya when they came to visit us last Spring in Cypress. Of course, Adam was my Best Man when Sandra and I were married."

"Yes, I remember when you were married," Agnes replied. "I went to see Sonya last week for the first time. I was determined not to like her. Within five minutes she had won me over. When I ask her if I could help with the wedding, she suggested that they get married away from Minnesota. She wanted to spare her ex in-laws as much embarrassment as possible. On my way home, I stopped in Minneapolis and discussed the wedding with her father. He's a Lutheran Minister. He agreed to come to Washington. I have arranged for the ceremony to be at the National Cathedral where I am a member. Are you familiar with the Cathedral?"

"Yes, I visited the Cathedral when I was stationed at our Embassy here."

"Do you remember the chapel where the Belgium Tapestries hang?" Agnes asked.

"The ones portraying David and Goliath?" he asked.

"Yes, that's where the wedding will take place," Agnes replied. "I don't expect a large crowd. We'll have a reception at the Army-Navy Country Club over by the Pentagon."

"Have you set a date?"

"We are looking at a week from Friday, at five pm. Adam will fly out of Cairo on this Friday. He'll fly to Minnesota to see their daughter, get Sonya released from the Mayo Clinic and fly to D.C. Monday afternoon."

"Then the baby survived?" Brian asked.

"Yes, the poor dear," Agnes continued. "She is hooked to an incubator. She weighs a little over four pounds now. They will keep her until she reaches six to six and a half pounds. Adam and Sonya will be able to come and get her then."

"Do they have any idea how long it will be?" Brian asked.

"The doctors have said November at the earliest and no later than Christmas," Agnes said.

"I really appreciate the update. Sandra will be relieved. She has been wondering how they were doing for a couple of months. I'll call her tonight and give her the good news."

"If either of you happen to get a call from Adam, please don't mention the wedding. I want to surprise them," Agatha concluded.

"I'll warn Sandra," Brian replied.

"And, Brian, could you join us for dinner at Army-Navy on this Friday?" Agnes asked. "It will be myself and my companion, Cecilia. She is a student at Georgetown. I provide her room and board and she cleans my house and takes care of me when I'm out of sorts."

"We would love to do that," Brian replied. "What time?"

"We'll meet you in the Lounge at six," Agnes said. "Bye, bye."

"Bye," he replied. "Thank you very much." They hung up.

Adam had tried twice to get through to his mother. Her phone was busy. On his third try, it rang through.

Agnes answered, "Hello."

"Hello, Mother," he began, "I've been trying to reach you."

"I was on the phone with Sonya," she began. "We were talking about your trip. Have you made reservations?"

"Were you able to find out about licenses and blood tests?"

"Yes, Dear," she responded. "If you can get here next Monday or Tuesday early, you can get everything done for a wedding Friday night. I've scheduled the ceremony for five pm. The reception will be at Army-Navy at seven.

"That sounds great. Does Sonya know?"

"I was going to call her in the next hour," Agnes replied, "unless you want to tell her."

"I have a half-hour before I'm going out to a function at the Australian Embassy. I'll see if I can get through. If I can't get through, I'll call you right back."

"Don't bother to call me back, Dear. I want to call Sonya later anyway. I'll make sure she knows everything," Agnes concluded. "Goodbye, Adam."

"Goodbye, Mother," Adam signed off. He immediately called Sonya. She was expecting his call.

"Hello, Darling!" she answered.

"How did you know it was me?" Adam responded.

"I've been lying here waiting for your call. It had to be you!" she responded.

"I've got good news," he continued. "Mother has set the wedding for five pm, a week from Friday. I will fly out Friday night. I expect to be in Minnesota early Saturday morning. We can go to Washington on Sunday. We'll get a license on Monday, and be married on Friday evening. How does that sound?"

"That sounds wonderful! What do you have planned for a honeymoon?"

"I thought we would hole up in a Swiss Air apartment for a month and never talk to anyone."

"Oh, Adam," she responded. "I love the thought, but you know we can't do that. You have too many obligations."

"Are there any restrictions on your sexual activities?" Adam asked.

"I thought you would never ask. I know you think you're more interested in sex than I am, but you're wrong. I'm happy to report that I'm cleared for sex. However, I'm advised that I shouldn't get pregnant for at least six months. The Doctor pointed out that Carol Agnes should not have been born until late November at the earliest. Even though I didn't carry her full term, I'm still recovering from the pregnancy. He gave me six months of pills. I just have one question?"

"What's that?" Adam asked.

"Is there any reason why Doctor Snyder should be interested in our sex life?"

"Ahhh, no," Adam replied slowly. "He was helpful in assisting Don Johnson in my efforts to prove my paternity. You don't need to worry about that. Both he and Don are bound by professional ethics not to discuss our problems with anyone."

"Well, that's a relief," she responded. "I was beginning to feel like everyone here knew I had an affair with you. I know I did, but I didn't think an affair in Egypt had to be of public interest in Rochester!"

"I suspect they're a little short on gossip in Minnesota. They won't even remember us until we come back to get the baby," Adam responded hopefully.

"I'm sure I'll think of a dozen things to ask you as soon as we hang up. Oh, I know, what about my clothes? I don't have a thing to wear. You'll remember, I came to Minnesota in a hospital gown."

"Oh yes," Adam replied. "I never got around to checking your apartment in Mohandisin. Some Embassy personnel went to check on your things a month after your fall. The apartment was occupied. We didn't even get your advanced rent back."

"What about the clothes I took to Cypress?" Sonya asked.

"I don't recall that you had any clothes on in Cypress," Adam replied.

"I wasn't naked when we went to see Brian and Sandra, smarty. I had an outfit on when we flew back to Cairo. They should be in your closet unless you've been entertaining other women since I left."

"Your clothes are still here. I'll bring everything I can find. Can you get away to shop this week?" Adam asked.

"I can hardly get out of my room, say nothing of going shopping. It seems that I'm the prisoner of my common-law husband who happens to be on the other side of the world!"

"Let me think," Adam responded. "I'm leaving here around ten pm next Friday. Even with bad luck, I should be in Rochester by noon Saturday your time. We can shop all Saturday afternoon either in Rochester or at the Mall of America in Minneapolis. Decide where you want to shop and get us a hotel reservation nearby. We'll go on to Washington Sunday morning."

"You don't want to go to D.C. on Saturday?" Sonya asked.

"I want a night with my common-law spouse. I have an idea that when we get to Georgetown, Mother is going to kick me out of the house. Common-law be damned, she isn't going to let me sleep with you until after the wedding." Adam concluded.

"I guess you know your mother pretty well, Sweetheart. She made reservations for you at the Willard for Monday through Thursday."

"And you didn't object!"

"Remember, Darling, I have experience with a mother-in-law. You don't pick a fight before you're married. I think it's particularly wise, considering that I'm a retread marrying an only son who could be considered a confirmed bachelor."

"I withdraw my objection," he replied. "You've done a marvelous job of making peace with Mother. I wish I could say the same for my efforts with your mother."

"Mother is beginning to mellow. She said she understood that I would be dead and buried if it wasn't for you. She is looking forward to meeting you again."

"I'm glad to hear that, Sonya," Adam said. "Now, I have got to get off this phone or our phone bill will be bigger than our hospital bill. I love you. I'll call you tomorrow."

"I love you, too, my Darling Adam. Goodnight." They hung up.

Adam's week went by fast. On Tuesday, he and Captain Baldwin took Spar 80 to Sharm El Sheik. An Army Captain, on leave from Germany, had died in a diving accident in the Gulf of Aqaba. According to the authorities, he was on a night dive with his diving club of Mannheim, Germany. They went down one hundred feet. The Captain had an air line problem. He drowned before he could reach the surface. The explanation was shaky, but there was nothing Adam could do. They picked up the body. It was in a body bag with a large amount of ice. The seats on the left side had been removed to accommodate the body bag. They returned to Cairo and put the body bag on a C-141, going to Ramstein.

Adam attended a luncheon for the military and Naval Attache's on Wednesday. The British Air Attache' informed Adam that Brian Scott was in Washington for a month. Adam called Sonya that evening.

"Is that you, Adam?" Sonya answered.

"Yes, Darling. I've got great news. Brian Scott is in D.C. for a month. I'll call Mother and have her invite him to the wedding."

There was a pause. "How did you find out?" Sonya asked.

"The British Air Force Attache' told me at lunch today. He said Brian is at National War College for a month."

"Oh, that's terrible! You're not supposed to know. Brian called your mother last week. Sandra is joining him this week. Brian's your Best Man and Sandra will be my Matron of Honor. You must not let your mother know!" Sonya pleaded.

"We never had this conversation. I can keep the secret and I guarantee I'll give a great performance at the wedding. Mother will not know that I know," Adam promised.

"Thank you, Dear," she responded. "Agnes is so enthused. She even asked me how soon I thought I could get pregnant. I told her that Dr. Snyder wants us to wait a while. He wants us to be sure I'm healthy before we try for a second child. She nodded her understanding and then added, 'I don't care if it's a boy or a girl.'"

"We are fortunate that we will be in the Near East for a while. We can have a nice long honeymoon," Adam replied.

"Where are we going for our honeymoon?"

"Third floor of the Swiss Air Building. That will give us time to make up for all the love making we've missed since we left Cypress."

There was silence. "Are you still there, Sonya?"

"Yes, I was just thinking. I'm thinking if we made love three times everyday, we could catch up in about a month and a half, excluding my menstrual cycles. However, there will be days when you won't be able to come home for lunch. Then, there are days when you fly and when you go to Khartoum. Even if I go along, I will probably be left with Marty for a day or two at a time. We'll fall behind again. On the other hand, if we went to Istanbul for a week or ten days, we could probably make love thirty or forty times."

"We're going to Istanbul, smarty." Adam replied. "I have to wait a couple of months before I take another leave. We have to be in Cairo for the annual military parade on October sixth. We will be going to El Alamein for the annual commemoration on November eighth, and we are trying to get authorization to visit Siwa Oasis before the Ambassador departs. We'll be staying overnight at Sidi Barani. Maybe we will have to be satisfied with not falling further behind."

"That will be fine with me, Darling. Will you call tomorrow?"

"Yes, Sonya, I'll call tomorrow. I won't call Friday as I will go to the airport from dinner at the Hulls. I won't call unless my airplane doesn't leave on time.

"I love you. See you on Saturday," Sonya said.

"I love you, too!" Adam hung up.

The next day, the Ambassador's office called and requested Spar 80 for a flight to Tel Aviv. Two Congressmen were in town and needed transportation. They were to be delivered to the airport for a two pm departure. Adam and Dave were waiting at the aircraft. The Congressmen showed up at four pm. The trip to Lod Airport was without incident. By the time they returned to Cairo, Adam was three hours late for his call to Sonya. As soon as he returned to the apartment, Adam ordered a sandwich from downstairs and then called Sonya.

You're late!" Sonya answered on the first ring. "Where did Spar 80 take you today?"

"Hi, Sweetheart. We went to Tel Aviv. How did you know we flew?"

"Sweet Emma called and told me you would be late. Are either of the Congressmen people we could vote against?"

"Not likely, Love. One's from Rhode Island and one is from Alabama."

"Are you packed?" Sonya asked.

"I'm going to finish as soon as I get off the phone and eat my sandwich."

"Where did you pick up a sandwich in Cairo?" she asked.

"I ordered it from downstairs," he replied.

"I won't keep you long. You need your rest because tomorrow will be a very long day by the time we get to bed Saturday night," Sonya said.

"Where are we staying?"

"We're in a Marriott near the airport. If you are really tired we can stay Sunday night and leave early Monday."

"Let's plan to do that. Mother's reservations for me at the Willard are Monday through Thursday aren't they?"

"Yes, they are, Love," Sonya replied. "How can I survive four days not seeing you when you're only blocks away?"

"Adjoining rooms have spoiled us, I guess," he replied.

"Let's elope," Sonya suggested.

"Great idea," Adam agreed. "However, you had better be prepared for an unforgiving mother-in-law for the rest of our lives."

"Cancel eloping," she responded. "We'll have to tough it out. I love you. Goodnight, Darling."

"Goodnight, Sweetheart." They hung up.

Adam slept late on Friday Morning. At noon, he stopped at the Embassy to read the message traffic and hit the snack bar for a light brunch. He played two sets of tennis with Dave Baldwin. He went back to his apartment to finish packing. After a long shower he donned his uniform, grabbed his bags and went down the back stairs to meet Mustafa. They loaded the bags in the trunk.

"Why so many bags, General?" Mustafa asked.

"I have to take some clothes for Sonya. You remember Sonya?" Adam asked.

"Aiwa," Mustafa replied in Arabic. They conversed in Arabic all the way to the British Embassy. Adam brought Mustafa up to date on his wedding plans. Mustafa knew that Adam had an eleven pm flight to the States. He would be back to pick Adam up at nine thirty pm.

The butler met Adam at the door and escorted him into the drawing room where cocktails were being served. The butler served Adam his usual Dewars on the rocks.

Alistair and Wanda Ames were the only other guests. Introductions were not necessary.

"You're in uniform, Adam!" Alistair remarked. "I would have worn mine had I known."

"I'm leaving for the airport in about three hours," Adam explained. "I like to travel in uniform, otherwise I would be more casual. I hope I'm not too overdressed your Ladyship."

"Nonsense," Lady Agatha replied, "I'll bet that you get marvelous service with the uniform and all those medals!"

"The only problem," Sir William interjected, "is the stewardesses in first class tend to be a bit long in the tooth. They're more likely to mother Adam rather than hustle him."

Lady Agatha responded, "Well, I don't think Adam has anyone on his mind except Sonya. You are going to get married?"

Adam nodded in the affirmative.

"Your mother invited us to the wedding. Unfortunately we aren't able to get away."

"Lady Agatha, do you know my mother?"

"Yes, Dear," Lady Agatha responded. "We met your parents in England when you were in the Academy. We had lost contact. The other day I called your mother."

"How did you get her number? I'm just curious. I would have given it to you had you asked."

"Actually, I got it from Emma, your secretary. You see, we have a grandson at the Embassy in D.C. I wanted him to meet a nice girl his age. Agnes told me about her companion, Cecilia Thompson. Our William, the Fourth, is dining with Agnes and Cecilia this evening at the Army-Navy Club. What do you think of that?" Lady Agatha concluded.

"Is your grandson in the Foreign Service?" Adam asked.

"Yes, why do you ask?" Ambassador Hull interrupted.

Adam replied, "Cecilia is a student at Georgetown. She's majoring in International Relations. She's fluent in French. She's five foot six, weighs about one hundred fifteen or one hundred twenty. She is blond, has a face of an angel. I don't think William has a chance!"

"She's at Georgetown? Is she Catholic?" Agatha asked.

"No," Adam replied. "She's Episcopalian. At least she regularly attends the National Cathedral with Mother."

"Your wedding is on Friday?" Agatha asked.

"Yes," Adam replied.

"Tell your mother I will attend. Will can't come. I will make the sacrifice. I have to meet Cecilia," Agatha concluded.

The butler came in, "Dinner is served."

They dined on Roast Beef and Yorkshire Pudding. Of course, there was a soup course before and a salad course after the entree. The meal was accompanied by an excellent Claret from Bordeaux.

This was followed by a Bread Pudding desert. Dinner was finished by nine. They returned to the Drawing Room for after dinner libations. Adam checked his watch and noted it was nearly nine pm. He had thirty minutes before Mustafa would pick him up. He opted for a Brandy. Lady Agatha said that she would forward her travel plans to her grandson and also to Agnes. As soon as Mustafa arrived, Adam said his goodbyes.

Mustafa dropped Adam at the TWA entrance at ten pm. They were boarding the New York flight. Adam checked his suitcases and boarded immediately. His first-class seat was near the right hand bulkhead in the front row. He would have plenty of room to stretch out and sleep. The stewardess brought him a Dewars on the rocks. By the time the 747 reached cruise attitude, he had finished his drink. He got up and took off his uniform blouse. The stewardess took the blouse and hung it up. She brought him a blanket. He tilted his seat back and went to sleep. He slept for over six hours. Adam was awakened by a shudder of the aircraft. The elderly lady in the seat next to Adam was gripping her armrests and pushing back in her seat. The crew had increased power on the engines.

"Ma'am" Adam addressed the woman. "You don't need to worry. We just got into the jet stream. The pilots are climbing to avoid the turbulence."

"How do you know?" she asked abruptly.

The co-pilot came on the intercom, "Ladies and Gentlemen, we've encountered a little clear air turbulence from the jet stream. We've been cleared to thirty-seven thousand feet. That should keep us out of the turbulence. We should be landing at Kennedy around two am New York time."

"I'm sorry," the lady addressed Adam. "When should I worry?"

Adam laughed, "If it looks like I'm worried, you can worry."

"Are you a pilot?" she asked.

"Yes, Ma'am," he replied.

"What's the largest airplane you've flown?"

"The B-52," Adam replied.

"Is it as large as the 747?"

"Yes, it is," Adam answered.

"Could you fly this plane?" she asked.

"Yes, I could in an emergency," Adam replied.

"Have you ever flown a 747?"

"No," he said, "but if the pilots were incapacitated for some reason, the stewardess would ask for pilots from the passenger list. I would volunteer. Since I have six thousand flying hours, I would have no problem maintaining airspeed and altitude as required. We would land at the nearest suitable airfield. The airline would send a 747 pilot to the tower to advise me on when to lower flaps and landing gear. My landing might not be quite as smooth as normal, but we would arrive safely."

The lady said, "Thank you!" Her grip had relaxed. She tilted her seat back, closed her eyes and went to sleep. She must have been exhausted as she continued to sleep until the pilots advised the cabin crew to prepare for landing at JFK. Adam nudged the lady. She awoke in a start.

"What is it?" she asked.

"We are about to land at Kennedy. The stewardess wants us to raise our seats and fasten our seat belts."

"Oh!" she replied. "Thank you! I had a wonderful nap. Thank you." She thanked Adam three more times on their way to baggage claim. It reminded him of his mother.

There was a shuttle bus waiting to go to La Guardia. Adam had nearly two hours to make his Northwest connection to Minneapolis. He took the shuttle. His flight was on time and he would be in Minneapolis by eight am local.

As soon as he deplaned at Minneapolis, he went to the Hertz counter and rented a Lincoln. He was anticipating more baggage for the flight to D.C. He collected his bags and took a shuttle to the Hertz lot. He had breakfast on his Northwest flight. He drove to Rochester without a stop.

At the Mayo Clinic, he stopped at the reception desk. "Ah, General McGregor," the receptionist said. "We've been expecting you. If you turn around you will see a lady who's been waiting for you." He turned.

There was Sonya sitting on a couch dressed in a hospital gown and slippers. He went over and took her in his arms and kissed her.

"You're not dressed?" he questioned. "Is there a problem?"

"Darling, there's no problem. I'm ready for release as soon as you sign for me. The reason I'm not dressed is because I don't have any clothes. If you'll remember, you brought me here dressed like this. Did you bring some clothes?"

"Yes, I'll run out to the car and get your bag. I have all your Cypress clothes. Are you sure we can't have a room here before you get dressed?"

"These rooms are way too expensive for what you have in mind. Believe me, I checked." They kissed again.

Adam rushed out the door. Everyone in the clinic knew who Sonya was and the story behind her medical problems.

"Sonya," the receptionist spoke. "He is drop dead gorgeous!"

"Yes, I know," Sonya responded.

"Does he have a brother?" the receptionist asked.

"Sorry, honey, he's an only child," she said. "I'll scold his mother for you on Monday!"

Adam returned.

"What's in the bag?" Sonya asked.

"The dress you wore to Cairo from Cypress. There are two sets of lingerie and two pairs of shoes. There is also another dress and two swim suits."

"My bikinis?" she asked.

"Yes." he responded.

"Throw them away. No bare mid-drifts for me!"

"Is it really that bad?" he asked.

"Come and I'll show you while I change. Dr. Snyder will meet us at the room. We'll go by the nursery and see Carol Agnes and then we'll come back and sign out."

The receptionist had alerted Dr. Snyder and he was at the room when they arrived. Sonya went in to change. When she was about to put her dress on, she called for Adam. She pulled down her panties and exposed the scar.

"It doesn't look so bad," he said.

"I know," she answered. "I just don't want anyone else to see it." She finished dressing, putting on her yellow sheath. "Let's go see our baby."

Dr. Snyder spoke, "Adam I would like to introduce Carol's pediatrician, Dr. Alice Kittleson." They shook hands.

Dr. Kittleson took over. "General McGregor, I would like to congratulate you on your successful efforts to get Sonya here safely and making the early decision for a C-Section. Your daughter is doing extremely well. All of her vital signs are normal. Her growth and weight gains are doing fine. I believe that you'll be able to take her home in three to four months."

"That's wonderful," Adam began. "We are returning to Egypt next week. That's not a healthy place to live. We will err on the safe side. I would like to plan a trip to pick her up around Christmas. How does that sound?"

"That should work fine and it is a good idea to wait a little longer," Dr. Kittleson stated. "It will add quite a bit to your bill."

"I didn't think about that, Adam," Sonya chimed in.

"It's not a problem, Sonya. I've been sending checks monthly. An extra month or two may preclude our having to rush back again."

The two doctors agreed that it was prudent to wait a little longer. Adam and Sonya took a last look at Carol Agnes and said goodbye to the two doctors. They checked out at the reception desk and went to the car. Sonya was weeping.

"What is it?" Adam asked.

"I'm not going to see the baby for four months!" she responded. "I've gone to see her every day since I've been able to walk."

"I understand, Dear, but we can't do anything for her until she can leave the incubator," Adam said. "We can only return to Cairo and get everything ready for her arrival." Adam opened the car door and ushered Sonya into the passenger side. He went around to the drivers side and slide in.

"Where to, Sonya?" he asked.

"Let's go check into the Marriott and then go to Nordstrom's. I want to buy one outfit to wear to your mother's on Monday. I'll wait until we get to D.C. to do some more shopping. I'll have three days before the wedding and I will enjoy shopping with your mother and Sandra."

Adam nodded his understanding and added, "You are going to have another shopper. Lady Agatha is coming to the wedding."

"Lady Agatha Hull?" she exclaimed.

"Yes, She called Mother to ask her to introduce her

grandson, William Hull the Fourth, to a nice girl," Adam said. "Do you know Cecilia Thompson?"

"Yes, she came out to Minnesota with your mother. I adore her."

"I suggested that William IV will adore her also. Lady Agatha said 'I'm coming to your wedding.' You can expect her to join you at some point."

"I'm flattered that she will come to our wedding, even though she has a ulterior motive. Obviously, she wasn't about to arrive without an excuse."

Adam didn't answer immediately. He was thinking about how this wedding was growing. If Lady Agatha stays with the British Ambassador, which she probably will do, then Mother should invite the Ambassador and spouse. Oh well, she will do what she wants to do.

"A penny for your thoughts," Sonya whispered.

"I was just thinking about how our wedding is growing. There's nothing we can do about it. We might as well relax."

"I agree, Darling," Sonya answered.

They were speeding up I-35 toward Minneapolis. Adam saw a restaurant on a billboard for the next exit. "How about some lunch. I haven't eaten since last night on the airplane."

"I'm ready," Sonya replied.

They had a quick lunch while they planned the rest of the day. They decided to stop at the Nordstrom's in the Mall of America on their way to the hotel. They would check in and eat dinner at the hotel. Sonya suggested that they attend her father's church on Sunday. Adam agreed. They would have to be up early on Sunday as the church was at least forty-five minutes away.

Sonya tried on three different dresses. Adam liked all three.

"Which one do you like the best?" she asked.

"I like the blue one best. It matches your eyes," he replied hoping he was guessing right.

Sonya asked the sales girl what she thought. Adam couldn't hear what she said. It must have been positive as Sonya took the dress. She went back to the dressing room and changed back to her sheath. Adam paid for the dress while Sonya finished primping. She looked radiant when she came out of the dressing room. They went to the Marriott and checked in. Sonya decided to try on her new dress again.

"Maybe I'll wear it to dinner," she said. She stripped down to her panties and bra.

"What's that scar on your left shoulder blade?" he asked.

"That's where they went in to pin or fix one of my broken bones. Is it really ugly?" she asked.

"I don't know. Your bra strap is in the way. Let me unfasten your bra." He unhooked the bra and reached around to her left breast. He fondled her breast until the nipple hardened.

"What are you doing, Adam?" Sonya asked.

"I'm checking out the body I knew in Cypress," he whispered. "Can I interest you in a little love making?"

"I thought you would never ask!" she said. "If we do, I must take a pill. Dr. Snyder says I shouldn't get pregnant for at least five months."

"How many pills do you have?" he asked.

"Two hundred-fifty," she responded. "When those pills are gone I want to get pregnant again with at least two more of your sons."

"Are you aware that the chances of having two boys after having a girl are really slim?" Adam asked.

"Then we'll keep having babies until I have two boys, or until you can't stand me because I'm too old and fat."

"I promise that if you get old and fat, I'll get old and fat with you. Take your pill."

"I already took it. I was hoping we would have time for some loving before dinner," Sonya responded as she was rolling back the bed covers.

They both slept after making love. Adam woke up first and realized their dinner reservation was coming up. "Wake up, Sonya," he whispered. "Dinner is in fifteen minutes. Can you make it?"

"I can if you don't care how I look and what I smell like."

"I'm the one that smells bad when I sweat. If you can stand me, I can certainly stand you. I'll get us a table in a corner where we won't offend any other patrons."

Sonya quickly brushed her hair and checked her eye shadow. Before she put on lipstick she went to Adam and kissed him. She put on her lipstick and they departed for dinner. They asked for a remote table and were escorted to a far corner of the dining room. Adam ordered scotch for himself and white wine for Sonya. They studied their menus.

"I like your hair short. It has so much more curl," Adam opined.

"They shaved my head when they tapped into my skull to relieve pressure from bleeding. When the hair finally grew back it came in curly.

"It makes you look younger," Adam stated. "I'll be accused of robbing the cradle."

"There are quite a few gray hairs among the gold," she responded.

"When did you come out of your coma?" Adam asked.

"After they tapped my skull. I became aware of my surroundings. I could understand what was being said, but I couldn't speak and I was afraid to move for fear of pain. Dr. Snyder noticed that my eyes were responding when they talked around me. He suggested they put me in a pool. When I got in the water, I began to move my limbs on my own. A few day later, I was talking. I asked for you."

"Yes, Dr. Snyder said your first words were to ask for me. I'm very flattered."

"I missed you so much," she answered. "I was afraid I would never see you again. Dr. Snyder said he imagined that you would come as soon as you could. I asked why he was so sure. He said that to start with that you were my common-law husband and you were paying my bills. I asked why you were my common-law husband and that's when I learned your blood test had proved that you were Carol Agnes' father. I was ecstatic. Your mother came the next day and we began planning our wedding. I couldn't call you sooner because you were in the Sudan."

The waiter appeared and they both ordered Walleyed Pike. Each ordered a glass of Sauvignon Blanc with the entree. They ate their dinners quietly. When they finished dessert and after dinner drinks, they returned to their room and went to bed. They made love again and then slept through the night, rising early to shower and dress for Church. On the way to St. Paul, traffic was light and they were in plenty of time for the ten am Service. Sonya's mother was in the Narthex of the Gothic style stone church. She was greeting visitors. When she saw Sonya she began to weep.

"Oh, Sonya, it's so nice of you to come to the service," Carol Carlson began. "I thought you were on your way to Washington." They hugged and then turned to Adam.

"Mother," Sonya began. "I want you to meet my fiancée, Adam McGregor."

"We met once before when Adam brought you to the clinic. Adam and I spoke on the phone months ago," Carol said. "I was terribly rude. I hope you can forgive me."

"Forgiven and forgotten, Mrs. Carlson," Adam replied. He leaned forward and kissed her on the cheek.

"Please call me, Carol," she added. "Thank you for naming Carol Agnes after me. I hope you two will be very happy."

Mrs. Carlson introduced Sonya and Adam to several other parishioners. Then she had one of the ushers show them to her regular pew. Reverend Carlson was preparing for the service and communion.

"Hi, Daddy!" Sonya called to get her father's attention.

"Sonya!" he exclaimed. "I thought you were on your way to D.C. and this is Adam McGregor," he addressed Adam. "We are indebted to you for saving Sonya's life and her baby. It will be my pleasure to officiate at your wedding. I understand from your mother that you are Episcopalian. Please join us in Communion today."

"Thank you, Sir, I will do that," Adam replied.

They settled into their pew and were joined by Sonya's mother just before the service began It was a large congregation. The church was nearly full. There were two assistant pastors. They were able to support three lines at the alter railing. The service was over in an hour and ten minutes.

Sonya's mother insisted that Sonya and Adam come to the Parsonage for brunch. They stayed most of the afternoon. Adam, Earl, and Pastor Carlson watched the final day of the PGA Championship. Sonya spent the time discussing the wedding plans with her mother.

The Carlson's received a phone call from their travel agent. The agent had been unable to get hotel reservations in D.C. for

Tuesday through Friday.

"What will we do?" Mrs. Carlson asked.

"Let me make a call," Adam volunteered.

He called the housing office at Bolling Air Force Base. They reserved a VIP Suite for Brigadier General McGregor for Monday through Thursday. Then he called his mother.

"Mother? This is Adam. The Carlson's are having trouble getting hotel reservations in D.C. I've made reservations for myself at the Bolling BOQ through Thursday night. Could you call The Willard and transfer that reservation from me to the Carlson's for Tuesday through Friday?" He listened to his mother's response and then they hung up.

"She'll call back in a few minutes," Adam announced.

Adam and Sonya were preparing to leave when Agnes called back. She confirmed the reservation and mentioned that the suite would sleep four if Earl and Rachel were planning to attend the wedding.

"Dear Mother," Adam added, "She thinks of everything."

Adam and Sonya thanked Carol for the brunch and departed for the Marriott. They planned an early dinner at the hotel. When they went back in the room, they crawled in bed to watch TV. By ten, they were sound asleep.

Monday morning, they were up at five am. Their flight was scheduled to leave at seven am, and would land at Washington National around ten local. They dropped off the rental and took a shuttle to the Northwest Terminal. First class was boarding. They took their seats and ordered breakfast. By the time the Boeing 727 leveled off, their breakfast was ready. The remainder of their flight was uneventful. There were a few cumulus clouds building, which suggested mid-to-late afternoon thunderstorms. They would occur long after their landing.

Cecilia was there to meet their flight. She took them to City Hall to apply for their marriage license. They went to Bethesda Naval Hospital for their blood tests. From there, they went back to the airport and Adam rented a Mustang. Before they parted, Cecilia informed Adam that he was expected at his mother's residence for cocktails and dinner starting at six. Lady Agatha and her grandson, Will, would also be attending.

"I understand that you and Mother had dinner with William Hull the Fourth on Friday night," Adam stated.

"Yes," Cecilia answered with an excited voice. "We had such fun. Will and I spoke French most of the evening. Your mother kept saying, 'What are you two talking about?'. His French is very good and mine is better than I expected. Will is at the Embassy for some training. He'll be assigned to Paris as a political officer when he completes his training."

"You found out all of that Friday night?" Adam asked, facetiously.

"No, Adam," she answered. "We went to the theater Saturday night and to the Redskin's pre-season game on Sunday. Your mother gave me her tickets so that was my treat."

"When did Lady Agatha arrive?" Adam asked.

"She came in late last night. We met her plane after attending the game. She was very tired. I'm not sure she was prepared to meet anyone other than Will. He explained that I had a car and he would have to hire one. He gets around her pretty well."

"He must be a diplomat!" Adam replied.

"What do you mean?" Cecilia asked.

"I mean, no one gets around or past Lady Agatha," Adam replied as he closed the car door. "I'll see you two tonight."

Adam went to Bolling and checked in to the BOQ. He called the War College and asked for Brian Scott.

Brian came on the phone. "Adam, you aren't supposed to know I'm here."

"You're the third person who's told me that. Nobody needs to know that I know you're here. Can you play golf?"

"I can play around twelve-thirty. I have to pick up Sandra at Dulles about six this afternoon."

"That's great," Adam replied. "I'll call for a twelve-thirty tee time. We should finish by four-thirty. You'll have time to get to Dulles even if the traffic is heavy."

"I'll be at Army-Navy by twelve-thirty," Brian concluded.

While the two officers were enjoying a round of golf, the women were busy discussing the upcoming wedding plans at Agnes' Georgetown Townhouse. Sonya said she was in a delima as to what to wear for a wedding dress, as she didn't want to wear white.

"How would you like to try on my wedding dress?" Agnes asked. "It's not white."

"Let's try it," Sonya exclaimed. She didn't want to disappoint her mother-in-law. Besides it couldn't hurt anything.

Cecilia went to the attic found the trunk and opened it with the key Agnes had given her. The dress was wrapped in white tissue paper. It appeared to be in good condition as it had been put through the preservation process. She took it downstairs to Agnes' bedroom. She donned the dress by unzipping it and stepping into the back. It was a strapless dress. The skirt came to her mid-calf. The powder blue color matched Sonya's eyes.

"What do you think?" Agnes asked.

"I like it," Sonya whispered. There were tears in her eyes. "What do you girls think?"

"It's perfect color wise," Cecilia commented.

"I think it looks better on you than it did on me," Agnes added. "It will need airing out after being in storage all these years."

"When we go shopping tomorrow, I'll get a blue garter belt and some blue hose. I don't think I want pantie hose," Sonya said while she turned in front of the full length mirror. "I really like it, Agnes. May I wear it?"

"Of course you can," Agnes replied. "I can't believe I was ever that small and trim!"

Sonya took the dress off. Cecilia shook it out and hung it on a hanger to air out.

"Changing the subject, Agnes," Sonya began, "how can I help you get ready for tonight's dinner?"

"You can't, Dear," she answered. "I'm having everything catered except the bar service. I'll let Adam take care of serving drinks and selecting the wines. All we have to do is make ourselves pretty by five-thirty."

Adam and Brian completed their golf round, then went to the locker room, ordered a beer, and took a steam bath. After showering, they dressed and parted.

"Remember, Brian, I don't know you're here. Be sure Sandra doesn't blow my cover."

"I won't even tell her I've seen you. That way she can't make a slip," Brian responded. "Golf tomorrow?"

"Anytime after noon," Adam replied. "I'm going to DIA in the morning."

"I'll be here at twelve-thirty. Sandra is supposed to go shopping with Sonya and your mother. I had a call from Cecilia. I guess she lives with your mother. She said she would pick up Sandra. By the way Adam, how did you know I was here?"

"Alistair Ames told me just before I left Cairo. I told Sonya you were here and she told me I wasn't supposed to know. We must keep the secret. I'll be sure to act surprised when I see you Friday."

"What about rings?" Brian asked. "As best man, I'm supposed to pull rings out of my pocket."

"I've ordered an Academy miniature with an accompanying wedding band. I should be able to pick it up in Annapolis Friday morning. If it's not ready, we may have to come up with a cigar band."

"How did you get from the Naval Academy to the Air Force?" Brian asked.

"It occurred because my father was Air Force. The Air Force Academy was open, but I had an appointment to Navy and my parents were in D.C. I decided to keep my Navy appointment."

"I had better hit the road," Brian said. "If I'm late getting to Dulles, Sandra will want to know with whom I was playing golf."

"Good thinking. See you tomorrow."

Adam stopped in the Grill Room and had a Scotch while he watched television. He drove to Georgetown, arriving at five-fifty. His mother met him at the door.

"Good evening, Adam," she greeted. "You are right on time. I want you to take charge of the bar. I expect Lady Agatha and Will any moment. Cecilia went to the Ambassador's Quarters to pick them up."

"Who's cooking dinner?" Adam asked.

"I'm having it catered from Rive Gauche, just up Wisconsin Avenue. They'll be here at seven or there abouts."

Adam went to the bar and picked up the ice bucket, took it to the kitchen and filled it. He went to the basement where his mother had a temperature controlled wine cabinet. He extracted two bottles of white wine and one bottle of red. There was plenty of beer in the frig.

Lady Agatha and Will arrived at the front door at six. Cecilia dropped them off and took her car around to the alley behind the house. Agnes met the guests.

"Please come in, Agatha," Agnes said. "I believe you know Adam?"

"My favorite General!" Agatha said as she approached Adam and gave him a peck on the cheek.

Sonya came down the stairs.

"This must be Sonya," Lady Agatha said approaching Sonya and taking both of her hands. She looked Sonya up and down.

"Adam certainly has an eye for beauty," Agatha added. "I have been anxious to meet you. Adam has been good enough to keep me informed of your progress."

"Thank you, Lady Agatha," Sonya replied warmly. "I must congratulate you on your handsome grandson." Sonya turned her attention to Will.

"I've been hearing great things about you, Will. Have you met my fiancée, Adam?"

Adam stepped forward and shook Will's hand. "I understand that you are in the Foreign Service," Adam said. "Congratulations."

"Thank you, General," Will replied.

Adam took cocktail orders and retreated to the bar. Sonya and Cecilia served the drinks as Adam made them. They all congregated in the living room.

"Tell me, General," Will began, "are the Israelis really going to return the Sinai to Egypt?"

"I think so," Adam replied. "They have given back the Western Sinai and the Sharm El Sheik area. They are on schedule to return the entire Sinai by April of 1983. I think it will happen because both countries have realized a tremendous increase in revenue from tourism. A majority of the tours now include both countries. Air Sinai which is run by El Al, has an office at Cairo Airport. Tourism has surpassed the Suez Canal as Egypt's largest revenue source. There is a great deal to see in both countries."

Will nodded his understanding and asked, "I understand you spend a lot of time in the Sudan. How are things going there?"

"Unfortunately, the Sudan is a basket case. The powers that be in Khartoum are not concerned with anything other than maintaining control. It's a shame because the country is blessed with an abundance of natural resources, particularly oil, while the government doesn't allow any exploitation until the government has been paid baksheesh. That's Arabic slang for graft."

"What about John Baranga and Ahmed Ibrahim?" Sonya asked.

"They are the exceptions and they can't operate in Khartoum. John Baranga has gone to the bush. We met him in Yei when we picked up his family and took them to Nairobi. His wife and children are in the States. I would guess that John is the leader of the revolt in the South. Ahmed is still in El Fasher," Adam responded. I have no idea how long he will be in Darfur. President Numerie tried to replace him last year. The citizens of El Fasher refused to accept Khartoum's candidate.

"Let's change the subject," Adam suggested. "A little bit of Africa goes a long way. Where are you going from here, Will?"

"I'll be in the political section in Paris," Will responded.

"That should be interesting," Adam replied. "I understand you and Cecilia are both conversant in French."

"I wanted her to come to Paris with me. She's determined to finish her course at Georgetown before we get married."

"Married?" Lady Agatha exclaimed. "You hadn't mentioned marriage to me. Do your parents know you are contemplating marriage?"

"Yes, Grandmother," he responded. "Cecilia and I will fly to London over Thanksgiving so that Father and Mother can meet Cecilia. I'm so glad that you came for Adam and Sonya's wedding so that you could meet Cecilia."

"How long have you known each other?" Lady Agatha asked.

"We met at a mutual friend's wedding," Cecilia interrupted. "It was almost six months ago. We've dated on most weekends and I've been to several Embassy functions with Will. He has helped me immensely with my French."

"Cecilia has helped me with my French," Will said. "You could say we have a French connection."

"It sounds like you aren't rushing into marriage," Will's grandmother responded. "I like the fact that you will finish your course, Cecilia. Will, I shall tell your parents that I'm quite impressed with both of you."

"Dinner is served," the waiter announced.

The dinner was excellent. Agnes was congratulated on her choice of caterers. The conversation shifted to plans for the rest of the week. Agnes informed her son that his presence was no longer needed until four pm on Friday. At that time, he was to come to the National Cathedral in his dress uniform. The wedding would be at five.

Adam took the hint and departed. He and Brian Scott played golf every afternoon. Adam spent his evenings at Army-Navy and/or the Bolling Officer's Club. He managed to run into a number of acquaintances from previous assignments. In the mornings, he went to DIA and the Pentagon to check in with the offices that had an interest in what was going on in Egypt and the Sudan.

The ladies had a wonderful time shopping with Sonya. Cecilia took note of all things involved in planning a large wedding. Sandra Scott joined the group at Brian's urging. That cleared the way for Brian to join Adam on the golf course.

Friday morning, Adam drove to Annapolis. He stopped at Tilgman's where he had done business before. He had taken them Sonya's wedding ring she had left in his apartment at Swiss Air for size. They made a miniature with diamonds from Adam's Class Ring and a diamond wedding band to match.

His next stop was at the BOQ Office at the Academy. He asked for a VIP Suite for the night. He explained that he was being married that evening and he and his bride would arrive between ten and eleven pm. The clerk said that the Severn Suite was available for one night only. That was very satisfactory to Adam. He was advised to pick up his keys from the Marines at gate eight. Gate three would be closed at ten pm. He returned to D.C.

Adam had checked out of the Bolling BOQ. He went back to Army-Navy to shower, shave and dress for the wedding. He called his mother and advised her to have Sonya pack her bags. She would need an overnight bag to take with her after the wedding. They would retrieve her other bags Saturday prior to catching their flight to New York.

"Do you have to leave so soon?" Agnes asked.

"Yes, I told the Ambassador that I would be back on Monday.

We'll be coming back to get Carol Agnes between Thanksgiving and Christmas. We'll spend some time with you then."

"I guess I'll have to settle for that," Agnes responded.

"I'll need to see you for a moment before the ceremony."

"What for?" she asked.

"I have a gift for the bride," he replied.

"What is it?" Agnes probed.

"Her engagement ring," he replied.

"It's a little late for that!"

"I know, Mother. I wanted her to have a miniature and it took some time to get it made. I think she'll like it. The wedding band goes with the miniature," he concluded.

"That is nice. I'll come up to the chapel as soon as you arrive," she answered.

They said their goodbyes and hung up. Adam finished dressing and left for the church.

Adam entered the Cathedral at the side entrance nearest the parking. His mother was right inside the door. He kissed her and handed her the miniature. Agnes looked at it and commented, "I would have thought a millionaire would have purchased a bigger diamond."

"A karat is as big as they can get into a miniature," he replied suppressing a smile.

"I'll give it to Sonya," Agnes replied. "Come meet your best man."

"I don't get to chose my own best man?"

Brian Scott was at the entrance to the wedding chapel. "Brian!" Adam exclaimed. "You're supposed to be at Cranwell!"

"I couldn't miss this wedding," Brian replied. "I've been at Fort McNair for the last month."

"You can both can the act," Agnes interjected. "Lady Agatha told me that you knew Brian was in town before you left Cairo. I called the pro-shop on Tuesday. Wanda confirmed that Group Captain Scott was your guest. You needn't pretend you didn't know. I would have known anyway when you never mentioned naming a best man. You should never try to fool your mother."

"Mother, tell Sonya to put the engagement ring on her right hand I will transfer it to her left after I put the wedding band on her finger," Adam changed the subject.

"Adam," Agnes replied, "where is your class ring and your wedding band?"

"I don't wear rings," he replied. "My class ring is on display at the Alumni House in Annapolis. I decided to donate it before I misplaced it."

"You should wear a wedding band!" Agnes complained.

"Tell Sonya she can use the figurative ring in my nose. It's always gotten you what you wanted!"

"Only when you were close enough for me to tweak your nose," she shot back. She kissed him on the cheek and added, "I'm going to get the Bride. Brian, you know where to take him." She hurried off.

There were about fifty people in their seats. An organ was playing in the background. Adam and Brian took their places. The organist began playing the Wedding March. Cecilia came down the aisle, followed by Sandra Scott and then the Bride, dressed in a pale blue strapless gown with a matching veil covering her head and shoulders. The veil was shear and Adam could make out Sonya's features through the veil.

Where had he seen that dress? In his mother's wedding album. She had conned Sonya into wearing her wedding gown. However, it was beautiful and it wasn't white. For a moment, he wondered why his mother hadn't worn white at her wedding. The ceremony was in full progress. As soon as her father said, "I now pronounce you man and wife, you may kiss the bride." Adam lifted her veil.

They simultaneously whispered, "I love you," followed by a tender kiss. It was as though it had been rehearsed. It hadn't been.

They departed in a limousine. The guests at the wedding were all invited to the reception. There was no need to delay the trip to Army-Navy.

When they arrived at the Club House, Sonya went to change her dress. She wrapped the wedding dress carefully. Cecilia would take care of getting it back to Georgetown. Adam remained in his uniform to be sure there was someone in the ballroom to meet the guests. The bar was open. Cocktails were served until the reception line was closed. Everyone sat down to dinner.

A disco was available for dancing during and after dinner. Shortly after dessert was served, Adam and Sonya got up to dance. After dancing, the newlyweds made the rounds of all the guests and then prepared to leave. Brian had driven Adam's Mustang rental to Army-Navy.

When Adam didn't take the Bolling Air Force Base turn off of I-395, Sonya asked where they were going.

Annapolis," he replied.

"Why Annapolis?" she asked.

"Did you look at your rings?" he asked.

"Yes, I love my rings. The stone is beautiful," she replied.

"Did you read the inscription around the crown?"

"No, I didn't have my glasses. I didn't want you to know your wife is nearly blind. I was afraid you would back out at the last minute."

"It says U.S. Naval Academy, Class of 1958," Adam replied. "We are going to spend our wedding night in the Severn Suite of the Naval Academy BOQ. It's not as nice as a Bridal Suite in the Willard, but it's a lot more private!"

"I like private!" she responded.

Adam drove directly to Gate eight at the Academy. The Marine Guard saw his one-star shoulder board and saluted. "I have your room packet General McGregor. Just a moment." He retrieved the packet and saluted again. Adam returned his salute and drove on to the BOQ.

The building was dark except for the entrance. Adam retrieved the key from the packet along with two small bags. Sonya reached to get two packages that were gift wrapped.

"Do we need those?" Adam asked.

"These packages have my negligee and your pajamas. Your mother insisted on buying them."

"I know," he replied. "We'll keep them for when she comes to visit or when we stop at her place with Carol Agnes. I'm used to your naked body. I avoid unnecessary change!"

They went in the door and up the stairs. The lights were on in the hallways. They proceeded to the third flight. The Severn Suite was the first room at the top of the stairs. Adam opened the door and invited Sonya.

"Aren't you going to carry me over the threshold?" she asked with feigned disappointment.

"Everything in its appointed time," he said. He turned on the lights. They were standing in a large room with a table and chairs in one end and a sitting room and a television at the other end. There was a kitchenette near the table. Adam opened the door to the bedroom. He turned on the bedroom lights and swept Sonya up in his arms and carried her into the bedroom.

Adam laid Sonya on the bed and proceeded to take off his uniform. Sonya stood up and unzipped her dress and took it off. She turned down the bed prior to unsnapping her bra. Adam noticed that her bra, panties, garter belt and stockings were all matching pale blue.

"I liked your choice of color for the wedding. Did Mother push her wedding dress on you?"

"Not at all. I just tried it and it fit perfectly. I didn't want a white dress. They're for virgins and first time weddings. I loved the blue color" she concluded.

"The blue color matched your eyes and set off your hair perfectly. You may be on your second marriage, but you couldn't have been more beautiful at your first," he said.

Thank you, Darling," she responded. "Flattery will get you everything you want in this marriage."

They finished undressing and met in the bed. They made love passionately until they were completely exhausted and then fell asleep.

Adam awoke at seven am. He took a shower and then aroused Sonya. She showered while Adam was settling the bill. They were ready to depart by nine-thirty. They arrived in Georgetown by ten-thirty. Cecilia made brunch for them. As soon as they could break away they left for Washington National. Adam turned in his car and they caught the first flight to JFK. They were in plenty of time to catch a direct flight to Cairo on TWA departing at four pm. They would arrive in Cairo around ten am local on Sunday.

CHAPTER 20

Adam asked Sonya if she wanted to go by St. Mathews. They would be in time for the eleven am service. She hesitated for some time before responding.

"I would rather wait until later. I'm sure that there are a lot of parishioners who will be aghast at my remarriage so soon after John's death. I need to be well rested for that first encounter. Do you know the name of the new pastor?"

"No, I don't," Adam responded. "Mustafa, take us directly to the apartment."

"Aiwa." Mustafa responded.

Sunday was a regular work day and the traffic was horrific. It took over an hour to get to Swiss Air. As soon as all the bags were in the apartment, Adam took a shower while Sonya unpacked her bags. She had purchased an entire wardrobe during her four days in Washington. It was wonderful having so many new outfits.

They had lunch sent up from the restaurant at noon. After lunch, Adam departed for the Embassy. Sonya noted that it was the first time they had been separated since their wedding. For a moment, she shuddered with fear that she might lose another husband. Her negative thoughts were interrupted by the ringing of the phone.

"Hello," she answered.

"Hello, Mrs. McGregor?   This is Lydia Sanford.   My husband, Don, is the Naval Attache'.   We were hoping that you and Adam were feeling up to coming to Maadi for dinner this evening. I will invite the entire office staff so that you can meet them.   If you are too tired from your trip, we can delay it until later."

"I was planning to take a nap," Sonya replied.   "I should be rested. If Adam can handle it, I certainly can. I would love to get out of the apartment for a couple of hours.   My memories of this apartment are rather frightening.   Let me talk to Adam and I'll call you right back."

"Don has discussed it with Adam and Adam left it up to you," Lydia responded.

"Then, as the pilots say, we're good to go," Sonya answered. "What time?"

"Around six," Lydia replied.

"We'll be there. Goodbye."

"Goodbye," Lydia said, and they hung up.

Adam arrived at the apartment a little after four. It was very quiet.   He assumed Sonya was napping.   He tip-toed into the bedroom. The bed was turned down. Sonya was laying on her side dressed in a robe. She stirred as Adam removed his clothes. As he turned to crawl into bed, she rolled on her back, spread her legs and opened her robe.

"What, no foreplay?"

"We don't have time, Darling. We're due in Maadi at six, she whispered as she reached for his erection and guided it into her vagina. After they climaxed, Adam began to raise up. Sonya held on to him. They dozed for a little while. At four-forty five, the alarm went off. They awoke with a start.

"What's that alarm doing on?" Adam asked.

"I wanted to be sure we had time to shower and get to the Sanford's by six.   If we're late they'll be whispering about us newlyweds."

They went into the shower together and bathed each other. "How did you know we would make love?" Adam asked.

"I didn't, Darling. We didn't have a nooner, and if we are ever going to make up for the months we lost, we'll just have to double up on the days we're together."

"I'm married to a sex maniac!" he said.

"Are you bragging or complaining?" she replied.

"That's my line," he said as he took her in his arms and kissed her with the shower pouring over their heads. She pushed away and said, "Are you trying to drown me?"

"No, I just wanted you to know that you're not safe from kissing and loving anywhere."

She kissed him again and jumped out of the shower. He stayed in and shaved. When he came out, Sonya was already half dressed. Her blond hair was nearly dry. The natural curls were forming as she brushed them.

They dressed casually as they expected to be having cocktails in the garden. Adam described the Sanford's house while they finished dressing.

"Now that I'm married, we could move to the Maadi house if you want to take over the Defense Attache's entertaining responsibilities," Adam commented while they waited for Mustafa to arrive.

"What would they do?" she asked, referring to the Sanford family that included two teenagers, one boy and one girl and two younger children.

"The Embassy would have to find them a house," Adam replied.

A horn beeped once. Mustafa was in the parking lot. They dropped the housing subject while they rode to Maadi. They arrived precisely at six-thirty pm. Adam instructed Mustafa to return at eleven pm.

The Sanford's had invited the entire Defense Attache's Office staff. Colonel Pete Marshall was the Army Attache'. His spouse had returned to the States for personal family reasons. Bobby Sanford, aged 13, was next followed by his sister, Ellen, aged 15. Warrant Officer, Ed Charles, and his wife, Emma, managed the Defense Attache's Office. Captain Sanford's secretary and her husband were next, followed by Colonel Marshall's secretary. Three NCO's representing the three services were there with two wives, one being a bachelor. Finally Sonya met the cook, Abdul and the sufragi (or house boy) named Mohammad.

Lydia Sanford then took Sonya on a tour of the house. It was a two story house with a detached double garage. The downstairs included a large kitchen, which Lydia explained was the exclusive territory of Abdul. The dining room had a table that could seat sixteen. There was a large sitting room and a closed-in sun porch. Upstairs, there was a large master bedroom with a large bathroom attached. There were three other bedrooms and a large common bathroom. All the floors were marble. The entire house was air conditioned. It was obvious that Lydia Sanford was expecting the General to expropriate the Defense Attache's quarters.

They returned to the patio and Adam took Sonya on a tour of the garden where there were all manner of plants. There was a row of banana trees along the far wall. The garden was surrounded by an eight foot wall. The top of the wall was covered with shards of broken glass. Large clumps of Poinsettia's, six feet high, lined the walls. Lydia explained that the Poinsettia's bloomed nearly all year. They returned to the bar area and Sonya refreshed her glass of wine. Then she took Adam outside. She gave him a short synopsis of her tour.

"Do you want to move out here?" Adam asked.

"Adam, it's lovely. If we were going to be here for two or three years, I would want to move. We are newlyweds. I love the privacy of the apartment and soon I'll have Carol Agnes. I'll be very busy and I want to travel with you at every opportunity."

"Fine, we'll stay in the apartment," he concluded. Sonya sought out Lydia again.

"Could we go back inside for a moment?" Sonya asked. They went into the screened in porch.

"Did you want to see some rooms again?" Lydia asked.

"Lydia," Sonya began, "we will be going to Minnesota in December to collect our baby. Truly, she will be newly born as she was only conceived in April. We will be returning to the States in late June next year. In addition to that, we are newlyweds. Could I possibly impose on you to continue to bear the burden of entertaining for the Office. I know I'm shirking my responsibilities, but I feel that I'm not prepared to take over here."

"What a lovely way of telling me I don't have to move." Both women laughed and hugged.

Don Sanford entered, "When are we eating?"

"I'll check with Abdul," Lydia replied as Sonya slipped out into the garden.

"When are we moving?" Don asked.

"We're not!" Lydia exclaimed. "I'll tell you about it later." She hurried off to the kitchen.

CHAPTER 21

Sonya enjoyed her freedom. She went riding or swimming during the day and accompanied Adam to various dinners at night. They made love every night possible. There was seldom time for love in the afternoon. The exception was Friday. That was the Muslim sabbath. On Fridays, they would lie in bed until mid-morning. Adam would run past his office to check messages before noon and then they would swim at the Meridien or play golf at the Pyramid golf course. Occasionally they would ride together at one of the stables out by the Pyramids.

Sonya found an Arabian Stallion she really liked. Adam agreed to make arrangements for her to have exclusive use of the horse until June. Rubayah, the owner of the stable, wanted a thousand dollars for the exclusive use of the horse and Sonya would have to provide for the horse's feed at fifty dollars a month. Sonya was ecstatic. Rubayah had promised to return the thousand dollars when Sonya released the horse. That evening Sonya repeated the deal to Adam. Adam agreed to the deal.

"However," he said. "Don't expect to get all of the thousand back."

"Rubayah said he would," she replied.

"Honey," Adam answered, "Rubayah and his forbearer's have

been trading horses for a thousand years. He will find a reason to back out when that time comes."

"Then you don't want me to purchase him?" she complained.

"No, go ahead. When June comes, I'll help you negotiate," Adam concluded.

They dressed for a cocktail party at the Australian Embassy on Sunday. Pete Marshall was at the function and he informed Adam that Tom Carson had called and requested that Adam bring Spar 80 to Khartoum for another trip to Juba. Adam phoned Captain Baldwin to alert him to the need to go to Khartoum.

"It's in the works General," Dave responded. "We'll be ready to go by eight am tomorrow. We have all kinds of seats. Does Sonya want to go?"

"She has asked to go. She wants to see Tom and Marty. We'll meet you at the airplane."

"There are some other aspects to the trip. I'll let you know all about it at the airplane, Sir," Dave added. Adam hung up and returned to the party.

"We're going to Khartoum in the morning," he whispered to Sonya.

"Wonderful! Can I go, too?" she exclaimed.

"Yes, you can," Adam responded. "We will be going to Juba on Tuesday. I don't know who all will be traveling with us. You may have to stay in Khartoum with Marty. Tom will definitely go to Juba with us. We'll sort everything out tomorrow when we arrive in Khartoum."

Adam and Sonya left the party early. They returned to the apartment. Adam ordered two dinners from the restaurant. By the time they had set the table and opened a bottle of wine the dinners arrived. They enjoyed their meal. While Sonya cleared the table and washed the glasses and silverware, Adam called the Mayo Clinic to check on Carol Agnes.

"How's our baby doing?" Sonya asked.

"She is doing fine," Adam responded.

Adam was unusually quiet as they prepared for bed. They made love as usual. Other than kissing and caressing, nothing was said. They both laid on their backs, catching their breath.

"Are you concerned about this trip, Adam?" she asked with a

whisper.

"Dave said there were some aspects of the trip that he didn't want to discuss over the phone. He'll bring me up to date in the morning."

"Does he not want me along?"

"No. The first thing he said was there were plenty of seats if you wanted to go."

"It's too bad Marianne isn't back," Sonya commented.

"I don't think Marianne is coming back," Adam volunteered. "I think she's getting a divorce."

Sonya raised up and leaned over Adam. "What a mistake!" She kissed him tenderly. "Good night, Darling. I love you."

"I love you, too," he answered.

The next morning they were at the airport and ready to go by eight o'clock. There were only the two pilots and Sonya. Sonya took a seat just behind the cockpit where she could see her husband. They made the usual refueling stop in Luxor. Sonya slept most of the way to Khartoum.

Tom Carson met the airplane as usual. They went to the Carson's quarters immediately. Marty Carson was there to welcome the newlyweds. She swept Sonya off to the guest bedroom for some girl talk.

"Sonya, you look wonderful. What's with the curly hair?"

"They kept my head shaved while I was in the coma. I had a couple of holes where they relieved pressure from internal bleeding. Of course, I was a vegetable. One day, I woke up. It was shortly after Adam made the decision to take our baby by C-Section. I have a terrible scar and curly hair. Also, no more bikini swimsuits for me!"

"And the baby?" Marty questioned.

"Carol Agnes is doing fine. We call every other day when we are in Cairo. She is gaining weight and we will probably be able to bring her to Cairo by Christmas.

"How did you come by Carol Agnes for names?" Marty asked.

Sonya explained the grandmother's connections.

"When was the C-Section performed?"

"The second of July," Sonya answered.

"When was the baby conceived?" Marty asked.

"In April," Sonya replied with an impish grin.

"That's before you came to go to El Fasher," Marty responded. "How long had you known Adam when you got pregnant?"

"I need to get this off my chest," Sonya began. "My husband stopped having sex with me after my second pregnancy. He believed sex was evil except for procreation. We were staying at the Meridien and I was taking advantage of the pool. I saw this guy, Adam, swimming laps. He was beautiful. He never looked at me. Two days before we were to move to our apartment, Adam took the room next to ours. He bought a basket of flowers with a card with the Olsen's name on it. I thought it was our room. I went in and there was Adam in a bath robe. He cut the strings on my bikini and pushed me onto the bed. I thought he was going to rape me. Strangely, I didn't fight it. He is a marvelous lover. He produced a bikini to replace the one he had ruined. I promised to return it the next day. When I did, we made love again. I told him I would never see him again. The next day, I stopped to say we were leaving the hotel. He had ordered lunch. We made love again and I said goodbye forever, thinking he was leaving Cairo. The next evening we were invited to the Embassy. Here was Adam in uniform. I was devastated. The next thing I knew, my husband had volunteered me for the trip to Geneina," she finished with a sigh, and then added, "How long did I know Adam before I conceived? Somewhere between a couple of minutes and three days. I think he knocked me up on the first encounter!"

"How did you know?" Marty pried.

"I had my first hint of morning sickness before we left Khartoum to return to Cairo."

"Did he believe you?"

"I didn't tell him until we slipped off to Cypress. By that time, he had asked me to get a divorce and marry him."

"Is Adam absolutely convinced that he is the father?" Marty asked.

"Yes, the blood tests on the baby confirmed that he is the father. Since my husband was dead, Adam was able to claim me as a common-law spouse. That gave him status to make the decisions."

There was a knock on the door. "What is it?" Marty asked.

"It's time for cocktails. We thought you guys were dead," Tom replied.

"We'll be right out," Marty responded.

"Sometimes I feel terribly guilty," Sonya stated.

"You couldn't have foreseen the terrorist attack," Marty interjected. "You weren't suppose to die."

"Thank you, Marty, I needed that," Sonya whispered.

They joined Adam, Tom and Dave on the veranda. Tom mixed drinks for the ladies.

"Tell us, Adam," Sonya began, "are we staying here or are we going to Juba?"

"Tom says we are all invited. The Ambassador and his wife are both going," Adam continued. "The Ambassador's wife wants some company."

"Is Juba a good place to shop?" Sonya asked.

"Only if you are looking for African made goods," Tom Carson volunteered. "Whatever is sold in Juba is made in Juba or very close by."

"What about Derek Douglas?" Dave Baldwin interjected.

"Haven't seen hide nor hair of Derek since our last trip," Tom replied. "He's probably out in the bush somewhere."

The evening came to a close and all were up early the next morning. Ambassador Barton and wife, Amy arrived at the airplane a short time after the Attache's and wives had arrived.

Amy Barton looked at Sonya.

"Haven't we met before?" she asked.

"Yes, Mrs. Barton," Sonya replied. "We were together on a trip to Darfur. I'm married to General McGregor now. It's a long story." Marty came to the rescue.

"Amy," she said quietly, "You remember I told you about the girl in the coma? That was Sonya."

"Oh, of course," Amy Barton replied. "I'm sorry, Sonya. I know all about the terrible problems. I just hadn't thought about it for some time and I didn't make the connection. How are you?"

"I'm fine now, although, I was in a coma for a long time. They do marvelous things at the Mayo Clinic."

Their conversation was interrupted by an invitation to board the aircraft. Ambassador Barton, Tom Carson and Adam were the last to board. They were engaged in conversation at the left wing tip.

Ambassador Barton spoke, "The reason I asked you to come down, Adam, is because we need to get Tyler Gordon and his wife, Ann, out of Juba. The CIA informed me that the regime in Khartoum is convinced that the AID mission is abetting the civil war in the south. They are spreading a rumor that the AID Mission works for Khartoum. The rebels are ready to wipe out our mission. Every one in the mission has departed except for Tyler and Ann. I have reservations for two nights for all of us at the hotel. We'll have dinner with the Gordon's at the hotel tonight. We'll spread the word that we are going to the Gordon's for dinner tomorrow night and leaving the next morning. Tomorrow morning I want all the ladies to go shopping in the Souk. Brigadier Adam Boutros will pick up the ladies about ten-thirty. The three of us will be with Tyler. We'll all head for the aircraft to arrive at eleven am. Captain Baldwin will be at the aircraft ready to crank engines as soon as we arrive. Leave your bags and toiletries in the hotel. The Gordon's are leaving every thing. I've already paid for two nights at the hotel. Any questions?"

"Why are the ladies here?" Adam asked.

"To lend credence that this is just a shopping trip. We are all volunteers in a plot to save the Gordon's. Sorry I couldn't give you an opportunity to back out."

"Works for me!" Adam said "Let's go through Rub Kona and top off the tanks. That way we'll have enough gas to get out if they refuse to sell us Jet A-l." They all nodded in the affirmative and boarded Spar 80.

As soon as they got airborne, Adam told Dave to put on his headset. Adam briefed Captain Baldwin on the entire mission and the need to make everyone act as though they were staying a second night.

"What do you think, Dave?" Adam asked after he had finished.

"As we would say in Nam, shit hot!" Dave replied. "The bad guys shouldn't read through it, particularly since we aren't returning to the hotel to retrieve bags."

They stopped at Rub Kona for fuel. When they landed at Juba, Adam and Dave noted the fuel readings. They had enough to get to Khartoum. Adam suggested that they forget about fuel lest they give the ground crews the impression that they might be in a hurry to leave.

Fortunately, their accommodations were much better than on their previous visit. Each couple had a suite with a private bath. All the rooms were on the ground floor. They had high ceilings and well screened windows with good cross ventilation. The air conditioner in the window was not capable of maintaining a cool temperature. The room had two twin beds.

"Which bed do you want?" Adam asked.

"Which ever one you're going to sleep in," Sonya replied.

"Aren't you going to be too hot," Adam replied.

"I'd rather sweat a little than be out of touch with you when the lights go off."

"Let's try one bed before we take a shower," Adam suggested. "You realize that we will be accused of making love whether we do or not. It goes with being newlyweds."

"You're right," she said emphatically as she turned her back to Adam. "Unzip me please."

He unzipped her dress. She stepped out of it and quickly pulled the covers down on the nearest bed. She released her bra, peeled off her panties, and laid on the bed welcoming him with outstretched arms.

"What no foreplay?" he asked.

"It's too hot for foreplay," she said. "Besides I don't recall you ever being big on going slow."

They made love passionately. By the time they had both climaxed they were perspiring from head to toe. They laid side by side on the tiny bed and slept deeply for nearly a half hour.

"What?" he asked with a start.

"The sun is going down," she responded. "We need to shower and dress or we'll be late."

The sun crashed and in less than a minute the room was pitch black. Adam quickly got lights on and ushered Sonya to the bathroom. She showered quickly and left it running for Adam. They were both finished in twenty minutes. They closed up the room and turned on the air, hoping it would cool a bit by the time they returned. As they entered the dining room, they saw the group of seven seated at a long table.

"Here come the newlyweds," Marty Carson cried out. "We thought you were going to pass on dinner."

"Yes," Ann Gordon chimed in, "It's to hot for making love. What were you doing?"

Ambassador Barton chimed in, "How long have you been married, Adam?"

"Let's see," Adam responded. "It will be two weeks on Friday."

"No wonder you're late," Amy Barton said, "We're lucky you're here at all. You should be on your honeymoon."

"We are," Sonya replied, "and we're gong to be on it as long as we keep going to exotic places." She turned and kissed Adam and added, "Eat your heart out girls!"

Amy Barton said, "Make it last as long as you can, Sonya."

"I intend to do just that," Sonya replied.

The ladies planned their shopping tour for the next day. Ann Gordon suggested that she meet Marty, Amy and Sonya at the hotel for coffee around eight-thirty. They could walk to the Souk in ten minutes and they would have a couple of hours to browse before the heat would get intense.

The party broke up shortly after the dessert and after dinner drinks. The Gordon's left for their quarters. Sonya yawned.

Marty laughed. "Oh, oh, Sonya is tired, Adam. I think she needs to go to bed."

"Marty," Sonya said, "You're supposed to be my friend. You know how exhausting travel can be."

"Of course, I do dear. It's particularly exhausting when you're in a different bed every night," Marty concluded with a wicked smirk on her face.

Sonya stuck her tongue out at Marty and grabbed Adam's arm, tugging him toward their room. As soon as they had brushed their teeth and stripped off their clothes, they tried the other bed.

"Marty," Tom Carson scolded, "Why are you picking on Sonya. You're supposed to be her friend."

"Don't worry, Tom," Marty replied, "That girl is so much in love that she doesn't care what anyone says as long as it doesn't harm her husband."

Amy Barton concurred. They all finished their drinks and

went to bed.

The next morning everyone gathered in the dining room for coffee and pastry. The ladies departed for the Souk for their shopping tour. When they were out of earshot of any strangers, Ann Gordon asked them to gather around her.

"Ladies," she began, "Around ten-thirty, a gentleman from the Sudanese Army will arrive to gather us up. We must climb right into the Land Rover as quickly as possible. The driver knows where to take us. Sonya, you're the youngest and most agile. Please get in first and climb to the other side. I'll sit up front with the driver. Amy and Marty, follow Sonya into the back.

"It sounds mysterious," Sonya commented.

"Not really," Ann lied. "We are due to meet our husbands at eleven, and we must not be late."

The ladies wandered through the shops. All of East Africa was represented. One shop had brightly colored fabrics from the Central African Republic. There were cured meats from Kenya. Some were beef and water buffalo. Others were from more exotic animals. One shop, run by Ethiopians, had exotic masks carved out of ebony. Nothing was expensive by Western standards. Everyone collected some souvenirs. At the end of the shopping area, they came to the Nile. Hippos were basking in the river. They looked like gigantic rocks floating in the river until their heads would come up to take a breath.

Ann turned them around and they headed back through the Souk. They came to a crossroad where a number of Africans were gathered. They were mostly Dinkas and Masai, according to Ann Gordon. None were Sudanese Muslims.

One of the native women was chanting in a falsetto voice. Ann realized in a moment that her chant was in English. She was singing, "We all love Numerie." Her tone and attitude dripped of sarcasm. A desert tan Land Rover suddenly appeared. The four women went directly to the Rover and climbed aboard as directed.

"Ladies, this is Brigadier Adam Boutros. He's been good enough to pick us up."

The ladies all acknowledged General Boutros and he responded by thanking them for being on time. They sped off toward the airport.

Meanwhile, Ambassador Barton, Tyler Gordon, and Adam were leaving the Gordon residence for the airport. They left the servants busy preparing the evening meal.

Both vehicles arrived at the airport a few minutes before eleven. Brigadier Boutros flashed an airport pass and instructed the guard to let the second vehicle follow him. They went directly to Spar 80, where Captain Baldwin was starting the right engine.

The passengers got out of the vehicles and moved to the airplane. Adam led the way and opened the entrance door. He instructed everyone to take a seat and strap in. Adam waved at General Boutros who had parked the Land Rover and was departing the airport in the Gordon's car. Adam closed the entrance door and moved up the aisle to the co-pilot seat. Dave Baldwin had the left engine started as he asked for taxi instructions. The tower cleared Spar 80 for take off.

"Spar 80, what's your destination?"

"Spar 80 is en route to Khartoum," Adam responded as they broke ground. As soon as the gear and flaps were up, Adam got out of his seat and went back to the cabin.

"I hope no one left the family jewels behind due to this sudden departure. However, it was necessary to get the Gordon's out of town. The most urgent question now is how many of you ladies need to go to the the lavatory?"

All four raised their hands. Adam went back to the little door by the entrance.

"It's not big, but it works. As soon as you've relieved yourselves, perhaps we can get Ambassador Barton to brief you on the need for this mission." He opened the door to the little bathroom. Adam made his way back to the cockpit.

"By the way," Adam added, "we are going to stay at low level across the Sud. You might look out the windows and see if you can pick up any exotic animals. We'll be stopping at Rub Kona in about three hours."

When everyone was settled in their seats, Ambassador Barton gave the women a short run down on the need to shut down the USAID Program in Juba. "Thanks to Adam Boutros, we learned that someone in Khartoum was spreading a rumor that the AID mission was supporting the insurrection in the south. At the same time another rumor was spreading in Juba. That rumor purported that the AID Mission was working for the Numerie Government against the possible insurrection. Washington decided it was time to get the AID mission out of country. Two families left on legitimate emergency leaves. Last week, Tyler's deputy and his wife went to visit the Karras' Coffee Plantation. They slipped over the border into Kenya. They're awaiting reassignment in Nairobi. Washington asked me to see if I could get Tyler and Ann out at the last minute. The Juba shopping trip was our ruse to drop in and slip out with the Gordon's. I apologize for the inconvenience and the loss of property abandoned. We didn't want to take a chance on losing someone."

"All's well that ends well!" Marty Carson interjected. Everyone nodded their agreement.

Adam and Dave kept the C-12 at about fifteen-hundred feet above the Savanna. It was high enough to allow them to scan in all directions and still be safe from detection from above. If the Khartoum Government was spreading false rumors about USAID, they might send a couple of Mig-21's out to intercept Spar 80. The low level flight would be safe to Rub Kona. They would fly on to Khartoum at night. The Sudanese did not fly their fighter aircraft at night—too many accidents.

As far as sight-seeing went, they did see a herd of Thompson Gazelles and a pride of lions enjoying the remains of some large animal.

At Rub Kona, they stopped into the base operations, used the facilities, had coffee, and generally wasted time. They finally departed fifteen minutes before sundown. They landed at Khartoum without incident.

Ambassador Barton thanked Adam for the support and the aircraft. He mentioned that he and Tyler Gordon went back a long way. Adam had suspected that the Ambassador had a link to the CIA in the past.

Adam, Sonya, the Carsons and David went to the villa to spend the evening. They had cocktails and dinner and turned in around ten pm.

Sonya spoke, "When did you know we were on a rescue mission?"

"The Ambassador briefed Tom and me just before we left

Khartoum. I briefed Dave on the flight to Rub Kona. Ann Gordon knew about the timing."

"Why didn't you tell the rest of us?" Sonya asked.

"You didn't have a need to know," Adam replied.

"Our lives might be in danger and we didn't have a need to know?" she questioned abruptly.

"Yes, my Darling. Everyone who knew about the timing had a specific critical mission. I had to know because of the airplane. David had to know because he had to be at the airplane ready to start engines. The Ambassador knew because he was directed to get the Gordon's out of Juba ASAP. Ann Gordon had to know because it was critical that you left the Souk with Brigadier Boutros on time. You three ladies were window dressing. It was absolutely necessary for you to act as you did. You all played your parts beautifully."

"Oh, I see," Sonya replied. "We were shills, but didn't know it."

"Do you think you could have played your parts as well had you known it was a ruse?" Adam asked.

Sonya was completely silent for quite a long time. Finally she spoke.

"My first inclination is to accuse you of not trusting me. I remembered how nonchalantly we wondered through the shops never looking at our watches, never glancing around to see if anyone was watching us. Ann Gordon played her part wonderfully. She kept us moving. I never saw her look at her watch. She was the perfect hostess. God, you live an exciting life!" She rolled over on top of his chest and kissed him passionately.

"I think I can go to sleep now," she whispered. "I love you more every day."

The next day they returned to Cairo. It was Thursday, October fifth. Adam went to work at the normal time. Emma Charles brought him up to date on the activities of the previous four days. Adam completed his after-action report on the trip to Juba and sent it off to DIA. He called a staff meeting.

The subject of the meeting was the Sixth of October Military Parade, scheduled for the next day. The parade commemorates the date that the Egyptian Army had invaded the Sinai in an effort to take it back from Israel. Even though the eventual outcome was a loss with the Sinai returning to Israeli control, Egypt celebrated the date as a victory.

The entire Military Attache' Corp in Cairo was invited to view the parade along with diplomats from every Embassy. The parade would feature units from every branch of the Egyptian Defense establishment. For the first time, the Military Attache' spouses were invited to the parade with their husbands.

Colonel Marshall had coordinated the expected activities with the Military Police. He explained the seating and parking arrangements. The parade was scheduled to begin at noon. Everyone was expected to be in their seats no later than eleven-thirty. No one would be admitted to the parade area after President Sadat and his Cabinet arrived in the reviewing area.

Warrant Officer Charles briefed the Attache's on travel arrangements. Mustafa would pick up Adam and Sonya at ten-thirty. The other two drivers would pick up the group from Maadi at the same time. He also read a message from DIA that requested maximum photography. He passed out cameras and three rolls of film to each Attache'. He reminded everyone, that starting the next day, there would be a four day Egyptian holiday. Except for hotels, the whole country would be shutdown. Adam asked if there were any questions. There were none.

"There are no scheduled events for tonight. We'll meet here briefly after the parade, turn in our exposed film to Gunnery Sergeant Olisen and hopefully have a nice holiday. If anyone goes out of town, leave a contact number here in the office. See you Tuesday."

Adam called Sonya to tell her he would be taking the afternoon off. "How would you like to go riding?" he asked.

"I'd love to go riding," she responded.

"Pack us a change of clothes. I'll get us a reservation at the Mina House. We'll stay overnight. We can eat Indian Cuisine. It's excellent."

"Sounds marvelous. I'll be ready when you get here," Sonya concluded.

They said goodbye and Adam told Emma Charles where he could be reached. Emma called the Mina House for his reservation while Adam was closing up his office.

Adam went by the Commissary on his way to the car. He

bought toiletries to replace the things they had left in the Juba Hilton. He figured if he forgot anything, they could buy it at the Mina House. Sonya met him at the door of the apartment.

"Adam, we left our toiletries in Juba," she said.

"I went by the commissary," he said, as he held up his shopping bag. "If it isn't in here, we'll buy it at the Mina House. Bring our swim suits and we'll use their pool after our ride."

"I packed them. Great minds run together," she commented.

They drove to the stable. Sonya's horse, Abul Kheer, was happy to see her. She fed him a carrot. Rubayah's nephew, Ishmael saddled Abul Kheer. He brought out another stallion named Ibn Bint Mahassen. That translated to the son of the daughter of Mahassen. The two stallions wanted to fight. Sonya and Adam were good riders and the horses gave up their animosity as the riders kept them apart. They rode out on the desert, just south of the Pyramids of Giza. They would be able to see the two largest Pyramids on their entire ride. They rode for nearly two hours, galloping for short periods. The horses seemed to enjoy the workout as much as the riders.

After the ride, they went directly to the Mina House. They checked into their room, donned swimming suits and went to the pool. After several laps they found two lounge chairs and stretched out to get some sun. Sonya noticed two women watching her. Sonya thought they were noticing that she was the only one at the pool in a one piece suit. Most of the women were in bikinis. Finally, one of the women came over to where Adam and Sonya were laying.

"Pardon me," the woman began, "are you related to Sonya Olsen? You look just like her."

"I'm Sonya," she replied.

"We thought you committed suicide," the woman continued.

"Oh, no!" Sonya laughed. "I accidentally fell off a balcony. I was paralyzed for almost five months."

"You used to wear a bikini, didn't you?" the woman pried on.

"Yes. I had a Cesarean section birth several months ago and I have a rather ugly scar," Sonya responded. "Are you a member at St. Mathews Lutheran?"

"Yes, we finally have a new pastor," the woman answered. "We were devastated at the loss of your husband and two sons."

"I understand," Sonya replied. "I was watching television of the aftermath of the terrorist attack when I had my fall. After I recovered, I married again. This is my husband, Adam McGregor."

"Oh!" the woman replied. "That was quick." She realized her blunder and stammered as she tried to recover.

Sonya bailed her out. "Adam was responsible for getting me to the Mayo Clinic. You could say he saved my life."

"Yes, well congratulations," the woman responded. "I must go. You should join us at St. Mathews while you're in town. All your old friends would love to see you."

"We'll try to do that," Adam interrupted. "Now we had better go dress for dinner. Nice to meet you."

The woman backed away quickly and departed with the other woman. Adam and Sonya departed for their room. When they got to the elevator and the door closed behind them, they burst out laughing.

"Do you remember her?" Adam asked.

"Yes," Sonya replied. "She's a bit of a gossip."

"You just supplied her with a real juicy story. I would like to be a mouse in the corner while they work out the time line. Would you like to go back to St. Mathews?" Adam asked.

"I wouldn't mind it," Sonya replied.

"Why don't we surprise them and take Carol Agnes to St. Mathews when we pick her up," Adam stated.

They arrived at their floor and proceeded to the room. As soon as they were in the room, Sonya turned down the bed. She peeled off her swimsuit and laid out on the bed. She held out her arms to Adam. "Come see me," she said. They made love. Later they dined on spicy Lamb the specialty of the Indian Restaurant.

In the morning, Adam woke up first. He gently shook Sonya's arm until she opened her eyes. ""Good morning, Darling," he whispered as he kissed her gently. "We have a big day ahead of us. Let's get some breakfast. We can shower at the apartment before we dress for the parade."

"What! No loving?" she murmured.

"You're insatiable," he whispered.

"If I am, it's your fault, lover." She kissed him and rolled out of bed. In ten minutes they were ready to leave.

After breakfast, they drove to the apartment. Because of the holiday, there was little or no traffic. They arrived at the apartment in time to shower and dress. Adam was in his service uniform. His five rows of awards were just below his Command Pilot Wings. Sonya was dressed in a linen suit. It was blue and matched her eyes. Her short hair was all curls.

"You are beautiful!" Adam said.

"And you're handsome," she replied as she kissed him. She went to the bathroom and put on her lipstick.

They went out the back and found Mustafa waiting in the parking lot. The trip to the parade ground took thirty minutes. Mustafa parked just behind the amphitheater that was built up behind the reviewing stand. The whole area was covered with a cantilever roof which provided shade for those invited to the parade. There were two seating areas. On the right the seats were occupied by members, mostly Ambassadors, of the Diplomatic Corps. There were seventy-five Embassies in Cairo.

The military Attache's were seated on the left side. They were arranged alphabetically. This put the American Contingent just behind the United Kingdom. Only the Attache' from Zambia was further up. There were a total of sixty-one Embassies that had military Attache' Offices in Cairo.

Alistair and Wanda Ames were sitting directly in front of Adam and Sonya. "I understand we are having dinner with Sir William and Lady Agatha next week," Alistair remarked.

"Yes," Adam replied. "It's next Friday."

"Darling?" Sonya questioned, "am I invited?"

"Of course," Adam replied. "I forgot to bring the invitation home."

"This must be Sonya," Wanda Ames said as she extended her hand to Sonya. "I'm Wanda Ames. You'll love Lady Agatha."

"Oh!" Sonya replied. "I do love her. We met in Washington and she came to our wedding. I look forward to meeting Sir William."

"You will love him, too," Wanda replied. "The two of them play off each other in a remarkable way. It's fun to be around them."

They were interrupted by the arrival of the official reviewing party. It was led by President Anwar Sadat. He was accompanied by the Vice President and Commander of the Air Force, Lt. General

Hosni Mubarak. Third in line was Lt. General Abou Ghazala, Commander of the Army.

The parade was scheduled to begin at noon. All the units were lined up to the left. They were led by a special unit dressed in white kilts and berets. They were running in place in preparation for the start. Suddenly, six of the reviewing party formed up in a triangle behind President Sadat. They marched across the parade route to the Tomb of the Unknown Soldier. Sadat made a short speech which couldn't be heard and then laid a wreath at the tomb. By the time the reviewing party returned to their seats, the parade had been delayed by twenty minutes.

Various military aircraft were flying over the area, crossing the route at a right angle to the parade route and then disappearing above the roof of the reviewing stand. The air display was on time but the ground parade was late starting.

At last, the ground parade began. The special units were followed by contingents from the Military, Naval and Air Force Academies. They were followed by various Army units interspersed with tanks, armored cars, military trucks pulling artillery pieces and a motorcycle unit. Two of the motorcycles wouldn't run and they had to be pushed until they could be cleared from the parade route.

The four US Attache's continued to snap pictures of every vehicle, mostly Russian built, and every aircraft flying past. The parade was entering its third hour when the Egyptian Air Force aerobatic team appeared on the horizon. At the same time, the Egyptian Artillery was passing in review. Four trucks in line abreast were towing howitzers. Adam stood up to take a picture of the four Mirage jets as they passed over head. As he snapped the picture he saw the two trucks closest to the reviewing stand fall out of line as though an engine had failed. A man in the truck bed stood up with a rifle and fired at the reviewing stand. At the same time, a man jumped from the cab with a sub machine gun followed by another soldier from the truck bed. They attacked the reviewing stand, throwing four hand grenades, none of which went off. The machine gunners emptied their weapons into Anwar Sadat's body.

The Egyptian Colonel who had escorted the Attache's to their seats called for everyone to get down. Adam laid down and pulled Sonya down with him. When the firing stopped, Adam stood up and took the remaining frames left on his film. He snapped as fast as the automatic winder would forward the film. Suddenly, Mustafa appeared.

"General," Mustafa spoke, "I think we should leave." Mustafa had tears in his eyes. "The President is dead," he added.

They quickly crossed to the Salah Salem and headed for downtown. There was no traffic.

Sonya finally spoke, "Look at my dress, Adam. I felt a sting during the shooting." There was a blood spot on her dress over her right shoulder blade.

"Man you are really unlucky," he said with a grin.

"What do you mean?" she asked.

"I did two tours in South East Asia and never took a hit. You show up at your first fire fight and take a ricochet."

"Stop being funny," she replied.

"It's not serious, honey. We'll have the dispensary look at it to make sure there's no metal in the wound."

They went to the dispensary. While Sonya was being treated, word came down that the Ambassador had called a meeting of the Country Team. As the Defense Attache', Adam was automatically a member of the Country team. However, the Ambassador had invited all of the Attache's because they were all eye witnesses.

Adam suggested that Sonya go to the apartment. She did not want to go as she was not in the mood to be alone. Adam invited her to go with him since she was also an eye witness. When they arrived at the meeting, Adam explained Sonya's aversion to being alone. The Ambassador understood. The Ambassador opened the meeting by explaining that the Egyptian spokesman had indicated that President Sadat was seriously wounded but that he was alive.

Mr. Richardson, the number two man at CIA suggested that the Government was busy trying to determine the extent of the assassination plot. One of the political officers suggested that the attack was coordinated with the air show to coincide with the aerobatic team.

"That can't be," Adam interjected.

"Why not?" the Ambassador asked.

"I checked the published parade schedule," Adam began. "The aerobatic team was right on time. The ground parade was an hour and a half behind schedule. That was partially due to a late start when President Sadat took the time to lay the wreath at the tomb. Several vehicles stalled creating further delays."

A messenger entered the room with a note for the Ambassador.

"It appears that the BBC has reported that President Sadat is dead," the Ambassador announced. "Hosni Mubarak and Abou Ghazalla are both all right. Evidently, General Ghazalla was hit by one of the grenades the attackers threw. The grenades were evidently duds."

There was a moment of silence while the enormity of the assassination sunk in. The Ambassador broke the silence, "What I don't understand is why none of the Military Police surrounding the area never used their weapons."

Captain Sanford answered, "I posed that question to Colonel Akim, our host at the parade. He explained that the M.P.'s had pistols but no bullets. His boss, the Director of Intelligence, had spoken in favor of arming the M.P.'s with ammunition. He said that Sadat had insisted that no one in the parade should have ammo."

A second message arrived from Hosni Mubarak. Mubarak acknowledged that Sadat was dead. Mubarak had assumed the Presidency. The ring leader of the five assassins was in custody. He was a Lieutenant in the Army named Islamboli. An enlisted man was captured with him. Three others not military but members of the cabal were being sought. They were all dressed in military fatigues. The three missing men were not active duty military. They had melted into the crowd of military uniforms that had descended on the reviewing stand. The message concluded with a report of casualties among the spectators. Stray bullets had found eight diplomats. Two were seriously wounded. There were also two American Officers wounded. They were visiting from the Joint Staff of U.S. Forces, Europe, in Germany. One was an Air Force Lt. Colonel and the other a Marine Major. They were hit by ricochets as they were not in the line of fire. Those two officers were sitting two rows ahead of the UK delegation. A short time later they learned that a Chinese Diplomat had died and that the Charge' d'affaires from Australia was still in serious condition. The Ambassador adjourned the meeting.

Adam and Sonya, along with the other three Attache's went

over to their office where Sgt. Olisen was busy processing film. Most of the pictures confirmed the pandemonium at the scene of the assassination. The one photo of immediate interest showed a man shooting an Egyptian Officer. Adam made a note to show that photo to the Ambassador the next day. Adam suggested they all go home and plan to come in at nine am in the morning.

Mustafa had gone to the Swiss Air apartment and drove Adam's Corvette back to the Embassy. The car was parked in Adam's regular parking spot.

Adam and Sonya drove to the apartment. They went upstairs and had a drink, then went down to the restaurant to have dinner. They ordered drinks and perused the menu.

"I'm not hungry," Sonya whispered breaking the silence.

"Are you tired?" Adam asked.

"Exhausted," she replied.

"I'll order us a fillet and a salad," Adam stated. "We'll turn in as soon as we're finished."

"I don't think I can make love tonight," she added.

"It's not required. Everyone has a let down after their first firefight. It takes a change of venue to get the shooting out of one's mind. You'll be okay in a day or two."

"I hope so. Right now, I can't get it out of my mind." Their steaks arrived. Adam ordered two glasses of Bordeaux.

As soon as they got to the apartment, Adam picked up the phone and dialed the long distance operator. He gave the operator Dr. Snyder's number.

"Hello, Mayo Clinic, is Dr. Snyder available." The answer was affirmative.

"Hello, Adam," Dr. Snyder answered. "Dr. Kittleson is with me. We were just discussing your daughter. Were you anywhere near the shooting today?

"Unfortunately, yes," Adam replied.

"Well, we've got some good news for you. I'll put Dr. Kittleson on the line. She'll give you the latest on Carol Agnes."

"Just a second," Adam replied. "I want Sonya to hear this." He handed the phone to Sonya.

Sonya said, "Hello." She listened acknowledging occasionally with an affirmative reply. Finally she thanked the person and gave the phone to Adam. She disappeared into the bedroom.

Adam chatted with the doctors for a few minutes. The news was all good. He hung up and turned to look for Sonya. She appeared from the bedroom in a bathrobe. She came over to Adam and kissed him. "I changed my mind," she said. "I want to make love."

"What brought the sudden change?" Adam asked.

"As if you didn't know," Sonya shot back. "Carol Agnes is doing better than we could have expected. By the time she is eight months old she will be at normal weight. We can go get her before Christmas. I can quit taking the pill and get pregnant again. By the time Carol Agnes is fifteen months old we'll have a son. One year later we can have another and our family will be complete."

She waited several moments for a response. Finally she said, "Well, say something."

"I don't want to seem negative. Surely you realize that the odds of having another girl are quite high."

"If we have another girl," she began, then hesitated, "No, if I have two more girls then we'll try one more time. We'll have three girls and one boy or we'll have four girls. How's that." She waited for a reply. Adam sat with a smirk on his face.

"Say something!" she demanded.

"I'm getting accustomed to the long range planning. I've been accustomed to living day by day. I have no problem with your plan. One girl and two boys would be fine. Two girls and two boys would be fine. We could spread them out a little more to give you more time to recover between pregnancies. There's no danger of me running out of sperm." He didn't mention that they had a similar conversation earlier.

"Now you're making fun of me again," she stated.

"I'm not either," he replied. "Let's go do some practice breeding."

"Oh, we're not making love anymore."

"Darling, we're always making love when we're naked. That includes hugging, kissing and breeding or practice breeding."

They went to bed.

CHAPTER 22

Cairo was somewhat subdued after the assassination of Anwar Sadat. Initially there were a lot of rumors about a possible cabal within the government. There was a lot of pressure on the Muslim Brotherhood. The authorities failed to make a connection between the Brotherhood and the five assassins. The two captured at the parade soon turned in the other three co-conspirators. The three were picked up at their agreed rendezvous on the Western Desert west of Giza. It would be nearly a year before they were tried and executed. Lt. Islamboli and his enlisted colleague would face a firing squad. The three civilians would be hanged.

For Adam and Sonya, it was a relaxing time. Official Cairo was in an unofficial mourning period. This created a situation where no one wanted to appear to be pleased with the demise of Anwar Sadat. All the Embassies avoided big parties. This cut back on the social obligations of the Attache' community and left a lot more time for Adam and Sonya to enjoy their love affair.

All Egyptians were not unhappy with the demise of Sadat. Adam became aware of this at the Cairo Airport. He had stopped into the weather office to check weather prior to a flight to Israel. The weather briefer, an Egyptian, who had always been pleasant before made a belligerent comment.

"Your buddy, Sadat, finally got his, didn't he?" the man said in a surly manner.

Adam raised his eyebrows and asked for the weather in Tel Aviv. The man produced a weather sheet and walked away. Adam decided to let the remark pass. When he returned from Tel Aviv, he made a call to an old friend, Brigadier Wahid Fahta.

Wahid's wife answered the phone. They spoke in Arabic. Wahid's wife informed Adam that Wahid had retired and was presently managing a beach hotel in El Arish. She gave Adam a number to call.

Adam returned to the office at the Embassy. He had Emma make a reservation for Sonya and him at Wahid's hotel in El Arish. While she was making the reservation, Adam called his contact at Egyptian Military Intelligence and informed them that he was planing to go to El Arish for two days on the beach. He would be flying over on Wednesday morning and returning Thursday. Mrs. McGregor and Captain Baldwin would be traveling with him in Spar 80. He added that he might take some of his enlisted men and their wives along.

His contact made a check to see if there were any military exercises in progress. There were none. The trip was approved.

Adam checked with Captain Sanford. The Sanford's had a small dinner party planned for Wednesday. He checked with Colonel Marshall. He could go. Sgt. Olisen and his wife would also like to attend for a day on the beach. He called Sonya and told her to pack for the trip. They would need swimsuits and casual clothes.

Adam called Alistair Ames to let him know they would be gone overnight. They would be back for Lady Agatha's dinner party Friday night. Alistair asked if Adam had any open seats. Adam took the hint and invited Alistair and Wanda to join the trip.

Adam went home late afternoon intending to take Sonya out for diner. She surprised him. She was cooking dinner.

"I didn't know you could cook!" he said teasingly.

"Of course, I can cook," she responded. "All girls from Minnesota learn to cook by the time they are eighteen."

"What are we having?"

"Meat loaf," she replied.

"What if I don't like meat loaf."

"You told me once that you liked everything," she responded as she continued to busy herself. "If you don't like it, you can't make love to me tonight!"

"Oh, you're mean. Where did you buy the ground beef?"

"I bought everything at the Commissary. I even bought a bottle of red wine to go with dinner."

"I think I'm going to like the meat loaf. When are we eating?" Adam asked as he sneaked up behind Sonya and patted her on the butt. She squealed.

"Don't bother me while I'm cooking," she said sternly.

"Maybe I should hire a cook." he said.

She washed her hands, dried them and turned around. She kissed Adam passionately.

"You can hire a cook if you want. For tonight, though, you are going to eat meat loaf, like it or not."

"Okay! Can we make love?"

"No!" she replied. "I'm busy cooking. If you hire a cook, I still won't be able to make love because I'll be busy telling the cook what to do."

"Are you mad at me?" Adam asked seriously.

"No. You could have given me more warning about this trip, however."

"I need to go see a guy in El Arish," Adam replied.

"It's a terrible time to go to the beach."

"No, it isn't," Adam countered. "The Med will be warm enough to swim through mid-November."

"It's not the water. It's me. I'm having my period. We can't make love either."

"Why not?" he ask with a grin.

"Because it will make a terrible mess."

"We'll use a towel. Besides, I heard that sex during menstruation eases the discomfort."

"Just where did you hear that?"

"Around the locker room."

"The men's locker room or the women's locker room?"

"The men's," he replied grinning.

"I didn't realize men were experts on menstrual cramps." she opined.

"Some men are experts on everything."

"Are you one of those men?"

"Heavens no! I don't believe anything until I've tried it myself."

She was about to ask if he had experienced sex during menstruation. She decided she didn't want to know. They went to bed and made love, Sonya made one trip to the bathroom. She went in the dark preferring not to witness the results. She noted that her fear of the dark had subsided. She knew it was because Adam was nearby. It gave her a warm feeling.

Adam got up first in the morning. He went in the bathroom and took a shower. Sonya got up when she heard the shower running. She took one look at the bed and then rolled the sheet and the towel together and threw them in the garbage can.

Adam came out of the bathroom. He noticed the bed was made up. "Was it pretty bad?" he asked.

"It looked like we had slaughtered a sacrificial lamb," she replied. "My cramps are gone. I guess your source was right!"

"I don't think we can draw conclusions from one test," he said. "Why haven't you had a case like this before?"

She paused to think, then spoke. "When we first met, you got me pregnant. Then I had my fall. I was pregnant and paralyzed for four months. This is my first period since my recovery. That's why you have never seen Sonya, the bitch, before. Now, you'll have to put up with her once a month."

"Au contraire, my love. You forgot that according to your plan, you will be pregnant by Christmas. That means you won't have a period until October. By December next year you'll be pregnant again. So I'm looking at two periods a year until you are finished propagating the planet. I can handle it," Adam concluded.

"I love you, Darling," Sonya replied. "Let's go to the beach." They finished dressing and went out the back door. Mustafa was waiting. They picked up Alistair and Wanda at their apartment and headed for the airport. They arrived in El Arish before noon.

Their hotel was a nice new building. All of the rooms had balconies facing the Mediterranean As soon as they were settled in their rooms, the women donned swimsuits. Captain Baldwin and Sgt. Olisen joined the ladies. Adam, Alistair, and Pete Marshall went in search of Wahid Fatha.

They found him in his office. He invited them to join him for lunch. They all ordered something to eat and drink. Adam began the conversation. "I called your house a couple of days ago. I was surprised to hear that you had retired," Adam commented.

"It was quite sudden," Wahid began. "This opportunity appeared and I decided to jump at it. My family will join me in the Spring when school is out. It pays well, plus I have my retirement."

"Can I ask you a question?" Adam queried.

"Certainly," Wahid replied.

"We have heard some comments around the airport that indicate a significant number of people are not unhappy about the demise of Sadat. Can you shed some light on the situation?"

"I can't give you any particulars. However, I can give you a general idea of what I think has happened. I have a cousin on my mother's side who was arrested and jailed by Sadat because he was entangled with the Muslim Brotherhood. Most of my mother's side of the family hated Sadat because of that incident. The other factor is a strong minority of the Army still want to have another go at the Israelis. They are upset with the Israeli-Egyptian Peace efforts. I don't believe the anti-Sadat animosity will ever combine into a workable opposition"

"Why not?" Alistair asked.

"There isn't any leadership to pull them together. Ten years from now, it may be different," Wahid replied.

"Why ten years?" Adam asked.

"Let me tell you a story," he began. "Have you ever heard the comment or joke; 'The Saudi's will fight the Israeli's to the last Egyptian.'" He waited for a reaction.

The three officers shook their head, no. Wahid continued, "It was just before we charged across the Suez Canal to retake the Sinai. I was out to Giza to plead for more water for the family orange groves. When I came out from the water commission, I met three old family friends. One said to me, 'Wahid, why don't you make peace with the Israelis? We are tired of our young coming home on stretchers.' I objected. I told them that this time we would win. About nine months later, I was negotiating a prisoner exchange. We were exchanging at a rate of one Israeli for twelve hundred

Egyptians. The old men were right. We had promises of attacks by Syria. They spent one day attacking the Golan and withdrew. The Saudis promised money. How much we got, I don't know. In spite of animosity toward the government, I don't believe the public would stand by for a revolt. Every time we have something happen, we lose millions in tourist trade. I'm hoping the Israeli's will help me keep this hotel full."

Wahid continued, "Another item of concern is the Muslim Brotherhood. The government is cracking down on the Brotherhood in order to infiltrate an outfit called Hizb Allah, or Army of God. Lt. Islamboli was a member of Hizb Allah. The government is going to try to purge the military of any radical suspects."

"Do you know a weatherman at the airport named Farid, Adam?" Wahid asked.

"Yes," Adam replied. "His comment after the assassination suggested that he was very anti-Sadat."

"He's been relieved of his job and is in jail. The authorities found a list of names in his apartment. It was assumed that it was a hit list. It included your Ambassador, Mr. Richardson, who we assume is CIA and you. You might want to take some precautions."

"That's very informative, Wahid. We really appreciate an inside view," Adam replied. "It's refreshing to meet someone who has a broad view of the situation. I will inform the Ambassador and Richardson that we need to take precautions."

"I should like to add my appreciation," Alistair added. "It's a touchy time for Egypt and it's good to know there are people being rational." Adam and Alastair departed.

Pete Marshall stayed behind. He and Wahid had been close and they decided to have dinner together. Pete had told Adam that he would try to spend some extra time with Wahid.

Adam and Alastair went to their respective rooms and put on swim suits. They joined the rest of the party on the beach. Adam went over to Sonya and kissed her. "Have you been in the water?" he asked.

"Yes," she whispered, "My period is over. I'm not a bitch anymore. At least I don't feel bitchy."

"Let's swim out to the float," Adam suggested. Sonya jumped up and raced Adam to the surf.

"I see the newlyweds are still on their honeymoon," Alistair remarked.

"They might as well enjoy each other now. They will be picking up their baby before Christmas," Wanda Ames volunteered.

They watched Adam and Sonya as they approached the float. Adam helped Sonya up on the float and then he crawled up beside her. They kissed.

Ted Olisen said, "Maybe they'll make love right in front of us."

"Don't be nasty, Ted!" Mary Olisen interjected. "You were just as amorous when we were newlyweds. Besides, General McGregor used to scare the wits out of me. He was always so serious or at least I thought so. He's so sweet to Sonya. Did I tell you they made reservations to go to Istanbul."

"How do you know that, Mary?" Wanda Ames asked.

"I made their reservations on Turkish Airways. They're staying at the Hilton. They even booked a night dinner cruise on the Bosporus. I think it's so romantic."

Ted got up and took Mary by the hand and led her to the water. He scolded her for talking about the General.

"When Mrs. McGregor made the reservations," Mary replied, "I asked if their trip was a secret. She said, 'No!' Besides, I haven't told anyone else and the Ames' are two of their best friends."

"Okay," Ted replied. "I guess it wasn't a secret."

"I'll tell you what is a secret, if you can keep a secret," she teased as they reached the water.

"Okay, I know you're dying to tell me, so tell me," Ted said.

"You knew that they were planning to pick up their baby before Christmas," she proposed.

"Yes," he answered.

"Well, General McGregor made reservations for his mother and Cecilia Thompson and the Reverend and Mrs. Carlson, Sonya's parents, to fly out for Christmas. The Carlson's will bring the baby to Washington, and they will all fly to Cairo from Dulles."

"Where will they all stay?" he asked.

"The Carlson's will stay at the Swiss Air apartment. Mrs. McGregor and Cecilia will stay at the British Embassy."

"Why the British Embassy?" Ted asked.

"That's the most exciting part," Mary replied. "Cecilia Thompson and William Hull, The Fourth, will announce their engagement."

"Who is William Hull, The Fourth?" Ted asked.

"He's the grandson of Sir William and Lady Hull. Sir William is the British Ambassador."

"That, I didn't know," Ted replied. "How did you get all of this information?"

"I made the reservations including a reservation for William to fly in from Paris on Air France." Mary Olisen was Swiss. She was fluent in English, French, German, Italian and Arabic.

"I guess being fluent in several languages has its advantages," Ted conceded.

They dove in and joined Adam and Sonya on the float. "General, are we on company time?" Ted Olisen asked.

"You don't have to take leave, Ted. However, this is not an official trip so you'll have to pick up the cost of your room. I'll buy dinner."

"I was just kidding, Sir," Ted replied.

"I know, Ted," Adam answered. "I'm pleased with what we've learned from Brigadier Fatha. I would not have wanted to draw attention to him by flying in and leaving right after we talked. Colonel Marshall is having dinner with Wahid tonight. The rest of us are window dressing."

The group had dinner together in the hotel restaurant. The area was developing into a beach resort. Because of the growth, the hotel had a full bar with plenty of imported wines from Greece, Italy and France.

Pete Marshall returned in time for a night cap. Adam suggested that they go up to Adam and Sonya's room. Alistair and Wanda joined them. Captain Baldwin stayed with the Olisen's.

"Did you get anymore info?" Adam asked Pete while Sonya took care of pouring drinks.

"Yes," Pete Marshall replied. He knew he could speak in front of Air Commodore Ames. "There has been a real house cleaning. Mubarak has fired at least three Major Generals, ten Brigadiers and a bunch of Colonels. Wahid was asked to retire, and he wasn't given a reason. He doesn't know if Abou Ghazala will survive or not. Because the artillery vehicle was involved in the transport of the assassins, there's a cloud over Abou. He came up through the artillery. It appears that the shakeup is more an effort by Mubarak to solidify his power than a house cleaning of people associated with the assassination."

"Have they rounded up the assassins?" Alistair asked.

"Yes, the three that escaped in the crowd have been picked up. Wahid said they are being interrogated and there is no doubt that they will talk."

"Good work, Pete," Adam added. "That confirms what we heard before and makes our trip worthwhile."

The next morning the group met for breakfast at eight am and departed for the aircraft by nine. They were back in Cairo by eleven. Mustafa was waiting at Cairo East with the car. He dropped Adam at the Embassy before taking the Ames' and Sonya to their apartments. Adam filed a report to DIA and then he called Sonya to see if she wanted to go riding. She picked Adam up and they went to the stable. They rode for an hour and then returned to the apartment. Sonya had made a stew. They had a cocktail and Adam opened a bottle of red wine to go with dinner.

"Are we still going to the Hull's for dinner tomorrow night?" Sonya asked.

"Yes," Adam replied.

"I really like Lady Agatha," Sonya volunteered. "She is sure to ask when we are going to pick up Carol Agnes. We should call tonight."

"I'll call Dr. Snyder while you are finishing the dishes," Adam offered.

"Will we be in the States for Christmas?" Sonya asked.

"I'm planning on being back here for New Years Eve. The military Attache's always have a formal dinner dance to celebrate the New Year. We'll have to leave D.C. on the twenty-ninth."

"Will we have time to see my parents?" she asked.

"We'll make time," Adam replied.

"Are we still going to Istanbul?" Sonya asked.

"Yes," Adam replied. He was relieved to be able to tell her the truth. "I've made reservations for the week after next. We'll be staying at the Hilton. It's right on the Bosporus."

"How long are we staying?"

"Four nights and three days."

"Will I have time for some shopping?" she asked.

"As long as it doesn't interfere with our love making. After all, we will be on our honeymoon."

"I promise that you'll get all the loving you can stand. I won't even take a negligee so we won't have to waste time taking it off. I do want to buy something to remind me of Istanbul."

"You can buy a prayer rug," Adam suggested. "or you might want to buy a leather outfit for riding this winter."

"Leather?" she murmured, "That sounds interesting."

"They make nice leather slacks with matching jackets. Of course, you'll look like a motorcycle honey!"

"Will you buy me a motorcycle?" Sonya asked.

"No!" Adam stated.

"Why not?"

"I had a motorcycle when I was stationed in Thailand. While I was there we lost five to the war and five to motorcycle accidents. I was never so glad to be rid of something as I was that motorcycle."

"What did you do with it?" Sonya asked.

"I gave it to my Thai girlfriend," he replied.

"Did she teach you how to make love?" Sonya asked.

"I don't know who taught who," he answered.

"Did she want to marry you?"

"It never came up," he replied.

"How come?" Sonya pressed.

"We lived in two different worlds. I was never going to adapt to the Far East. I really don't think she could have been happy in Washington."

"What happened to her?" Sonya asked.

"The last I heard, she married an Aussie and moved to Singapore."

"Was it fair for you to give her the motorcycle when you knew how dangerous they are?"

"She knew," he replied. "She wanted to buy the motorcycle anyway. I just gave it to her."

"Will you teach me how to make love the way she did?" Sonya asked suppressing a smile.

"No!" he replied emphatically.

"Why not?"

"Because I like the way you make love. You don't wait to climax, you participate."

She stood up and proceeded to strip.

"What are you doing?" he asked.

"I'm getting ready to participate," she said as she headed for the bedroom dropping her bra and panties on the way. Adam followed close behind.

Afterward, they lay quietly catching their breath. They got up and showered together, put on robes and Sonya made dinner while Adam poured cocktails. After dinner, Adam called Minnesota. They turned in early.

Friday, Adam went by his office to check the message traffic. The daily paper was on his desk. The Arabic headline described a jail break. One of the escapees was Farid Bashir, the weatherman at the airport. Adam called CIA and asked Richardson to meet him at the Ambassador's Office.

"What's up, Adam?" the Ambassador asked.

"Did you see the article in the daily?"

Richardson replied, "Yes!"

"I sent you both a note about my conversation with Wahid Fatha in El Arish. This guy Farid Bashir is the one who admitted to having a hit list that included the three of us. Since he is out of jail, I thought we should discuss the situation."

"I always have a security guard with me," the Ambassador replied. "What do we do about the two of you?"

"I'm on the Egyptian list, authorizing a weapon," Richardson replied. "I suggest we add Adam to the list."

"Do you have a weapon, Adam?" the Ambassador asked.

"Yes Sir, I have a .38 caliber pistol."

"I can get you on the list," Richardson added.

"Are you a good shot, Adam?" the Ambassador asked.

"Not bad," Adam replied. "I generally qualify every year."

"I suspect this guy is out of the country," Richardson added. "However, he probably has contacts that can tell him when Spar 80 is traveling. Adam may be his target of opportunity. I suggest you let us run a check whenever you are on the road."

"I'll have my secretary keep you posted," Adam replied.

Adam returned to the apartment for breakfast. Adam and Sonya went to the Pyramids to play nine holes of golf, followed by an hours ride on the desert. They were home in plenty of time to shower and dress for dinner. Their invitation to the Hull's dinner party read casual. That meant coat and tie for Adam and a cocktail dress for Sonya. They arrived at the Ambassador's quarters precisely at six. The Ames' were just ahead of them. As soon as they were inside, Lady Agatha took Sonya aside and asked her about the baby.

"Adam called last night. Carol Agnes is growing each day. We can pick her up just before Christmas. We'll spend a short time with my parents and then stop in D.C. to be with Agnes and Cecilia. We'll be back in Cairo in time for the Military Attache's New Years Eve affair."

"Oh! That sounds wonderful." Lady Agatha replied. "You must bring that baby by as soon as you can."

Cocktails were served on the veranda.

"Will you be at El Alamein for Memorial Services?" Sir William asked Adam.

"Yes Sir," Adam replied. "Colonel Marshall has volunteered to hold down the office. They rest of us will be going for the festivities and will do some swimming."

"Families going also?" Lady Agatha asked.

"Yes. The Sanford's are taking their two oldest children along and Captain Baldwin is also going."

"Are you sending anyone to the AXIS Powers Memorial Service?" Sir William asked.

"We are discussing it. Colonel Ehrlich, West Germany's Attache' asked that question. I've discussed it with our Ambassador. I think we probably will send someone. It may be myself and Sonya."

"What does Washington say?" Sir William asked.

"There's always someone concerned that we might be paying homage to Nazis. With forty-three hundred soldiers in a mass grave there have to be a few Nazis. On the other hand the Germans have been good members of NATO. I'm inclined to favor an appearance."

"I have the same problem with London," Sir William replied. "Let me know a day ahead, if you can."

"Yes Sir," Adam replied.

Casual conversations continued until the butler appeared and announced that dinner was being served.

Lady Agatha led the conversation. "Adam, Sonya tells me you will go to the States to pick up your daughter over Christmas."

"Yes, Lady Agatha. We'll be back in time for New Years, after spending some time with both of our families."

The remainder of the dinner conversation revolved around Egypt after the assassination. Everyone had noted that the lack of visa requests for Egypt had seriously affected tourism in Egypt and Israel. Ever since Sadat and Begin had made peace, most tours from Europe and the Western Hemisphere involved both countries.

Lady Agatha excused herself to go to the kitchen. When she was out of sight, she came back to where she could see Adam. She motioned for him to come with her.

"What's up?" Adam asked.

"Is our secret still intact?" she asked.

"Sonya hasn't indicated that she suspects anything," Adam answered.

"What do you think about going to Luxor or Alexandria while our guests are in town?" Agatha asked.

"I think we should consider it," Adam began. "Of course, Sonya and I may have to stay home depending on the baby. I'll be sure to get a list of what we shouldn't do from our pediatrician as soon as the baby arrives."

"I'll make some reservations," she continued. "I'm sure with the tourism down, we can add people without a problem. How about two days in Luxor between Christmas and New Years and an overnight in Alexandria after New Years."

"That sounds great," Adam replied. "If all is going well, we could get together a couple of days in Israel also."

"That will be lovely," Agatha responded. They returned to the group.

The party broke up shortly after eleven. Adam and Sonya drove to the Swiss Air apartment. They brushed their teeth, disrobed and went to bed.

CHAPTER 23

Adam and Sonya's Turkish Air flight, a Boeing 727, landed in Istanbul a little after four pm. Adam rented a car, an Alfa Romeo, and they drove directly to the Hilton. By the time they were checked in, it was nearly time for dinner. They quickly unpacked and changed into informal clothes. Adam wore a turtle neck with a sports jacket. Sonya wore a sleeveless sheath, light green. She carried a matching green sweater in case the dining room was cold.

There was a bar overlooking the Bosporus. They took a table by the window where they could watch the ships.

"I don't see any docks," Sonya commented.

"The docks are in the Golden Horn," Adam replied. "The Bosporus is too deep for docks."

"What will we do tomorrow?" she asked.

"I'll make a reservation for the dinner cruise on the Bosporus tomorrow night. I thought we would take a drive to the Asian side. When we return we can go to the Mosques south of the Horn. We'll explore the areas on both sides of the Golden Horn," he added.

"When do I get to go shopping?"

"I'll inquire at the desk and see where we should go. I suspect they will recommend the Souk," he said.

"Is the Souk like the one in Cairo?"

"It's not as big and the shops have better items, in my opinion. Istanbul is the most cosmopolitan city in the Middle East. You won't see many people here that won't be dressed like Europeans rather than Arabs."

"How many times have you been to Turkey?" Sonya asked.

"This is my second trip to Istanbul. When I was flying Phantoms at RAF Bentwaters, we would deploy to Incirlik Air Base. Incirlik is a joint Turkish and NATO airbase down near the Syrian border. It's not far from Tarsus the home of Saint Paul of Epistle fame. Are you ready for dinner?" he asked.

"Yes," Sonya responded. "What do you recommend?"

"Lamb Shish Kabob is my favorite Turkish meal," he answered. Adam paid the bar bill and they went to the elevator to go to the roof top restaurant.

They were seated by the windows where they could look over the Bosporus. It was just as the sun went down. The lights on the ships were having an interesting effect with light reflecting off the clear, but dark, water pouring from the Black Sea to the Agean at a fantastic speed.

A waiter appeared and Adam ordered appetizers, Shish Kabob over rice with mixed vegetables, salads for after the entree' and a bottle of Turkish Red Wine.

"I hope this wine is better than Egyptian Wine," Sonya whispered.

"It is," Adam replied. "The Turks have some excellent wines. They also make their own Ouzo."

As they were enjoying their meal, a combo was playing swing music. They danced for a while. They finished with mood music. The slower the music the closer Adam held her.

"Darling," Sonya whispered "If you are trying to get me in the mood, you've succeeded. Shall we go up to the room?"

"That would probably be more acceptable than making a scene here in the dining room, although we could explain that we are on our honeymoon. I'm sure everyone would understand."

"I agree," Sonya replied, "but do we really want to go through all that? Besides we're wasting time."

"Right! Let's go," Adam responded as he paid the check.

They went to the room. Adam opened the door and turned on

the light. Sonya turned the light out. "You don't want the light?" he asked.

"No," she replied. "Maybe there's a camera like there was in Cypress."

"How did you find out about that?" Adam asked.

"When I was coming out of my coma, I overheard one of the nurses ask how they had determined paternity for our baby. Dr. Snyder told her he had witnessed a clandestine film where I had stated that you were the father. That had to be in Cypress."

"Yes, it was in Cypress. The night after we had been to see the Scotts"

"Can I see the film?" she asked.

"I suppose so. It isn't good quality. We are certainly identifiable. My mother wanted to see it. I told her it was X-rated and she couldn't see it."

"No wonder she was so cool to me when she first came to Minnesota," Sonya said.

"How did you turn her around? When I left Washington, I was convinced it would take years to get her to accept our marriage. I talked to her after her trip to the Mayo Clinic and she informed me that the two of you had made plans for the wedding to be in Washington and your father would help officiate. I was amazed. What did you say to her?"

"She seemed quite cool at first. She came with my mother. We walked to the nursery. They brought Carol Agnes to the window so we could see her. We just stood there for several minutes. I thought how could she believe that tiny baby could be yours. I began to cry. She asked why I was crying. I told her that I was hopelessly in love with you, that I would rather lose you than make you unhappy. The next thing I knew, we were planning our wedding."

"Why in Washington? Was that her idea?" Adam asked.

"No, she asked if I wanted to be married in my father's church. I said, no, because it was too close to the Olsen's. That's when she suggested National Cathedral. I called my father. He completely understood my concern for the Olsen's and agreed to come to Washington."

While Sonya was talking, Adam was intermittently disrobing the two of them. By the time she finished, they were both naked.

They stood by the window and looked out over the Bosporus. A full moon shown in the window. They kissed tenderly at first and then passionately.

"A penny for your thoughts?" she asked.

"Love really does conquer all," he whispered.

Sonya took his hand and led him to the bed. They rolled back the covers and Sonya stretched out on the bed, inviting Adam on top of her. They made love slowly and passionately. They woke up when Adam felt a chill. He rolled over and pulled the covers up. They slept soundly. The next morning they were up and ready for breakfast at nine. They had breakfast sent up to the room.

"Where are we going today?" Sonya asked.

"I thought we would check out a museum. Did you ever see a movie called 'Topkapi'?" Adam asked.

"Yes," she responded, "Peter Ustinov was in it. They tried to steal a dagger for the emerald that was on the scabbard."

"Correct," Adam added, "I want to show you the dagger and the emerald."

"How exciting," Sonya responded.

"We'll also visit the Mosque that was a Greek Church."

"Was a Greek Church?" Sonya questioned.

"I'm not absolutely certain, but the history of the building goes something like this: The Roman Emperor, Constantine converted to Christianity. He built St. Helen's in honor of his mother around 500 AD, I think. His mother had made a pilgrimage to Israel. Around a thousand years later, the Ottoman Turks conquered Constantinople. They changed the name to Istanbul and made it the capital of the Ottoman Empire. The church became a mosque."

"I love traveling with you. You have all of this information," Sonya stated.

"I thought you loved traveling with me for the sex," he added with a smirk.

She responded immediately, "Don't be silly, Darling. I live with you for the sex. All the rest are fringe benefits."

"Why didn't I meet you ten years ago?"

"If I had met you ten years ago, I would have run away and hid. I would have been frightened to death. I almost died of fright that afternoon in the Meridien. I thought I was going to die. You were so gentle I had to see what would happen. Once I found out what I had been missing, I couldn't dream of giving it up."

"I thought I had lost you when I saw your limp body on top of that car," he replied. I took heart when I got you to Rochester. I said a prayer for you every day. I think the happiest day of my life was when I heard that you and my mother were planning our wedding. It was as if a great stone had been lifted off of me. I could breathe again."

Oh, Darling," Sonya answered, "I never realized how much you went through. Now it's over. Soon we will go and pick up our daughter and we can be a family and have more children. We are so lucky and blessed, Adam."

"Yes, we are," Adam Replied. "Let's go see some sights."

They went to St. Helen's first. They walked around the grounds to look at the Minarets. They went inside. Considering its age, the building was in marvelous condition. Because it had been turned into a Mosque, all of the sculptures depicting saints had been covered with Arabic lettering in keeping with Islam's ban on human pictures and sculptures.

They went to the Topkapi Museum. They spent three hours browsing through the artifacts. After they had seen everything they had planned to see, they decided to return to the hotel and rest up for their dinner cruise on the Bosporus.

The dinner cruise was fully booked. Adam and Sonya arrived fifteen minutes before the departure. They were shown to their table in the dining area. They would be joined by two business men, one American and one Englishman. They went on deck where cocktails were being served. Sonya selected a white wine and Adam asked for scotch. The barman didn't have Dewars. He recommended Famous Grouse as an alternative. Adam accepted the barman's suggestion most willingly.

They strolled along the railing to the bow and looked out at both shores. The shore line seemed to be neat and clean. It was a welcome change from the dust that covered everything in Cairo. Adam noticed how dark the water looked. He commented about it to one of the stewards.

"It comes from the Black Sea," the Steward stated. "We think it's a combination of the depth and the color of the stone lining the bottom. The water doesn't appear blue until it is well south of Istanbul."

Adam thanked the Steward and they wandered back to the bar for a refill. The sun was sinking fast and it was beginning to get chilly. Adam returned to the dining room to retrieve Sonya's coat. Sonya stood by the railing as two men approached.

"Excuse me, Madam," one of the men began, "are you Mrs. McGregor?"

"Yes, I am," Sonya replied.

"My name is David Strange and this is my colleague, Malcomb Avery. We will be sitting with you through dinner."

"How do you do!" Sonya replied shaking both gentleman's hand. Adam appeared and slipped Sonya's coat over her shoulders.

"Darling, these gentlemen will be joining us for diner. Meet David Strange and Malcomb Avery. Gentlemen, my husband, General McGregor."

"Oh!" Malcomb Avery said, "I knew of an Adam McGregor in Viet Nam. Any relation?"

"If you are talking around sixty-nine and seventy, I'm your man," Adam replied.

"I was in the RAF at that time," Malcomb replied. I was seconded to an Aussie Phantom Squadron at Phan Rang. I believe you spent a night with us."

"I did," Adam answered. "We had an oil leak after a mission. It was discovered by my wingman when we were checking each other's plane. Phan Rang was the closest Phantom Base. We dropped in for a couple of days. Your maintenance did a good job for us."

"As I recall we tipped a few drams of Scotch while you were there."

"As a matter of fact," Adam replied, "you introduced me to Famous Grouse. Famous Grouse didn't show up in the States for ten years. I was surprised to find that the Hilton stocks it."

The dinner bell rang. It was just beginning to get dark and they filed into the dining room. They dined on a starter of white fish caught locally, followed by lamb Shish Kabob. Excellent side dishes of vegetables were available, as were both red and white wines.

David Strange initiated the conversation, "Since both of you were in Viet Nam, I would be interested in your opinions on the war."

Adam and Malcomb looked at each other deciding who should go first. Malcomb volunteered.

"Since I only had one tour, and Britain wasn't involved, I"ll go first. We in Britain were happy that we weren't directly involved like we were in Korea. We thought that Viet Nam was a terrible place to fight and that the enemy, both the Viet Cong and North Vietnamese, were too well supported to ever give up. We were convinced that the war was not winnable. In addition, the war cost America billions. We saw the whole thing as a terrible waste. Your turn, General."

Adam nodded his head and began. "There certainly are a lot of Americans that would agree with you. However, I'm not one of them. First, I would point out to you that you can't look at Viet Nam objectively without considering where the Soviets would have been putting their effort if we had simply allowed the Communists to have Viet Nam without a fight. Thailand would certainly have been threatened. Would the Soviets have turned their attention to Africa or Spanish America? Our supply lines would have been shorter. Would surrounding countries have cooperated the way the Thais did? We might have exchanged one quagmire for another. Incidentally, it looks like the Soviets may have found their own quagmire in Afghanistan right now. We shall see. Let me also address the subject of cost."

They were interrupted by the arrival of coffee and dessert.

Adam continued, "The financial costs of war are highly overrated. When we lose a Phantom or a Thud anywhere, the media broadcasts the replacement cost of the airplane. We in the military only care about the welfare of the aircrew. It doesn't matter if the airplane was shot down in combat or crashed at it's home base, it was part of our Gross National Product. World War II brought us out of the Great Depression. Our economy is in a sad state now because the government quit buying GNP and switched to social programs. The multiplier on GNP may be close to two. There is no way to calculate a multiplier on social programs. It may even be negative."

"Adam, are you suggesting that we should go to war for economic reasons?" Sonya asked.

"Absolutely not!" Adam responded. "All I'm saying is financial reasons are not valid for avoiding war. Engaging in war must be a decision based on a trade off between human costs and political gains. Once the decision to go to war has been made, it's always better to win than to lose."

"What about a draw?" David Strange asked.

"If there is such a thing, I would suggest that both sides lost," Adam concluded.

"What brings you to Istanbul?" Malcomb Avery asked.

"We're on our honeymoon," Sonya volunteered.

"How long have you been married?" David asked.

"Almost two months," Sonya replied.

"That's a long honeymoon," Malcomb added.

"We returned to Cairo the day after our wedding," Adam added. "I promised Sonya we would come to Istanbul as soon as I could break away. It's one of my favorite cities. At one time I thought that San Francisco, Hong Kong, and Istanbul were my three favorite cities. I've since added Sidney."

"I wouldn't argue with that list," David interjected. "Although I haven't been to Hong Kong. How many of those cities has Adam taken you to, Sonya?"

"Only Istanbul," She responded. "I'm just a country girl from Minnesota, but now I know where I want to go."

"It looks like you are in for building your air miles, Adam," Malcomb concluded as the boat approached the dock. They returned to the hotel.

"Do you have time for a nightcap?" David asked.

Adam looked at Sonya. She nodded yes.

"Sure," Adam replied.

They all took the elevator to the bar on the top floor. The view was spectacular as the weather was perfect. Sonya ordered a white Crème de Menthe on ice. Adam introduced David and Malcomb to Asbach, a German Brandy.

"How is Egypt reacting to the assassination?" David Strange asked. "Are things back to normal?"

Adam responded, "The tourist trade is taking a real hit. Before the assassination there wasn't a room available in any of the first rate hotels. Now all the hotels have vacancies. Because many tours included both countries since the peace treaty, it has also hit Israel. Israel's agreement to return the Sinai seems to be on track."

"What about the assassins?" Malcomb asked.

"In my opinion, they were on a suicide mission. They didn't appear to have an escape plan. Even though three of them escaped in the confusion, they were all picked up within three days. They will stand trial and get the death penalty."

"Is this an organized cabal?" David asked.

"The claim is that they are members of Hizb Allah, Army of God. It doesn't appear to have any connection to the Muslim Brotherhood. The Brotherhood has been active in Egypt and the Sudan for years. However, their efforts have been stymied by numerous arrests by both the Nassar and Sadat regimes. Historically, radical Islam appears to raise it's head every century or so. I don't have any proof, it's just my opinion. I'm guessing that the impetus for this outbreak has it's origins in Iran and the takeover by the Mullahs. Only time will tell."

They chatted on about the Middle East and travel while they finished their drinks. Then they parted company. Adam and Sonya went to their room. The blinds were open and a full moon shone in the windows. They left the lights off. They kissed in the moonlight and began to take each others clothes off. They went into the bathroom and took a shower together and then went to bed.

"Have you noticed that you aren't afraid of the dark any longer?" Adam asked.

"Not as long as I can touch you, my love," she replied in a whisper. They made love for a long time and then slept until daylight.

After a leisurely breakfast in the hotel, they went down to the Bosporus and found the Palace the Ottomans had built right by the water. It took them three hours to go through the Palace and the grounds. It was a beautiful building and the grounds were equally attractive.

They went back to the Alfa Romeo and drove around the city. Eventually, they stopped in an area where there were several leather shops. Sonya had a great time trying on different leather combinations and then modeling them for Adam. She finally settled on olive green colored slacks with matching jacket. She just happened to also find matching boots.

The two returned to the Hilton in time for cocktails and dinner. Sonya was wearing her new outfit and heads were turning in her direction. "Adam," she said quietly, "I think people are staring at us."

"Sonya, they're staring at you. They couldn't care less about me," Adam replied. "They're wondering if you are my mistress or my daughter!"

"Your daughter!" she exclaimed. "Do I look that immature? Maybe I should smoke a cigarette."

"In that outfit you look seventeen to twenty-something. You don't smoke and neither do I, so where would you get a cigarette?" Adam asked. "Besides I think you should enjoy this while it lasts. Let's dance." Sonya nodded her approval.

Sonya looked older on the dance floor. Her three inch heels and her long legs brought her forehead up to Adams chin. As they swirled around the floor, Sonya noticed the stars were diminishing They returned to their table when their entree's arrived. They finished dinner, had a night cap at the bar and went to their room. Adam left a call for six in the morning. Sonya had stripped to her panties and bra and was headed for the shower. Adam reached out and grabbed her hand.

"Let's make love before we shower. We won't have to shower in the morning then," he said. She didn't reply. She simply dropped her bra and panties on floor, pulled down the covers and laid out on the bed. She held out her arms.

"If you're waiting on me, you're wasting your time," she giggled. Adam undressed, turned out the lights, and joined Sonya on the bed. "Aren't honeymoons just great?" he said.

"This is my first honeymoon," Sonya replied.

"It's my first honeymoon, also," Adam answered. "It doesn't have to stop here."

"How will we know it's over?" she whispered as they kissed.

After a considerable amount of kissing and fondling, Adam replied, "How about if we declare it over when you get pregnant again."

"How about between when the doctor tells us to stop having sex and when we stop?" replied Sonya.

The next morning, they were up early. Their return flight to Cairo would depart at eight am. They hurried to the airport returning the car and arriving at the check-in by 0630. As they entered the queue for departure, Adam looked at the line of incoming passengers. Arriving from Rome, he recognized Farid Bashir, the Egyptian fugitive. They were about to disappear into the departure area when Farid spotted Adam. Farid stared at Adam until they disappeared.

They arrived back in Cairo mid-morning. Mustafa was at the airport to meet them. Mustafa dropped Adam at the Embassy and took Sonya to Swiss Air. Sonya changed clothes and went to the desert to ride Abul Kheer. She would be back in time to shower and change for their function at the French Embassy.

Adam spent the remainder of the day catching up on his paper work. In just another week they would be spending three days at the El Alamein battle field. Adam met with the Ambassador that afternoon.

As soon as Adam was alone with the Ambassador, he related seeing Farid Bashir entering Turkey at the Istanbul Airport. He told the Ambassador that he had informed CIA of the incident.

"Did Bashir see you?" the Ambassador asked.

"Oh, yes! We exchanged nods," Adam replied. They went on to the plans for El Alamein.

"About the problem of the Axis Power's Memorial," the Ambassador began. "The Pentagon favors sending someone. State is concerned that we will raise the possibility of paying homage to some Nazis. What do you think?"

"All the German and Austrian dead are buried in a single mass grave," Adam answered. "There are no head stones, just a long list of names that isn't complete. I think the presence of myself and my wife would be appreciated without creating a stir. I think the Brits may also participate. I can talk to Alistair Ames and see what he says."

"Let's do it," the Ambassador replied. "If you can get Air Commodore Ames to go along, fine. I'll suggest it to Sir William."

"Yes sir," Adam agreed and departed.

That evening Adam and Sonya arrived at the French Embassy just as Alistair and Wanda Ames were entering.

"Hello, Adam and Sonya," he called out. "I had a call from Sir William. He suggests that the four of us attend the memorial service at the German-Austrian Memorial."

"Our Ambassador agreed," Adam replied. They went in to the function.

The day before their departure for El Alamein, Adam had a short staff meeting. He announced that he and Sonya would be taking the Corvette to El Alamein. That would leave one vehicle for Colonel Marshall. He suggested that one or two of Captain Sanford's children could ride with Captain Baldwin and Mustafa. Everyone was familiar with the hotel accommodations as this was the third year they had been to El Alamein. The hotel was right on the beach with direct access to the water. Although it was November, the water was still quite warm and the sun was bright. Equipment for wind surfing would be available.

Adam and Sonya departed at seven the following morning. By eight, they were speeding up the desert highway toward Alexandria. It was a two lane road in bad condition at times and heavily traveled. The truck traffic was particularly heavy. It wasn't long before they were confronted with two trucks, one trying to pass the other. Adam slowed down and eased the Corvette over onto the desert. When the trucks passed, he eased back onto the asphalt paving and resumed his speed.

"Is that normal?" Sonya asked.

"Very normal," he replied. "We'll have to pull off several times between here and Alexandria. It's better after we leave Alex as the traffic is much lighter."

They chatted about the coming holiday period. Sonya asked about plane reservations. Adam made up a story with details on when they would be in Minnesota and Washington. He added his plans for traveling with Carol Agnes.

"She'll have to sleep in our bedroom for a while," Sonya mentioned. "That's going to put a crimp in our love-making."

"We can change it to practice breeding?" Adam asked, smiling.

Sonya looked at Adam's profile, waiting for a smirk to appear on his face. He continued to look straight ahead.

"What's the difference between making love and practice

breeding?" she asked.

"The climaxes are more subdued."

"The heck with that," she responded. "I don't want to make love without climaxing."

"You can still have a climax," he answered "You just can't wake the baby."

"I have a month and a half to learn how to control my enthusiasm for love making. You can critique me every day," Sonya concluded.

"We'll start tonight, okay?"

"Yes, my Love," Sonya replied. "We'll definitely practice breeding tonight."

"Sex, sex, sex!" Adam stated, "That's all you think about."

"Wait until we have three babies on our hands and you'll see if sex is all I think about. I want you to know I'm a good mother," she responded.

"I've never doubted that, Sweetheart. I'm sure you can train me to be a good father," Adam responded as he turned off the main highway to by-pass some of Alexandria's traffic.

"I think you'll take to fatherhood quite well," she said. "You certainly did a fine job of caring for me and Carol Agnes while I was in a coma."

"It was a labor of love," Adam replied. He pointed out items of interest as they drove west on the coast highway. Occasionally there was a view of the Mediterranean Sea. Mostly it was desert with a stand of date palms covered with dust here and there.

They were the first to arrive at the hotel. As soon as they had checked in, they decided to go for a swim. Sonya donned her new one-piece swimsuit.

"Do you like it?" she asked as she turned full circle.

"I love it," Adam responded. "With your figure you'll look good in any swimsuit. Everyone will wonder why you're not in a bikini."

Sonya frowned at Adam. "I will not wear anything that will expose my ugly blue scar in public, so quit bugging me!"

"Yes, dear," he answered dutifully. They headed for the water. After a short swim, they went to the snack bar and had a sandwich and a beer. While they were eating, Dave Baldwin arrived.

"How was the trip, Dave?" Adam asked.

"Without incident, Sir," he responded. "Mustafa can dodge those trucks on the Alexandria Highway with the best of them."

"We had a couple of challenges, too," Adam replied. "Are the Sanford's here?"

"Yes Sir. They arrived right behind us."

"Do you all know about the Ambassador's party tonight?" Adam asked.

"We know about the party. We don't know where it is," Dave replied.

"Mustafa knows where it is. Sonya and I will ride with you and the Sanford's can follow us. The Ambassador has access to a beach house across the bay. It will take us about twenty minutes to get there. Let's gather about five-thirty in the lobby."

"Yes Sir, I'll pass it on to the Sanford's," Dave answered. "How's the water?"

"Considering that it's November, it's fairly warm," Sonya interjected.

"Where's your bikini, Sonya?"

"Never mind, David. It's none of your business," Sonya fired back.

"Sorry, Ma'am," he replied with a grin.

"It's all right, David. My husband has been bugging me, so I'm supersensitive!"

They went back to the water and had a try at windsurfing. Adam maneuvered the board until the wind caught them. He pulled Sonya up beside him and they headed across the small bay. The wind was perfect and they were able to cross in about ten minutes. Coming back took longer as the wind was not as favorable. They fell off twice. It was getting late. They headed for the showers. By the time they were dried off, it was time to get dressed for the evening.

"I guess I'll have to wait until we return to get my first lesson in practice breeding," she commented.

"I promise to start your training as soon as we return to the room," Adam replied.

She was about to put on lipstick when Adam stopped her and kissed her passionately.

She feigned a swoon. "Do we really have to go out?"

"Duty calls and we must answer," he replied. "We can't disappoint the Ambassador and his wife. Besides they throw a good party. They bring their chef from Cairo."

They went down to join David for the ride around the bay. The Sanford's arrived at the same time as Adam and Sonya. David was waiting with Mustafa and Captain Sanford's driver, Ali. Fifteen minutes later, they arrived at the Ambassador's Quarters. A bar was set up on the veranda overlooking the bay. They all lined up to order drinks.

The Ambassador and his wife were on the veranda waiting for the guests to arrive. They were joined shortly by Sir William, Lady Agatha and the Ames'.

"Adam, are you and Sonya set up to go to the German Memorial tomorrow?" the Ambassador asked.

"Yes Sir, we set it up with Colonel Ehrlich at the German Embassy. Air Commodore Ames and Mrs. Ames will go with us. The Austrian Ambassador will officiate this year. We will have time to drive to the Italian Cemetery for their function after the German-Austrian function."

"Very good," the Ambassador replied. "Sir William, I assume you are okay with these arrangements."

"Yes, Avery," Sir William replied. "We discussed it with London. They concurred on having the Defense Office send an emissary. They didn't want me to go."

"I got the same hint from Washington," the Ambassador replied.

Sir William reminded every one that he and Lady Agatha would be hosting a party at their beach house the next evening. The Hull's were staying in a house owned by the British Government. He reminded everyone to come casual as they would be sailing on his yacht during the cocktail hour.

After dinner, they broke up into small groups. Adam and Sonya played bridge with three other couples. They rotated between tables after each rubber until all teams had played each other. When they were finished, they sought out David and departed for the hotel. Mustafa was waiting at the car. They were back at their hotel in twenty minutes.

Dave Baldwin decided to have a nightcap. Sonya suggested

that she wasn't feeling up to a nightcap. Adam took the hint and they went up to their room.

"Are you okay?" Adam asked as soon as their door was closed.

"Of course, I'm okay," she said. "I'm ready for some practice breeding."

"Get your clothes off," Adam replied.

"Can I brush my teeth first?"

"Of course! I'll get undressed while you're in the bathroom," he answered.

She came out of the bathroom in the nude. Adam had stripped to his shorts. He patted her bottom as she walked past.

"Hurry," she whispered.

"I will, I promise," he replied.

When he came out of the bathroom, he was surprised to see the lights were off. He groped his way to the bed and found her in the middle.

"I thought you were afraid of the dark," he said.

"I used to be," she started, " but I met this man in Khartoum and as long as he's nearby, I just close my eyes and I'm all right."

He kissed her on the lips, on her neck and down to her tummy and proceeded to make love. When her climax began, she started to moan. Adam kissed her again.

"Remember," he whispered, "soon we'll have a baby close by, so we can't make too much noise."

"I'm trying to have a quiet climax. It's very difficult," Sonya replied.

"It won't be too long until the baby will be able to sleep in her own room," Adam added. They hugged and fell asleep.

Adam and Sonya were up early the next morning. They had a light breakfast and then dressed for their visit to the German and Austrian Memorial. They picked up the Ames' at their hotel.

The memorial was of modern construction, primarily of cast stone. There were no individual graves as found in the British Empire Cemetery. It was estimated that the mass grave beneath the edifice, contained slightly over four thousand corpses. The internal walls bore the names of German and Austrian soldiers that were known to have been in the force that was overrun at El Alamein. The list was not complete.

The Austrian Ambassador gave a short memorial speech. Wreaths were laid around the center of the memorial by personnel from the various embassies that were present. Adam and Alistair did the honors for the US and the UK. Both officers were impressed with the demeanor of the proceedings.

After introducing the wives to the dignitaries, Adam introduced Sonya to Colonel Ehrlich and his wife. The Ames' were long time friends of the Ehrlich's. Colonel Ehrlich took them on a quick tour of the memorial and thanked them for attending the service. They departed for the Italian Cemetery.

Most of the Italian victims were buried in individual graves. A significant number of Italian soldiers were taken prisoner at El Alamein. These prisoners were employed to identify the Italian dead and to bury them in marked graves. A Catholic Chaplain had flown in from Italy and he performed a mass. After the mass, the four visitors paid their respects to the Italian Ambassador and the Italian Attache's and families. Adam and the Ames' were very familiar with the Italians. Adam introduced Sonya to the Attache's whom she hadn't met.

Mustafa was waiting in the parking lot. As soon as they were all in the car the conversation began.

"With all those dead bodies, there has to be some Nazis involved," Alistair said.

"I don't think there's any doubt about that," Adam rejoined. "However, I can certainly understand Colonel Ehrlich's position. There had to be some draftees in the bunch , also."

"Someone has to tell me about El Alamein," Sonya interrupted. "I have no background on the Second World War."

Wanda Ames broke in "You're in trouble now, Sonya. Alistair lectured on the North African Campaign at Cranwell. He can bore you for hours."

"Not so, Sonya," Alistair replied. "I can make it as long or as short as you like. I can talk about El Alamein without doing the whole North African Campaign. We'll talk about it over a cocktail at the party tonight."

"Agreed," Sonya answered.

They dropped Alistair and Wanda at the hotel. They would

meet at Ambassador Hull's quarters at six pm.

That evening, Sir William invited everyone to go sailing on his yacht. Adam, Wanda Ames, Captain Sanford and his children joined the group. The yacht was a single mast, twelve meter boat. It could sleep six comfortably. Adam and Don Sanford helped raise the sails as they headed out to sea. Sir William shut down the engine as soon as the sails had caught the wind. They returned just before dark and just in time for an excellent buffet dinner.

Sonya and Dave Baldwin spent the time with Alistair learning all about the importance of El Alamein in the Second World War. Just before the party broke up, Lady Agatha cornered Adam.

"Does she suspect anything?"

"No," Adam replied. "She asked if I had the tickets. I told her they were in my briefcase at the office with our passports and everything we needed for the trip."

"I talked to your mother just before we left Cairo. They will all be in on the same airplane. I'm really looking forward to Christmas and seeing Will and Cecelia. We'll talk several times between now and then."

"I'm sure we will," Adam replied. "I'll keep you posted. Sonya will be surprised!"

The next morning everyone left for Cairo.

Adam and Sonya were only ten miles east of El Alamein when they had to abandon the roadway to avoid a collision with two trucks that were racing westward. Adam eased the Corvette into the desert, avoiding two palm trees. By shifting down, he was able to keep moving and they went safely back on the road, leaving a cloud of dust behind.

The Corvette and Adam were none the worse for wear. The same could not be said for Sonya. She berated Adam for reckless driving. She suggested that he wouldn't be satisfied until she was dead and Carol Agnes was an orphan to be raised by aging grandparents. She raised the specter of her culpability in the death of her two sons. Finally, she burst into tears, sobbing uncontrollably until she fell asleep.

It took Adam an extra hour to get back to Cairo. He was careful to avoid rough areas in hopes that he wouldn't upset Sonya. When they arrived at the Swiss Air Building, Adam parked next to the stairway. He carried Sonya up the stairs. She woke up in time to go into the apartment on her own. She went immediately to the bedroom and laid down.

Adam unloaded the car and called his office. He informed his secretary that Sonya was ill and he wouldn't be coming in until the next morning unless it was absolutely necessary.

At five local, Adam called the Mayo Clinic and fortunately he was able to catch Dr. Snyder. He described Sonya's symptoms. The doctor confirmed that Sonya had a similar breakdown while she was waiting for her release. He described how Agnes and Carol had come to the rescue. He suggested that Adam should try to ignore the outbursts unless he felt she might hurt herself. If she didn't revert to her near normal self, he suggested they move up the planned Christmas trip of the three parents. He advised Adam not to confront Sonya under any circumstances.

Shortly after the phone call was terminated, Adam heard the shower running. He went into the bathroom and asked if he could join her.

"I was wondering where you were," she responded. "I had about decided that the honeymoon was over."

He joined her in the shower. They dressed and went down to the restaurant for dinner. Sonya had blotted the incident from her mind.

CHAPTER 24

It was December twentieth. For all Sonya knew, they were leaving for Minnesota the next morning. She was returning from her bridge club. Mustafa had driven her because Adam wanted the Corvette. When Mustafa dropped her off at the Swiss Air Building she noticed that the Corvette was there. Adam was already home she assumed. A thought ran through her mind that she could easily entice her husband to make love to her.

She was dressed in powder blue. She had on a sheath that zipped up the back. Her lingerie and shoes matched the sheath. Her lingerie consisted of a bra, panties, a garter belt and nylons. She stepped out of her shoes as she closed the door behind her. She reached over her back and started the zipper of her dress down, reaching around with the other hand to pull the zipper all the way down. As she stepped out of the sheath, she called out.

"Darling, I'm home and I'm ready for some practice breeding."

She had just unhooked her bra and exposed her breasts, when the door opened from the spare bedroom. Carol Carlson appeared.

"Sonya," she said. "Be quiet! You'll wake the baby."

"Mother!" Sonya blurted, as she quickly refastened her bra.

"What are you doing here?"

"Your husband invited us for Christmas. We brought your baby. Are you in the habit of stripping in the living room?" The last sentence was emphatic.

Sonya quickly retrieved her dress. She stepped into it and pulled it up just as her father entered the room.

"Sonya," he exclaimed, "your face is very flushed! Are you ill?"

"Oh, no Daddy! I'm just so surprised that I can hardly breathe. Where is Carol? I must see my baby."

"She's in the bedroom in her basket," Reverend Carlson replied. "She was a good traveler, but she woke up often. We think it was the noise."

Sonya didn't answer. She crept into the bedroom to look at the baby. "Oh, Momma," Sonya whispered. "She's so tiny!" Sonya picked up the baby.

"Dr. Kittleson assures us that she will grow faster now that all of her vital functions are normal. She told us to remind you that under normal conditions, she should still be in your womb. We have special formula for her to last until April. Dr. Kittleson would like to see her when you return to the States."

"Has Adam seen the baby?" Sonya asked.

"Yes, of course!" her mother replied.

"What did he say?"

"He said, 'She really is a miracle.' He had tears in his eyes."

Sonya put the baby back in the basket. She led her mother to the kitchen and suggested they brew a pot of coffee.

"Sonya," her mother began. "You haven't explained the striptease in the living room."

"Mother," Sonya began as she heaved a sigh of exasperation. "All I can say is that Adam and I enjoy a very active sex life. I encourage him because we both love it."

There was an awkward pause. Carol spoke. "When you called out to your husband, 'I'm ready for some practice breathing' you actually said, 'I'm ready for some practice breeding'?"

"Mother!" she exclaimed in frustration, "I knew you wouldn't understand."

"On the contrary, my dear daughter. I've had a few climaxes

in my life, too. Enjoy it while it lasts!"

Sonya turned and watched her mother's back. Carol was laughing. Suddenly, Sonya realized it was going to be a wonderful Christmas.

She was just finished with setting up the coffee pot when Adam arrived. Reverend Carlson and Carol were back in their bedroom.

"I take it that you've seen Carol Agnes," Adam whispered in Sonya's ear.

"Yes, she's beautiful. However, in the future, I suggest you not surprise me like that." She related the encounter with her mother, including the partial strip.

"What did she say?"

"She demanded to know what I meant by practice breeding!"

"Oh, no! What did you say?"

"I told her that I knew she wouldn't understand, but that we had a very active sex life. I told her I encouraged you."

"What did she say?"

"She said she had a climax or two herself. She suggested we enjoy it while we can. She was laughing as she left the room." They were kissing when Sonya's father came in the kitchen.

"Harrumph," he cleared his throat. "I heard you were making coffee."

"Yes, Daddy! It's almost ready," Sonya replied. "Have a seat in the living room and I'll bring everything in there."

"What are we doing for dinner?" Sonya asked as she busied herself with the coffee.

"I made reservations downstairs," Adam replied. "Mother and Cecilia will be arriving about ten pm."

"Where are they staying?"

"With Sir William and Lady Agatha," Adam replied. "Lady Agatha was the mastermind of the whole thing. William the Fourth and Cecilia are announcing their engagement. Will's parents will be here, also."

"When are they getting married?"

"Sometime in the Spring. I think Agatha is negotiating the time and place with Will's parents. It may even end up in D.C. at the National Cathedral."

"If it is to be at National Cathedral, are we going to be in the states?" Sonya asked.

"I talked to Air Force Personnel early today. They tell me the Chief of Staff bumped me off the Major General's list because I haven't been to a senior service school."

"What's a senior service school?" she asked.

"They are called War Colleges," Adam replied. "The Army has one at Carlisle, Pennsylvania. The Navy's school is in Rhode Island and the Air Force has a school in Montgomery, Alabama. The National War College is at Fort McNair in D.C."

"Why haven't you attended one of them?" she asked.

"I was on the list for National War College when my predecessor in Cairo got himself fired. Because I spoke Arabic and had been in Saudi Arabia, I was a natural to fill the vacancy. I was asked to volunteer."

"If you hadn't volunteered, we would never have met," Sonya observed as she moved into his arms and kissed him.

"If you two love birds can take a break, I would like some coffee." Reverend Carlson suggested as he peeked in the kitchen.

"I'm sorry, Daddy," Sonya responded as she reached for the coffee pot. She followed her father into the living room. "We're still honeymooning, Daddy!"

"I noticed," he responded. "I'm sorry I intruded. You should keep your love affair going as long as you can. Your mother and I have."

"Have you had any contact with the Olsen's?" Sonya asked.

"I've talked with John's father. He's resigned to the fact that you would be dead, too, if you hadn't met Adam. John's mother is more unforgiving. I suspect she will carry her bitterness to her grave."

"What about the Carlson's?" she asked.

"They asked about you all the time. I hope you can attend one of our family reunions when you get back to the states. It would be good for you to see your cousins and have them meet Adam and Carol Agnes."

"We will do that," Sonya agreed. "Is it still in Fairmont in June?"

"Yes, the second Sunday in June."

They were interrupted by Adam. He suggested that they go downstairs to the Swiss Air Restaurant for dinner. Sonya bundled Carol Agnes and they all went to dinner.

After dinner, Reverend Carlson and Carol went to bed early. Sonya rocked Carol Agnes to sleep while Mustafa drove Adam to the airport to pick up his mother, Will and Cecilia. They returned to Swiss Air because Agnes insisted on seeing the baby. Of course, Carol Agnes was asleep, but her grandmother didn't care. She just had to see her only grandchild. After Agnes had finished oohing and ahing over the baby, Mustafa drove Agnes, Cecilia and William to the Hull's residence.

The next evening, they all gathered at the Hull's for dinner. Adam and Sonya had suggested that they leave the baby with a sitter. Neither Lady Agatha nor Agnes would stand for that. They took the baby with them and the baby slept most of the time.

The dinner was a spectacular affair. William's parents had arrived. There were eleven for dinner. Lady Agatha insisted on an even number so they set a place for the baby although she was allowed to go to a side room and sleep.

The dinner conversation was largely Lady Agatha telling everyone about the wonders of Luxor. She had made reservations at the Winter Palace in Luxor for two days. Sonya was the first to back out. She would stay with her baby. Sir William insisted that he couldn't go. Adam refused to go because he wanted to be with Sonya and the baby. They whittled the list down to seven and Adam suggested that they could go on Spar 80.

"Can you do that?" Sonya asked.

"I'll ask our Ambassador tomorrow. I'm sure he'll approve it for Lady Agatha," Adam replied.

The next weekend the party went to Israel. Adam and Sonya took the baby and flew over on Air Sinai with Agnes and the Carlson's. Cecilia and William had returned to the States. William's parents had returned to England.

Adam borrowed a car from the Naval Attache' in Tel Aviv. He was a classmate of Adam's at the Naval Academy. In three days they managed to get to Jerusalem, Bethlehem, the Sea of Galilee, the Mount of Olives and Nazareth. Reverend and Mrs. Carlson were awestruck. The party returned in time for the New Year's Eve Ball at the Mina House.

There was an argument about who would stay at the apartment with the baby. Agnes insisted that the Carlson's should go to the ball and that Sonya must attend with her husband. She finally convinced everyone that she was right. Reverend Carlson had brought a tuxedo and Mrs. Carlson had a ball gown that was full length, red satin. Adam was resplendent in his Mess Dress uniform with five rows of medals and citations. Sonya was beautiful as always. Her light blue full length dress matched her eyes. The dress was strapless. Her tan from the summer and the trips to the Sinai and El Alamein was still even and attractive. She wore a blue sapphire pendant that drew attention to the slight cleavage showing between her breasts. Her blond hair was slightly longer, but the natural curls were still even and easy to manage.

Agnes was the first to comment. "Adam," Agnes began, "I do believe you've married an angel."

"Looks can be deceiving," Carol said with a smirk on her face.

"Mother!" Sonya injected.

"I'm kidding," Carol replied. "You look marvelous. I'm sure Adam is pleased to have you on his arm."

"The dress is very pretty, Sonya," Reverend Carlson interceded. "That's a beautiful necklace."

"Adam bought it for me while we were honeymooning in Turkey," Sonya responded as she went over to Adam and kissed him on the cheek.

Adam kissed his mother and thanked her for staying with Carol Agnes. Then he went to the closet and took out two furs. He placed the mink stole over Carol's shoulders and helped Sonya into the fox jacket. They were at the door when the phone rang.

"Adam McGregor," Adam answered. He listened for several moments without expression. "Let me check with my wife," Adam answered putting his hand over the phone.

"Sonya, how would you like to go to Rome?" Adam asked.

"Where is Rome?" she responded.

"Last I checked it was in Italy," Adam replied without expression.

"Rome, Italy?" she questioned. "Of course, I want to go."

Adam returned the phone to his lips, "If you can make it work, Scotty, we are ready to go." He listened for a few moments and then added, "Call me when you have the details worked out. Goodbye."

"What was that all about?" Agnes asked.

"That was an old friend at personnel. He wants to send me to the NATO Defense College."

Sonya broke in, "Is that like a War College?"

"It fills the square," Adam replied.

"You would get promoted?"

"Maybe. At least the lack of War College wouldn't be an excuse to keep me off the list. Let's go to the ball. I'll fill you in on the way."

They said good bye and went out the back door. Mustafa was waiting in the parking lot. As soon as they were in the car, Sonya and her parents in the rear seat and Adam in the front. Sonya demanded to know about the phone call.

Adam responded, "Scotty is the one who suggested that I might have been left off the Major General's list because I hadn't filled the War College square. He has a replacement for me in Cairo. We would leave next month."

How long would we be in Rome?" Sonya asked.

"Through the middle of July," he replied. "It's a six month course."

There was silence for a minute. Finally, Reverend Carlson broke the silence.

"Let me get this straight," he began. "You are going from a two year tour in Cairo to a six month tour in Rome. When do you work, General?" he remarked with a twinkle in his eye.

"Generals don't work, Dad," Adam replied, "they just tell others to work!"

"What a nice job!" Carol remarked.

"I love it," Sonya butted in. "The life of a General's wife is pretty good, too!"

Reverend Carlson laughed heartily. "When can we come to see you?" Reverend Carlson asked.

"I was thinking about that possibility," Adam replied. "It may be necessary to bring Carol Agnes to you and have you take her to

Doctor Kittleson. You could bring her back to us and spend some time in Rome. Is there any problem with you getting away?"

"Not since I retired," the Reverend replied.

"Doctor Kittleson suggested April to bring Carol Agnes," Sonya interjected. "What's the weather like in Rome in April?"

"The Med is still cold," Adam replied. "It improves a lot in May and June. Could you possibly get away for three weeks?"

"I guess so," Reverend Carlson said.

"I will be going on a tour of North European, NATO capitals. Wives are invited to go along everywhere. I would like to take Sonya with me if you and Carol could come and stay with the baby."

"Try to keep us away," Carol remarked.

"Then all we have to do is wait until Scotty calls back, hopefully with good news."

"Darling, where does the North European Tour take you?"

"This is the Itinerary," Adam explained. "We start out in Bonn, Germany, on to Amsterdam and The Hague. We go to Copenhagen, followed by Oslo. We leave Oslo for British Aerospace near Blackpool. The wives stay a day or two in Norway. After two day's at British Aerospace, north of Liverpool, we will rejoin the wives in London for three days. We finish with Brussels and Paris."

"Daddy!" Sonya exclaimed, "I could visit Uncle Harold's family in Bergen. How far is Bergen from Oslo, Adam?"

Adam replied, "Bergen can't be more than a couple hours from Oslo by train."

They arrived at the Mina House and the Rome conversation was put on hold. Adam took the Carlson's around the room and introduced them to a large number of Attache's and their spouses. When they met Commander Piangiani, Adam remembered that Gino Piangiani was a graduate of the NATO Defense College.

Gino immediately launched into a description of life in Rome and the experience of being at the War College. Adam slipped away to refill cocktails. When he returned Sonya was beside herself.

"Oh, Adam," she began, "I wish I had never heard of Rome."

"Why, for heaven sakes?"

"I want to go so bad, I'm sure you won't get the assignment," she said.

"We'll just have to wait and see," Adam replied. "Scotty has never failed me before."

Sonya cheered up and began to enjoy the evening. Sonya danced with her father for the first time since she was in her teens. Adam danced with Carol.

"I want to thank you, Adam," Carol said.

"What for?" he asked.

"For bringing happiness to my daughter. I tried hard to dislike you. As one problem was solved after another, I began to realize how important you were to Sonya. You've become very important to our entire family. You've become the family magician who fixes everything."

"Thank you, Carol. I really appreciate those kind words," Adam replied. "However, I must admit when I first met Sonya, my intentions were questionable. Maybe Sonya is the magician. Every time she meets someone she has a new friend for life. I know that I will love her 'til death do we part."

"Thank you, Adam," Carol finished.

There was an excellent dinner, more dancing and the welcoming of the New Year. Shortly after midnight, Adam motioned that it was time to go. Most of the Attache's were staying the night and Carol apologized for making Adam and Sonya leave the party.

"Actually," Adam said, "It was Carol Agnes who made us decide to return to Swiss Air."

When they arrived home, Agnes told Adam that he was to call Scotty as soon as he got in. It was around two pm in Texas. Sonya watched nervously as Adam listened and made notes.

"Thanks a lot Scotty," Adam finally said. "I'll keep in touch."

"Well?" Sonya exclaimed, "What did he say?"

"He said we need to be in Rome by the fifth of February. We need to ship the car tomorrow. We're going to Rome, Italy!" Adam replied.

"To Rome! Darling, you're wonderful," Sonya moaned. "Thank you! Thank you!" She kissed Adam passionately.

"We both need to thank Scotty. He made it happen."

"Oh, Adam," Agnes said, "I almost forgot. You had a call from Tom Carson in Khartoum. He said Ahmed Ibrahim needs to talk to you. You should call Tom Carson tomorrow." Agnes departed for the Hulls.

CHAPTER 25

Adam called Tom Carson as soon as he arrived at his office. Tom advised him that Ahmed Ibrahim had requested that they visit El Fasher on their next trip to the Sudan. He asked when they could come down.

"Can you get us clearance to Darfur next week?" Adam asked.

"That soon?" Tom inquired.

Adam explained that he would be leaving for Rome in early February. His last opportunity to visit would be the month of January. Tom agreed to try to set up the trip immediately. By noon, Tom called back to confirm that the trip was on for the second week in January.

"Will Sonya be able to come down?" Tom asked.

"I doubt that I could keep her off the plane," Adam responded facetiously. "Of course, she'll have to bring the baby."

"Can the baby travel?" Tom asked.

"She's already been half way around the world without a whimper," Adam replied.

"I'll call you back before the end of the day," Tom concluded.

Adam enlisted Dave Baldwin to drive his Corvette to Alexandria for shipment to Ostia, Rome's nearest port. Mustafa followed with a car to bring Captain Baldwin back to Cairo.

Adam learned that his replacement had been in Saudi Arabia. He was on the Colonel's list but he would be junior to both Captain Sanford and Colonel Peter Marshall. Adam stopped in Don Sanford's Office.

"Hi, Don," Adam got Captain Sanford's attention. "We must have been clairvoyant when we decided to leave you in the DATT'S quarters."

"How's that?" Don asked.

"It's official, Don. I'm leaving in a month for the NATO Defense College in Rome. You'll be assuming the Defense Attache' duties as senior O-Six. Congratulations."

"What about your replacement?"

"He's on the Colonel's list, but he hasn't pinned on yet. DIA may want to extend you for a few months while they are sorting out seniority."

"I just got notified that my replacement has been changed to Pakistan. I know I'm here until December. Lydia and the kids will be ecstatic."

"Good," Adam replied. "I'm glad I'm not screwing up your rotation."

"Not at all," Don replied. "We are going to miss you and Sonya. I think you'll like Rome better than Cairo."

"I was there once for a couple of days. Both Sonya and I are really looking forward to the assignment."

"We would like to have a farewell for you," Don continued. "What's your availability?"

"We are going to Khartoum next week. We'll be gone six or seven days. Pick a date between the fifteenth and the end of the month," Adam suggested.

"How about the last Friday in January," Don suggested. "That won't interfere with any Egyptian functions."

"Sounds like a winner. I'll check with Sonya and have her call Lydia and Emma Charles to seal the date."

When Adam returned from lunch, he found a message from Khartoum. Tom Carson had heard from Ahmed Ibrahim. The Governor requested that they come out to El Fasher for three days. He wanted to take them to Tundubai. Tundubai was a village on the

Chad border where trucks came into Darfur from Libya. They were returning Sudanese workers from Libya to their homes. The workers were paid in Libyan currency. The Libyan Government would not allow them to take the currency home. The Sudanese bought merchandise, primarily televisions and air conditioners, for resale in the Sudan. Khartoum had set up a customs house in Tundubai to extract customs. Tundubai had become a vibrant community. Ahmed Ibrahim would be giving a speech to further his campaign for re-election. Tundubai was about two to three hours from El Fasher via Land Rover. If they departed at eight am, they would be able to spend two to three hours in Tundubai and still return to El Fasher before dark. It all sounded very interesting. The results should make for interesting reading at DIA.

Adam made arrangements to brief the Ambassador and CIA on the mission. Tom Richardson met with the Ambassador and Adam the next day. Adam briefed them on the mission.

"It sounds like a routine boondoggle," the Ambassador commented.

Adam suggested they step out on to the Ambassador's balcony. Once they were out of earshot of anyone, Adam began, "I think it's suppose to look like a boondoggle. I expect Ahmed to have a special request for aid to get him and his family out of the Sudan."

"That's certainly a worthy cause," Tom Richardson interjected. "I'm afraid you would be on your own. The agency could only provide peripheral support on a very short term."

"I understand," Adam agreed.

"You realize, Adam," the Ambassador interjected, "Spar 80 can not be part of your plans. We would jeopardize our access in the Sudan."

"Of course, Sir!" Adam replied. "I would never involve Spar 80 or the Defense Attache's Office in any rescue effort. That's a sure way to get kicked out of the country. It would be bad enough to lose Attache's, but losing the aircraft, and the access it allows us would be a disaster."

"Let us know if you are successful after the fact," Tom Richardson concluded with an understanding smirk. "CIA will be pulling for you."

"It's worth looking into," the Ambassador agreed.

"Ambassador Barton speaks very highly of Ahmed Ibrahim. It's too bad Khartoum doesn't have a few leaders like Ahmed Ibrahim. With all the potential oil revenue that Chevron has uncovered, the Sudan could become the richest country in Africa in addition to being the largest."

"I fear that the current leadership in Khartoum is more likely to squander the possible largess than to take advantage of it," Adam concluded.

The Ambassador and Tom Richardson nodded their concurrence as the meeting concluded.

Adam returned to the office to complete the plans for the trip to Darfur. He called Dave Baldwin in and briefed him. They would leave on Friday, spend one day in Khartoum and travel to El Fasher on Sunday. They could go to Tundubai Monday or Tuesday and return to Khartoum on Wednesday. They would be back in Cairo late Thursday. The only passengers would be Sonya and the baby. There would be seats available for other passengers. Dave would check with the Consulate for possible travelers.

Next Adam called Sonya to tell her the plans. She wanted to know if she could take the baby to Darfur. Adam suggested that the flight would be fine but the off road trip to Tundulai might be a little rough. They decided to wait until they got to Khartoum to decide. There was no question that Sonya would take Carol Agnes to Khartoum. She wanted to show her baby to Marty Carson.

Sonya heard the baby crying and went to the crib. Of course, the baby needed changing. She completed this chore and then rocked Carol until she went to sleep. Sonya busied herself by going through her clothes to decide what to put in shipping to Rome and what to keep in carry on. Her mind wandered as she planned. She realized that Adam hadn't made love to her for several days. She wondered if he was losing interest. On a whim, she called Lydia Sanford to see if Ellen would be available to baby-sit for two nights. Lydia suggested that she bring the baby to Maadi. Between Lydia and Ellen, there would always be someone nearby.

Sonya called the Meridien and booked the room where she and Adam had their first encounter. The room was available for two nights. She packed two bags with changes of clothes and swim suits. The Corvette was already gone. She called Adam's office to see if one of the drivers was available to take her and the baby to Maadi. Mustafa was at the back door in ten minutes.

Mustafa drove Sonya and Carol Agnes to the Sanfords. Then he dropped Sonya at the Meridien. She instructed Mustafa to bring Adam to the Meridien after work. As soon as she got to the room, she changed into her swimsuit and went to the pool. She swam some laps and sunbathed for twenty minutes and then went to the room for a shower. After the shower she combed out her hair and put on her makeup. She was lounging in the bathrobe when Adam knocked on the door.

"Who is it?" she called out as she approached the door.

"It's your husband," he replied.

She opened the door and ushered him in. She kissed him quickly and then turned toward the turned down bed and peeled off her robe. She stretched out on the bed and spread her legs reaching out with her arms to invite him to make love to her.

"I need a shower," he said.

"Later," she said. "I love the way you smell when you're a little bit sweaty."

"I take it that you're ready for some more practice breeding," he said, as he proceeded to shed clothing onto the floor.

"Actually, I'm ready for breeding," she responded. "I'm off the pill and I decided that I would like to get pregnant."

"I'll delay my shower and service Madame as requested. If it doesn't take, Madam may rest assured that I will be available for further service."

"Quit joking around and make love to me," Sonya demanded.

There were no more complaints. Afterward, they laid side by side. "What made you decide to come to the Meridien?" Adam asked.

"You remember when we were visiting the Scott's in Cypress," Sonya began. "When you and Brian were away with the boys, I had a bout of morning sickness. Sandra spotted it immediately. She asked how long we had been together. I related the whole story about our encounter at the Meridien and the trip to El Fasher and Khartoum. She asked how long I had been having morning sickness. I told her that my first time was the last morning in Khartoum. She suggested that I was pregnant by my husband. I said that wasn't possible because we hadn't had sex since my last pregnancy. She said, 'Then Adam must have knocked you up on the first encounter.' I decided that was the luckiest day of my life and I wanted to come back to the scene of my good fortune."

Adam responded by kissing her tenderly and making love to her again. They spent another night in the Meridien and then departed for Khartoum.

Tom Carson met Spar 80 at the usual parking area. Sonya emerged from the aircraft carrying Carol Agnes in her arms. The baby woke up at the sound of Tom's voice. She didn't cry. She looked at Tom, blinked and went back to sleep.

"I usually cause babies to cry," Tom began. "She doesn't seem the least bit interested."

"All she does is eat, sleep and poop," Sonya said. "She wakes up once or twice at night. She usually goes to sleep before we put her down."

"How old is she?" Tom asked. "She's so tiny."

"She's just six months," Adam tossed in as he walked up. "She's our little miracle."

"Well, Marty gave me orders to get that baby to the house as soon as possible. You'll all be staying with us until we leave for El Fasher on Monday."

"Sounds good, Tom," Adam replied. "It's just the three of us and Dave Baldwin."

"Dave's wife hasn't returned?"

"No, and it doesn't look like she will," Adam concluded as they boarded Tom's Land Rover.

Marty Carson was at the door of the villa when they drove up. She came out to the Land Rover.

"Let me see this baby," she demanded. Sonya uncovered the baby's face for Marty.

"She's so tiny," Marty remarked.

"Under normal circumstances, she should be a new born," Sonya remarked.

They went in the villa and took the baby to the bedroom where Adam and Sonya would be sleeping. Sonya changed Carol Agnes' diaper and put her in her basket. The baby went to sleep. Sonya and Marty went to the kitchen and had a glass of wine. Tom took Adam and Dave outside where he had a bar set up. It was time for cocktails.

"Have you given any thought to having more children?" Marty asked.

"I told Adam I wanted two boys to go with Carol," Sonya responded.

"Good luck," Marty answered. "The odds are in favor of more girls."

"I know. I'm still young and I want to try to give Adam at least one boy."

"When will you start trying to get pregnant?" Marty asked.

"Yesterday," Sonya said in a whisper.

"You are anxious. I don't believe I would want to be pregnant in this part of the world."

"Oh!" Sonya began, "Didn't Tom tell you? We are leaving for Rome in February. We'll be at the NATO Defense College until July."

"Let's go outside," Marty suggested. As soon as they arrived on the patio, Marty accosted Tom.

"Tom, why didn't you tell me Adam and Sonya are leaving for Rome?"

"I forgot to mention it. I knew you would find out when they arrived! Sorry Dear."

"All right," Marty replied. Then she turned to Adam and spoke, "When did you find out?"

"I received a call from Air Force Personnel on New Year's Eve. I've never been to War College. It was rumored that I was deleted from the Major General's list because I hadn't been to War College. A good friend at Personnel got me the assignment. Who in their right mind would turn down six months in Rome?" Adam concluded.

"Then this will be the last time we will see you in the Sudan?" Tom remarked.

"I'm afraid so," Adam replied. "When are you rotating?"

"We leave in June," Tom began. "I've asked for ROTC duty in the Mountain States. We want to retire in the Denver area. I'm hoping for duty at Colorado U or Denver U. A two year assignment would take me to thirty years."

"What part of June?" Sonya asked.

"My replacement is due in by the fifteenth. We plan to leave the next week," Tom replied.

"You should stop in Rome on your way home," Adam suggested knowing that was Sonya's intention.

"That would be fun," Marty chimed in. "We've never been to Italy. Surely, you will have a flock of visitors while you are there."

"We tentatively have that all worked out," Sonya began. "We have to take Carol Agnes to the Mayo Clinic for a checkup in the Spring. I plan to take her back in April. My parents and Adam's mother will bring her back to Rome in late May. They will stay and take care of the baby while we are on our North European tour. We'll be back the third week in June. By the time you get to Rome we should be qualified tour guides."

"Tom," Marty ordered. "Refresh our drinks and turn your gazelles loose while I try to digest all this. There has to be a reason it won't work." Marty went into the kitchen to start dinner. Sonya followed her to lend a hand. Marty was crying.

"Marty! What's the matter?" Sonya asked.

"I feel so guilty, Sonya."

"But why?" Sonya pressed.

"When you first came to Khartoum, I suspected that you were stalking Adam. I watched you looking at him. I knew you were in love and I thought you were a tramp because I knew you were married. When you had your accident, I thought God had punished you for your sins. I wished you were dead. Then Adam came down and told us that you were going to survive and I began to realize that he loved you. I'm Catholic and I couldn't accept that the death of your husband and children wasn't God's punishment for your sins. I hated you for involving Adam. You came to visit after you were married and I began to see how much you and Adam loved each other. As a Catholic, I have always wanted to visit Rome, see St. Peters and see the Pope. Now thanks to you and Adam, I will get my wish. I couldn't accept your kindness without clearing my conscience of the evil thoughts I've harbored. I hope you understand and can forgive me."

"Marty, I understand. Quite frankly I didn't like myself very much. I had terrible guilt feelings about my feelings for Adam.

When I saw the pictures on the television of the attack at St. Mathews, I wanted to die. I remember backing away from the TV. I don't remember the fall. I must have fainted before I went over the railing."

"What happened when you came out of the coma?"

"I didn't know where I was. My first thought was that I was in an asylum. I asked a nurse where I was. She said, 'You're in the Mayo Clinic.' I said, 'How did I get here?' She said, 'Your husband brought you.' I was about to respond when Dr. Snyder came in the room. He introduced himself and told me that Adam had brought me to Rochester. He asked me if I remembered Adam. I said yes, but that Adam was not my husband. He explained that Adam had claimed me as his common law spouse because he was the father of our daughter. He explained that my parents who were my next of kin had agreed to Adam's claim when they learned that Adam was Carol Agnes' father. So here we are!"

"Did your parents say why they had agreed to Adam's claim to be your common law spouse?"

"My father would have opposed Adam. However, my brother Earl looked into the cost of keeping me at the hospital. He warned my father that they could not afford my bills. He recommended that they acquiesce to Adam's claim. Of course, when Carol Agnes was born, the blood tests confirmed that Adam was the father.

"The baby was premature?" Marty asked.

"Yes," Sonya continued. "She really is a miracle. She should still be in the womb. Dr. Snyder wanted to abort Carol Agnes. Adam insisted on a Cesarean birth. Fortunately, it worked. Of course, it doubled the cost of our stay in the Clinic."

"Are you guys making dinner or just gossiping?" Tom called into the kitchen.

"Everything is on schedule," Marty called back. "Have another drink. We'll eat in forty-five minutes." She turned to Sonya.

"Sonya, let's stay here. I want to hear the rest of this epic love story uninterrupted. We would be left in El Fasher while the men go to Tundubai anyway. We wouldn't want to expose Carol Agnes to that cross country trip."

"As much as I would like to see Mr. Ibrahim again, I agree that the baby is not ready for that trip and I don't relish a day in El

Fasher with the men gone," Sonya agreed. "I'll announce our decision." Sonya went out into the yard.

The two Thomson Gazelles were bounding around the perimeter of the spacious lawn. They each had two spiraling horns sticking straight out of the brows. They didn't run. They bounded from one stop to the next stopping occasionally to eat and drink. Sonya watched the Gazelles for several moments.

"They're so cute, Tom. Where did you get them?"

"They were orphaned by some hunters," Tom explained. "We brought them home when they were babies. We've had them for six months. They have really matured in the last three months."

Sonya remembered that she had come out to deliver a message. "We will be eating about dark. You'll have to come in to fill your plates. By the way, Marty and I and Carol Agnes will forgo the trip to El Fasher."

"That's probably a good idea," Adam agreed. "The overland trip will be brutal."

After dinner the two couples played bridge until ten. By ten-thirty, they were all in bed. The following morning everyone was up by seven. The women made breakfast for the travelers. The men were on their way by eight-thirty.

Sonya took care of the baby while Marty made breakfast. As soon as fresh coffee was ready, Marty called for Sonya. Sonya brought Carol Agnes in her basket.

"Now," Sonya began, "Where were we?"

"You were telling me about the birth of Carol Agnes."

"Yes," Sonya replied. "It was three weeks later that I came out of the coma. Dr. Snyder had me put in a pool to start the therapy needed to get my muscles working again. I was able to talk and I began to get my memory back. I got to see my baby through the glass for the first time. Dr. Snyder explained that Adam had made the decision to take the baby. That's when I learned that Adam was legally my common law husband. I wanted to talk to Adam but he was not in Cairo. I received a call from Adam's mother, Agnes. She announced that she was coming to see me. I was petrified. I had no clothes and no makeup. I was not able to leave the hospital to do any shopping. I was going to meet my prospective mother-in-law in a hospital smock."

"My God!" Marty interrupted as she poured more coffee. "What did you do?"

"I met her in my hospital gown."

"What a way to meet your mother-in-law!" Marty said. "Was she really terrible?"

"I was in a fit of depression. Dr. Snyder called my mother and told her I needed some help with my depression. Mother called Adam's mother and suggested they both come to Rochester to meet with me. Mother scolded me and left me with Agnes. She was abrupt. I didn't know what to think. She wanted to see the baby. We went to the incubation room and looked at Carol Agnes. She commented that she was so tiny. She asked me if I loved Adam. I answered, yes. She said, 'I guess he must love you. He's never paid this much attention to any woman since his divorce.' She asked if I wanted to get married at my father's church. I said that I would rather not get married in Minnesota because of my dead husband's family. She said, how about getting married in Washington. I said, I just want to get married as soon as possible. She asked if I had talked to Adam. I said, I had tried but Adam was in the Sudan. She said, tell him we are planning your wedding and we need to know how soon he can get to the States. She was grinning. She really surprised me when she said, 'He's a terrible rake. Maybe between the two of us we can turn him into a decent husband and give me a grandson as well.' We've been good friends ever since."

"My word," Marty responded. "What did Adam have to say?"

"He called Dr. Snyder to inquire about my health. I was in the office and Dr. Snyder gave me the phone. I said, hello, am I speaking to my common law husband? There was a pause and he said, 'Sonya, is that you?' I said, 'Yes, when are you coming to get me and our daughter?' He was silent for a moment. Then he said, 'I'll make arrangements immediately. I need to call Mother and bring her out. I promised she would meet you.' I said, 'She was here yesterday.' There was another long pause. He said, 'How did you get along?' I said, 'We have the wedding planned. It will be in Washington as soon as you can get here, pick up me and Carol Agnes and get to D.C.' He asked me how I liked Agnes. I said, 'She's wonderful. She likes me better than she likes you already.' He said,

'I'll call you tonight with my schedule.' It was such fun."

They both laughed. "Do you think he's jealous of your relationship with his mother?"

"No. He may have been for a few days, but not now. He's happy. His mother is pleased that he's married and that she will finally have some grandchildren. We really had a great time over Christmas with both my parents and Agnes. They'll all visit us in Rome."

******

Meanwhile, Spar 80 had landed in El Fasher. Ahmed Ibrahim was there to meet the aircraft. He informed all three officers of where they would be sleeping. Dave Baldwin would be in the Guest House and Adam and Colonel Carson would be in the rooms occupied by Adam and Sonya when they had visited on their trip to Geniena. They all gathered at the Guest House for drinks and dinner. They went over the plans for the trip to Tundubai the next day. The Governor invited Adam and Tom Carson back to his quarters where they shared some fine brandy and learned the real reason for the trip.

"Gentlemen," Ahmed began, "I've asked you here to request your help. I desperately need to get myself and my family out of the Sudan. As you know my wife and two sons are virtual prisoners in our quarters in Khartoum. I must get the President's permission to visit my family. They dictate the length of my visits."

"Do they ever let your family out of Khartoum?" Adam asked.

"Only once a year. They let her and the boys attend an anniversary celebration of the Catholic Church in Wau. I'm not allowed to join them. They make certain that I'm here in El Fasher when they are in Wau. In order to join them, I would have to have access to an airplane. An overland trip to Wau by Land Rover would take several days."

Adam replied, "Let Tom and me think about this overnight, Ahmed. We can try to come up with an answer before we leave on Tuesday." They finished their brandies and parted.

Adam and Tom met in the adjoining bathroom. Tom was about to brush his teeth. "Adam," Tom began, "This sounds like a job for Spar 80."

"No way, Tom!" Adam responded. "My Ambassador says we can't involve the Kingair because the loss of access would be a disaster. CIA agrees with him."

"You're thinking about picking up the whole family on the same day? If you don't do it with Spar 80, how are you going to do it?" Tom concluded.

"Let's leave the logistics to me, Tom. You need to be sure that Mrs. Ibrahim and her two sons are together in Wau on the right day."

"You're crazy, Adam!" Tom exclaimed. "You're on your way to being the Chief of Staff. Why would you jeopardize your whole career for Ahmed Ibrahim?"

"Tom, my chances of Chief of Staff are not nearly as good as you suppose. However, that's not my big problem. I've been in the Middle East for four years. In that time I've met three men whom I consider extremely important to the future of the Middle East. Anwar Sadat, John Baranga, and Ahmed Ibrahim. Sadat is dead. John is on the run and Ahmed Ibrahim is in danger and he's a hostage. We got John Baranga's family out safely. I want to get Ahmed and his family out if we can."

Tom continued, "You think there is a better chance to get them out of Wau than Khartoum?"

"Gudrun's house in Khartoum is under twenty-four hour guard. Any effort to get her and the boys away from the house would probably arouse the whole town. At least in Wau, her watch dogs would not be able to call out the Army."

"Okay, Adam," Tom replied. "I will be in my last days in Khartoum. If I become Persona-non-Grata, it won't be a big deal."

"How about our old friend, Derek Douglas?" Adam asked.

"The fat man?" Tom said. "I haven't seen him since Juba. I'll ask around." They went to bed.

Everyone gathered at the Guest House the following morning. They had coffee and rolls made with honey. The Governor had three vehicles lined up. His Range Rover was first. Two military Land Rovers would follow. Adam and Tom would ride with Ahmed in the Range Rover. Dave Baldwin would ride in one of the Land Rovers. The third vehicle was to be a spare in case one vehicle broke down.

El Fasher had less than twenty miles of paved road. It was only a short time to the end of the road. The three vehicles spread out in line abreast traveling across the semi-arid landscape. The two military drivers were careful not to get ahead of the Governor's vehicle.

The terrain was relatively level with an occasional group of small hills. Every two or three miles they would come upon a Wadi. The military drivers would fall in line behind the Governor to find a place to cross the Wadi. There was some sparse vegetation, scrub trees, and cactus. A few Acacia trees were spread along the banks of the Wadi. The Governor kept his speed up going over fifty mph on the level areas and slowing for the Wadi's. Needless to say, the ride was rough and not conducive to conversation. Everyone was worn out by the time they reached Tundubai.

Their first stop was at the Customs House. There were nine trucks lined up for inspection. Four were Mercedes. Three were Volvos. The other two were British built. All the trucks were built for desert travel. They each had six gigantic wheels. The tires appeared larger than large aircraft tires. All the tires were engine driven. The truck beds were loaded with boxes. All appeared to be appliances. The labels were mostly televisions and air conditioners. They would bring a premium in Khartoum.

The town mayor was the Governor's host. After the visit to the Customs House, they were escorted to the Mayor's version of City Hall. It was the newest building in the town. They were served lunch with coffee, tea and Pepsi Cola.

The local dialect was a mystery to the Americans. Adam could pick up some Arabic words, but not enough to understand the conversations. Ahmed apologized for the inconvenience. He would be giving his speech in the local dialect. He would translate for them on the return ride to El Fasher.

The central square of Tundubai was set up for the Governor's speech. Adam, Tom and David were provided seats on a stage at the back of the square. The area between them and the dais was filled with native men and an occasional boy. There were no women present. While the mayor was giving his introductory remarks, five camels lined up behind the VIP seats. Each camel had at least two men on top where they could see the dais over the heads of the VIPs. About halfway through the Governor's speech, the camel drivers decided to change riders on one camel. When the camel was poked with a stick to get it to kneel down, it complained loudly. The speech was interrupted while the culprits changed places. When the Governor resumed speaking, there was a large roar of laughter and clapping from the crowd.

"What did he say?" Tom whispered to Adam.

"I think Ahmed made a joke about the camel's wisdom and it's contempt for political speeches," Adam whispered to Tom.

The speech went on for another ten minutes. When it was concluded, the audience responded with enthusiastic applause and several rifle shots in the air. Dave whispered to Adam, "Are they firing blanks or should we cover our heads?"

"No, and you're too late," Adam replied. They made their way through the crowd to join Ahmed and proceeded to the Rovers. They started back for El Fasher. One of the Land Rovers hit a rock resulting in a flat tire. The driver and another soldier were left to change the tire. The rest went on to El Fasher.

Adam, Tom and Dave were invited to Governor Ibrahim's quarters for dinner. They enjoyed cocktails and a leg of lamb dinner. Ahmed served an excellent Bordeaux with dinner. After dinner, the four enjoyed after-dinner drinks for an hour. When they broke up, Adam stayed behind for a few minutes.

He spoke, "Ahmed, would you mind taking a drive out to the aircraft?"

"Not at all. Do you need to check on Spar80?"

"I'll explain on the way," Adam responded.

They got into the Governor's Range Rover and drove to the airport. They were followed by a Land Rover. The trip took ten minutes. Adam went to the airplane and removed a briefcase. They returned to their quarters. They went into the Governor's den.

"What's in the briefcase?" Ahmed asked.

"Maps, a manual on the aircraft, some forms, nothing important."

"Then why the hell did we go?" Ahmed pressed.

"First, I wanted to see how long it would take to get to the airport. By the way, are you sure this room isn't bugged?"

"It isn't," Ahmed replied. "My bedroom is bugged. The one in here doesn't work. What else did we accomplish?"

"I noticed there was a soldier at the airport. Is someone always there?"

"Only if there's an airplane there."

"Could you walk to the airport without being seen?"

"Yes, if necessary," Ahmed replied. "What else?"

"Did you notice that the full moon lit up the airport quite well?"

"Yes, I suppose so," Ahmed replied.

"Okay, here's the plan. If your wife is allowed to go to Wau, she will be there on June seventeenth. There will be a full moon on the night of June seventeenth. An airplane will pick your family up in Wau between nine and ten pm. The same airplane will pick you up between eleven-thirty and midnight on the same evening."

"How will I know it's still on?" Ahmed asked.

"You will be notified if it's off. Otherwise be prepared to be at the airport alone at the appointed time."

"How will I know it's the right aircraft?"

"If the aircraft lands without lights and without clearance, you'll have to assume it's the right aircraft."

"Will I know the pilots?"

"If all goes well, you'll know the pilot," Adam promised. "We can't put it off for another year because one pilot can't make it."

"That's five months from now," Ahmed noted.

"We can't get your wife out of Khartoum without an International Incident. Getting you out of Darfur with your family still in Khartoum would probably end up in a hostage situation. Be thankful the almighty has seen fit to coordinate the church celebration in Wau with a full moon."

"You're right, of course!" Ahmed replied. "I will remember that no news is good news. I'm in debt to you my friend. Somehow, I'll pay you back someday."

"Between you and John Baranga, I've learned more about the Middle East and Africa than from all of my other contacts and travels. I apologize for my Nation's lack of interest in the areas."

They shook hands and parted. The next morning they joined for breakfast. Spar 80 departed for Khartoum at nine am. They were all back in the Carson's quarters by three pm. The men took turns in the shower and everyone was ready for cocktails at five. When they were all in possession of a libation, they proceeded to the patio where they could watch the gazelles perform.

Marty mentioned that Gudrun Ibrahim had spent the midday with them. Her two boys were with her.

"Did she mention going to Wau in June?" Tom asked.

"She said she had requested permission to go for the annual celebration of the opening of the church. That would be in mid-June. She wanted to know if Spar 80 might be available to take them to Wau."

"It's hard to say that far in advance," Tom responded. "That's up to Cairo to say."

"Press Adam to get it done," Sonya interrupted. "He's probably already got a plan to rescue the Ibrahim's, don't you Darling?"

She looked over at Adam. He was staring at her like he had never looked at her before. She realized she had opened a taboo subject.

"What about it, Adam?" Marty said. "Have you got a plan?"

"I'll be in Rome," Adam replied. He had calmed himself. "I can't imagine how I could possibly be involved in anything in Africa or the Middle East for the foreseeable future."

"Oh, excuse me," Sonya said rising from her chair.

"Where are you going?" Marty asked.

"When nature calls you have to answer," Sonya replied. She was gone for a relatively long time. Adam decided to check on her. She was in the bedroom. He walked in without knocking. She was crying.

"Oh! Darling!" she began. "I was just joking. I didn't realize you really have a plan."

"I do not have a plan!" he replied. "If I had a plan it would be none of your business. You are never to broach this subject again. Do you understand."

"Yes, Darling! I understand. Can I go along?"

"Damn it, Sonya!" he said with teeth clenched. "You just promised to never mention it again."

"Yes, Darling! I promise!" She had her fingers crossed. They returned to the group.

The conversation reverted to the prospective visit of the Carson's to Rome. Adam gave Tom a rundown on his itinerary for the North European tour. Adam would give the Carson's an update on his travels during June once he had a firm schedule. The Carson's agreed that they would plan to spend two weeks with Adam and Sonya on their way back to the States.

After dinner, the Carson's and the McGregor's played bridge until eleven. Everyone turned in for the night. As soon as Sonya and Adam were alone in their bedroom, Sonya began to pout.

"You certainly were friendly this evening," she remarked. He didn't reply.

"Did you hear me?" Sonya pressed.

"Yes, I heard you!"

"Are you still angry with me?"

"Sonya, I don't think you appreciate the sensitivity of what we were talking about. I don't want to talk about it until we get back to Cairo."

"Can we make love?" she asked.

"Of course! Get your clothes off!"

"I'll be ready just as soon as I finish in the bathroom," Sonya responded as she disappeared into the bathroom. When she returned to the bedroom it was completely dark.

"Darling," she whispered, "you know I'm afraid of the dark. Where are you?"

"Right here," he said as he swept her up in his arms and carried her to the bed. He kissed her before he laid her on the bed. They made love for a long time. The baby slept right through the night.

They left Khartoum the next morning at nine and arrived in Cairo at three pm. Adam went back to the office. After checking the message traffic, he went to the commissary and picked up two steaks and some veggies for cooking and for a salad. At the apartment, Sonya bathed and fed Carol Agnes. She was ready to make dinner when Adam returned.

Adam poured himself a Scotch on the rocks and opened a bottle of wine for Sonya. "Any sign of morning sickness?" he asked.

"Not yet," she replied. She had Carol Agnes in her arms as

she fed her the special diet. "Our daughter is beginning to grow hair," Sonya added.

"I noticed that in Khartoum," Adam replied. "I thought she would be a blond. It looks like her hair will be dark."

"It's too early to tell," Sonya replied. "My mother says I had dark hair until I was three."

The baby finished her bottle and promptly went to sleep. Sonya put Carol Agnes in her basket in their bedroom. She returned to the living room.

"Can we discuss your plan now?" she asked.

"No!" he replied.

"Why not?"

"You don't have a need to know."

"As long as you understand that I'm going with you," Sonya responded.

"We'll see," he responded. "Maybe you'll be pregnant and won't feel like traveling."

"By that time, I'll be over the morning sickness and feeling fine. I won't be far enough along to worry about an early birth. I carried both of my boys to full term. I was in the peak of health between the fourth and seventh months. The rigors of travel will not bother me and I will make a marvelous shill."

Adam didn't answer immediately. He was thinking. Finally he responded.

"The shill role may not be a bad idea. Promise me you will not discuss this with anyone. If, by the time to travel, you are feeling good and we haven't had any leaks, I will consider taking you along."

"You're a tyrant," she exclaimed as she crossed to his chair and sat in his lap. "I love you so much, I don't care. How about a little more breeding after dinner? I want to be sure that I'm ready for my role."

"I think that can be arranged," Adam replied. They had a leisurely dinner and went to bed early.

CHAPTER 26

When Adam arrived at the office the next morning, his replacement was there to meet him.

Lt. Colonel Joe Dugan saluted smartly as he introduced himself. Adam returned his salute and shook his hand.

"This was short notice, Joe," Adam commented. "Do you have family coming to Cairo?"

"Yes Sir." Colonel Dugan replied. "The kids and Margo will come over as soon as school is out. I have two boys and a girl."

"Good, that will leave plenty of time for the Embassy to arrange for suitable quarters. In the meantime you can stay with my wife and me at Swiss Air. We will be leaving next week. The Swiss Air flat is paid up through the end of February. That will give you plenty of time to look at the available housing."

"Are you sure I won't be imposing, General?"

"Not at all," Adam replied. "Our spare bedroom comes with a full bath and our baby doesn't cry. At least she hasn't so far."

"How did you get a baby that doesn't cry?"

"It's a long story. I'll let Sonya fill you in," Adam continued. "Have Mustafa run you by your hotel and pick up your gear. You can swing back by here and pick me up about four. We'll have some time to chat before we leave for our farewell party at Captain Sanford's quarters in Maadi."

As usual, Friday was an easy day. The Egyptian offices were closed and message traffic from out of country was light. Adam was ready to leave the office at four. Colonel Dugan and Mustafa were waiting in the Embassy Courtyard when Adam appeared. They drove to Swiss Air. They unloaded the car and Adam asked Mustafa to return at five-thirty.

They went up to the apartment. Adam called out for Sonya, "Are you decent?"

"It depends on what you have in mind," Sonya called back.

"We have a house guest!" he exclaimed.

"Go in the living room. I'll be out in a minute." She appeared in a sheath dress. "Adam, be a dear and zip me up."

"Yes, Dear! Joe, this is my wife, Sonya." He went behind Sonya and zipped up her dress. Sonya extended her hand.

"Welcome to Cairo, Joe," Sonya said. "Please excuse our informality. We're newlyweds and we still fool around a lot."

"You can't be too new," Joe replied as he shook Sonya's hand. "I understand you have a baby."

"Yes, we do!" Sonya said. "However, the time line is kind of jumbled. I'm sure you will hear all about it in due time."

"I didn't mean to pry," Joe replied.

"Not to worry, Joe. It's really an open book," Sonya continued. "However, it does take some time to tell."

Adam interrupted, "Joe and I are going to have a drink while I give him a rundown on the office staff and some of my best contacts. Mustafa will be back to pick us up at five-thirty."

"Do you like Scotch, Joe?" Adam asked.

"Yes, Sir!" Joe replied.

"Ever had Famous Grouse?"

"No, but I've never had a Scotch I couldn't drink."

"Me, too." Adam replied as he opened the liquor cabinet.

They chatted for nearly forty minutes. Joe took notes on the kind of information he could trade with certain Attache's and what he could expect in return. Adam also gave him a rundown on the Attache's from behind the Iron Curtain. It was time to leave for Maadi. Adam checked the back door. Mustafa was in the parking lot.

"Are you ready, Sonya?"

"Yes, Darling. Carol Agnes is in her basket. She's sleeping so carry it carefully. I have her baby kit." They departed.

"How old is she?" Joe asked.

"She's coming up on eight months," Adam replied.

"How long have you been married?"

There was a slight pause. "Five months," Sonya volunteered.

"Oh!" Joe responded. "I'm sorry."

Adam and Sonya broke out laughing. "Don't worry, Joe," Adam injected. "You can get the whole story from anyone in the office tomorrow. It's too long to tell tonight."

Ellen Sanford met them a the door. She immediately took the baby's basket and kit. She assured Sonya that she would stay with the baby until they were ready to depart.

Don Sanford followed his daughter and took the McGregor's and Joe Dugan out to the garden. There was a large group already assembled. A make-shift receiving line formed as individuals and couples slowly came over to wish the McGregor's bon voyage and to introduce themselves to Joe Dugan. Sir William and Lady Agatha led the procession followed by Alistair and Wanda Ames. Colonel Ehrlich was there with his wife who was visiting from Germany. Sonya counted thirty nine guests total. Several parties departed for other functions. The remainder stayed for the buffet dinner that was spread out on the veranda. Numerous tables were set up in the sun porch, dining room, and den. Everyone was able to find a seat. The Sanford's had borrowed servants from Pete Marshall and Dave Baldwin so that wine glasses and other beverages could be replenished throughout the dining event.

Sir William and Lady Agatha left early. Before they departed, they informed Adam and Sonya that William and Cecilia would be married in London on the fifteenth of June. Adam volunteered that he would be on the North European tour with the NATO Defense College. He was sure that he could get away for the wedding. If not, Sonya would certainly be there.

By eleven pm, most of the guests had departed. Adam and Sonya, the Sanford's, Pete Marshal, Dave Baldwin and Joe Dugan gathered in the living room to finish their drinks. Adam announced that he, Sonya and the baby would be leaving for Rome on Tuesday.

He invited everyone to Swiss Air for a final get together on Monday evening. Everyone agreed. They would come early, cocktails at five, dinner at six-thirty.

Sonya went to the bedroom where Carol Agnes was sleeping. Ellen was awake but yawning. Sonya tried to pay her. She refused to take anything. They all departed by eleven-thirty.

Adam and Sonya were busy over the weekend. There was packing to do and there was the problem of selling Sonya's horse, Abul Kheer, back to the stable. They went out Saturday morning. Of course, Rubayah renigged on his promise to return all of Sonya's money. Sonya was too upset to haggle. She took the baby out to see the horse. Adam continued to negotiate the price. Finally, Adam conceded that he must close the deal because they were leaving on Tuesday.

"Rubayah," Adam began, "You owe me a thousand Egyptian Pounds. I know you aren't going to pay me that amount. If you will pay me eight hundred pounds, I will throw in a bottle of Scotch."

"Make it two bottles" Rubayah replied.

"Done!" Adam agreed. He would bring the Scotch the next day.

Adam found Sonya in the stable with the stallion. Adam relayed the terms of his deal. Sonya was visibly upset. "He told me he would give back all of our money," she said as the tears welled up in her eyes.

"Welcome to the Middle East. Promises have short lives here," Adam replied.

"How much is the Scotch worth?" she asked.

"Fifteen dollars, American," Adam replied. "It runs about seventy Egyptian Pounds per bottle in Cairo."

"What will we do with all those Pounds in two more days?"

"Joe Dugan will take them off my hands before we leave," Adam replied.

Adam concluded his deal with Rubayah early Sunday morning. When he returned to the apartment, Sonya and Carol Agnes were dressed to leave.

"I would like to go to St. Mathews one last time," she suggested.

"I'll grab a quick shower," Adam said. "We can make the

eleven am service."

"Then you don't mind?" she asked.

"I think it's called closure. I've always regretted missing services for lost comrades. Failing to pay last respects has a way of remaining in the back of ones mind forever. I'm sure you have thoughts about John and the boys often."

"Yes, I do! Sometimes, I look at myself in the mirror and break down crying."

Adam picked Sonya up and carried her to the bed. When he laid her down, she rolled up into a ball and began to sob. He brought her a box of tissues. He kissed her on the forehead and left her to mourn.

Sonya was sleeping when he returned from his shower. He finished dressing and then gently woke her.

"We can still make it to the service if you are up to it," Adam whispered.

They arrived at St. Mathews a few minutes before the service began. The greeter was new and he had no idea who they were.

"Welcome to St. Mathews," he stated. "My name is Dennis Johnson. I'm with USAID. I'm new in Cairo."

"We're the McGregor's," Adam replied. "Mrs. McGregor's former husband, John Olsen was the previous pastor here. We're leaving on Tuesday and this is our last opportunity to say goodbye."

"Please have a seat where ever you are comfortable," Dennis replied with hesitation. He obviously knew who the McGregor's were via rumors from the congregation.

They selected an empty pew a few rows from the front on the left. No one sat near them. Adam laid Carol Agnes out on the pew between himself and Sonya. The baby was sleeping as usual. There was considerable whispering going on until the choir started the procession with the opening hymn. The pastor, Joseph Ericson, brought up the rear. Pastor Ericson introduced himself to those attending for the first time. Adam looked at the program to see if there was a title for the sermon. There wasn't. He hoped it wasn't on original sin. It turned out to be about the Prodigal Son. Adam thought, at least there was no direct correlation between the sermon's theme and the sins of Adam and Sonya. After the service, Adam carried the baby and followed Sonya as they joined the queue of departing worshipers. Several people spoke to Sonya.

"Sonya, you look wonderful. We had heard that you were in a coma," a woman commented.

"I was in a coma for five months," Sonya replied. "Our daughter was born by Cesarean section because I was beginning to lose weight. Shortly after her birth, I came out of the coma."

"How old is the baby?"

"She's seven months. She was taken prematurely, so she isn't nearly as big as normal."

"She was conceived while you were still married to John," the woman continued.

"Yes. I had made up my mind to leave John and Adam is the father of this baby."

"Aren't you ashamed to have deserted your husband in his time of need?" the assault continued.

"It certainly is dichotomous. As my husband points out to me, if I had been with my family that Sunday, I would be dead." She turned to meet Pastor Ericson, who had heard some of the conversation.

"Thank you for attending our service. I understand that you are leaving Cairo."

"Yes, Pastor. My husband is being assigned to the NATO Defense College in Rome."

"Congratulations," Pastor Ericson turned his attention to Adam. "I'm sure you will enjoy Rome, General." He turned back to Sonya, "Has your baby been baptized, Sonya?"

"My father, who is a Pastor, baptized her before we left the Mayo Clinic."

"Very good. We wish you God's speed."

The McGregor's hurried off to the car where Mustafa was waiting. They were not interested in more conversation with the parishioners. Mustafa dropped them back at the apartment. They spent the afternoon writing thank you notes. Sunday evening, after having dinner, they made phone calls to the States informing the family members that they were leaving Cairo on Tuesday. They would be living in the Residence Garden in the EUR suburb of Rome.

Adam paid a last visit to the Embassy on Monday morning

then returned to the apartment. Sonya bundled the baby and they took her along to the Swiss Air Restaurant where they had lunch. Adam noticed that Carol Agnes was making sounds.

"What's with Carol Agnes?" he asked.

"She just found out that she can make noises," Sonya replied.

"No more sleeping through the night, I guess," Adam opined.

"Don't worry, Darling," Sonya replied, "I'm practiced at taking care of babies and I know what they need as long as the baby isn't ill."

"You mean that I don't have to do diapers?"

"Well, you may have to help out when I get big as a house. That won't be for months, though."

"Do you think you're pregnant?" Adam asked.

"I don't think so," Sonya replied. "I haven't had any morning sickness. I'm due for a period in the next week or so. If my period is on schedule we'll just have to start over."

"I can live with that," Adam replied with a smile on his face.

Sonya added, "I'm living with a sex maniac and I'm not complaining."

"Let's finish our lunch and go put the baby down for a nap," Adam suggested.

Adam made reservations for the farewell party that night. They would have cocktails in the apartment and then go down to dinner in the restaurant. They went up to the apartment and put Carol Agnes in her basket.

"Oh, Adam!" Sonya exclaimed. "I meant to tell you that I found a cannister of old eight millimeter film when I was packing. Should we just leave it?"

"No we don't want to leave it. It's kind of a family heirloom."

"What do you mean, family heirloom?" Sonya asked indignantly.

"Do you remember our five days in Cypress?"

"Yes, of course. That was when I really fell in love with you."

"A couple of Aussie Entrepreneurs rigged up a camera and photographed us whenever we were in the room. We talked about it sometime back. I think it was when we were in Istanbul."

She responded. "I remember now. You wouldn't let your mother see it."

Adam replied very calmly, "That's the film."

"What was on the film?" she pressed on.

"The camera came on whenever we entered the room. It stayed on as long as we were moving and talking."

"Did they film us making love?"

"Every time."

"Did you kill them?" she questioned.

"No, I thought about it. I decided to view the film. Fortunately, there was a passage on the film when you identified me as the father of Carol Agnes. That's how I was able to claim you as my common law spouse and how I was able to make the decisions on your treatment."

"I want to see the film," Sonya stated.

"Okay." Adam agreed. "When we get to Rome, we'll find a projector and we'll view it together. Maybe we can keep it around for when we need sexual stimulation."

"I'm really bad, huh?" she asked.

"I would say you're really good," Adam replied with a smile on his face.

The party was successful. Ellen Sanford took care of the baby while the adults went to dinner. The party was over early.

******

Mustafa came in the morning and drove them to the airport. Their plane departed at ten am. By mid-afternoon, the were in their Residence Garden apartment. The Residence Garden was an apartment hotel that catered to long-term patrons. Several students arriving for the new class at the NATO Defense College were all ready in residence.

Sonya changed Carol Agnes' diaper and put her down for a nap. Adam helped the Bell Hop get all the bags into the correct rooms and Sonya began unpacking. Adam hung up his uniforms, suits and jackets.

"Sonya," he said, "I'm going to go down to the desk and check on the Corvette. I'll be right back."

"Give me a kiss before you go." He kissed her passionately.

"How can you leave me after a kiss like that? I'm ready to make love, besides I may be in my prime for pregnancy."

"Hold that thought!" Adam directed. "We can try the bed before we go out to eat." He kissed her again and then left the room.

Adam inquired at the desk about picking up his car in Ostia.

"Your car is here," the clerk answered. "It came into Cittavechia not Ostia. The shipping company delivered it. We paid the company and added the cost to your bill. Don't let it scare you. It's in Lira and translates to less than one hundred dollars."

"Great," Adam replied. "What do I need to do to get it licensed?"

"You have a grace period. Check with your Embassy. If you aren't remaining over six months, you may be able to keep your Egyptian license"

Adam took the keys and went out to the parking lot. The car started up. He saw that it was low on gas. He went to the nearest gas station and filled the car. He used his credit card without a problem. When he returned to the hotel lobby, he noticed an Army Colonel at the desk. When the Colonel had finished his business, Adam approached.

"Excuse me, Colonel," he said, "My name is Adam McGregor. Are you by chance here for the NATO course?"

"Yes Sir, General McGregor. I saw your name on the list. My name is Ed Poole. What can I do for you?"

"We just checked in and I'm looking for a place to have supper."

"Why don't you join us. We are going to a Ristorante' out on the Apian Way. We've been told it's quite good."

"I appreciate that Ed, but we have a tiny baby with us. I think we need something closer to the hotel."

"I have two teenage daughters that would be glad to baby-sit for you. The restaurants don't open until eight pm. Our kids are over at the local play ground, enjoying the rides and eating junk food. They won't be going with us. They will be back in the hotel long before we leave. Our suite is 211. Join us for cocktails around six-thirty."

"I'll run this by the boss," Adam replied, "and I'll call your room."

Adam went up to the apartment and told Sonya about his meeting with Ed Poole. Sonya wasn't happy about leaving the baby with complete strangers. Adam suggested they stop in for cocktails and if Sonya was still uncomfortable, they would back out of dinner and eat at a local Tratoria. Adam called the Poole's.

They finished putting things away and decided to join the locals in a siesta from one to four. They made love and fell asleep. They woke up at four, took a shower together and then checked on Carol Agnes. She needed a change and Sonya fed her some formula. At six-thirty, they went down the hall to Apartment 211. Carol Agnes was asleep in her basket.

Ed Poole introduced them to his wife, Diane, and daughters, Belle, age sixteen and Dora, age fourteen. While Ed filled drink orders, Sonya and Diane took the baby into the master bedroom.

"So this is Carol Agnes," Diane said.

"Adam told you her name?" Sonya asked.

"No," Diane replied. "I know all about you and Adam. I've been looking forward to meeting you."

"Do we have a mutual friend?" Sonya asked.

"Yes and no. I first heard about you through Marianne Baldwin."

"I wouldn't call Marianne our friend," Sonya replied defensively.

"Neither would I," Diane replied. "I got the real story from your mother-in-law."

"How do you know Agnes?"

"I played bridge with her at the Army-Navy Club. She had just returned from Cairo. Someone asked when Adam was leaving Cairo and she announced that he would be in Rome for six months. We had lunch together. She told me all about you and Adam and the baby. You are really high on her list."

"She is a dear. She will visit us here in the spring. We'll have a party and you and Ed are invited. I can't wait to tell Adam."

"I understand your parents will be here, as well," Diane continued.

"Yes, we plan for them to be here to care for Carol Agnes while we are on the North European Tour. Will you go on the tour?"

"No, the girls will be in school. I will stay and ride herd on them while Ed is traveling."

They returned to the living room and had a glass of wine. Sonya went over to Adam and whispered, "We'll go to dinner. The girls will be excellent baby sitters."

"How can you tell?"

"I'll tell you tonight."

The four adults went to dinner at eight. After being seated, the waiter poured wine while a second waiter distributed menus. The menu consisted of ante pasta, pasta, fish, foul, meat, salads, and finally desserts, Each course serving was quite small. Follow-on courses were not served until everyone was finished, with the exception of the fish, foul or meat course. It was assumed that one of these choices would be the main course and this serving was ample. The salad and dessert courses were similar to the earlier quantity courses. The meal stretched over two and a half hours.

There was ample time between courses for conversation. Adam and Ed swapped experiences in Southeast Asia. Ed was a graduate of West Point, Class of sixty-two. They traded memories of the nineteen fifty-eight Army-Navy game won by Navy.

Diane volunteered that she had met Ed when he was at West Point. They were married right after graduation.

"Were you married at the Academy, Adam?" Ed asked.

"Yes," Adam replied. "However, that marriage was annulled in the first year. Sonya and I are newly weds." Adam looked at Sonya. She was smiling.

"What else can I say?" Adam asked.

"Darling, let Diane explain our situation to Ed. She has your mother's version."

"Do you know my mother?" Adam asked.

"Yes, we met at the Army-Navy Club. When I learned that you were coming to Rome, I asked if you were going to the NATO Defense College. We talked for two hours after that. I know all about Carol Agnes, the Mayo Clinic, your confrontation with the blackmailers."

"Oh, my God!" Sonya interrupted. "I didn't know about the blackmailer until recently. How did your mother know?"

"She was badgering me about how I was certain I was Carol

Agnes' father. I told her that you had stated that I was the father on the film. She wanted to see the film. I told her, no!"

"I'll bet I would enjoy that film," Ed interrupted with a grin on his face.

"Sorry, Ed," Adam replied. "It's not for public consumption."

"Has anyone else seen it?" Diane asked.

"The blackmailers, Sonya's doctor, and my lawyer. Thanks to my lawyer, I was able to convince Sonya's family that I should be making the decisions concerning the baby. Of course, after the baby was born, a blood test confirmed that I am the father."

"Sonya, did you have anything to do with all this?" Ed asked. "I was in a coma," she replied. "You could say I slept through the whole production. I suspect Diane can fill in the blanks right?"

"Oh, yes! Agnes told me everything. She is really quite proud of you both. She can't wait for more grandchildren."

"We are working on that," Sonya stated. "I hope to have two boys to go with our daughter."

"Good luck, Sonya," Diane added. "You realize that odds favor another girl."

"I know." Sonya agreed. "I can hope. Besides, I'm young and I don't have to stop trying for several years."

The party broke up and they returned to the Residence Garden. Adam and Sonya gathered the baby's things and returned to their suite. Sonya checked Carol Agnes' diaper and then laid her in her basket. The baby made various noises for several minutes before falling asleep. Sonya went into the bathroom to brush her teeth. When she came out of the bedroom it was dark except for moonlight coming in the window. Adam brushed by her as he made his way to the bathroom. When he came out, he saw that she was in bed covered only with a sheet. He took off his clothes and approached the bed.

"Can I make love to you?" he whispered as he laid down beside her.

"Yes, you can!" she whispered back. "I have a feeling tonight is the night. Maybe if you breed me more than once, I'll have twins or even triplets."

That was the end of the conversation for the night. It was some time before they went to sleep.

CHAPTER 27

The next morning at nine am, Adam joined Ed Poole on a five block walk to the Defense College. The College was located on the second floor of a commercial building. A major bank occupied the ground floor. The floors above the second floor were occupied by various businesses.

Ed escorted Adam to the administration office. Adam signed in and received an entry badge as soon as he had his picture taken. Adam was advised to bring Sonya in for issuance of a badge. Wives would be invited to join their husbands for lunch in the mess. Children would also be invited if they were thirteen or over. They, too, would need badges.

Regular classes would begin the following Monday. The thirty-eight students would be divided into six syndicates; four would have six students and two would have eight.

Syndicates would meet at eight am. Each syndicate would be led by the senior military officer in the group, and would have at least one civilian. All classes would be conducted in English or French. Although France no longer participated in the College, there were a number of students that were more proficient in French than English. After DeGaulle took France out of the NATO Alliance, NATO Headquarters moved to Belgium and Italy invited the Defense

College to Rome.

The second hour was dedicated to language training. Students were required to study French or English whichever was not their most predominate language. Students that were anticipating assignments in Italy were encouraged to study Italian.

There would be a lecture most days from ten to eleven am. The lectures would be in English or French with simultaneous interpretation for those students not proficient in the lecturer's language. There would be a coffee break after the lecture. The lecturer would conduct a question and answer period after the coffee break. The bar opened in the mess promptly at noon. Lunch was served at one. At three, the syndicates met for a short time to discuss assignments for the next day. If a paper was required, the Syndicate leader would ask for one page outlines from each member and the leader would write the paper. There were no grades.

The NATO Defense College was established during the Eisenhower administration. It's main purpose was to develop a camaraderie among officers who would serve on the staffs of NATO installations where ever these installations might be established.

The present Commandant of the College was a Lieutenant General from the Danish Army, named Rolfe Pedersen. Adam was called to the General's office after he had signed in. The General informed Adam that Adam was the senior officer attending and he would be the Class President. Adam asked if that was open for discussion.

"I suppose we can discuss it with Brigadier Roger Smythe of the Royal Marines," General Pedersen replied. "Please enlighten me on your problem."

Adam explained the need to take Carol Agnes to the Mayo Clinic in April, during the North Atlantic tour. He also explained that he might have to leave the North European Tour for a special project in June.

The General suggested that Adam get together with Brigadier Smythe. The General would accept whatever the two Brigadiers agreed upon. Adam inquired at the Administration office and found that Brigadier Smythe was also staying at the Residence Garden. Classes would begin the next day. Adam returned to the hotel and suggested to Sonya that they visit the church of "Saint Paul's Without the Walls." The church was nearby.

Adam rang Brigadier Smythe's suite and invited him for cocktails at five. They bundled up Carol Agnes and went for a drive in the Corvette. They stopped at the U.S. Embassy and stocked up on Wine and Spirits. They drove to the church. After a tour through the grounds and the Church, they returned to the hotel in time to freshen up before the arrival of Brigadier Smythe.

Their guests arrived promptly at five. The Brigadier was joined by his wife, Diedre, who had arrived in Rome that afternoon. Sonya introduced the Smythe's to Carol Agnes, who slept right through the experience. Adam filled orders for Scotch and Soda without ice.

Adam and Roger discussed Adam's problems. Roger had no problem with assuming the Presidency of the class. Diedre would be spending most of her time back in England. He would have considerable spare time on his hands.

The next two months seemed to fly past. The daily lectures were informative and interesting. On one occasion, the lecturers had to cancel. The Commandant asked Adam to fill the slot and talk about the Middle East. Adam was happy to respond. He described his tour in Saudi Arabia in detail. Most of his discussion about Egypt revolved around the Sadat Assassination. One of the students asked when Adam had learned that Sadat was dead. Adam explained that the Egyptian Government was slow to acknowledge Sadat's death for reasons that were not explained. The first confirmation of Sadat's demise had been announced by the BBC. This produced a chuckle from the audience. Adam opined that the Egyptians were trying to confirm that the assassination was the work of fanatics and not part of a cabal within the military. Adam then spent considerable time talking about the Sudan including the prospects for a new civil war in the South and ongoing problems between Darfur and Khartoum.

After the coffee break, there was the usual discussion period. Adam answered questions and gave his opinions on each query. Almost all the questions on Egypt concerned the assassination and the impact on the Egyptian-Israeli Peace Agreement. Adam explained the impact of the assassination on tourism in both Israel and Egypt. That factor would hold the peace agreement together. He suggested that the return of the Sinai would continue on schedule because of the advantages to both countries. The remainder of the period was spent discussing the Sudan oil and Darfur. Finally, the Commandant interrupted and suggested that the bar was open. They adjourned for cocktails and lunch.

The wives and older off-spring were treated to a lecture on ancient Rome. Their host was a Canadian named Edward Logan. He was an ancient Rome expert with a PHD. He taught at the University of Rome and he moonlighted at the War College. Edward also arranged weekend bus trips to various places of historical importance. The trips ranged as far South as Monte Cassino and as far North as Siena. Each class was treated to an overnight trip to Florence to see Michelangelo's famous statue of David. That trip included a visit to the Etruscan Tombs on the way back to Rome.

Edward was truly gifted with knowledge of Italy's Ancient History. His only problem was his affection for Italian wines. His tours always finished at one pm near a favorite Ristorante. They would stop for lunch-a long lunch-and then return to Rome. Edward would sleep all the way back to Rome. Still, the tours were great. Edward had been doing the tours for many years. He knew the right people to get into museums that were normally closed to most groups.

Adam and Sonya found plenty of opportunities to make love, both in the afternoons and the evenings. By the first of April, Sonya was able to confirm that she was pregnant. She was having morning sickness on a regular basis. Adam suggested that Sonya get an appointment at the Mayo Clinic at the same time that Carol Agnes was to receive her checkup. They would be leaving for the States on the North American Tour by the middle of April.

The North American Tour was very popular with the Europeans. For many of the officers, it would be their only opportunity to visit the States and Canada. Another aspect of this year's tour included a stop at Lisbon en route to Washington and a stop in Iceland on the return from Canada. The Iceland stopover negated the need to go to Iceland on the North European Tour. Adam checked the new schedule. They would be in Brussels on the fourteenth, fifteenth and sixteenth of June, leaving for Paris on the seventeenth. He would need access to an airplane preferably in

Belgium on the sixteenth.

The North American tour was scheduled to depart Rome on April fourteenth. The U.S. Air Force would supply a VC-135 Boeing Jet for the trip. They would leave Rome in the morning, stopping in Lisbon for two days proceeding on the sixteenth to Andrews Air Force Base outside of Washington. They would spend four days in D.C. receiving briefings at the Pentagon and visiting the National War College and the Industrial College of the Armed Forces at Fort McNair. The class was programmed to visit McDonnell-Douglas Aircraft Company in St. Louis. The class would next go to Ottawa, Canada, for briefings on Canada's involvement in NATO. After three days with visits to Montreal and Quebec City, they flew to Iceland for two days before returning to Rome.

Wives were encouraged to join the class in Washington and Canada. However, they were required to fly commercial from Rome to D.C. and from Canada back to Rome. This didn't affect Sonya. She was flying to Washington to spend the four days with Adam and Agnes. All three of them would fly to Minneapolis and pay their visit to the Mayo Clinic while the rest of the class was in St. Louis. Adam would join the class in Ottawa. Sonya and Agnes would spend a couple of days with the Carlson's before returning to Washington. Sonya would fly back to Rome the same day Adam would leave Iceland for Rome.

Their visit to the Mayo Clinic was very successful. They met with Dr. Snyder and Dr. Kittleson. Both doctors were satisfied with Carol Agnes' growth. They recommended that she begin eating regular baby food and they surmised that her growth would be much faster over the next six months.

Dr. Snyder performed an exam on Sonya. He confirmed that she was definitely pregnant. He guessed that she was probably a month to six weeks along. They could expect a new baby before Christmas. It was too early to project gender. Adam left for Ottawa and Sonya, Agnes and Carol Agnes left for Washington.

Adam enjoyed his visit to Canada. He had been to the Banft and Lake Louise area. This was his first visit to Montreal and Quebec. There was also a short stop in Halifax.

The trip to Iceland was a first for Adam. The government briefings were short. They were treated to a day long bus trip out of

Reykavik. The U.S. Air Force C-135 had flown into the Air Base at Keflavik. Although April days were quite long, there was still evidence of a long hard winter.

During her days back in D.C., Sonya spent a good deal of time with Cecilia. Cecilia had all kinds of questions about married life. She and Will had set the date for the wedding. It would be on June eleventh at St. Paul's Cathedral. Sonya thanked her for selecting a date when she and Adam would be in London. They had worked around the four days when the NATO class would be in London. The wedding would be in one of the chapels at St. Paul's not in the large sanctuary.

"What did your parents say about your marrying an Englishman?"

"They were upset" Cecilia replied. "They were really upset when they learned that the wedding would be in London. My father said I was marrying too far above my station. Fortunately, Agnes took my part. She convinced them that Will was genuine. They agreed to the wedding, but insisted they would not attend. Agnes bought them tickets and finally my mother got my father to agree to the trip. Now they are excited about it. It's their first trip abroad."

"What about your attendants?" Sonya asked.

"That may become a problem. I was maid of honor to my best friend last December. She was supposed to reciprocate. However, she had a miscarriage last week. She is not recovering very well and her doctor will not agree to her travel until she shows considerable improvement. I need a backup. Will you be my backup?"

"Of course. However, I must warn you, I'm a little bit pregnant," Sonya replied. "By June, I will be beginning to show. I may have to find a dress at the last minute, depending on what size I need"

"How exciting!" Cecilia exclaimed. "When did you find out?"

"My doctor in Minnesota confirmed the pregnancy a couple of days ago. However, I was sure a couple of weeks ago. I have a telltale morning sickness for several days within two or three weeks after I've conceived. It happens every time."

Cecilia thought for several moments, then decided not to ask anymore questions. She already knew most of Sonya's background from her discussions with Agnes.

The doorbell rang. It was Agnes. She had forgotten her key. She had been shopping with an old friend. She had bought an evening gown and wanted Sonya and Cecilia to see it.

"Will I have occasion to wear a gown in Rome?" Agnes asked.

"Absolutely," Sonya replied. "The NATO school will have a couple of functions requiring black tie. They also recognize each country's national days. The Embassy will invite the NATO class for the Fourth of July. I would say you need at least two frocks, one for Spring and one for summer."

"We're leaving tomorrow. I don't have time to shop for another dress now."

"Rome has stores," Sonya replied, "and you can shop in London when you come for Cecilia's Wedding."

"I thought I was taking care of Carol Agnes while you are on your North European tour," Agnes replied.

"My parents will be in Rome and our Army friends have two daughters that love to stay with Carol Agnes."

"You have to come to my wedding," Cecilia added. "I wouldn't even have met Will if not for you."

Agnes had tears in her eyes. "I guess I worry about too many things," Agnes agreed. "I think sometimes that I spend too much money. There won't be any left for my grandchildren."

"Oh, Agnes!" Sonya interrupted. "You don't need to worry about money. Adam went over his investment portfolio with me recently. He's highly diversified. The total value is near forty million. That's after paying for myself and Carol Agnes and it doesn't include his Air Force income."

"Nearly forty million?" Agnes exclaimed. "My portfolio is below twelve million. We both began with fifteen million. How can that be?"

"I asked Adam that very question" she confided. "He pointed out that your cost of living is much higher than his or at least it was until he met me. He told me that for half of his career he practically lived in his flying suit. He paid no Real Estate taxes. I couldn't believe your tax bill on your home in Georgetown. Adam has never owned a home. He gambles sparingly. He drinks sparingly. He hasn't bought a new car since he bought the Corvette. If he hadn't had to write checks for my accident and the baby, he would have well over forty million."

"How much was that bill, if I might ask?" Agnes said.

"He wouldn't tell me. He said it was half of what it was worth and a third of what he had expected."

"I've got to quit picking on that boy," Agnes stated.

"Adam said that if you stopped picking on him, since that is your job, we would have to call the doctor!"

They went to dinner at Army-Navy. When they returned they packed their suitcases in preparation for the flight to Rome on the next day.

Adam's flight returned two hours ahead of Sonya's flight from Dulles. He borrowed Ed Poole's station wagon and went to Rome's International Airport to pick up Sonya, Agnes and the baby. They were all tired and ready to go to bed. Adam suggested that they all have a siesta for a couple of hours, then they would decide what to do about dinner. As soon as the baby was settled Adam and Sonya went to their bedroom.

"Do you realize we've been apart for a week?" Sonya scolded.

"Seven and a half days," Adam responded. "Surely, you can go a week without sex." He had a smile on his face.

"It's not just the sex," Sonya replied. "I have terrible dreams when we're apart."

"The sex helps you sleep?" Adam asked.

"Will you get off the sex?" she whispered. "We can have sex as soon as we are ready for bed."

"Last one to the shower has to arrange the towels," Adam said as he dropped his trousers and continued to strip.

"You're the sex maniac! All this conversation was to get me in bed and make me feel it was all my desire."

She picked out two large towels and hung them on the shower wall where they could be pulled down from inside. Then she slid in the door. Adam had the water temperature set perfectly. They took turns washing each other all over, stopping to kiss passionately from time to time. They were drying off when there was a knock on the door.

"Yes?" Sonya answered.

"I wanted to say goodnight," Agnes replied. "I thought you were never going to get out of the shower."

"That was my fault," Sonya lied. "I was enjoying the hot water."

"Carol Agnes has a clean diaper and she is sleeping. I'll see you both in the morning."

"Goodnight, Mom!" Adam added as he turned the shower on again.

They let the shower run while they turned down the bed. Then Adam went back and shut off the shower. The moonlight was sufficient to light the bedroom. Sonya was lying in bed waiting for him.

"Do you still want to see the film of our time in Cypress?" Adam asked.

"I've seen it." she replied.

"When?" Adam asked.

"I borrowed a projector from the Hotel. I watched for fifteen minutes. I burned the film," she concluded.

"Okay." Adam responded. He leaned over and kissed her.

"Thank you, Darling," Sonya whispered.

CHAPTER 28

The time between the North American Tour and the North European tour was less than seven weeks. The time seemed to fly past. Adam had spent part of each day looking for an airplane. He had decided what he wanted. He was looking for a Kingair C-90, the forerunner of the Spar 80 model. The C-90 was a prop jet similar to the Super Kingair. However, it was smaller, five passenger seats instead of seven. It had a conventional tail assembly rather than Spar 80's T-Tail. He also expected the price to be considerably lower.

Adam made a call to Beechcraft in Wichita, Kansas. He inquired about C-90's and found that there were only five C-90's in Europe. All were government owned. The only aircraft known to be available was the property of the West German Government. They were asking six hundred thousand dollars. The aircraft had landed with the nose wheel up. It had been repaired and Beechcraft considered the aircraft totally flyable. The only negative about the aircraft was that the latrine had been removed and replaced by an additional fuel tank. This extended the range of the plane by ten percent. Adam considered this to be an advantage for his purpose. He next called the Embassy in Cairo. Dave Baldwin informed him that Colonel Ehrlich had returned to Germany and that he was due to retire in July.

Adam called Gerhard Ehrlich's quarters in Bonn. Mrs. Ehrlich answered. She informed him that Gerhard would be home after six pm. Adam called Gerhard before going out to dinner. He asked Gerhard if the C-90 was still available. Gerhard confirmed that it was. He assured Adam that the aircraft was in good flying condition, but that it looked awful. "It is painted in Luftwaffe gray. The iron crosses are painted over and the aircraft serial number is barely legible," Gerhard stated.

"What do they want for it?" Adam asked.

"One million, one hundred thousand marks," he replied. "That's around four hundred thousand dollars at the current exchange rate. They'll require a certified bank draft at the time of sale."

"That's great, Gerhard," Adam answered. "I will be in Bonn on the first and second of June. I would like to take possession at that time. Would you be able to deliver the aircraft to Brussels between the thirteenth and fifteenth of June?"

"I can do that, or I can fly it to Rome on the second," Gerhard replied.

"I need the aircraft prepositioned in or around Brussels by the fifteenth of June at the latest. The fewer people who know about the aircraft, the better I will feel."

"No problem," Gerhard replied. "Do you want me to pressure the authorities to give you a new paint job?"

"Actually, I like the nondescript paint job. I have in mind a special paint job when I get the aircraft back to the States," Adam answered.

Later that week, Adam called his accountant in Washington. He gave him instructions on providing the necessary bank draft by June first.

The NATO War College North European tour started on the first of June, 1982. The RAF provided a Bristol Britannia turbo-prop for the duration of the tour. Wives were not allowed on the aircraft for the first and last legs of the trip. No one could remember why this rule had been established. Five wives, including Sonya, had decided to follow their husbands. They had reservations on Lufthansa for the trip from Rome to Bonn. The final leg from Paris to Rome would be on Air France. All the other legs would be on the Britannia.

A German Military bus met the Britannia. The students were taken to the Department of Defense for briefings on Germany's military commitments to NATO. The wives were met by Colonel Ehrlich's wife, Ingrid. The wives visited the home of German composer Ludwig Von Beethoven followed by a shopping tour in Bonn.

Colonel Ehrlich called Adam out of the briefings long enough to complete the purchase of the C-90. Early the next morning, Gerhardt Ehrlich took Adam to see the aircraft. They inspected the exterior and started the engines. Other than the grotesque paint job the aircraft was fine. Gerhard would fly the C-90 to Brussels on June the thirteenth.

That evening the Minister of Defense hosted a dinner party. It was a formal affair. All the officers were in Mess Dress. The civilians were in black tie and the ladies were in evening gowns. Sonya was particularly beautiful in a dark green strapless evening gown. The last day in Bonn was taken up with a tour of the Cologne Cathedral followed by an invitation to dinner at the home of Wilhelm Klapper a class member from the Ministry of Defense.

They departed for The Hague early on the third. The first day was taken up with NATO oriented briefings followed by a dinner. The second day was spent in Amsterdam with visits to the Reich's Museum and a view of all the Dutch Master's paintings.

The stop in Copenhagen lasted three days. The first day was taken up with the usual official briefings. The ladies enjoyed a visit to Royal Danish Pottery Factory. Day two involved a bus trip to Elsinore Castle, famous as the setting for Hamlet, followed by a second dinner at the country home of Lieutenant General Rolfe Pedersen, the NATO War College Commandant.

Day three was open for the group to enjoy Copenhagen. Adam and Sonya slept in until ten am. They had a late breakfast and then walked across the square to Tivoli Gardens. They strolled through the gardens for an hour and a half, and then they returned to the hotel.

"This is a nice room," Sonya commented. "However, I would have preferred a shower to a bathtub."

"So would I," Adam responded. "I haven't taken a bath since I was in the Far East."

"I'll bet you took your Geisha Girl to the baths," Sonya probed.

"I don't remember anything that happened before I met a girl at the Meridien in Cairo."

"You're a liar," Sonya suggested as she crossed the room to kiss Adam, "but I love it."

"Let's take a bath together," Adam suggested as he went to the tub and began to fill it. While he monitored the heat of the water filling the tub, he stripped off his clothes. Sonya was naked when she entered the bathroom. Adam looked at her.

"Turn sideways," he ordered. She complied.

"Are you sure you're pregnant?" he asked. "You don't show it at all."

"The doctor confirmed it and I have had morning sickness. This is my fourth pregnancy. I should know."

"You're not going to make a very good shill." he commented. "I better leave you in Rome."

"You are not leaving me in Rome! You better shut the water off or we'll have a flood when we both get in the tub," Sonya replied emphatically.

Adam complied and they both entered the tub. The water came within three inches of the top.

"Don't make waves!" Adam suggested.

Sonya lifted her right leg up and began to apply soap to her calf. Adam extended his left leg and ran his toe up Sonya's left leg.

"Adam!" she said "What are you doing?"

"I was just checking to see how your leg feels under water."

"If you want to make love," she began, "just say so."

"I always want to make love to you," he replied.

Sonya stood up, grabbed a towel and quickly began drying off.

"First one in bed gets the bottom!" she announced as she dropped the towel and proceeded to the king sized bed.

Adam dropped his towel and followed Sonya when he heard her throw the bed covers back. She was lying across the bed with her legs spread in anticipation. They kissed passionately until Sonya was out of breath. She began to pant heavily as she had her climax. Adam climaxed simultaneously with her vaginal climax. They both were still breathing heavily. When Adam tried to move, Sonya held on to him. He found her cheek and tasted her salty tears. Then he kissed her lips tenderly and then passionately.

"Can we do that again tonight?" she cooed.

"I wouldn't be a bit surprised," Adam whispered in her ear, adding, "if we skip the bath, maybe the bed will be dry by tonight."

"What will we do to get me in the mood?" she asked facetiously.

"I'll think of something," he said, kissing her again.

They slept for an hour. Then Sonya took a bath while Adam shaved. He took his bath while she combed out her hair and put on makeup. They got dressed. Adam kissed Sonya again before she put on her lipstick. They went to meet Ed Poole and three other officers. They all walked down to the harbor for drinks and some seafood.

During cocktails, Ed Poole asked Sonya what she had planned for Oslo while the class was getting the Defense briefings.

"I'm taking the train to Bergen to visit relatives for the day," she replied.

"How do you happen to have relatives in Norway?" Ed asked.

"My family name is Carlson," she replied "My grandfather emigrated from Norway. There were seven in his family. One stayed in Norway. I'm going to visit the offspring of that man."

"Are they expecting you?" Ed asked.

"Yes. We made a phone call. They are planning a mini-reunion and a luncheon. I will be back in Oslo for dinner," Sonya concluded.

Everyone finished dinner by nine pm. The sun was beginning to set as they strolled back to the hotel. It would be twelve before darkness would set in. There was no hurry.

"Adam," Sonya began when they were back in their hotel room. "When are we going to the Sudan?"

"When you get more pregnant," he replied.

"I can't get more pregnant, Darling. Pregnant is pregnant!"

"When you're in London, buy some clothes for an expectant mother," Adam replied.

"I was planning to shop for those things in Paris," Sonya replied.

"Paris will be too late."

"Will we be in London for Cecilia's Wedding?" Sonya pressed.

"Yes, we will," Adam replied.

"Are you going to tell me when we are leaving?"

"Yes," Adam replied

"When?" she pressed.

"When we're ready to leave."

"You're going to leave me, aren't you!"

"No, I'm not leaving you. I've applied for Visas for both of us. You have an important part to play," Adam responded.

"Where are we going?" Sonya continued.

"Abu Simbal," Adam replied.

"Egypt?" she questioned.

"Yes, Egypt," Adam replied. "We're going to visit the Ramases the Second stone carving. They were moved up the mountain face when the Aswan High Dam was built to form Lake Nasser."

"You've been there before."

"Yes, but you haven't."

"I think I'd rather go to Paris," Sonya said.

"Too late," Adam responded. "Besides, I may need you. Remember you're supposed to be a shill, a pregnant shill."

By the time the conversation was over they were both naked. Adam felt Sonya's abdomen.

"Are you sure you're pregnant?"

"Just as sure as I am that you're the father of Carol Agnes. However, I don't mind if you keep trying to breed me," she said as she puckered up for a kiss.

They laid out on the bed and Sonya pulled Adam's erection into her vagina. They climaxed together. Adam rolled over on his back.

"How long can we keep making love?" he asked.

"Until Dr. Snyder says we should stop. However, as my belly gets bigger, we will have to invent new positions."

"I don't have any experience with that sort of action," Adam complained.

"Neither do I, Darling. We'll have to wing it because I don't intend to ask anyone." They fell asleep after kissing tenderly.

The Britannia departed Copenhagen at nine am. They were in Oslo before ten. A bus picked up the NATO Officers and took them to the Defense Offices. The ladies took a cab to the SAS Hotel, dropping Sonya at the Train station. Sonya caught the train to Bergen.

The Defense briefings were completed in an hour. The visitors were treated to a buffet luncheon that included locally harvested sardines and other seafood delights from the North Sea. After lunch, the group was taken to the Kon Tiki Museum in Frogner Park. After the tour, they returned to the SAS Hotel to change clothes and get ready for dinner.

Sonya returned from Bergen by six pm. Adam was waiting to take Sonya to dinner. Sonya took a few minutes to repair her makeup. They were on their way out when they received a message that they would be leaving for London at nine the next morning. There was no explanation for the change.

Ed Poole joined them for dinner at a restaurant near the hotel. When they arrived at the restaurant, they ran into three other NATO members. Two were from West Germany and the third from the RAF.

"Did you hear about the change?" Squadron Leader MacDonald asked.

"Yes," Adam replied. "What happened?"

"We have been invited to view the dress rehearsal for the Queen's Birthday Parade."

"What's the difference between that and the real thing?" Sonya asked.

"Tomorrow's parade will be exactly like next Saturday except the Queen won't be there for the rehearsal tomorrow. The real thing is the following Saturday. The British Defense Establishment doesn't like to make mistakes when the Queen is involved," Squadron Leader Mac Donald replied smiling.

"What will happen on Sunday?" Adam asked directing his question to Kevin MacDonald.

"We'll be free to do as we please," Kevin concluded. "On Monday, we will fly to Blackpool to visit British Aircraft Corporation. We'll leave for Brussels on Tuesday."

"That's great," Adam responded. "We have a wedding to attend on Sunday afternoon."

"Oh, where?" Kevin asked.

"St. Paul's, in one of the Chapels." Adam replied. "William Hull the Fourth, is marrying my mother's ward."

"I know Will Hull from Eton. He's in the Diplomatic Service. How did he meet your mother's ward?" Kevin asked.

Adam replied, "Will's grandfather and grandmother have known my mother for years. Will's grandmother, Lady Agatha Hull, called Mother and asked her to find Will a nice girl to date while he was in Washington for several weeks. That was last summer. They hit it off and Will and Cecilia announced their engagement over Christmas. Sir William and Lady Agatha are coming up from Cairo for the wedding this weekend. My mother is coming up from Rome. She has been caring for our daughter while we've been traveling.

"Is your daughter coming also?" Kevin MacDonald asked.

"No," Sonya broke in. "She's in the care of my parents. They arrived in Rome this week."

"You don't suppose I could come to St. Paul's just to wish Will the best," Kevin asked.

"I'll see to it as soon as we get to London," Adam promised.

They finished dinner and returned to the hotel. The next morning the Britannia left for London at nine am. A bus met the aircraft at an RAF base north of London. They were delivered to the Best Western Hotel in Kensington. Adam and Sonya took a cab to Brown's Hotel in Mayfair where Adam had made reservations for his mother. Sonya and Adam were in an adjoining suite. Sonya unpacked and waited for Agnes. Adam left for the defense briefings in White Hall. Agnes arrived shortly after Adam had departed.

"Hello, Mother!" Sonya greeted Agnes.

"Well, hello!" Agnes exclaimed. "I thought you wouldn't be here until tomorrow."

Sonya explained the changes in their itinerary. "How's our baby?" she asked.

"She's wonderful!" Agnes replied. "She's making all kinds of noises. Your parents arrived three days ago. They were amazed at Carol Agnes' progress. Your mother says she feels years younger having a baby in the room."

"Have you heard from the Hulls?" Sonya asked.

"Yes," Agnes replied. "They arrive from Cairo tomorrow. They will be staying here at Brown's. They will return to Cairo on Tuesday. I'll return to Rome on Tuesday. I believe you and Adam go to Brussels on Tuesday Morning.

"That's right," Sonya answered. "How would you like to help me shop for maternity clothes?"

"I would love it!" Agnes said. "There are all kinds of stores nearby. If we can't find anything here, we can take the tube to Harrod's."

"I also need to shop for wedding gifts for the bride and groom. We could do that at the same time. Do you know what color of dress she will wear?" Sonya asked.

"Unless they have changed their minds, she'll be wearing 'our' dress," Agnes stated.

"The blue one?" Sonya asked in shock.

"She tried it on," Agnes continued, "and it fit perfectly. Will liked it."

"He saw her in her wedding dress?"

"These are modern kids, Sonya. They don't believe in bad luck," Agnes answered. "I said, 'take good care of it because my granddaughter may want to wear it.' Cecilia said, 'Wouldn't that be wonderful, four generations married in the same dress. If Will and I have a daughter, we could make it five.' Who can argue with that kind of confidence?"

"We certainly won't rain on their parade," Sonya concluded. They left the hotel and headed for Bond Street.

Adam returned to the hotel around four. He called The Guinea, a restaurant on Berkley Square and made reservations for the three of them for dinner. He was just off the phone when Sonya and Agnes returned laden with purchases.

"Did you make dinner reservations?" Agnes asked Adam after she had kissed him.

"Yes, Mother. We are going to The Guinea at eight."

"How far is it?" Agnes asked.

"It's about a ten minute walk," he replied.

"Why so late? We'll have to walk back in the dark."

"Not on this trip, Mother," Adam added. "It doesn't get dark until after eleven. By the way, there is a Squadron Leader Kevin Mac Donald in our class. He knows Will Hull from Eton. He would like to come by the wedding and wish Will and Cecilia the best. Do you suppose that could be arranged?"

"I think so. I talked to Lady Agatha. She said that she had received a number of regrets because of people traveling. She said there will probably be a lot more gifts than guests. What have you done about the reception?"

"It's all arranged at the RAF Club," Adam replied. "I called from Rome in April. My money is still good. I'm glad I kept my membership. There will be an open bar as soon as guests arrive from St. Paul's. The Club is prepared for as many as one hundred. We can give them a final count at seven pm. Dinner will be at eight."

"Who is paying for all this?" Agnes asked.

"We'll discuss it over dinner," Adam replied.

They departed for The Guinea. The sun was still up as they headed for Berkeley Square. The Guinea was at the far end of the square. It had grown from a pub to a first class restaurant. The three of them were ushered to a small table for four. A waiter appeared immediately to ask if they would like something to drink.

"I would like a Famous Grouse on the rocks," Adam replied.

"Is that Bourbon or Canadian, Sir?"

"No," Adam replied. "It's Scotch Whiskey. I'll have a Bushmills on the rocks."

"Yes, Sir," the waiter replied. "We have Bushmills Malt. It's thirteen years old and quite expensive."

Agnes interrupted, "It's quite alright, young man. He's very wealthy and he's showing off for his wife and his mother. You may rest assured that he knows his alcoholic beverages. Adam pick a wine for Sonya and myself."

"Are you having fish or meat?"

"I'm having fish," Agnes replied.

"Me, too," Sonya Added.

"Bring a bottle of Muscadet and three glasses," Adam directed. The waiter departed.

"Who's paying for this reception?" Agnes asked.

"I am, Mother," Adam replied.

"But, why?" she said, "She's my ward."

"Yes, I know," he answered, "but you can't afford it."

"I can so!" she exclaimed. "I have several million dollars left. How much do you have left?"

"Mother, we've been through all this before," Adam said. "You haven't had a payday since father died, except for the stipend the Air Force sends you. That doesn't pay your taxes in Georgetown."

Their meals arrived and the conversation subsided while they enjoyed a fine meal of Plaice. After dessert and coffee they departed. The sun was down, but the sky was still bright. As they were leaving Berkley Square, they passed the Rolls Royce dealership. There was a two-year old Bentley convertible in the show window, priced at thirty-nine thousand nine hundred pounds.

"Adam, how much is that in dollars?"

"Around one hundred thousand," he replied.

"You wouldn't spend that kind of money on a car, would you?"

"No, Mother," he replied as he moved on up the street. "Let's stop in the Horse and Carriage and have a night-cap."

"What's the Horse and Carriage?" Agnes asked.

"It's that funny looking building over there," Adam commented as he pointed at the three cornered Tudor structure that had survived modernity. It looked like it could collapse at any moment.

"As long as you get me home by dark," Agnes replied. "I can't walk on these brick sidewalks in the dark."

Adam promised they would be back at the hotel before dark. He ordered two small sherries for the ladies and a half-pint of Adnams Bitter for himself. Most of the patrons were young and well behaved. A couple of young men were becoming belligerent. The pub manager ran them out before they got into a fight.

Sonya declared that she was getting tired. She suggested they leave. They were back in their suite before dark. Sonya went directly to bed.

Adam stayed up until his mother went to bed. When he went into his bedroom, he noticed that Sonya was wearing a negligee. He thought the honeymoon is over. However, a couple of hours later, Sonya got up and went to the bathroom. When she returned, she stepped out of her negligee and crawled in beside Adam. Adam awoke and they made love.

Adam, Sonya and Agnes had a proper breakfast in the hotel dining room. As soon as they had finished eating, Adam ordered a cab. It was a short ride to the Admiralty where the Horse Guards were preparing to enter the parade ground. They presented their tickets and were shown to their seats among the Defense College guests.

The Cold Stream Guards were already in place wearing their bearskin helmets. The sun was out and the temperature was rising rapidly. The heat began to take its toll on the guards and occasionally one would pass out and be carried away on a stretcher. Other than the fainting, the dress rehearsal went well. As soon as the Horse Guards were in position, Her Majesty's horse appeared. The Queen's Lady in Waiting was in the side saddle. The following Saturday the Queen would ride the horse.

When the dress rehearsal concluded, Adam suggested they walk back to the hotel. Their route took them up Pall Mall to Buckingham Palace. After watching the guards perform for a few minutes, they proceeded through Saint James Park toward Piccadilly. Agnes reminisced about how long it had been since she had first seen the guards at Buckingham Palace. It was shortly after World War II. Adam was seven or eight and they had come to England to join Major General McGregor, Adam's father. The old Army Air Corps had been re-designated as the U.S. Air Force and General McGregor was the first Air Force Attache' and Defense Attache' at the Embassy in London.

"We lived in Mayfair," Agnes said. "Do you know where Mayfair is, Adam?"

"Yes, our hotel is in Mayfair," he replied.

"Oh, how exciting!" Agnes responded. "Maybe we can find our house."

"I know where it is," he offered. "It's a short walk from the hotel."

"Do you suppose we could visit it?"

"No, Mother. I don't think that's a good idea."

"Why not?" she pressed.

"Because it's owned by Arabs and I doubt that it has been

kept up to your standards. However, there is an Anglican Church nearby. I suggest we go by the house on our way to church tomorrow."

"We have agreed that we will raise our children in the Anglican Faith," Sonya replied. "It was Adam's suggestion."

"Adam? Is that true?"

"I was never as good as you wanted me to be. However, I've never been as bad as you may have imagined."

"I'm beginning to appreciate that," Agnes replied. "I'm going up to rest. Why don't you two go out and enjoy yourselves."

Sir William and Lady Agatha were checking in as Sonya, Adam and Agnes entered the lobby. After greetings all around they were invited up to the Hull's Suite. Adam explained that his mother had been walking and was ready for a rest. He and Sonya were going to walk up to the RAF Club and check on arrangements for the reception.

Adam and Sonya took Agnes to their suite. They proceeded to walk to the RAF Club on Piccadilly, just a block and a half from Hyde Park Corner. Adam provided a final guest list and suggested seating arrangements. As soon as their business was concluded, they left the club and strolled back into Mayfair, stopping at the Shepherds Tavern. Adam had a pint of Adnams. Sonya settled for a glass of fruit juice.

"Are you on the wagon?" Adam asked.

"Yes, Darling," she replied without hesitation. "Dr. Snyder and Dr. Kittleson want me to return to Minnesota for the delivery. Is that possible?"

"Of course," Adam replied. "I expect to be assigned back to the States. Now that we have an airplane, I can fly you to Rochester on a moments notice."

"When did you buy an airplane?" Sonya asked, surprised.

"A couple of weeks ago," he replied without further explanation.

"You're going to get Ahmed Ibrahim!"

"Not so loud. He's not well known, however, anyone who has met him won't forget him!"

"Am I going along?" Sonya whispered.

"I believe that was your desire."

"How can you make love to me nearly every night and then tell me about something as important as this in a pub?"

"Bedrooms can be bugged," he answered.

"Bars aren't?"

"We didn't know we would be here until a few minutes before we walked in. We'll walk out in a few minutes and no one will remember us. What better place to discuss top secret business?"

"We certainly have privacy when we are having sex."

"Yes, but I have other things on my mind then."

"Like what?" Sonya said out loud. She immediately realized others were listening.

Adam whispered, "What will you bet that Mother is asleep. Let's go back to the room and see what happens."

They walked out of he Shepherd's Tavern and turned left, heading toward Curzon Street. As they approached the intersection, Adam saw a familiar face across the street. The man was headed down Curzon toward Barkley Square. As far as Adam could tell Farid Bashir had not seen them. Adam stopped at the restaurant on the corner of Curzon. He was reading the menu in the window as he watched Farid Bashir continue down Curzon Street in the reflection.

"What are you doing?" Sonya asked.

"I was just checking prices to see if we would want to come here for dinner. Let's go up to the Red Lion. It's one of my favorite pubs."

The Red Lion was only a block and a half up an alley. Adam ordered a Scotch with a splash of soda and a fruit juice for Sonya. He asked the barman to call a cab for them. The cab dropped them at Brown's.

"Is that you, Adam?" Agnes asked.

"Yes, Mom?" Adam answered.

"I'm going in to take a bath," Agnes advised. "I'll let you know when I'm finished."

They made love again and took a cat nap before Agnes woke them up. It was five o'clock. They were due at the Hulls in thirty minutes. They went into the shower together. As soon as Agnes was dressed she tapped on their door again. When there was no answer, she went back to her room. She reemerged at five-thirty to find them dressed and ready to go.

"That was quick," Agnes commented as she headed for the door.

"We can hurry when we have to," Adam added.

"I suppose it helps when you have someone to wash your back," Agnes replied as she went out the door trying to suppress her grin.

Sonya raised her eyebrows and said, "Do you think she's upset?"

"I think she's laughing her butt off," Adam confided.

They arrived at the Hull's suite just as Will and Cecilia arrived. Sonya took Cecilia back to Agnes' suite and moved her into the third bedroom. Sonya stayed with her while she freshened up and changed clothes.

"How's Agnes doing?" Cecilia asked.

"She seems to be doing fine. Is there a problem?"

"No, but she says she is going to miss me. I'll miss her, too."

"Well, you can't let that bother you. You'll have a new husband to look after in just one more day. We will return to the States in a month and a half. It looks like we will be stationed in Washington for awhile. We'll probably move in with her. She loves Carol Agnes and I'm due in December."

"Oh, Sonya! That's wonderful. Does Agnes know you're pregnant?"

"No, I was going to let Adam tell her. If he doesn't you can do it."

Cecilia finished her spruce up and they returned to the Hull's Suite.

Lady Agatha offered both women a glass of wine. Cecilia took a glass, but Sonya refused. Lady Agatha was taken aback.

"What's the matter, Sonya? Are you pregnant?" Lady Agatha ask jokingly.

Sonya and Cecilia broke out laughing. "What's so funny?" Agatha asked.

Cecilia began, "Sonya is pregnant and she said, If Adam didn't tell his mother, I could tell her. Now everyone knows."

"Adam!" Agnes scolded. "Why haven't you told me?"

"Well, Mother, I was going to let Sonya tell you." By then everyone was laughing.

"We were going to tell everyone here this weekend," Adam volunteered. "I had hoped to break the news a little more quietly."

"Are you feeling well?" Agnes asked Sonya.

"Yes. I expect to deliver around Christmas. We've decided that I will go back to Rochester for the delivery."

"Do your parents know?" Agnes asked.

"No. You can tell them when you get to Rome on Tuesday. We won't be back until the weekend," Sonya concluded.

After cocktails, the whole group went to The RAF Club for dinner. Agatha and Agnes hatched a plan to make sure the bride and groom were separated before midnight and that they didn't see each other until the wedding.

Sunday morning, Adam got everyone up and they took a cab to Church. They passed the house where the McGregor's had lived. Adam spotted Farid Bashir in the yard. They had lunch in a pub. They arrived back at the hotel on Agnes' schedule. Everyone got bathed and dressed. Cecilia was a nervous wreck. Adam got her a glass of sherry. Everyone except Cecilia was dressed for the evening. Cecilia would put on her wedding dress at the Cathedral.

Adam had hired a Limo for the wedding. Cecilia, Agnes, Sonya and Adam boarded the Limo at three. They were at Saint Paul's by three-twenty. The three women went to the changing room to prepare the bride. Adam was dressed in his uniform. He had a shoulder holster with a .38 caliber revolver under his jacket. He wandered through the Cathedral as he had several times before. He arrived at the Wedding Chapel in time to escort Agnes and Sonya to their seats in the front row. Will's parents and grandparents were seated directly across the aisle. The Wedding March began at four pm. The wedding was completed by four-twenty.

Will and Cecilia departed for their hotel. They were booked into the Dorchester on Park Lane. Their bags were packed for their honeymoon and prepositioned in the hotel. They quickly changed clothes and proceeded to the RAF Club for the reception. The reception and dinner lasted until after ten. As the Bride and Groom were saying their goodbyes, Cecilia whispered in Sonya's ear. Sonya responded quietly. Adam was watching.

"What did the Bride say?" Adam asked.

"She said she was scared," Sonya replied.

"What did you say?" Adam asked.

"I told her that all Brides are scared on their Wedding night."

"You weren't afraid on yours," he said.

"The hell I wasn't!" she whispered back.

"You could have fooled me," Adam concluded with raised eyebrows.

"I was over it by the time you went to sleep."

Adam paid the club bill while Sonya found Agnes. They departed for their hotel with the Hulls.

The next morning, Adam joined the NATO class for the trip to British Aerospace where they toured the Tornado Assembly line. Sonya and the four other wives went shopping after Agnes had departed for Rome. They took an afternoon train to Luton where they met the Britannia. They were all in Brussels by late afternoon.

On Tuesday, the class received briefings from Belgium's Military and Political hierarchy. On Wednesday, they toured the Battlefield at Waterloo. That evening before dinner, Adam met with General Pedersen. He informed the General that he and Sonya would be leaving for Rome.

General Pedersen responded, "I understand that you bought an airplane."

"I didn't know it was public information, General," Adam replied.

"The Civil Aviation Authority at the airport left word that your aircraft had arrived," the General continued. "I think they were primarily interested in collecting their parking fees."

"I knew about the fees," Adam answered. "I will pay them in cash before we depart."

"I don't intend to make a fuss over your absence from the Paris visit. Frankly, I wouldn't go if I didn't have to go. I do need to know when you expect to be back in Rome."

"I will be back in class when they resume next Monday," Adam promised. "If I'm delayed I will get in touch. If you don't hear from me, feel free to notify Washington that I'm missing."

"You realize you could be jeopardizing your career," the General added.

"Yes, I do," Adam replied. "I appreciate your concern, General."

"I wish you God speed," General Pedersen added as he returned Adam's salute.

Adam hurried back to the hotel to pick up Sonya and their bags. They were at the airport at nine am. Adam paid for the parking and they proceeded to the aircraft. They were airborne en route to Venice, Italy by nine-thirty.

Farid Bashir contacted his old office at the Cairo Airport. He asked an old friend to check on a clearance for a Kingair 6769. He found out that the aircraft had been cleared to Abu Simbel via Luxor, with a stop at Aswan, if required. The aircraft would exit Egypt via Cairo, not later than June 18th.

CHAPTER 29

Kingair 6769 was cleared to Venice at twenty-four thousand feet. They were cleared to climb to altitude by the time they crossed into Luxembourg. They proceeded on a southerly heading arriving over Italy in two hours. By twelve-fifteen, they had landed in Venice. The aircraft was refueled while Adam filed a new clearance for Iraklian Air Base on Crete. As soon as they were airborne, Sonya joined Adam in the cockpit.

"Adam," she expounded, "this is the ugliest airplane in the world. Why did you buy it?"

"The price was right, Sweetheart," he replied. "We'll get a new paint job before we take it home."

"Where are we going now?"

"We're going to Iraklian Air Station on Crete. I have reservations in the VIP Suite. We'll get a good night's rest and leave early for Luxor. We'll refuel in Luxor and fly to Abu Simbel. I want to see if I can refuel at Abu Simbel. If we can, we'll come back that way. From Abu Simbel, we'll go to Rub Kona and refuel. At eight pm, we'll fly to Wau and pick up Gudrun and the boys. We'll leave immediately for El Fasher and pick up Ahmed at midnight. We go back to Rub Kona and top off. We'll fly to Abu Simbel where you and Gudrun will go see the statues and tombs while I refuel. Ahmed and the boys will have to stay on the airplane. When you return we will fly to Israel and land at Lod. The Defense Attache's Office will arrange to fly Ahmed and family to the States. We'll spend an overnight with the Naval Attache' and leave for Rome on Sunday. We'll be back at the Residence Garden for dinner Sunday night. Any questions?"

"How did you arrange all of this?"

"I sent back channel messages to Cairo, Khartoum and Tel Aviv. Everyone notified Tom Carson when their actions were completed. Tom mailed me a letter last month to say everyone had been alerted. In the absence of any further communication, I'm assuming that we can pull it off. Oh, by the way, when you and Gudrun go to Abu Simbel, I want you to speak Norwegian. Gudrun will speak German. I'll speak Arabic. That's another reason for the ugly airplane.

"What do you mean?"

"The plane is not the typical American owned private plane. I want us to look European as much as possible and not draw attention to ourselves."

They arrived in Crete at five-forty five local time. Adam had the aircraft refueled. He paid with his credit card. They locked up the aircraft and went to operations to file a clearance to Luxor. The clearance went through without a problem. The office in Cairo had done their job. They checked into the BOQ.

The Base Commander provided a car and driver. Adam and Sonya went out in the local area to find a restaurant. They enjoyed a fine Greek meal of Lamb and Red Wine. They were back in their quarters by eight-thirty.

Sonya was in bed when Adam finished in the bathroom. "Do you want to make love to me?" she asked as he approached the bed.

"Of course," he replied as he slid in beside her. "We may not be able to have sex again until we get to Israel. We will leave for Luxor about ten tomorrow."

"Why are you cutting off my sex life? You know that's all I live for," Sonya whispered.

"I don't think we are going to bed again until we get to Israel. We may be able to stretch out for a few hours while we are waiting at Rub Kona," Adam replied as he ran his fingers over Sonya's breasts.

Her nipples were hard. They made love and then slept until morning.

The next morning, they had breakfast at the all-ranks club. They departed Iraklion at nine am. And landed at Luxor by three pm, Cairo time. They refueled and left for Abu Simbel.

Adam went into Operations and inquired about Jet A-1 fuel. He was told that they had very little fuel available and that he would have to pay cash in Egyptian Pounds. The price was two pounds per liter. That was highway robbery, however, it would be acceptable under the circumstances. Adam told them he would be back in about forty hours and he would need four hundred liters. Adam had picked up one thousand Egyptian Pounds for the trip.

"Where are we going now?" Sonya asked as they proceeded to the Kingair.

"Aswan," he replied.

"Can I ask why?"

"Sure," he replied. "I told Cairo that we would be cycling between Luxor, Abu Simbel and Aswan. I don't want to disappoint the authorities. Besides Aswan is a nice place to visit."

"Aswan, it is then," Sonya commented. "You never fail to surprise me. Are we staying overnight?"

"No, we'll leave for Rub Kona around midnight."

The flight to Aswan was less than thirty minutes. As soon as they had locked the aircraft, they went to operations and Adam filed a clearance to return to Abu Simbel. They caught a taxi and took a tour of Aswan to include the old Aswan Dam. On the return to the airport, they saw a Greek Restaurant advertising Gyros.

How about a Gyro and a glass of wine?" Adam asked.

"Sounds good," Sonya replied. "Besides, I need to go potty. Order the sandwiches while I'm gone."

Adam proceeded to the bar and placed an order for two gyros and two glasses of red wine.

Before the order was completed, Sonya returned. She got Adam's attention and motioned for him to follow her.

"I'll be right back," he told the server.

Sonya led Adam into the women's bathroom where two Egyptian men were confronting a tall, good-looking blond who was trying to defend herself with her high-heeled shoes. Adam recognized the taller of the two men. It was Farid Barack. Adam was wearing a leather vest that covered his shoulder holster, carrying his .38 special with a silencer.

Farid Barack recognized Adam. He reached inside his coat. Adam drew first and fired, killing Farid. The other man raised his hands. Adam couldn't leave a witness. He fired again killing the second antagonist.

Sonya and the blond were both in a state of shock. Adam spoke to the stranger, "I don't have time to explain. You'll have to go with us."

"I'm flying to Khartoum tomorrow," she said in broken English. "I must meet friends at the German Embassy in Khartoum tomorrow evening."

"You're in luck. We can get you there tomorrow night," Adam replied. He directed the driver to take them to the airport. They went directly to the airplane. The woman remained reluctant to board the aircraft.

"Sonya, use your Norwegian. See if you can explain to her that if she remains here, she will be arrested."

While Adam did a quick inspection and ran his checklist, Sonya explained to the woman the realities of being a woman accused in the Middle East. She finally relented and got on the aircraft.

Adam had filed for Abu Simbel, however, he turned south and headed for Rub Kona. He was betting that the Abu Simbel Operations would shutdown and the Kingair wouldn't be missed. He was right. He climbed out to twenty-four thousand feet and put the Kingair on auto-pilot. He called Sonya and asked her to bring the German woman to the cockpit. Between Adam's German, he had learned in high school, and Sonya's Norwegian, they were able to communicate with their passenger. Her name was Greta. She was twenty-five years old and very pretty. She was on her way to Khartoum to meet her fiancée who was at the Embassy.

Adam laid out the whole plan for Greta. They would spend most of the day at Rub Kona in the Chevron Oil Company's complex. They would leave Rub Kona early enough to land at Wau just before nine. At Wau Airport, Greta will leave the C-90 and board Spar 80 for a flight to Khartoum. In Khartoum, Colonel

Carson, the Defense Attache' would take her to the German Embassy. Adam did not tell her that she would be taking the place of Gudrun Ibrahim and her two sons on Spar 80.

At this point, Sonya went to pieces. She came to the cockpit, sobbing. "Adam!" she exclaimed, "I can't go on. I want to return to Rome. I know we will be killed if we continue. I can't leave our daughter without a parent and I can't lose another baby. I'll go crazy."

Adam didn't respond. He was looking at the instrument panel and checking all the gages.

Sonya shouted, "Adam! I'm talking to you!"

"Sit down, Sonya," he said quietly as he nodded toward the co-pilot's seat and indicated that she should put on the headphones. When they were both on the inter phone, Adam continued.

"Sonya, it's too late to turn back. We would be complicit in the murder of Ahmed Ibrahim, his wife and their two children."

"You just killed two men!" Sonya exclaimed between sobs.

"Sonya, when we were in El Arish, you'll remember I met with Wahid Fahta. Wahid told me that Farid Bashir was a member of the Muslim Brotherhood. Farid had left his job at the airport and was stalking our Ambassador Richardson from CIA and yours truly. I have been carrying my .38 ever since. If I hadn't killed him, he would have killed me, you and our guest He couldn't leave witnesses and neither could I."

Sonya was silent for a long time.

"Do you understand, Sonya?" Adam asked.

"I'm trying to understand," Sonya replied in a whisper. "Being married to a killer takes some getting used to."

"To the best of my knowledge, I've never killed anyone who wasn't trying to kill me," Adam responded.

Sonya returned to the cabin to talk to Greta.

Kingair 6769 arrived in Rub Kona just after six in the morning of June seventeenth. Adam found an empty office and laid down on a sofa. He slept until mid-afternoon. Sonya continued to entertain Greta. Around three pm, Sonya woke Adam.

Adam went out to check on the aircraft. It had been refueled and it was ready to fly. Adam took Sonya and Greta to the Chevron Snack Bar. They had coffee and some lunch. Adam paid for the fuel and advised flight operations that he would be back for more fuel around three in the morning. He didn't bother with a flight plan. They took off at six-fifteen. They arrived over Wau at eight forty-five. Adam circled the field once and then landed. He taxied to the apron and parked next to Spar 80. Don Sanford and Dave Baldwin were standing by Spar 80 with Tom Carson. Adam introduced them to Greta. Tom Carson knew about Greta.

A few minutes later a Land Rover pulled up. It was driven by a Sudanese Soldier. Derek Douglas was in the front seat. Derek got out and ushered Gudrun Ibrahim and her two sons toward Spar 80. Derek made conversation with the soldier while Gudrun and the boys ducked under the tail of Spar 80 and climbed aboard Kingair 6769. Greta was seen entering Spar 80.

Adam had the King Air running and he taxied the minute the door was closed. Sonya made certain the passengers were strapped in properly, and then she joined Adam in the cockpit. As soon as they were airborne, Adam turned to the Northwest heading for El Fasher. When the aircraft reached cruise altitude at twenty thousand feet, Adam invited the boys to visit the cockpit.

The ten year old asked if they were going to meet their father. Adam responded in the affirmative. Adam showed the boys all of the instruments and explained all the levers and switches. When the boys began to yawn, Adam suggested they get some sleep so they would be awake to meet their father.

Adam turned off the running lights when they were thirty minutes out of El Fasher. He was not concerned about traffic as any airliners would be well above them. It was eleven-forty pm when Adam made a fast decent to ten thousand feet. It was clear and the moon was directly above them. He could make out El Fasher and he began a slow spiral downward. He dropped the landing gear. As soon as he had a down and locked indication, he pulled the circuit breaker to shut off the landing lights. He hoped Ahmed Ibrahim had seen the lights for a moment. He continued to spiral down with the engines in idle. When he was fifteen-hundred feet above the ground, he eased the throttles up to reduce his descent rate to eight hundred feet per minute as he turned around slowly to line up with the field. He touched down on the end of the field and allowed the aircraft to slow on its own with throttles still in idle. The aircraft rolled across the crushed rock in the middle of the landing strip. When the

Kingair rolled onto the hard surface, Adam eased to the left side of the runway. He told Sonya to watch for Ahmed. He would be dressed in white.

"I see him, Adam. He's in the shadows on my side of the runway," Sonya said quietly.

"Go back and open the door as soon as I stop," Adam ordered. Adam put the aircraft into a hard right turn. As the air craft reversed it's direction, Adam saw Ahmed sprint toward the aircraft. He braked to a halt.

"Open the door, Sonya!" She unlatched the door and pushed it outward. The minute the ladder was down, Ahmed stepped in and turned to close the hatch. He expected gunfire. None was forthcoming. They were successful. Adam pushed the throttles forward for take off. They had been on the ground for one minute and fifty seconds.

"Grab a seat and fasten your seat belts until I get a little altitude. You'll have to save your greetings for a few minutes," Adam commanded. Everyone complied.

Adam turned East and climbed to twenty-one thousand feet. As soon as he leveled off, he turned off the seatbelt sign and Ahmed and Gudrun were able to greet each other properly. Ahmed came forward to thank Adam for the rescue.

"We're not out of danger yet," Adam explained. "We will land at Rub Kona and refuel. We'll leave there for Abu Simbal as soon as we can. Sonya and Gudrun must go visit the Ramses II tombs while I get refueled. As soon as they return we will take off for Cairo. While we are airborne, we'll refile for Tel Aviv. The Defense Attache's office in Tel Aviv has documents ready to get you into the States. You'll fly to Washington on El Al this evening. Our trip into the Sudan is strictly under the table. We had no clearances. Abu Simbal is expecting this airplane, myself, Sonya and a blond German woman, named Greta. Gudrun must speak German and answer to the name of Greta until we are airborne again."

"I guess the boys and I will have to remain on the aircraft at Abu Simbal," Ahmed surmised.

"Yes," Adam responded. "Please make full use of the bathroom facilities at Rub Kona."

"We will and thanks for sticking your neck out. I was getting desperate. I don't think there was one chance in a hundred that Gudrun, the boys and myself could have ever escaped without help," Ahmed stated. "We are forever in your debt."

"Don't worry about that!" Adam replied.

"Where did you get the aircraft?" Ahmed asked.

"I bought it from the Luftwaffe," Adam replied.

"I'll reimburse you," Ahmed suggested.

"Not a chance," Adam replied.

"Why not?" Ahmed asked.

"Because I've wanted a C-90 for years," Adam replied.

"This airplane looks awful," Ahmed opined.

"It was just what I was looking for to complete this mission. The aircraft is in fine shape. I plan to have it repainted and then fly it home to the States. I'll keep it until I'm too old to fly. It really is the perfect aircraft for Sonya and myself."

Sonya was chatting with Gudrun and the boys while Ahmed was in the cockpit with Adam.

"Sonya is the woman who came with you to visit Geniena, isn't she?"

"Yes," Adam replied. "We were married last year."

"I thought she was already married," Ahmed pried.

"Her husband and two sons were killed by terrorists in Cairo," Adam said. "Sonya had an accident and she was in a coma for several months. I had taken her to the Mayo Clinic in the States. Shortly after her recovery we were married."

The remainder of the flight was routine and they landed at Rub Kona just after three am. They were airborne for Abu Simbal by three-thirty and landed just before nine.

Sonya and Gudrun took a taxi to the ancient crypts. They returned in an hour. The Kingair was airborne for Tel Aviv by ten-thirty.

Adam got in touch with his old office at the Embassy. Colonel Marshall was called to the H.F. Radio.

"This is Adam, Pete. I need a favor. Can you change my clearance to Tel Aviv? I have plenty of fuel and I need to get to Tel Aviv before dark."

"We'll give it a try. I see no reason for Cairo to object."

Colonel Marshall returned to the radio and confirmed the

flight plan change. Adam altered course for Tel Aviv. The Kingair C-90 landed at Lod Airport in the late afternoon. Navy Captain Eric Sampson, an Academy Classmate of Adam's, met the airplane. Sonya opened the door and exited the aircraft first.

"You must be Sonya," Eric began, "I'm Eric Sampson, the Naval Attache'. You and Adam will be spending the night with us. My driver will take you to our quarters." Captain Sampson turned to Ahmed as he exited the aircraft.

"Governor Ibrahim!" he greeted. "We have made arrangements for your flight to the Sates. We need to take you and your family to the Embassy for some I.D. pictures and special passports."

"I had hoped we could rest overnight," Ahmed replied.

"Unfortunately, the Government of the Sudan has suggested that you are the victim of a kidnapping. The Government of Israel would be very embarrassed if your presence here became known. It's expedient that you leave Israel as soon as possible."

"I understand," Ahmed replied. He turned to Sonya. "Sonya, we thank you for all that you and Adam have done for us."

"We'll look forward to seeing you when we return to the States in July," Sonya replied. They parted company. Adam and Sonya were taken to the Sampson's Quarters.

"Hello, Adam," Mrs. Sampson greeted them. "Sonya, I'm Evelyn Sampson. I've known your husband since he was a Midshipman. We are so happy to have you in our home. Can I get you something to drink. We'll have dinner as soon as Eric gets home. He had to take the Ibrahim's to the Embassy. CIA will take care of getting them on the El Al flight to Dulles. I don't think Eric will be gone long."

"We would like to grab a quick shower," Adam suggested. "We've been on the go for about forty hours."

"You must be exhausted," Evelyn replied. "We have an ample guest suite. You can make yourselves at home. Come this way." By the time Adam and Sonya had showered and dressed, Eric had arrived. They all sat down to enjoy a cocktail.

"I know you've been at the NATO Defense College, Adam. How did you get involved with rescuing the Ibrahim's?" Eric inquired.

Adam gave them a quick rundown on his association with Ahmed to include Ahmed's virtual incarceration in Darfur. He explained the basic plan and all the people who were involved.

"Where did you get the airplane?" Eric asked adding, "It looks like a relic!"

Adam explained his desire to own a Kingair C-90, and what his plans were for the future.

"I take it that the Air Staff didn't have a dog in this hunt," Eric suggested. "Is that going to get you early retirement?"

"It may," Adam replied. "As of now, I don't have a follow-on assignment. The Chief of Staff is still upset with me because I didn't marry his daughter, Marianne. He appears to be blocking any further promotions."

"It's lucky that you have twenty years in service. At least you're assured of retirement," Eric added.

"That's right," Adam replied. "We just passed twenty-two years since graduation."

Evelyn announced that dinner was on the table.

"Any chance that you could stay over a couple of days?" Eric asked.

"We would love to. My mother and Sonya's parents are in our hotel waiting for us to return. I really need to be back at the school, ASAP."

"What time do you want to leave tomorrow?" Eric asked.

"We gain two hours. If we leave by ten, we should be in Rome in the early afternoon," Adam replied. "We're stopping in Crete for fuel."

"I'll go by the office and check my messages," Eric suggested. "I can return around nine and get you to Lod in time for a ten am departure. Can I file a clearance for you?"

"That would be great," Adam replied. "I would like to stop at Souda Bay if you can arrange it. Tell them I'll pay by credit card."

They enjoyed their dinner and an after dinner aperitif. Then they went to bed. Adam fell asleep the minute his head hit the pillow.

The next day went as scheduled. They had a thirty minute stop at Souda Bay Naval Air Station and landed at the Rome Airport at four pm local. They were in EUR by five.

CHAPTER 30

Fortunately, Adam had the weekend before he had to return to classes. He could use the time. The Chief of Staff had called Lt. General Pedersen asking for Adam. The Chief was livid when he learned that Adam had taken leave and left Brussels in his own airplane. Adam would have until Monday afternoon to decide what he would tell the Chief.

It was a busy weekend. Sonya engaged the Poole girls to babysit with Carol Agnes. Adam hired a limousine for the day. They went to St. Peters to see Michelangelo's Pieta and the Vatican Museum. They got to the National Museum just before they were closing. They were able to see the Greek Statue of the Discus Thrower, probably one of the oldest and best marble statues ever carved. The Roman Legions had brought the statue to Rome during the reign of Caesar Augustus. They spent the afternoon in the Catacombs. Reverend Carlson was particularly pleased. He said that he had always wanted to go to Israel, Rome and Egypt to see places where Jesus, St. Peter and St. Paul had traveled. He had now seen them all in less than a year.

They ended the day with dinner at one of Rome's best restaurants near the Spanish Steps. On Sunday, they went back to the Vatican in hopes of seeing the Pope. They were successful. On the return to EUR, they stopped at St. Peter in Chains Church. The church was not active anymore. It still contained Michelangelo's statue of Moses. That was the only thing left in the church except for the wall decorations.

The NATO College class was back together on Monday. They had a normal day with a lecture from a Professor of Nuclear Science at Oxford University. After the lecture and the question and answer period, the class retired to the bar for a cocktail and then went to lunch. Sonya, Agnes, the Carlson's and Carol Agnes had all come over to enjoy the lunch. All of the classmates and families came by to pay respects to Adam and Sonya's families. The lunch was longer than usual. Adam was still there when the phone call arrived. Adam was called to General Pedersen's office to take a call from the Air Force Chief of Staff. Adam answered the phone.

The Chief began, "Where the hell have you been, General McGregor? I understand you left your class in Brussels."

"Yes Sir," Adam responded. "I took my wife to Crete for a weekend while my mother was here to take care of our baby."

"Who authorized that?" the Chief persisted.

"Lt. General Pedersen authorized my taking leave, Sir."

"Did you travel space available?"

"No, Sir," Adam returned. "I bought an airplane from the Luftwaffe. We traveled in the aircraft."

"What the hell do you need with an airplane?"

"I've always wanted a twin turbo-prop. The Luftwaffe had this Kingair C-90 for sale. It was quite reasonable so I bought it."

"How do you expect to get it back to America? Your assignment is already confirmed to Fort Richie. You will be reporting there by the fifteenth of August. I will block your promotion to Major General as long as I'm in the Air Force. What will you do with your C-90?"

"No problem, General. I expect to fly the C-90 to the States. I appreciate your reasonable reporting date. I've always wanted to spend a couple of days in New Foundland. My wife and baby will enjoy the rest."

"Listen you smart ass, you career is over. I'm sending you to the one-star graveyard. You'll never get promoted again. What do you have to say?"

There was a long pause. "What do you say, Adam?"

"I didn't know that my promotions would ever depend on whom I married. I'm very happily married. We will be happy to spend a tour at Fort Richie. At least I can be assured of being around for the birth of our second child. It's due in December."

"Smart ass!" The phone went dead. Adam went back to the table. He was smiling.

"What happened?" Sonya asked.

"The Chief wasn't very happy. I guess he expected me to be a little more humble. Anyway, we are going to Fort Richie to the alternate Command Post. I will be home for the birth of our second child. If the Chief is still around, I will probably have to retire in three years. That's all right, also. We aren't going to worry about it."

The three grandparents decided they would take the baby for a walk over to the nearby amusement park. Adam and Sonya returned to the Residence Garden. Adam decided to take a shower and he began to strip. Sonya had stripped to her panties. Adam reached around her back and fondled the nipple on her left breast. As her nipple hardened she turned and fondled Adam's testicles. The response was an instant erection. They turned down the covers and fell into bed. They had developed this approach to sex to avoid all noise. They proceeded with a long sexual encounter. Afterwards they fell asleep.

When they heard noises at the door, they jumped out of bed. Adam went into the shower. Sonya donned a bathrobe and went to the door. Agnes came in with Carol Agnes while the Carlson's went on to their room. Sonya suggested they come back for cocktails at six. Everyone prepared to go out to a restaurant for dinner.

When the Carlson's arrived, they all gathered in the living room and Adam took drink orders.

"How would you all like to take the grand tour of Italy before you go back to the States?" Adam asked.

"What do you have in mind?" Reverend Carlson asked.

"There's a bus tour next week starting in Venice with stops in Milan, Pisa, Siena and Florence, ending in Rome! It takes eight days. I'm taking the C-90 to Venice Friday after classes. We could take you up there and you could return on the bus tour."

"What about Carol Agnes?" Sonya asked.

"The Poole's have volunteered to take care of Carol Agnes. That would preclude her having to make the train ride back," Adam replied.

"We're coming back on the train?" Sonya asked.

"Yes, we'll come back on Sunday. We can all have dinner in Venice Saturday night. There's a great restaurant near the Rialto Bridge."

"Sounds like an offer we can't refuse," Carol opined. Reverend Carlson nodded his agreement. Sonya reminded Adam that the Carson's would be arriving over the weekend.

Adam replied, "I made reservations for them here. Ed Poole will meet their airplane."

The Carlson's and Agnes were ecstatic at the prospect of touring Italy by bus. They got together with tourist brochures and made lists of the things they didn't want to miss. During the week the grandparents made sure they spent as much time as possible with their granddaughter. Carol Agnes was standing up by herself and she was trying to take her first step.

Belle and Dora Poole were always available to sit with the baby. They seemed to enjoy caring for Carol Agnes and they liked the money. Their mother would scold Sonya for over-paying them. Sonya would tell her that Adam paid for everything. Talk to him.

After lunch on Friday, Ed Poole took the group to the airport. The C-90 was ready and they were off to Venice by three. The Beechcraft Technical Representative met the aircraft. He was there to monitor Aero Navaldis' painting of two U.S. Air Force Kingairs. One more would not be a problem.

Adam discussed the paint scheme with the Tech Rep. He wanted to make sure his aircraft would not look like a U.S. Government Kingair.

They spent Saturday seeing some sights in Venice. They rode a Gondola down the Grand Canal and visited Saint Marks Cathedral. They stayed in the Hotel Lisboa on St. Marks Square. They had an early dinner at the restaurant near the Rialto Bridge and returned to the hotel early. The next morning, Sonya and Adam caught an early train to Rome. They were back at the Residence Garden by three pm, Tom and Marty Carson were there to greet them.

"Have you seen our baby?" Sonya asked.

"Yes, we have" Marty replied. "She's beautiful."

"I'll call the Poole's and have the girls bring her over," Adam volunteered. "After all, we haven't seen her for two days."

"Don't pick on me!" Sonya admonished him. Adam made the call while Marty and Sonya went out on the balcony.

"How are things in Khartoum?" Adam asked.

"They're still upset at losing the Ibrahim's," Tom began. "They can't figure out how they all got away. Their people in Wau insist that Gudrun and the boys got on Spar 80. We insist the only one on Spar 80 was the German woman. They sent people into Rub Kona. There was no record of Spar 80 going into Rub Kona. There was no record of your C-90 being in the Sudan. They were really upset when they learned that Ahmed and family are in the States."

"How did they find out?"

"Ahmed appeared on Black Entertainment TV in New York. The Sudanese Delegation at the UN reported on the show."

"President Numerie must really be pissed," Adam surmised.

Tom replied, "There's no doubt about that. The Army is making moves to oust him. We'll have to wait and see what happens."

"Sounds like it was a good time for you to leave Khartoum," Adam added.

"They were about to declare me 'Persona-Non-Grata' when my replacement showed up. I guess they decided to drop it. I think they were too embarrassed to create any waves."

The Poole's arrived with Carol Agnes. Adam took drink orders. He went to the kitchen and got three lemonades for Belle, Dora and Sonya. Sonya appeared from the bedroom in maternity clothes.

"Sonya!" Marty Carson exclaimed, "Are you pregnant?"

"Yes," Sonya responded. "I can't hide it any longer."

"When is the baby due?" Tom asked.

"We're guessing sometime in December," Adam volunteered. "As soon as we get back to the States, Sonya will go to Rochester and see Doctor Snyder and Doctor Kittleson. They were her doctors for Carol Agnes' birth. We expect to get a more definitive date for the delivery then."

"That explains the lemonade," Marty said. "Doesn't it frost

you that the men go right on enjoying their cocktails while you have to go on the wagon?"

"It would, Marty," Sonya replied. "I'm the one who quit taking the pill. I can hardly blame my husband when I turn up pregnant."

"There's always abstinence," Marty interjected with a smirk on her face.

"Oh, right!" Sonya answered. "I've been married ten months and I'm supposed to give up sex?" Everyone laughed.

The phone rang interrupting the levity. Adam answered.

"Hello," Adam answered. The call was from Air Force Personnel.

"Scotty!" Adam replied. "What are you doing at work? It's Sunday." Adam listened for some time, then he replied, "Scotty that's great. I really appreciate the good news." Adam hung up.

"What is it, Darling?" Sonya asked.

"The Chief of Staff has been fired. I'm back on the Major General's list."

"Has your assignment been changed?"

"Yes, Sonya. I'll be assigned to the Air Staff at the pentagon until my promotion comes through. That will probably be in October or November. Then we will be going to Japan where I will be the Deputy Commander of US Forces, Japan."

"Our baby will be born in Japan?" Sonya asked.

"We'll cross that bridge when we get to it," Adam answered. "We'll see what the doctors at the Mayo Clinic say about your traveling that late in your pregnancy. I may be able to delay my reporting date. If not, you can stay with your parents until you need to go to Rochester. We'll talk it over with your parents and my mother next weekend."

"You don't happen to need an Army Liaison officer in Japan?" Ed Poole asked facetiously.

"If we do, I'll keep you in mind, Ed," Adam replied seriously. They all went to dinner in Ed Poole's Van.

After classes on Monday, Adam made a call to the Personnel Office on the Air Staff. He talked with the aide to the three-star Chief of Personnel. The aide explained that the Secretary of State had recommended that Adam be rewarded for his successful rescue of Ahmed Ibrahim and his family. The Secretary emphasized that the CIA and State had both debriefed Governor Ibrahim and that the Governor had provided them with excellent information. The Chief of Staff blew his top at which point the Secretary of State hung up. He phoned the Secretary of Defense and informed him of the Chief's attitude. They both consulted the president who promptly suggested that the Chief of Staff retire.

Needless to say, Adam was pleased. He reiterated the story to Sonya as soon as he got back to the hotel. Sonya heaved a sigh of relief, knowing that Adam's nemesis was retired.

The Carson's stayed for another week to see the main sights in and around Rome. Reverend Carlson, Carol and Agnes left the following Tuesday. They tried to take Carol Agnes with them. Sonya wouldn't hear of it. She said they would see the baby when she went to Minnesota for her check up. Agnes was pleased because Adam had asked her if they could move into the Georgetown house while they waited for orders to Japan. Agnes would be seeing a lot of the baby.

The remaining time at the War College flew past. The second weekend in July, Adam flew to Venice and picked up the C-90. He was very pleased with the paint scheme. The metallic-silver on the bottom had been spruced up. The gray on the top was replaced with white and a blue strip was placed between the two paint schemes. It looked like a new airplane. On Sunday, he took Sonya and the baby out to see the airplane. Sonya was pleased with the appearance of the airplane. She finally realized there wasn't any facilities for the baby.

Adam took them on a tour. The extra gas tank had been replaced with a new room with a toilet and sink. In the baggage area, he retrieved a wooden cradle. He placed it between two seats that faced each other and secured it with the lap belts. Velcro straps across the cradle would secure Carol Agnes during take off and landing and any turbulence.

"How can we cross the Atlantic without the extra fuel tank?" Sonya asked.

"Every day you act more and more like my mother," Adam commented with a chuckle.

"It's a mother's job to worry about her kids. We'll soon have two."

"We're not going to cross the Atlantic," Adam responded. We'll fly to Prestwick, Scotland on day one. We'll cross to Keflavik, Iceland next. Then, we go to New Foundland, which will be the longest leg. Our final leg will be to D.C. There are no legs longer than seven hours. I'm taking a thirty-day leave so we will only travel when the weather is good. I've flight planned the whole route."

"Sounds terrific," Sonya agreed.

CHAPTER 31

Adam shipped his Corvette two weeks before the graduation. He wanted to be sure it was in Washington by the time they arrived.

Ed Poole received his assignment. He was to join the Army Staff at Brussels. Ed mentioned that they had decided to send the girls to Ed's parents in Pennsylvania for the remainder of the summer if he could get them space available out of Naples.

"Why don't they go with us, Ed?"

"Do you have room?" Ed asked.

"Sure," Adam replied, "It's just Sonya, the baby and myself. We've rigged a crib for Carol Agnes that takes two seats. That leaves three seats open."

"I'll talk it over with Diane," Ed said. "We can spring it on the girls at dinner tonight if Diane agrees."

It was the Carson's last night in Rome and they were all going out to their favorite restaurant on the Appian Way. Adam had rented a Fiat for the remainder of their stay in Rome. The Carson's rode out to the restaurant with Adam and Sonya. As soon as they were all seated at the table, Diane asked Belle and Dora if they would like to go to the States with Adam and Sonya.

Belle answered immediately, "Would we go in General McGregor's airplane?"

"That's correct," Adam interjected.

"Can that little airplane cross the Atlantic?" Dora asked.

"No, not directly. We will stop in Scotland, Iceland and New Foundland to refuel, eat and sleep. It will take at least five days to get to the States."

"Wow! What fun!" Belle replied. "Will Grandpa Poole meet our airplane?"

"Yes," Ed Poole responded. "I will notify Grandpa when you will arrive in Washington."

"What's your dad's nearest airport, Ed?" Sonya asked.

"They're only five miles from Scranton Airport. That would be out of your way." Ed added.

Adam replied, "I doubt that it would be more than thirty minutes longer to stop in Scranton."

Ed replied, "That's too good to turn down. My dad doesn't like to drive more than four to five hours in a day. He would have to take two days to come to Washington and back."

"It's settled then," Adam concluded. "We'll call your dad before we leave New Foundland. It will take about four hours from Gander, New Foundland to Scranton."

"What about weather?" Diane asked.

"August is a good time to cross on this route. We will watch the weather and stay an extra day or two in Iceland if necessary." The deal was struck and the group settled down to eat dinner.

There was a good deal of conversation about the groups individual assignments. Ed Poole was on the Colonel's list. He would probably get a command in Germany within the year. Tom Carson had his retirement assignment at Colorado U in Boulder. He would be there for two years and retire with thirty years service. All three had served in Viet Nam and had passed through Japan. There was considerable interest in Adam's assignment--once he received his second star. They all promised to keep in touch. The Carson's left the next day.

One week later, Ed and Diane Poole took Adam, Sonya, Carol Agnes and their two daughters to the C-90. The Poole's would leave the next morning for Brussels. The C-90 was fully loaded by the time all the luggage was aboard. Two suitcases had to be strapped in the extra seat. The flight to Prestwick was without incident. They arrived by five pm local. They took a taxi to a local hotel that happened to have a two bedroom suite. They dined in the hotel's dining room. Adam tried to get the girls to try Haggis. They all preferred to have hamburgers. Adam was surprised that Sonya opted for a burger also. Later that evening, Adam suggested that they make love. For the first time since they met, Sonya didn't want sex. She was not feeling well.

When they undressed for bed, Adam noticed that Sonya's abdomen was expanding. She slept well that night and seemed to feel better in the morning. They left for Iceland at nine am the next morning.

They gained two hours in local time between Scotland and Iceland. It was early afternoon when they arrived in Keflavik. Adam had made arrangements for the VIP Suite at the VOQ. As soon as they were checked in, Adam called the Infirmary to see if a doctor was available to see Sonya. The hospital normally referred pregnancies to a hospital in Reykavik. The flight surgeon would be happy to check for vital signs, however.

Belle and Dora stayed in the suite with Carol Agnes while Adam took Sonya to see the doctor. After the doctor and a nurse had checked Sonya's pulse and other vital signs, they called Adam into the room.

"Congratulations, General," the doctor began, "you are going to be the father of twins."

"You know that already?" Adam asked.

"There is definitely two heart beats. We don't have the equipment to tell the sex of either baby. Your wife thinks she is four and a half months pregnant. I think she could be a month further along than that. I understand you are on your way to the States. Could you stay one more day and let her rest completely? I would like to check her again before you depart. If everything is okay we will send you on to Gander. You should be able to go to the States the following day."

"That's no problem. I had planned for an extra day here," Adam replied.

Adam rented a car and took Belle and Dora to Reykavik. They took a drive around the Capitol and then traveled to the area where the original Vikings had first settled. On their return to

Keflavik, they took a side trip to some hot springs. Adam explained that the hot springs provide hot water to heat most of the homes in Reykavik. They were back in Keflavik by six pm.

Sonya was feeling better. She said that Carol Agnes had slept most of the afternoon as had Sonya. Keflavik was a small airbase. They had an all ranks club. Sonya bundled Carol Agnes up and they all went to the club for dinner. When they returned to the VOQ, the baby was asleep and Sonya decided to turn in. Adam and the girls stayed up to watch the sunset while they played Hearts.

The next day, Adam took Sonya back to the flight surgeon. The doctor cleared Sonya for the flight to New Foundland. He suggested that they get Sonya home and in the care of an obstetrician as soon as possible. They went on to Gander. Belle and Dora took turns sitting in the co-pilots seat so that Sonya could relax in a seat that tilted back. They departed Gander at seven am the following day. They arrived in Scranton at eleven am. The girls grandparent's were there to meet the C-90. Adam explained that Sonya wasn't feeling well and he wanted to get her home as soon as they could get refueled. They were able to clear customs at Scranton.

Adam landed at a small airport just north of the District line in Maryland. He called his mother to tell her they were on the ground and would be home for cocktails. They took a cab to Georgetown. Agnes met them at the door. Adam was carrying the baby. Sonya entered first.

"My goodness, Sonya," Agnes began. "You have really grown."

"Yes," Sonya replied catching her breath. "It looks like we are having twins. I think I would like to lie down for awhile."

"You poor dear," Agnes replied. "Adam, you shouldn't be traipsing all over the world with Sonya pregnant."

"It looks like we may have got the dates wrong," Adam responded. "The doctor in Keflavik thinks Sonya is further along than we had guessed. He recommended that we get her to an obstetrician. I think we'll rest up a day or two and then we'll fly out to Rochester."

Adam checked in with Personnel at the Pentagon. He explained his personal problems and his need to continue on leave for another week. The following day, Adam packed up the family including his mother and flew to Minneapolis. They spent the night with the in-laws. Agnes and the baby remained with the Carlson's while Adam flew to Rochester with Sonya.

Doctor Snyder and Doctor Kittleson were there to welcome Sonya. After completing all the tests, they confirmed that she was carrying twins.

"There are two boys, aren't there?" Sonya asked.

"Yes," Dr. Snyder confirmed. "Was that a lucky guess?"

"I think they are already fighting," she responded weakly.

The doctor's insisted that Sonya remain at the hospital. Adam and Agnes returned to Washington later in the week. Carol Agnes remained with the Carlson's. The Carlson's insisted that they should get a chance to spoil the baby before the family moved to Japan.

Adam was promoted to Major General the following Thursday. That evening Doctor Snyder called to say that he and Doctor Kittleson had decided it was necessary to take the babies by Cesarean. Sonya's discomfort was serious and the babies were sufficiently mature for birth.

Adam signed out on emergency leave. He called the airport and had them prepare the C-90 for a six am departure. He alerted the Carlson's to be at the airport by nine am. They would all fly on to Rochester and be at the hospital by eleven am. The doctors wanted to start the operation at noon. The flight went as planned and the operation was over in an hour.

Dr. Snyder informed the family that both boys were fine. They were probably not identical twins but they were equally healthy. The mother was doing fine. The doctor wanted to talk over something with Adam and Sonya as soon as Sonya was awake.

"Is there something wrong with Sonya?"

"Nothing serious," Dr. Snyder replied.

Everyone gathered at the windows to view the two babies. They appeared just fine. They were almost identical in size and weight. Sonya came out of the anesthesia in a little over an hour. Dr. Snyder and Dr. Kittleson called Adam to the recovery room.

Dr. Snyder began, "Everything went well with the delivery. What we are concerned about is there was some evidence of more fetal tissue in the womb. We think you had one or two more eggs that didn't develop. If Sonya were to get pregnant again, she might have multiple babies again."

"So what are the options?' Adam asked.

"Well, of course, you could choose to abstain from having sex."

Sonya spoke, "Forget that!" She was emphatic. Everyone laughed.

Dr. Kittleson broke in, "You could take pills or we could tie your tubes. We recommend the latter."

"What do you say?" Sonya asked Adam.

"Two boys and a girl, all healthy, make a good family," Adam replied. "Let's not press our luck."

They named the two boys Adam Dougal and John Paul. Adam decided he didn't want an Angus and Sonya opted to name the younger boy after her two sons. Sonya stayed on for ten days to see that all was going as planned. Adam returned to the Pentagon until Dr. Kittleson gave Sonya the okay for the boys to leave the NICU.

Adam returned to pick up the whole family including his mother who had stayed in Rochester to take care of Carol Agnes.

They had been back in Washington for two weeks when Agnes noticed that neither Adam nor Sonya had put pajamas in the washing. Agnes decided to have some fun.

"Sonya, do you and Adam still shower together?" Agnes asked with her back turned to Sonya.

"Who told you that we shower together?"

"Your mother told me," Agnes replied.

"I don't know how my mother would know that," Sonya responded.

"She told me she noticed that you showered together when we were in Cairo last Christmas."

"I can't imagine how she could know what went on in the bathroom."

"She also told me about you stripping for practice breeding," Agnes continued. "She also said you admitted to a very robust sex life."

"I think," Sonya began, "I think," she repeated, "that our sex life should be our business."

"I totally agree, Sonya. Maybe you should throw a negligee or pajamas in the wash occasionally."

Agnes turned around. She was laughing.

"I guess we are rather obvious," Sonya admitted, smiling.

Adam remained at the Pentagon for two more months. They lived with Agnes. In early December, they moved to Tokyo. Agnes went along to help Sonya with the babies. Adam decided to leave the C-90 at the airport in Maryland. He didn't want to tempt fate by flying to Alaska, the Aleutians, and on to Japan in winter weather.

EPILOG

Major General A.D. McGregor and family arrived at Yokota Air Base near Tokyo on the fifteenth of December 1982. The quarters had been rehabbed. All they had to do was move in. Sonya and Agnes each carried one of the boys. Adam followed with Carol Agnes.

Lt. General and Mrs. Thompson stopped by to welcome them and suggest that they take two days to get over the jet lag. The babies were fine as they slept most of the flight from Dulles to Tokyo. Adam was able to sleep, but Sonya and Agnes were really tired. By the weekend, they were all ready for a night out at the Yokota Officers Club. The club had changed a lot since Adam had visited during Viet Nam. Agnes chided Adam about running into old girl friends. He pointed out that he hadn't been there in over twelve years. He didn't expect to see anyone he had known.

The winter flew by and Agnes decided it was time for her to return to Washington. There were a number of teen-aged girls in the housing area. Sonya had no trouble getting sitters for the babies. The hardest part was explaining how she managed three babies in such a short time.

Adam took leave in June to fly home with Agnes. He picked up the C-90 and flew it back to Yokota stopping in Minneapolis to see the Carlson's. He stopped in Anchorage for overnight and then flew to Yokota via a stop at Attu in the Aleutians. He was back in Tokyo for the weekend. Sonya had hired three senior girls to baby-sit. She had reservations at the Tokyo Hilton for the weekend. She and Adam made the most of it.

The C-90 was useful for weekend travel. They took day trips all over Honshu and overnight trips to the other Islands. They also visited Korea and Okinawa. The plane was always full. The waiting list ran the gambit from junior enlisted to Adam's boss. They always took an interpreter although both Adam and Sonya were reasonably fluent by the time they departed Japan.

Adam's boss retired in 1984. Adam was promoted to Lt. General and assumed command of U.S. Forces, Japan. After two years he returned to the Pentagon as the Deputy Chief of Staff for Logistics. They moved in with Agnes again. Agnes succumbed to cancer at eighty-five. It was most difficult for Carol Agnes and the boys. They had become attached to their grandmother. Agnes had spent long periods with them nearly every year.

Adam bought a forty acre horse farm in the Virginia Hunt Country while at the Pentagon. After selling his mother's house, her estate came to over twenty million after taxes. Adam put a short strip in at the farm and kept the C-90 in a hangar there. After the townhouse sold, he commuted to the Pentagon via Reagan Airport. A staff car provided transportation to the River entrance and back to the airport. If the weather was bad, he would stay at the Crystal City Marriott. Usually, Sonya would join him and they would eat at Army-Navy and enjoy a quiet evening away from the three youngsters.

Adam was promoted to General in 1989 and he assumed Command of U.S. Air Forces Europe at Ramstein Air Base, Germany for three years. Carol Agnes was eight and the boys were six. They all attended school on base.

Adam retired when they returned to the States in 1992. The children finished school at local private schools around Middleburg, Virginia. Carol Agnes graduated in 2000 and entered the University of Virginia that September. Adam and John finished two years later. Adam entered the Air Force Academy and John entered the Naval Academy at the same time.

The C-90 continued to serve the family to attend reunions in Minnesota, Air Force-Navy games in Colorado and Annapolis. They never missed the Air Force-Army games no matter where they were played. They attended the Army-Navy game every year.

Friends and neighbors often asked why Adam and John didn't go to the same Academy. Sonya explained that she was happy to have them separated. That way they couldn't fight. They both played defensive safety in football. They were rarely on the field at the same time. In lacrosse, they were mid-fielders. The Navy lacrosse Coach asked Sonya how he could keep John out of the penalty box. Sonya's answer was to keep him on the bench if his brother was on the field.

Carol Agnes married her high school sweetheart on graduation day at the Naval Academy in 2004. Her husband went into Nuclear Submarines. Their first duty station was Bremerton, Washington. The first grandson was born in April 2006.

John and Adam graduated the same day in 2006. Adam took the C-90 to Colorado Springs while Sonya drove to Annapolis for John's graduation. That evening they were all back in Virginia for dinner at the Red Fox Tavern in Middleburg. Carol Agnes arrived at Dulles in time for Sonya and John to pick up her and the baby. Carol Agnes' husband was on a cruise somewhere under water in the Pacific.

John and Adam were both going to be flying jets. Neither of the twins had steady girl friends.

That evening when they went to bed, Adam noticed that Sonya was very quiet.

"What's the matter, Sonya?"

"I'm afraid for my children," she began. "When I met you, you had been to war. I was spared the fear of losing you. My boys and my son-in-law are destined to go in harms way. I fear for their safety."

"It will be ever so for mothers," he said as he kissed her tenderly.

THE END

This page intentionally left blank.